THE

AFFAIRS

of

GERMANTOWN

by

charles savary

Eternally, for Jamie

CHAPTER ONE

"Are you frightened? Are you afraid, Lacy?"

"Oh, my God, yesss! Oh, my God, I'm so afraid! I'm so, so afraid!"

CHAPTER TWO

Lacy Knight sat in a remote clearing at the edge of the Mississippi River near Memphis, Tennessee. She'd gone there a lot recently to sort things out, and she always went alone.

It wasn't as if anyone missed Lacy, though. They might have pretended to, but most folks were content not to deal with her these days. Everyone was emotionally drained from the toll that doing so took on them. Because whoever's life she touched wasn't the same once she became involved with them.

Lacy was like a whirlpool, disrupting calmer waters before drawing everything into itself. Love from the people who cared for her, a few of whom had offered it to her unconditionally. Envy when they competed for her attention, and resentment when she didn't give it to them. And then anger. Ferocious, unyielding, retaliatory anger. Nothing escaped. It all swirled together like as much debris before getting sucked into the blackness.

So many things could have turned out differently for the girl whose family had abandoned her. No, they didn't drop her off at an orphanage or leave her on anyone's doorstep. But ever since coming into the world, the baby who stared up longingly into her mother's eyes, searching for that assurance that she was safe and that no one would be allowed to harm her, had to champion herself.

Instead of being nurtured and reassured in life, she had to create emotional triggers in others to bolster her self-image. She'd gotten pretty good at doing that.

Lacy never had the opportunity to develop emotionally, psychologically, or in any other way that might've helped her become a confident, self-assured, beautiful young woman for which she had every ounce of potential to be.

Instead, Lacy faced each wave that rolled into her life without help from anyone. There was no one to encourage her, no one to offer her advice, and no one to congratulate her when she managed to get things right. She was left alone to figure everything out.

Lacy was beautiful because her parents were beautiful, albeit only in the most superficial ways. They also had demanding careers and tunnel vision that obstructed the view of all the disturbing goings-on in their little girl's life that might ordinarily trigger the concern of a loving parent.

There'd been no romance between her parents, no lightning strike, nor any planning beyond a scheme. There weren't any salad days or scrimping to make ends meet until they struggled to the next phase of life. They didn't engage the world as a team, reinforcing each other and facing life's challenges with a unified front.

Money flowed like the Mississippi River a few feet from where Lacy was sitting, and, as a result, she had no want for material things because they were only the presentation of an American Express card or the punching in of an ATM code away.

None of that mattered now, though, as Lacy's glossy, troubled eyes reflected the Memphis lights that shone on the cold, dark water in front of her. None of it mattered one damned bit.

In a rare show of vulnerability, Lacy had cried, though. Although she knew it wouldn't do any good, she cried and cried.

***

A few hundred yards away, Jerome parked his Suburban and looked over at his wife, Ardella, who was asleep on the passenger's side. He knew she was exhausted because she'd worked a double at the front desk of the Days Inn.

"Baby? Baby. Baby," Jerome said, tapping Ardella's shoulder and waking her up, "we don't have to come down here tonight. We can go home and get out here early if you want. Those cats ain't goin' nowhere."

Ardella came to life then and sat up straight, taking in her surroundings, relieved she hadn't fallen asleep behind the front desk.

"No, no, baby. I'm good. I just can't go nowhere in a car when I'm tired. You know how I am," Ardella said, stretching forward in her seat.

Then, Ardella and Jerome started the tasks that came with a night of catfishing. Jerome grabbed his fishing pole and their cooler, full of Snapple and bottled water. Ardella would tote her pole and their picnic bag of tuna fish sandwiches and Andy Capp's Hot Fries.

"You go on, sugar," Ardella said, "I'm gonna call and see where Lil'J is."

"Okay, Momma," Jerome said before he turned and shuffled off toward the shore.

***

"Gat-damn," Jerome said, noticing the pitiful little white girl sitting in one of the sling chairs he kept hidden for Ardella. He stashed that and his tacklebox in a thicket behind the posted signs about ten yards away. That was easier than driving back to the house whenever he'd forgotten them.

The girl's back was to Jerome, and she hadn't noticed him yet. So, he could've easily tiptoed back to the truck and driven off with his wife. But he knew Ardella wouldn't have gone for that. Not when she'd come off a double, helped him load up, and ridden across town to go fishing with him.

Ardella and Jerome hadn't seen her in a while, but the girl sitting in their chair had haunted their fishing spot for the past few months, and it always seemed to have been at the least opportune times. Jerome thought she should've had better things to do than hang out with a middle-aged black couple on a Friday night, so her presence always begged several questions.

Jerome and Ardella were friendly to the girl just the same. They both felt sorry for her. A girl that pretty, dressed that well, spending a Friday night by herself? It was a damned shame. Something really must've been wrong in her life.

"Unh, unh, baby! I ain't gon' let you steal my spot, now!" Jerome kidded.

The girl didn't say anything back, though. She just continued to stare out at the river. Clearly, she was in no mood to carry on any small talk.

She was probably on something, just as Jerome and Ardella had always suspected whenever she came around. Nobody rattled on like that girl could, talking ninety miles an hour about nothing and flittering from one emotion to the next without any notice or reason. Jerome imagined he was probably witnessing the aftermath of one of those awful binges as he stared at her. But whatever emotional state she was in, he could tell she didn't want to talk to him.

"Ok, then," Jerome said, "but what'd you do with my tackle box, baby?"

***

Ardella heard her husband scream out from the distance. She dropped her phone and pole and started tearing through their picnic bag until she found Jerome's pistol. Then, she hurried toward the darkness he'd disappeared into moments before.

"Jerome?! Jerome?! Jerome!!" Ardella shouted, getting no answer.

Once Ardella started down the gentle slope to the waterline, she saw Jerome kneeling on the sandy mud, shaking his head, and holding the hand of someone who said something horrible to him. It was a woman. Whatever she said as she bobbed her head up and down, she said it with a lot of emotion.

Ardella got closer to them and saw that Jerome wasn't in danger. Nevertheless, she raised the pistol and pointed it toward the ground in front of him and the woman. As she approached the two, she recognized the female as being that crazy-ass white girl who came around sometimes. She couldn't imagine what the girl was saying to Jerome being so horrible that he'd screamed out how he had. But Ardella had always felt like that girl was trouble.

For starters, the girl was a chatterbox. She never stopped talking. She jumped from topic to topic and went from laughing and cutting up to crying or getting angry before you knew it. Never at them, though. It seemed she reserved her most intense emotions for the other people she always talked about. Her parents. Her brother. Her boyfriend. Her other boyfriend. And then about some big girl that bullied her at school all the time.

Sometimes, the girl told Jerome and Ardella how beautiful their lives seemed and that they were just like she wanted hers to be. Then she'd prattle with no break in her chain of thought. She'd tell them about things in a stream, speaking as they occurred to her.

She wanted a man—a good man like Jerome—to take care of her and protect her. Then she wanted a son, too. She wanted a little boy to dote on and dress up as a little soldier or in a football uniform. She wanted a small house but didn't want it to be in the city or anywhere close to Memphis. She thought she'd like Mississippi, though. Yes. That was it. Mississippi. That was where she was going to move. Mississippi. She'd move to Mississippi in the country somewhere. She'd get married, and she'd have a little boy. Stuart. She wanted to name him Stuart. And Stuart and her husband would go fishing together like Ardella and Jerome did. They'd fish. And they'd play backgammon. And she'd make them dinner. It was all going to be perfect. Just perfect. Life in Mississippi with Stuart and her husband was going to be perfect. She, her husband, and Stuart would have a wonderful life together in Mississippi. It would be just like "that black lady's from *Instant Mom.*"

"What the hell is goin' on?" Ardella demanded.

Jerome looked up at Ardella, and it stunned her to see he was crying. He shook his head and gasped as if trying to find words, but he never spoke.

That's when Ardella realized what was going on. That damned girl had threatened Jerome. She'd pretended he did something to her and was going to try and have him arrested. That's why she'd been jawing so much when Ardella walked up.

Lacy didn't intend to cause any trouble, though. She didn't mean to intrude on their good time or blather about little to nothing. Lacy assured Jerome about that before Ardella arrived, which is what had upset him so terribly. But her assurances hadn't come with words. Rather, they'd been delivered through a glance and her body language.

And that's because Lacy couldn't speak. And Lacy couldn't speak because someone had removed Lacy's tongue.

Whether or not Lacy had been alive at the time wouldn't be determined until her autopsy—as would the origins of the clubbing that the back of her head had sustained. That was also when they'd analyze the fluorocarbon test line her murderer had used to sew her eyes open. The forensics team would conclude that her killer used those things available at the scene and that they hadn't brought with them.

As Jerome tried to jar Lacy from what he had presumed was a comatose state, he entangled his hand in the fishing line, which her killer had also rigged to hold up her head. But when Jerome yanked his hand away, the gesture turned her into a macabre marionette whose head jerked back and forth before it finally tilted backward and stared at Ardella.

"No! No! Stop! Don't come down here!" Jerome hollered. "Call the police, Ardella! Call 911! Dial 911!" he sobbed as he accepted the reality of what was seated a few inches away from him.

CHAPTER THREE

"I won't tell anyone, Lacy. I promise."

Dr. Joshua Odom was responding to a student who had just revealed that she had insatiable sexual longings. She went on to say that she was currently having an affair with her volleyball coach, a thirty-eight-year-old woman.

However, the last thing Josh's patient disclosed was a bit more problematic for him. In addition to her coach, Prissy Tillman, the girl had recent trysts with two other Restoration Academy for Girls faculty members—simultaneously. Josh was in a quandary because he knew one of the men. Headmaster Gil Wallace was Josh's old fraternity brother. And though they'd become less familiar over the years, Josh still considered Gil a brother and a close friend.

The things Lacy said were substantiated by nothing more than her lurid descriptives—some of which were astounding. But Josh could envision Gil doing what the girl said he'd done. In school, Gil had been renowned at Baker College for being a sexual hound dog.

So, Josh thought it was funny when he heard that Gil, who'd barely scraped by in college, had accepted the chancellor's position at a non-denominational Christian school a few years before. And he did it with woefully limited practical educational experience.

Gil's school, Restoration Academy, got away with charging a fortune despite its lack of academic prestige. Moreover, its substandard credentials allowed the school to charge more because it was the last hope for rich girls who'd been kicked out of private and boarding schools everywhere else.

Gil heading up a naughty girls' school. Josh thought it was just one of those funny ironies of life that make you laugh and shake your head before you move on. Now, he was concerned it might be a lot more than that.

Josh knew he should pick up the phone after the girl's session and notify the authorities. But apart from him being close friends with one of the girl's alleged predators, there were other factors Josh had to consider.

According to her workup history and physical data, Lacy was eighteen. However, it was unclear how old she was when the indiscretions occurred. Regardless of Gil's role in her migration into womanhood, she was presently a consenting adult.

Something else that irked Josh was that Lacy was so blasé about the whole matter. She talked as though she confessed to staying out late or skipping class.

Then, that gum. That Goddamned gum she didn't stop chewing the entire time as she spoke. It certainly didn't garner any sympathy from Josh.

"Thank you, Dr. Odom. Oh my God, my Dad would kill Mr. Wallace and Coach Marvin if he found out," Lacy sighed.

Josh decided to address the issue that bothered him so much.

"Lacy, if you don't mind my saying so, you seem very accepting of your circumstances. You don't appear to be troubled at all by what's happened to you," Josh asked the brazen young woman.

Josh was even more put off by Lacy's politically correct response that discounted any consideration of morality or the implications of her having slept with two grown men.

"Well, I mean, we used protection. I'm not stupid, Dr. Odom," Lacy said, rolling her eyes.

Josh laughed a little through his nose and shook his head.

"Yeah, well, I suppose that's good news, Lacy, but," he started before she interrupted him.

However, this time—and Josh couldn't tell if it were a performance—Lacy wavered a little as she spoke, and her voice broke.

"I know it was wrong, Dr. Odom. I didn't mean to sound like a bitch. I just…I don't know what to do, so I'm here. I told my Mom it was because some girls fat-shamed me during P.E. and that I just needed to talk to somebody. And I didn't exactly lie about that either because a lot of them do call me stuff. Mean stuff."

Though Josh was still uncertain about her sincerity, it was a chance to discover what environmental factors may have caused a high school academy student to behave in such a way.

"How does that hurt your feelings, Lacy? In what way does what they say hurt you?" Josh asked.

Lacy shook her head as though she wished she'd left that part out. But Josh continued probing.

"Lacy, I'd like you to tell me what they called you. And I want you to tell me if they did anything else, alright? Did they physically harm you, or was it just the things they said that hurt you? I won't tell anyone, Lacy, and you won't get anyone in trouble. But it's information that would help me help you. It might seem that I'm just being nosy, but that's not true. Anything like that you tell me remains confidential."

Lacy sniggered, then said, "Shyuh, right. You sound like Miss Fogel. She wasn't going to tell anybody anything either. Then she wound up getting Tollie McCormick suspended with all her bullshit, 'Oh, I won't tell anybody, Lacy.' Whatevaz, Miss Fogel. Worst freakin' day of my life."

Josh pounced on Lacy's comment about the other professional she'd spoken with.

"Why was anything—Miss Fogel, did you say? I assume that's a school counselor? How did Miss Fogel cause one of the worst days of your life?"

Lacy went on to explain. Sort of.

"Yeah. You wouldn't understand that because you've never seen Tollie McCormick. Freakin' bull-dyke. She's like six-two! Her brother is Roland McCormick? You know, Roland, the Chicago Bear? Yeah, that's Tollie's brother. And the bitch is built just like him. Dr. Odom, she beat me up so bad. Swung me around by my hair and pinned me on the ground. And all I could do was, like, lay there while everybody called me stuff and hollered at me."

Josh still found it curious that Lacy was so bothered by the name-calling.

"You keep saying people calling you names hurts you, Lacy. But you also seem very mature to me, and that should be something you could handle. The pinning down? No. That's unacceptable, and Miss Fogel was right to intervene on that count. But name-calling? Come on, Lacy. You're a big girl, and anyone that name calls shouldn't register with you as anything but immature," Josh insisted.

"Bingo! That's the one!" Lacy said.

"What's the one, Lacy? What do you mean? I'm afraid you've lost me."

"Big girl! They call me 'big girl' for one thing! And big booty girl! And big titty girl! And big…"

"Okay, okay, I understand," Josh said.

He sighed and creaked back in his chair, studying Lacy.

Lacy may have been eighteen, but she'd obviously developed early. She was buxom and had all the features of a more mature young woman. He wasn't sure, but if he took a guess, he'd bet she'd been that way since she was eleven or twelve—possibly even earlier. And in adolescent social circles, that could foster resentment from girls of a similar age who hadn't developed as soon.

The later bloomers subconsciously viewed girls like Lacy as a threat. Instinctually, their brains told them, 'She will get all the males, and there won't be any left for you.' Since it wasn't the Stone Age, and they couldn't bash her head in, they'd ascend to destructive psychological tactics. Name-calling. Taunting. Spreading rumors. It could manifest in any number of ways. But seldom did it result in taking physical action against another female.

Had this been a struggle among boys, they might have beaten another boy down, if not worse. But it was different for females. Societal pressures, many of the same ones that aggravated the behavior, forced them to be less overtly aggressive. Young girls were so much more sophisticated.

Josh needed to know more about Tollie.

"Why do you suppose Tollie became physical with you, Lacy? Did you do anything to her first?"

"Uhhh—hello?? No! I didn't do anything to her! She did it because she's a big gorilla! That's why she did it!"

Josh looked up at Lacy in the corners of his eyes with a faint smile before Lacy continued.

"Okay, well, maybe I did call her a gorilla. But she *is* a gorilla! I didn't start anything with her, though! She started it with me! Big, fat ass gorilla."

"So, you called her a gorilla. Do you think that's why she attacked you and held you on the ground?" Josh asked.

Lacy went silent. She fidgeted, twisting her hair with her left hand and tapping her right one on her knee. Josh realized then that she was withholding information.

"Lacy?" he asked quietly, "Lacy, look at me, please."

"Oh, my God, what?! What is it?!" Lacy blurted.

"Lacy, I want you to tell me why Tollie McCormick became physical with you. And I want you to tell me something distinct from her status as a gorilla."

Lacy sniffed a little laugh and then smiled at Josh.

Lacy was a pretty girl, and she looked more like a woman being coy than a teenager bearing her soul to a psychiatrist. Josh could see how her precociousness could get her into trouble. He just couldn't believe that Gil, as bad as he was, would take advantage of a student that way, no matter how mature she seemed. Hell, all of Gil's children were older than Lacy, and two were girls. Had things gotten so bad between Gil and his wife, Michelle, that he needed to vent his sexual frustrations with a child? He'd never come across that way to Josh.

"Yes? Are you leaving anything out?" Josh continued.

After a long pause, Lacy started talking again. She spoke as though she were giving in, surrendering to whatever Josh might suggest. But it was more than that. It was like she was surrendering to everyone else. All the other girls and what they thought about her. And what the men thought about her, in her mind, justifying their abuse.

Josh then understood Lacy's relationship with an older woman. He could see it from both sides. While it was still unconscionable, he believed Lacy's route to her coach, Prissy Tillman, led to a place where she felt safe, free from resentment and ridicule. She was encouraged and reassured rather than demoted and oppressed. Miss Tillman, however perverse her motivation was, tried to protect and nurture the girl. Josh supposed that was better than the alternatives Lacy had.

"She's probably jealous that I messed around with her boyfriend," Lacy suggested before off-handedly adding a wrinkle, "or maybe 'cause I messed around with Roland, too."

And though Josh wanted to, he couldn't act as appalled as he felt. He couldn't even act like he was surprised. He could take her to the woodshed psychologically, which was his initial compulsion. Then he felt like that had happened to the girl enough. But he was so aghast at the prospect of what Lacy suggested that he had to confirm it.

"When you say messed around…"

"I fucked them. I fucked both of them," Lacy said as cooly as she'd related her other affairs.

Josh had to suppress his revulsion and instead focus on treating the patient. However, he couldn't help thinking, if only for a moment, *what a whore*. He allowed his judgmental feelings to come and go, though. He had to learn as much as he could about Lacy Knight.

"I see," Josh said, trying to stall to regain his focus.

Then Lacy snickered. And it was like she poked at something already tensed and ready to explode.

"Lacy, I really don't see anything amusing here. You came to me today because you supposedly wanted help, and I'm trying to help you. But if this is nothing more than a way to get out of class, or if you think you're going to leave with an Adderall prescription, then we can stop right now, and you can go back to school."

It was one thing to be cavalier about whorish behavior, but if it had all been a ruse from the outset, then Josh, indeed, was going to get his pound of flesh before he dismissed the girl. He refused to get played by a teenager who'd first described symptoms that sounded like compulsive sexual behavior disorder but quickly moved on to a run-of-the-mill chronic low self-esteem aggravated by a hostile environment and the patently irresponsible, self-indulgent acts of adults who took advantage of their relationship with a student.

"No. No. No. I'm sorry, Dr. Odom. I wasn't laughing at you. I swear. I was laughing at myself. You didn't even have to be in the room, and I would've laughed. And I wasn't really laughing at myself, either. I was just thinking about what a slut I've been and that it was so bad that even a shrink didn't want to talk about it. I just…I don't know what to do. Everybody else is doing normal stuff, but I'm sitting at Prissy's, listening to KD Lang and watching *Beaches* while she gets wasted on Franzia. I mean, she's got that box sucking air by ten o'clock every night, and then I have to make sure she goes to bed. Even Tollie Gorilla has a dude while I'm babysitting Megan Rapinoe. What a life, huh?"

Then, Lacy introduced a new variable in the equation.

"And I hate to break it to you, but I can get Adderall anytime I want it," Lacy continued.

After a moment, Josh asked, "From where?"

"My brother takes it. He's taken it forever. But, my God, the dude is twenty-four, lives at home, and works part-time at Game X Change. If that's what Adderall does, then I'm sorry, you can keep that shit."

"Alright, then," Josh said, noticing the clock behind the bookshelf.

He managed his office by himself, electronically, and computerized everything when possible.

An auto attendant scheduled Josh's appointments using a menu-driven phone-based system. His patients could book an appointment for themselves through an app. Everything, including their identity, insurance information, and payment method, was certified before they entered the front of the building and walked out of the back. There was no waiting area or lag time between sessions, which also lessened the likelihood of fellow patients running into one another. Instead, they exited at the end of a long corridor behind his office.

But the minute hand was on the eleven, so it was time to wrap things up with Lacy—only for the time being, Josh hoped.

"Well, Lacy. At the risk of sounding cliché, there's much more to unpack here. But I'm afraid we have to end our session this morning. On a forward-thinking note, I'll revisit the things you've told me and be prepared to discuss them at length on your next visit. Does that sound amenable to you?"

Lacy looked back at him through squinty eyes for a moment.

"First, you'll have to tell me what amenable means. But I'll let you know after that," Lacy giggled.

"Well, I suppose I should've asked, does that sound like something you'd be willing to do?" Josh said, checking himself for failing to remember he was talking to a high schooler.

In fairness, that had been easy to do because Josh's discussions with teenagers were ordinarily limited to harrowing tales of teen angst and why-am-I-here-type reflections. *"I'm failing all my classes,"* and *"My parents took away my car."* Those folks?

They're the ones he gave Adderall. And he did it just as fast as he could get his iPhone in hand and transmit the prescription to the pharmacy.

But Josh's average patient interactions didn't include an ersatz porno star whose dalliances with school officials were the featured attraction. Not only that, but Lacy was a brutally honest and exceedingly intelligent young woman, even if she wasn't so educated. Medication might ease her symptoms for a while, but they'd only be to her detriment in the long term. Then, there was the glaring absence of parental guidance in Lacy's life. She'd hardly mentioned them except to say how her father would've reacted to others because of *their* behavior instead of *hers*. Josh imagined that because of that and her age, Lacy's parents would play but a tiny role in her road to recovery.

Lacy was going to make Josh sing for his supper. But on the backside of that, she would have to work as hard as he did, with the difference being that he was getting paid the whole time. Through Restoration Academy, Lacy had the federally subsidized Empowered Youth coverage for adolescent mental health, which was pretty damned good insurance.

Just before closing the door, Josh was interrupted by Lacy turning in the corridor and saying, "Dr. Odom, you didn't write anything down the whole time we talked. How are you going to *revisit* anything?"

Man, the girl was observant, Josh thought. "It's documented, Lacy. Don't worry about that," he assured her.

"You were recording me the whole time?" Lacy asked, craning her neck forward like she was outraged.

"Not exactly. Well, yes, and no. Everything we discussed was instantly transcribed into a digital memorandum. This way, it protects you and me both. And it also helps me with your treatment,

Lacy. Our session doesn't end just because you're no longer sitting in front of me. I'll devote a lot of energy to what you told me and develop a course of action. It's all clinical. No one will ever hear or read that information but me. I promise."

Lacy slowly eased back into her comfort zone, maintaining eye contact with Josh. Then she smiled again and said, "Alright, Doctor O. You're in charge."

Josh nipped Lacy's address of him as 'Doctor O' in the bud.

"Lacy, my name is Dr. Odom," he said, smiling.

"Gah! A thousand pardons, m'Lord!" Lacy complained.

Josh couldn't help laughing this time, but he said, "Now go."

A few seconds later, as he watched Lacy move down the corridor over the security camera streaming to his phone, Gil's reprehensible decisions started making more sense to Josh. Lacy might have only been eighteen, but she sashayed down that hallway like she was strutting toward a pole she'd grab before twining her legs around it and twirling.

CHAPTER FOUR

"Shhitt," Josh said at the screen the next morning, staring at his first appointment. The name "Prissy" had grabbed his attention. It was the coach who had been in a relationship with his eighteen-year-old patient from the previous day.

Since Josh already knew more about Prissy Tillman than he ordinarily would, he skipped her demographic info and scrolled down to Medical History. Nothing extraordinary jumped out at him. Asthmatic, compliant. Adolescent to young adult eating disorder, resolved. Recurrent endometriosis, resolved.

Then Josh clicked on the "New Patient Questionnaire" tab, and alcohol was mentioned in the first sentence under the "*Why are you coming to see the doctor today?*" section.

Chardonnay. Seven or more glasses a day. Then, of the eighteen bullets in the Symptoms checklist, the only one that wasn't checked was "Hallucinations."

Josh hoped Restoration's employee coverage was as good as Empowered Youth's because if her girlfriend, Lacy, was a little ill, then Prissy should've been considered terminal.

Prissy's checklist was encompassing for a reason, though. And though Josh was a conscientious practitioner, he couldn't help being greedy as he inventoried everything wrong with Prissy Tillman.

Then Josh thought about something else. Maybe Prissy checked all those boxes for other reasons. Maybe she was seeking information. She might have wanted to frame things so that there was no way a competent psychiatrist would let her leave without establishing a protracted treatment plan. Perhaps she believed that could buy her time to try and bilk information or advice about dealing with Lacy.

Prissy could also be a pill-head. She might've already made the rounds of every dentist and physician in Shelby County and worn out her welcome.

But that didn't seem very likely to Josh. If Prissy drank "7 or more" glasses of Chardonnay a day, she self-medicated differently.

Or maybe it was just as Prissy's symptoms list indicated, and she would've been better served with an "All of the above" option. She could veritably be dogged by all the conditions she'd selected. If that were the case, she was quite a disturbed individual.

Still, the timing of it all was a red flag for Josh. Prissy showed up the day after her girlfriend, one of the most promiscuous teenagers Josh had ever sat across from, presented for treatment. It was too worrisome not to keep his guard up much more than usual.

***

"That's impressive," Josh responded to Prissy's description of her investment portfolio.

That was after Prissy talked about growing up as the only child of radial tire magnate Carter Tillman. Josh hadn't made the connection before the session started, but the circles in which Josh and his wife, Liza, moved were littered with Tillmans. They were pretty much poster children for a dysfunctional wealthy family.

In 1968, Carter Tillman and his older brothers, D.T. and Hollis, started a tire-changing business at the gas station their father owned. They all worked hard, but Carter was the proliferative businessman of the three.

While D.T. and Hollis were at Memphis State for a few years before drinking their way back home, Carter stayed with it, opening two additional stores. From that point, D.T. and Hollis were just along for the ride. But together, the boys opened ten more stores, stretching their concern into Arkansas, North Mississippi, and Georgia. By 1985, they had an empire with stores in every major city in the Southeast. Tillman Tires' revenue approached that of South Central Bell.

But Carter's world was set ablaze in 1986 when his wife, Virginia, died in a one-car accident. It left him a widower and single father of a two-year-old Prissy. Incapable of living alone without Virginia, Carter married only three years after that.

Carter's new wife, Jennifer, was an aerobics instructor who had been casual acquaintances with Virginia at the spa where she worked out. Jennifer wasn't at all promiscuous. Carter could never carry on with a woman like that. But there were profound reasons she was still single in 1980s Memphis, Tennessee.

Jennifer was hard-driving, just like Carter. A perfectionist. Very demanding. And together, they reared Prissy in a world that included Laura Ashley dresses, cotillion dances, and Estee Lauder bonuses, none of which was either appealing or affirming to the heartbroken little girl. If Virginia had been running the show, she probably would have noticed the signs that Prissy wasn't like all the other girls her age and within their social strata. But the fact that Virginia wasn't there left Prissy alone. Confused. And even more melancholy than she should have otherwise been.

However, Prissy did grow up going on hunting trips with her father while her stepmother suited up and came along—such dreadful outings, from start to finish. Instead of showing an interest in makeup, fashion, and homemaking, Prissy was drawn toward less feminine distractions like the outdoors and athletics. Ironically, the latter may have saved Prissy's life.

Carter attempted to keep Prissy as close to him as possible. He wanted to protect her, so he encouraged her interest in such things to ensure he could have her at his side as he intended to groom her to take over Tillman Tires one day.

But Jennifer? Well, Jennifer became a calculating, insufferable, unapologetic bitch. She didn't want Prissy around and made no competent attempt to conceal it.

In a major and unlikely coup for Jennifer, and as Carter lost steady ground to single malt scotch, Prissy was transferred to a boarding school in the Northeast just before starting junior high. She was only home for holidays, and her summers consisted of meeting her father and Jennifer at their Fiji estate before going on mother-daughter getaways to various European locales. Those trips were a covert attempt by Jennifer to maintain distance between Prissy and her father. And while the European jaunts were memorable, it was for all the wrong reasons.

After matriculating to Princeton, Prissy did exactly what Jennifer had wanted her to do all along: she revolted. It got to the point where Prissy intentionally distanced herself from Carter rather than having to be provoked.

The hunting excursions stopped, with Prissy always citing some pressing academic or athletics conflict. Attending school on a track and field scholarship, she loved running, how the sport pushed her to her limits, and the endorphin rush it provided.

Prissy's avoidance was carried over from prep school, and she continued to boycott any activity involving Jennifer, which, by default, included doing anything whatsoever with her father.

At the nadir of her existence, after returning to Princeton for her senior year, the tide turned, if only briefly, for Prissy. That's when she met Aurora Silva, during Women's Lacrosse Club.

Aurora was also on the women's soccer team, and although she had never been attracted to women before, Prissy was infatuated with Aurora, or "Roe," as everyone called her. She coveted the shape of her body and her athletic prowess, and, apart from that, they developed an odd kinship after discovering each other's pasts.

Their circumstances in life were somewhat similar. But while Prissy's stepmother was responsible for all her anguish, Aurora's biological mother fueled hers.

However, Prissy felt Roe's situation was much worse, and in the most unlikely turn, Prissy had compassion for Roe. She felt sorry for the bright-eyed, beautiful Brazilian who perpetually smiled and made both men's and women's hearts race whenever she came around.

Roe was the first woman Prissy had ever been with. She was the first anything Prissy had ever been with. But once the awkwardness was over, and they established their respective ground rules, Prissy and Roe couldn't keep their hands off one another, and they ended up a couple.

They went to movies together, ate out together, went to ball games together, and even stayed at each other's apartments sometimes, but—at Roe's insistence—not always. If Roe hadn't taken a stand early on, Prissy would've held on too tightly and eventually moved in with her. Prissy adored her exotic woman, and she wanted her all to herself.

There was a problem, though.

While Roe felt the same way Prissy did, she had a wandering eye. And hurting Prissy even more, sometimes that eye fell upon men. Rumors circulated about Roe and her sexual exploits, with a jealous competitor once telling Prissy that Roe had even been with more than one football player at a time.

But rather than put up a fight, Prissy just gave in. Despite being very attractive and intellectually engaging, her insecurities made her convinced she could never truly rate with Roe because it was apparent to Prissy that Roe was attracted to men. And that devastated her.

After earning her degree in education, Prissy packed it all in and moved back to Memphis with her tail between her legs. That only resulted in Jennifer picking up stakes and house-hopping with Carter to the different homes he'd acquired over the years, leaving Prissy to fend for herself. Prissy made attempts to follow Carter, but they were always short-lived.

Because the messages were the same no matter where Prissy tried to recapture whatever vestiges remained of her relationship with her father.

You are not wanted here anymore.

You are not welcome.

Go away.

***

At that point in the session, Josh felt like he'd leaned over to take a sip of water, only to learn that it was a firehose he'd pursed his lips around. And he'd mentally re-checked every box Prissy had as she recounted the horrific circumstances that had brought her to his office that day. She had done a remarkable job of self-diagnosis. So, Josh no longer suspected her of anything but being a downtrodden soul who'd been victimized her entire life and was poised to experience the same tragedy whether or not she realized it.

Then, Josh's skepticism crept back in. Surely, Prissy wasn't cunning enough to lie to him. Surely, she only wanted him to ponder as he did now to chart a course to mental well-being. She wasn't clever enough to enlist him to help her get what he imagined she wanted, which was Lacy. Was she?

But after reflecting on Prissy's narrative and listening to its sobering crescendo, the conversation invariably returned to her current status, including her inheritance, her anxiety, and her relationship with Lacy Knight.

"You know, I've gotten my tires at Tillman's my whole life. I just put a set of Pirelli's on my wife's Mercedes," Josh said in an unusual attempt to make casual conversation during one of his sessions.

Josh thought he might humanize himself, making Prissy a more comfortable patient, receptive to any suggestions he'd have because he knew that someone as war-torn as Prissy might be mistrustful.

"Oh. Well, I'll let them know. Maybe I can get you a retroactive discount," Prissy said snidely.

There it was. It was the first bite of cynicism Josh had gotten from Prissy, but he sensed there was much more where that came from. He was surprised it had taken that long to present itself.

"I'm sorry, Prissy. I was just thinking aloud," Josh said, trying to cover his tracks, "Let's get back to this person you were discussing—the romantic interest. You'd said that you loved her. Like you hadn't loved anyone for a long time, and by that, I presume you mean since Roe. But then you said there were obstacles you didn't feel could be overcome in your relationship. How so, Prissy? If you love someone and they love you, I just can't imagine any obstacle being so great that it can't be dealt with."

Prissy appeared to perk up a little as if Josh opened a window for her to tell him what was really happening that made her so miserable.

"It's not so much an obstacle as it is a postponement. At least, I hope that's all it is. Certain things have to happen before we can be together. But even if they do, I'm not sure she'll feel the same way about me. And that's the scariest part."

"You seem secretive about these obstacles, Prissy," Josh said, "you haven't once said what any of them are. And now you're telling me the main one is…time-dependent? Are you saying the potential for the relationship has a shelf-life? That's very confusing if you are. And it doesn't sound like the sort of durable bond you need. It sounds quite the contrary."

Prissy acted wounded. Whatever enthusiasm Josh had managed to spark, it was like he'd immediately suffocated it with a blanket.

"Are you even listening to me? That's what I just said, Dr. Odom. I said that's the part that scares me the most."

"Oh, I'm listening to you, Prissy. And I heard you say that. But you also said that before you could even consider this person, something had to happen first. That life with this person is being postponed. And without any more information, I'm telling you that it doesn't sound formulaic for a happy, secure relationship with someone. To me, it sounds more like a recipe for disaster."

Although Josh had only tried to explain himself so that Prissy wouldn't lose confidence in his opinions, that's not how she interpreted him.

"Look. I'm thinking maybe this wasn't such a good idea," Prissy said, collecting her phone from the arm of the chair and dusting off her soccer shorts.

Prissy prepared to do what she'd always done, and that was to pack up and leave. The situation was no different from what it had been for any people she'd ever loved or had conflicts with. She'd abandon Dr. Odom and any hope she might have for a relationship with Lacy—legalities aside. Because Josh was damned sure that she wouldn't go to another therapist, and he wasn't simply being arrogant. She just wasn't one to try and try again. Prissy didn't face adversity head-on in her personal life as she did with athletics. That's where she'd always channeled all her productive energy. She was drawn to long-distance running because she had complete control over its outcome.

"Prissy, please sit back down. Take a few deep breaths. I'm afraid I pushed you a little too hard. But in my defense, I think you're approaching a breakthrough on your first day, and that's commendable and uncommon. Your decision to come here today was the biggest stride. I don't want you to give up on that. Do you want to? It's only when we apply ourselves to something with consistency and perseverance that we achieve anything. It can be difficult and very taxing, and sometimes you might feel like you can't go anymore. But I want you to relax because we're through here today."

Josh's phone rang.

"You, see? You've gone way farther than the time allotted for your session because I lost track of time. This is my wife reminding me about our lunch date. It's something we do every Friday. She'll bring a picnic lunch, and we'll sit behind that oak tree outside and plan our evening. I think she wants to help her friend set up for Artwalk. But I'm going to lobby for a game of Trivial Pursuit at the house."

Josh was chauvinistically and homophobically trying to come up with the most lesbian things he could think of to calm Prissy down and make her contemplate how life could be. It may have been manipulative, but sometimes, he thought, you had to do what you had to do. And besides, he did have a lunch date.

"Take your call, Doc," Prissy said with a smile, "I'll go online and book again for next week. Same Bat time, same Bat channel?"

Good. Josh had calmed her sufficiently to keep her as a patient. He was growing just as curious about how this ordeal might play itself out as anyone would be.

"Uh, yes, that's excellent. But, Prissy, could I please ask that you refer to me as Dr. Odom? I'm admitting I want to establish that boundary with you, but it's only for your sake."

For a moment, Prissy looked confused. Then, she appeared a tad aggravated, but ultimately, she smiled again.

"Whatever you say, Doc…Tor-Odom," she said playfully before turning and walking out of the door without being escorted or told where to go.

Man, Josh thought to himself. Maybe he'd done a better job than he thought if he got someone like Prissy to kid around.

"I've got one more to see, then I'm on my way," Josh said after returning the call he'd silenced.

CHAPTER FIVE

"They suck!" Gil Wallace blurted, gnawing on a big bite of ribeye in his left cheek, "They got no O-line, man. I mean, that kid they got in the portal can toss it, and he can move. But he looks like Mahomes playin' with a bunch of Cub Scouts. Bama's gonna eat his damn lunch. It's a joke!"

Josh and Gil sat in Madeline's, the trendy new steakhouse geared toward a younger clientele. It wasn't like traditional steak houses that were dark, where people could sit in virtual obscurity, only being noticed when they wanted to. Madeline's was as bright as a lit stage. Its pastel yellow exterior and the bay windows serving as its facade put everything and everyone on display. It was very different from what Josh had envisioned when Gil suggested where they'd meet. He'd pictured something between a Ruth's Chris and a Fleming's. But it felt more like a greenhouse than a steakhouse.

"I can't remember the last time I sat and watched an SEC football game," Josh responded, "I just don't care anymore, you know? I got better things to do on a Saturday these days."

"I do, too. But I just don't do them!" Gil said, laughing as he wiped the A-1 from the corner of his mouth.

"We really ought to try and go to at least one game this year. If it ain't an Ole Miss game, we could even head up to Knoxville. I friggin' love Neyland Stadium. We could make a trip of it, dog. Rent an RV. Load it down and take a booze cruise. You down?"

Josh snickered. Gil hadn't changed a lick since college. He was a giant frat boy whose interests were as mundane as his mannerisms.

Gil was more reserved if you caught him in front of parents or students. Josh was getting what Gil projected around his friends and frat brothers. He'd only ever gotten brief glimpses of the real Gil. He was a social chameleon, and Josh wondered if he'd been suffering from borderline personality disorder the whole time.

Looking back at Gil as he thumped two Splenda packets for his tea, Josh said, "I don't think Liza would let me. Especially if I told her that you were going."

Josh wasn't entirely kidding.

"Shit, man. Bring her! I promise to behave!" Gil laughed.

"Is Michelle gonna go for that?" Josh asked.

Immediately, Gil's expression changed, and he rolled his eyes. He knew Josh was trying to find out if he and his wife had patched things up since the last time they spoke. But he wasn't going to let him get away with it.

"Shit. Who said anything about Michelle? I just meant you, me, and Liza. We could have a real good time, man," Gil said with a dirty little grin.

"What's the matter? You afraid Liza might like it too much? Come on, man. I'm telling you, it would be fun! We could take turns driving the RV. And we could take turns driving her, too," Gil continued.

Gil was only trying to get a rise out of Josh, and both men knew it. But they also both realized that if Josh rubber-stamped it, Gil would be more than willing to accommodate. He'd always been such a freak.

"Not funny, dude," Josh said, halfway smiling.

"Aw, maann. I bet Liza would do it! Call her! Get her on the phone!" Gil said, just loud enough not to cause a scene among the other lunch-goers at Madeline's.

"Gil," Josh said, erasing any remnant of a smile and lowering his tone.

"Okay, okay. You know I'm just messing around. Quit bein' so sensitive, dog," Gil said before directing his attention over Josh's shoulder.

"Oh, here she comes, here she comes," Gil whispered as their waitress approached the table.

"Hey, Mr. Wallce," the server said while filling their tea glasses. "How are you today?"

She spoke in the sing-song manner that people do when addressing a regular, almost like it was a rhetorical question.

"Oh, I'm good, Kelsey! How're you doing, precious?" Gil said, sitting up more erect and gleaming his big white teeth.

"I'm fine. How are your steaks?" the pretty young redhead asked.

Josh didn't want Gil to have a chance to flirt anymore, so he spoke up first.

"Delicious. Everything's wonderful."

"Good! Good! Are you boys going to have dessert today? We've got free ice cream when you purchase a Mississippi Mud.

And, Ohma' God! It is sooo good! I can't eat too much of it because it's so rich, though. And it also adds layers to my butt before I'm even done eating!" Kelsey giggled.

Josh urgently headed Gil off again. He didn't even want to imagine what he would've done with that. Kelsey didn't make it easy, either. She was clearly inviting Gil's advances.

"No, thank you, hon. Tell you what, though. I'd love to have a cup of pineapple sorbet."

Then Gil thrust himself into the conversation and spoke like a big perv.

"I'd like some of that Mississippi Mud and some ice cream. I wonder if it'll do the same thing to your butt if I'm the one eating it?"

Josh cringed. How did the guy get away with shit like that? And he was that way with utter strangers. It was impressive. Reprehensible and stomach-churning. But impressive. Then Josh was even more confounded by Kelsey's demeanor. She wasn't as put off or disgusted as she should have been.

"Well, maybe we just need to find out," Kelsey said, arching an eyebrow as she stared at Gil.

Josh felt invisible. But he'd always felt that way around Gil, particularly if they were in the company of young ladies--although he wasn't sure Kelsey qualified. Gil was loud, arrogant, and had the strongest libido Josh had ever witnessed, and he'd witnessed a bunch.

In college, whenever Gil walked into a bar or showed up at a 'late-night,' it was like flipping a switch. Every female head turned in his direction before swiveling back and discussing something through giggles. That same switch caused another phenomenon among the males at whichever venue.

However. they didn't giggle. They eyed Gil just as intently as the girls did, but the expression on their faces told Josh there was nothing they'd like more than to beat the mortal hell out of Gil. And it looked like they wanted to take their time doing it.

After Kelsey went to fetch the men's desserts, Josh decided to try to get back on topic.

"I take it that you and Michelle haven't figured things out yet."

Gil took on the same wounded expression as before.

"What's to figure out, Josh? She's leaving me. Or I guess I should say she's making me leave. Got my walking papers last month. So, it's all over but the crying. Well, that and I'm supposed to be looking for a permanent place to live. Unreal, man."

Josh couldn't believe Gil was even pretending to be shocked that Michelle was leaving him. He had the unfortunate vantage of someone who had known the couple forever, and his career also made him reach the pessimistic conclusion that no one ever really changed.

"You're not saying anything," Gil said, snapping Josh out of his trance.

"Oh. I'm sorry, Gil. I was listening. I just got distracted, thinking about how long you two have been together and what a shame it is. Have you told the girls?"

That made Gil even glummer as he poked his fork at the fat on his plate.

"Yeah," he said, continuing to look down.

"And how'd that go?" Josh asked.

Gil looked up and started shaking his head.

"Not as well as I'd imagined it would. It's weird, too, because they've been there this whole time. They've heard the shouting. They've seen the ruts I've left in the yard. But they acted like this was all something brand new to them. They were devastated."

Josh shifted into psychiatrist mode.

"I suppose that's to be expected, Gil. I'm not saying that makes it any better, but they're grown now. They made it through all those dicey times, and so did you and Michelle. They've entered a phase of life where you just assume home is home, Momma is Daddy's wife, and they'll always be there. Can you imagine having that taken away just when you're trying to create your own family? It's got to be tough, Gil."

Gil still seemed distressed, and he got a little testy, too.

"I...I just don't know what to say to that, Josh. Of course, I realize all that. And I know I'm the one to blame. It still hurts, though. You know? I mean, it really hurts."

"What about Clint?" Josh asked.

Clint was Gil's boy. The youngest. He was a big, good-looking kid like Gil had been. But compared to Gil, he was a bit of a milquetoast. He was "all up in the church," according to his father.

"Won't even talk to me. I saw him play last weekend in South Haven. Went down on the field to congratulate him, but he walked right past me like I wasn't even there."

"What did you do?" Josh asked.

"What *could* I do? I just turned around, walked to my truck, and went to the Comfort Inn where I'm staying."

Josh's mind raced, and he tried to think of a way to bring a little levity into the discussion.

"Cool, man. I heard their Continental Breakfast is the shizzle my nizzle," was all he could come up with.

It was enough because Gil burst out laughing.

"You really should never talk like that, bro. You sound like Tom Brokaw vacationing in South Central."

After that, they both started laughing, and they laughed for a good minute before calming down. Gil finally spoke but devolved into the same pitiful state as before.

"Listen, Josh. You've always been a good friend to me, man. Always. And it means a lot to me."

"I think a lot of our friendship, too, Gil. Liza loves you, too. She's not ready to let me hang out with you at the Comfort Inn or anything, but she does."

They became quiet as Josh stared at Gil, who appeared to be in deep thought.

"Have you found a new place yet? I mean, will you lease an apartment or just buy a place?" Josh asked.

Gil surprised Josh when he spoke up in a peppy tone.

"Actually, I have, Josh. I'm going to see what I can do about finally selling Momma and Daddy's place, and then I'm moving to Mississippi. I'm looking at a house about twenty miles from the school. But it'll give me a little distance, so I won't be running into people all the time like I am now."

Gil continued light-heartedly, saying, "I won't have to stop what I'm doing and go to lunch with people that never bother calling or checking on me and just hit me up out of the blue."

Josh tried to hide his embarrassment when he looked up at Gil. But Gil had already broken into a chuckle, so Josh laughed. He knew he'd better explain himself, though.

"Come on, Gil. I don't ever go to lunch with anyone. I just hadn't thought about you in a long time, and you popped into my head. Thought it'd be nice to visit with you for a while."

Gil put his hand in the center of his chest and feigned an expression as though he were moved.

"Oh. That's so touching. I feel so…so special inside, Joshua."

"Shut up, man," Josh groaned with a smile.

Gil had always found a way to make Josh laugh and was a master at diffusing uncomfortable situations. That was another of his few traits that were enviable to Josh.

***

The men sat in the restaurant for another hour and a half, talking about trivial things. They both avoided discussions about Gil and Michelle, and Josh put his concerns about Lacy on the back burner. But just as Josh pulled out his wallet to pick up the tab for lunch, Gil stopped him.

"Before we go," Gil began, "can I talk to you about something that's been bothering me."

Josh stopped fumbling with his wallet and looked up at Gil, who looked back at him like his golden retriever, Scout, did when she was in an obedience crisis. It was whenever the pooch had done something bad and was willing to acknowledge something bad had been done. She just didn't want to take ownership of it.

"Of course you can, Gil. I blacked out my whole afternoon to visit, so we can discuss whatever you'd like."

Gil's eye contact diminished as he spoke to Josh. He went from being assertive, almost staring Josh down at times, to cutting his eyes around and weaving his head as though whatever was fighting to get out of his mouth would make him heave.

Josh gave him space. If he knew Gil as he thought he did, then he'd eventually bring it all to bear because he'd been the one who asked permission. Josh was going to let Gil tell him everything.

"You know, you get older, your life can go a few ways. You're either prepared to finish the rest of it with the same person you've been with for that long or, if you find yourself like I do, you have to choose another path. Man, I've destroyed everything Michelle and I built together, and while I'm willing to try and put it back, she's not. And I can't say I blame her for that. Goddamn, I…I can't make someone try any harder than they've already tried for years while I sat on my ass and did nothing. It's like, you know, there's all this stuff, man. Stuff I wasn't a part of. Stuff I wasn't around for. I missed my whole gah-damned life, Josh. I missed my kids' lives, too."

Repentance—that's what Gil was giving Josh. But it did *not* suit him at all. He labored over his speech with a lot of 'you know' and 'man,' and it appeared that, at any moment, he could clam up and shut down. Josh didn't want that to happen, so he threw Gil a life ring.

"Gil, you didn't miss anything. Your role may have been diminished as a father, and you might have been a jackass at times. But you should realize that your children love you, Gil. If they didn't, they wouldn't be trying to punish you as they are. It's their way of taking you to task for what you've done, and while all the wounds are still wide open, they'll heal. They'll accept whatever new visage you take after that's happened. It's a reorganization, Gil. You can either refuse to accept that and be miserable for the rest of your life, trying to pretend that nothing happened, or accept whatever status they're willing to give you in their new lives. But make no mistake, Gil. That's going to be up to them. And you'll have to take what they give you and build on that. You see?"

"Jesus Christ, man. You're making this even harder than I thought it would be," Gil said, fighting emotions.

"I'm sorry. I didn't mean to do that," Josh said, trying to calm him.

Gil sighed and began shaking his head.

"No, no. It's alright. It's all a part of the decision point I'm at in life, and I guess I needed to hear that. But there's something I don't want to leave unsaid before you go. I just don't know if I'm brave enough."

Josh continued trying to coach Gil through his emotions.

"I've listened to you throughout your marriage to Michelle, so I know just about everything there is to know already. What's one more piece of kindling on the pile?"

Gil smiled and cocked his head sideways.

"I don't know, man," he said, laughing again, "this is a big old chunk of wood I'm about to lay down!"

Josh reluctantly backed off. He wanted the whole truth, but he thought he might endanger that by pressing too hard.

"Then don't tell me, Gil. If it's not something you're comfortable discussing, let's just postpone it for another time. Unless I die or something, I'll always be here to listen to you. So, let's just visit this again when you're more comfortable. I'm not going anywhere."

Gil smiled and nodded at Josh like he was comforted by his friend's words.

"Maybe that's the best move. Maybe you're right. But I am going to lay the groundwork for you, okay? I don't think you'd be able to deal with all I've got to tell you if I just dropped it on you cold."

"Say as much or as little as you'd like, Gil. I'm listening."

Gil started back up, speaking slowly as though he wanted to ensure Josh absorbed every word.

"Do you remember how you felt when you started dating Liza? You acted all goofy, telling everybody how awesome she was and how you felt like she'd be the one you ended up marrying. But that feeling? Do you remember that feeling?" Gil asked.

"Of course I do," Josh insisted.

"And you didn't give a shit that she was Vietnamese, right? You didn't care what anybody thought, not even me or Scott or Michael. You just didn't give a damn, you know? You knew we would give you grief over it, but you didn't care. And then when we all wore those rice paddy hats and installed that big tailpipe on your Accord? Oh *shit*, that was some funny *shit,* man!"

Gil seemed to immerse himself in the past and laugh like he was in college again. Even though it would be short-lived, he was concealing his emotions by kidding around.

That little tailpipe stunt had pissed Josh off. But he saw the humor in it for the first time since it had happened. He had to drive around for a week with his car sounding like a Kawasaki Ninja until he could get to a mechanic to "fix" it.

"That was messed up, what y'all did," Josh said, giving in to a snicker.

"I know, I know. It was messed up. We were way outta' line with that one."

Gil got serious again.

"But we're not kids anymore, Josh. And I'd never make fun of you or ridicule you for someone you chose to be with—no matter what society thought about it. I hope you realize that. And I'm telling you this because people always make snap judgments, especially when it involves their friends' choice of mate. Sometimes, you've got to break the rules, though, Josh. Sometimes, you must forget what your friends, society, or anybody else thinks about that person. It shouldn't matter who the person is or where they come from. It shouldn't matter if they're white, black, Asian, Mexican—whatever. And it shouldn't matter how old they are, either."

Wait a second. Hold the phone. Was Gil building toward telling Josh he was in love with that little vixen he'd double-teamed with that coach in his office? Was Gil even capable of emotions like that, given the situation? He'd screwed almost every good-looking girl at Baker, but he never fell for one of them. Refused even to date them.

So, was Gil now saying that one of his many dalliances had led him into a relationship with an underaged bimbo? Had she broken his heart? Were the cosmic tables of love now turning on the mighty Gil? Was this his penance for a life of screwing around?

Dear God, Josh hoped not. And he hoped that wasn't what Gil would tell him either. So much so that he wanted to stop him from talking anymore. But Gil interrupted Josh's pondering.

"Josh, I've found somebody like that. We're similar in so many ways. We both like cooking. We both love going out to eat. They laugh at my jokes, and I laugh at theirs. And it shouldn't matter, and you might be grossed out if you knew more. But we have record-breaking kinky sex. It's nonstop physicality, but for the first time in a long time—for me, at least— it's like there's emotions behind it. They honestly make me feel the way I used to feel about Michelle, and I hope the way she felt about me. Somebody's finally letting me be who I've always wanted to be, and I want to invest myself in something for the first time in a very long time, Josh. I don't want anybody else, man."

Josh had to put a stop to everything. It was headed off the rails quickly, and he didn't want to be caught up in the aftermath of Gil telling him he was in love with a child that Josh knew good and damn well didn't feel the same way about him.

"Gil, I'm sorry. But I need you to stop talking now," Josh said, trying not to sound cold.

"Huh?" Gil asked.

"I said I want you, no, I need you to stop talking right now. Don't say another word," Josh continued.

"What the hell, man? Are you serious right now? 'Cause if you're kidding, then quit messing around. I'm trying to tell you something. I'm sorry for the tailpipe, alright? We were just kids, I mean, what do you want from me? You can't still be pissed about all that."

Josh struggled for a second, but he realized he had to bring the impromptu psychiatric session to a halt.

"Gil, I know about Lacy, alright? I know everything. And I shouldn't tell you that because I'm breaking the law, and I could be debarred because she's my patient. So, just shut up, okay? Just don't say anything else."

And Gil didn't say anything for the longest. Then, when he did speak up, he was a different person.

"You unbelievable little prick. Is that why you asked me to lunch today? To try and get me to confess to something?"

Gil leaned forward, gritted his teeth, and growled. And the sudden metamorphosis scared the hell out of Josh.

"I ought to get up and beat the hell out of your ass.."

"Gil, I und…"

"No. *You* shut the hell up, Josh. Because if you say anything else to me, that's exactly what I'm going to do to you. I'm going to beat you within an inch of your life."

Gil shot up from the table and marched toward the door. He was so distracted that he left the napkin tied around his neck, which Kelsey swooped in and snagged.

Gil looked fearsome. He stopped, and all six-foot-four inches of him stood like a Roman Centurion who'd materialized in Madeline's. Then he barked toward the table, "Oh, by the way. You remember that guy Brad? The freshman I ran out of Kappa house, and everybody was pissed at me because I did?"

Everyone in Madeline's was now tuned in and intrigued to find out if Josh remembered this Brad fellow.

"Well, I did that because he was bangin' Liza, Josh! That's right! While you were at that MCAT prep course in Nashville, Liza was getting pounded by that little bastard, so I ran him off!"

The maître dis reached toward Gil, saying, "Sir!"

But Gil pushed him backward, and the frail man knocked over the podium and sandwich board describing the dessert special Gil had just finished. Everyone in the restaurant gasped, but then they all looked at Josh as Gil bounded out of Madeline's.

"Shhhhit," Josh said under his breath.

CHAPTER SIX

"*What* did he say?" Liza asked in bed beside Josh.

Josh realized he'd crossed a line the moment he finished speaking.

"I can't believe he said that," Liza whispered, "I don't know what to say. So just give me a second, okay?"

Her composure didn't last very long, though. She fussed with the down comforter covering them both, then reached over and turned the bedside lamp on.

"And he said this in front of people? In Madeline's?" Liza continued.

"He did," Josh responded, rolling on his side and turning his back to her.

They were quiet for several seconds before Liza finally said, "Wait a minute. You *believed* him? You believed that giant, egomaniacal asshole?"

Liza was a virtuous woman—at least, that's how Josh had always viewed her. And he was just as chapped as she was that someone as morally bankrupt as Gil Wallace had dared to tarnish her image. Still, part of him couldn't help wondering if Gil had been telling the truth.

"And you didn't say anything? You just let him drag me through the mud without saying anything?"

Liza was livid. Her little five-foot-tall frame could terrify anyone whenever she became as angry as she was.

"I wanted him to shut up, Liza," Josh said, stretching his head over his shoulder, still lying on his side with his back to her, "What would you have had me done? The guy could grind me into a pulp! He'd just threatened to do that to me a second before!"

Liza looked confused as she stared back at Josh, and he could tell she was just beginning to analyze everything.

"I don't understand. Why were you talking about me at lunch with Gil? No, wait, what in the hell were you even *doing* at lunch with Gil? And why was he threatening to grind you into a pulp?"

Josh said nothing because he couldn't talk about why he'd called Gil and asked him to lunch. Without disclosing confidential patient information, it wouldn't make sense to Liza. He had no right to call Gil on the grounds he had, and he knew it.

Liza reached over to the nightstand and put in her contact lenses. That couldn't be good, Josh thought—Liza preparing to be on the move.

"What in the hell are you doing?" Josh asked, sitting up in bed.

"I'm going to talk to that son-of-a-bitch! That's what I'm doing!" Liza hissed, grabbing the keys to her Mercedes and leaping from the bed.

"Wait, what? What do you mean??" Josh begged.

The little firecracker swiveled around and held her keys up as she glared at him, and Josh heard a distant chirp from the garage.

"I…am…going…to…*talk* to him!" Liza shrieked, moving toward her closet and rifling through her shoes until she found her Ugg boots. She hunched down, pulled them on, then wrapped herself in the mid-length silky pink robe she yanked off the armoire, cinching its belt.

"Are you out of your damned mind, Liza?" Josh said, raising his voice, which he might've done once or twice the whole time they'd been married.

Liza didn't answer, which frightened Josh. She started toward the door, and Josh realized that if he didn't stop her, she'd do exactly what she said she'd do.

She didn't bluff. She didn't threaten. Liza acted. So, Josh jumped up and ran her down just as she reached the door. But as he pulled her backward, she grabbed the doorframe with her right hand and tugged.

"No, no! Let me go!" Liza insisted.

Feisty as she was, though, there was no way she could overpower Josh. She was too petite. But that didn't mean she wouldn't put up a fight.

They continued to struggle until, at one point, Liza had both feet on the wall, holding onto the doorframe, grunting and pulling with everything she had. Once Josh got close enough, he reached around her waist and hurled her onto the bed. Liza raced on her hands and knees, making it to the other side of the bed so she could stand on solid ground between it and the wall. But then she was cornered.

Josh had to calm her down somehow. It wasn't going to end well if he didn't. He held his hands out to his sides and started reasoning with her. He couldn't be too passive with her, though. He had to deal with her assertively to some extent.

"Liza? Liza, I'm sorry, alright? I'm sorry, and I should've called Gil on his BS. That was stupid of me, and I'm sorry. Okay?"

Liza's chest heaved, and mascara began to run from the corners of her eyes. She looked like a caged animal someone had taunted.

After a second, Josh calmly continued.

"I want you to calm down and think about what you're doing, and all you're doing is letting Gil win."

Liza continued to breathe heavily as she looked at him, but she wasn't saying anything as Josh went on.

"Gil said that to be hurtful because his life is in shambles, Liza. Lord knows he and Michelle have been in a tailspin for a long time, but they've just come crashing to the ground. And Gil doesn't know what to do, so he wants to be as disruptive as possible. It's nothing but his way of crying for help, Liza. He's alone, and he's terrified, honey. Please, just calm down, and let's not even talk about it again tonight, okay? We'll talk about it tomorrow, and we'll laugh, and that will be the end of it. Do you hear me, Liza?"

Josh saw he was gaining ground because Liza's breathing slowed.

Damn, she was beautiful, Josh thought to himself. All piss and vinegar. Her spunk had always enticed him. He took her hand and guided her back over the bed, where she fell onto him as though she'd just finished a marathon. She was exhausted from the adrenaline rush.

When Liza got that way and was most vulnerable, she wanted to be with Josh. But she didn't want to 'make love' with him. Liza wanted sex. She wanted animalistic, passionate sex. And when Liza wanted it that way, so did Josh. It was like some pheromone-infused signal they sent out to one another. So, Josh obliged her.

What Liza didn't realize was that Josh had entered a different realm. In that place, Josh wasn't Josh anymore. Liza was still Liza, just a lot younger. She was a twenty-year-old college student. But Josh was Brad Lawrence, that ridiculous simpleton that flunked out of Baker shortly after Gil ran him out of the frat house. Josh wasn't anywhere around, though. He was off studying for the MCAT. But his naughty little girlfriend was there. And Brad would do all sorts of stuff to her while Josh was gone.

Just as oblivious as Liza was to Josh's assumed identity, he was ignorant of the fantasy that simultaneously titillated her. In it, she'd left Josh at the house, torn out of the driveway, and raced to confront that son-of-a-bitch, Gil Wallace. Yes, she'd messed around with Brad behind Josh's back. And yes, it had been a purely physical romp. But that was her business. What right did Gil have to tell Josh anything?

Liza imagined being in for a surprise when she got to the Comfort Inn. She'd bang on Gil's door, and he'd rip it open. Then he'd yank her into his room and do exactly what was being done to her—except he'd be a lot more forceful.

"Harder! Harder!" Liza moaned as Josh upped his pace.

Josh and Liza were on the same plane, but they were miles apart, each perceiving they were in control. Suddenly, though, that place became inhospitable to them both. Their existence there was unsustainable. It was too much. Too intense.

And as they simultaneously experienced an exodus from that place, they both shouted.

"Oh, my God," Liza said as the carousel lost momentum and stopped.

**

Near the airport a few miles away, Gil Wallace lay in bed, staring at the ceiling. He had so many things on his mind, but foremost was how he'd behaved at lunch that day.

Josh had always been good to him. He drove two hours to Oxford to bail him out of jail the time he got in a fight after an Ole Miss game. Then, he helped Michelle and him move from Knoxville into that old house in Jackson before she got her Master's at Milsaps. Josh stood by him when the rest of the fraternity wanted to kick him out for beating the hell out of Brad Lawrence—even though Josh hadn't known why he'd done it.

Josh was a true blue. He was the kind of guy you could call on anytime, and he'd try to help you. He didn't deserve Gil to have talked to him the way he had at lunch. Liza didn't deserve Gil saying anything either, even if she had stepped out on Josh. They were just kids when all that damned stuff happened. Gil wondered if he'd ever be able to patch things up with them.

Gil thought about his son, Clint, and if he'd had a good game that night. The weekend before would've been hard to top, though. Five hurry-ups. Three sacks. He imagined that Clint would still be chasing down quarterbacks in a year, except he'd be doing it in a college stadium somewhere.

Lastly and most passionately, Gil thought about Michelle. He tried to picture what she was doing. Was she thinking about him? Was she thinking about everything he'd put her through and sorry she'd ever met him? Or did she even miss him? Did she feel alone? Was she sad? Was she crying?

Unable to keep thinking about Michelle, Gil rolled over and took the room phone off its receiver.

"Hey," he said after a few seconds, "I need to see you."

Gil was greeted with an onslaught of complaints and threats before he interrupted.

"I know, okay? Just listen to me for a second."

The fussing stopped long enough for him to speak again and say what was on his mind.

"Listen. I can't be alone tonight. I need to see you."

"I realize that," Gil continued after a moment of listening, "I know! Damn it, I know! "

Gil remained silent as he listened for several more seconds.

Then, Gil Wallace, the aging lothario and Restoration School for Girls headmaster, started to cry.

"Please," he whispered, "please, don't do this to me. I can't take it anymore. Alright, I'm sorry. I know. I'm just so emotional right now. "

Gil waited a few moments before getting the answer he wanted.

"Oh, sweetheart, thank you. Sweet Jesus, thank you so much. Yeah, that's right. It's the Comfort Inn on American Way. I'm in Room 235, a little down from the elevator."

Gil sighed before committing to what he'd had such trouble saying ever since things got started.

"Honey, I love you. I love you so much."

***

After Liza parked in the Comfort Inn parking lot, she stopped and sighed. Was she really about to do this?

Josh always slept like he was in a coma, and he'd been that way since residency. He'd stay zonked out for hours, especially after everything she'd laid on him that night. She figured he'd be asleep until at least noon.

She lowered the vanity and looked at herself again, but everything was tight. She wore the lighter base Josh liked because it made her look like a geisha, and she would happily play that role tonight. She'd do whatever Gil wanted and give herself to him however he saw fit.

Just as Liza clicked into the hotel's vestibule and the doors closed behind her, she heard a pleasant male voice saying, "Miss! Miss!"

She continued into the lobby before turning back to see who was speaking to her. Then, when the doors slid open again, a tall, svelte man wearing a white shirt, black jeans, and shiny black shoes strolled into the lobby behind her. He was smiling and looked like he'd just stepped out of one of those teeth-bleaching pamphlets from the dentist's office. He was ruddy, with longer black hair, pulled back across his head with blue eyes.

"You dropped this, ma'am," the man said as he approached.

He held something, but Liza didn't notice because she couldn't stop staring at him. He was that good-looking. And by the time he was close enough that he could've wrapped his arm around her waist and drawn her to him for a kiss, she'd already begun to fantasize that he would. And the way he smelled—it was clean—icy clean.

"Here you go," the man said through a wash of minty breath that suddenly made Liza even more self-conscious. Had she brushed her teeth enough? The man made her feel ugly.

Pushing her hair over her right ear and looking down at the man's hand that had, regrettably, never made it so far as caressing her cheek, Liza noticed that he was handing her the golden-bowed tube of Satin Allure lipstick that had fallen out of her purse.

"Thank you," Liza said, too insecure to say anything more.

The man smiled again and winked at her. Then he moved past her toward the elevators.

Liza wanted to follow him. She wanted to go wherever he was going.

Then Liza remembered why she was at the Comfort Inn, but that was the only thing she remembered. She didn't even know what room to go to.

***

"235, 235, 235," Liza kept reminding herself after she left the front desk.

When the elevator reached the second floor, Liza stepped out and turned right as instructed. But there was the beautiful man again, facing a room door. She heard the door creak open and a man's voice say, "Hey!"

Though she couldn't see the person inside the room, Liza realized it was the man's father or another relative because of how the voice spoke to him.

Liza was going to get her money's worth from Gil that night. But she was so taken with the young man that she started fantasizing again. She fantasized about finishing with Gil and then waiting in the lobby until the young man returned to his car. She wanted to be near him again. She wanted to see him up close. To touch him and for him to touch her.

'What the hell is wrong with you?' Liza asked herself as she tried to move by the open door without the men noticing her. As she got closer, she ducked her head and looked at the floor so she wouldn't make eye contact. Then, as she got to where they stood, she saw the good-looking man's shiny black shoes and his father's enormous bare feet standing on the tile entrance to the room. She hurried past and continued toward her destination.

235, 235, 235. Liza was on her way to the best sex of her life. It was going to be non-stop for hours to come.

235, 235, just a few more seconds until 235, where passion awaited her. She'd see just how tough a mood Gil was in tonight. She'd tame him just like she tamed Josh.

235, 235, 235.

Liza looked to her left to get a fix on where she was and noticed the number "232" on a wall placard next to a door. It was just before happening. She didn't care what emotional state Gil was in. She was going to bring him around.

Liza looked at the wall again and saw 234, 236, 238. Damn it. She'd walked too far. She twisted around in the opposite direction. That's when she saw the handsome man and realized that it wasn't his father who had greeted him because whoever had opened the door was clutching the good-looking man's cheeks and kissing him as lustfully as she'd wanted to.

The other man pulled the handsome man into the room as he protested, "No, no. I really can't. I've got to get back. I just wanted to see you for a minute."

Liza looked to her left as she moved past the room in the opposite direction. She was sure she had passed Gil's room again because she was so distracted. And when she saw "231," she realized she'd done just that. So, she turned around a second time and headed back toward Gil's room.

When she got to 235, she knocked lightly on its door. She waited a few moments, but no one answered, so she knocked again—still nothing.

Liza thought back a few moments, trying to regain her wits. Then she walked to the end of the hall while Googling the number for the hotel. When she reached the end, the woman she'd spoken to earlier answered at the front desk.

"Uh, yes. Could you give me Gil Wallace's room again? I assure you he's waiting on me, but I think I got the number wrong, and I don't want to wake anybody else up."

Before the girl could give her the room number, though, Liza heard someone unfasten the latch in the direction of room 235, so she walked back toward Gil's room. But as she stopped in front of it and the door opened, she saw the good-looking man staring back at her, and he looked confused.

"Is everything okay, sweetheart? Is something wrong?" he asked.

Liza looked between the man and the placard that read "235." Realizing she was in deep trouble, she said, "Oh, no. No, sir. There's nothing wrong. I just had the wrong room."

Liza turned and hustled toward the elevator, leaving the man with the same confused look standing in the doorway. As she hurried into the elevator, Gil Wallace just missed seeing her when he stepped into the hallway next to the good-looking man who looked back at him, shrugged, and shook his head.

"Some nutcase, Gil, I mean, I don't know," he said.

Gil looked toward the elevator and then at Stephen. Then he cupped his hand on Stephen's head, kissed him, and walked him into room 235. A moment later, the door closed behind them.

"Oh, my God, oh, my God, oh my God," Liza whispered on the elevator.

She was coming to the realization of what a horrible mistake she'd averted. She'd just dodged a life-altering, marriage-ending nightmare of a landmine.

But when the doors opened, and Liza flew out of the elevator, alternating between sprinting and walking so she wouldn't alarm anyone, Liza didn't know the half of it.

CHAPTER SEVEN

It was going to be a pass play. Clint could sense it.

Blinks, twitches, posture angles—his brain took everything in, deciphering what it all meant. In essence, his instinct toggled to the "on" position, transforming him into a killer.

Clint was the All-State, 5A nightmare that made high school coaches and offensive coordinators lie awake at night, trying to devise a way to stop him. He was the perennial blue-chip athlete.

But all Clint Wallace knew at that moment? It was going to be a pass play.

As anticipated, the quarterback dropped back, and then he rolled right. He examined the field and the position of his receivers before he pump-faked. That caused half of the secondary to flinch as they contemplated narrowing the distance between themselves and the potentially designed run that could take place. But it never happened.

Instead, number seven for the Merciful Cross Crusaders reared again, except this time, he was going to throw. But just as he started to send the ball on a rope to the end zone, a flash of light came simultaneously with a cracking sound.

The quarterback couldn't move his arms and could no longer stand upright. All he could do was fall forward like a felled pine tree.

Clint Wallace lingered over him as the pain came to the all-division quarterback. Coaches on both sides hollered, "Ball! Ball! Ball!" but Clint didn't hear them as he gazed down at his bounty that hadn't moved for several seconds. Clint's teammates slammed into him, shouting in his ears and bringing him back into reality.

"Yeah! Thass what I'm 'talm baht!"

"Argh! Argh! Argh! "

"Get it bay-bay! Get it! They ain't shit!"

After Clint hit Trent Rogers, the ball exploded away from the Crusader quarterback's arm, but it wasn't because he'd passed it. It was because he'd been delivered a blow so hard that he'd go to the hospital later that night, unable to breathe without crippling pain. Then Vondrelle Stewart, who'd go on to be an All-American safety at Georgia, scooped the ball up and ran into the end zone, clenching the win for the St. Michael Cardinals, spoiling their nemeses' undefeated record. The stadium erupted as fans raced down and charged the field.

Clint had no interest in celebrating, though. He just wanted to get on the bus, go home, shower, and be with the newfound love of his life, whom he'd met over the summer at Camp Redemption. She'd moved to Memphis from Nashville to live with her aunt, just so she could be closer to him. He'd never felt about anyone the way he did about Lucille. She was his muse, and he was her captain.

***

"You know, God has a plan for all of us. And I can't speak for him, but my heart tells me his plan for you doesn't include drinking, Aunt Bette," Clint preached as he stared at Lucille's aunt.

"Hmm. I see," Bette replied, seething and red-eyed, under the influence of a lot of white wine. "Well, you know what?"

Clint shrugged and shook his head.

"Fuck you, Clint. Fuck you, and fuck your God," she snapped, "and you can take him, your Bible, and that little whore and get the abzolute fffuck outta my houzze."

Clint didn't act shocked at all. He was well-versed in dealing with a drunk. And while he chose to disregard Aunt Bette's stinging comment about God, he did take exception to the one she made about Lucille, who was upstairs getting dressed.

"Don't call her that," Clint warned, leaning forward on the sofa and glaring into Aunt Bette's bloodshot eyes as she sat in an oversized leather wingback, glaring right back.

The slight, bird-faced woman eased forward as she mocked Clint's position. Hands on her thighs, hunched over and looking mad at the world. It seemed like she was taunting Clint, and he imagined that she was either so stupid or so wasted that she couldn't comprehend how badly he could hurt her if he wanted to. He could snap her neck like a chicken's without rising from the sofa if she were within arm's reach.

About that time, Lucille came bubbling down the stairs.

"Hey, honeybunches! Aunt Bette, why didn't you tell me he was here?"

Even in the conservative flower print dress she wore, Lucille was stunning. She had classic good looks. Her hair was up in a bun, and she looked more like she was heading to the beach for a bonfire than seeing a movie.

Bette didn't answer Lucille. She and Clint looked like a couple of street dogs, growling and gauging each other's intentions. By the time Lucille reached the pair, Clint had stifled the fantasy that played out in his mind. The one where he coiled Aunt Bette's hair in a circle and repeatedly bashed her face into his knee until she stopped breathing.

Realizing he'd forgotten his manners, Clint shot up from the sofa in observance of a lady entering, which melted Lucille's heart. All Aunt Bette did was roll her eyes.

"Aunt Bette, we're going to see…" Lucille started before turning toward Clint and asking as if yet another time, "*Deep Water*?"

"*Ant Man and The Wasp*," Clint countered.

Lucille looked disappointed.

"Oh," she said, "Okay. I guess we're going to see, uh, *Ant Man and the Wasp*, then."

Feeling he needed to explain, Clint said, "I know you wanted to see *Deep Water*, sweety, but I was reading some stuff, and it turns out it has a lot of sex and violence. I just don't think it's appropriate to take you to see something like that."

Aunt Bette couldn't take it anymore and let out a big "Ha!". She settled down, though, when Lucille shot daggers at her with her back to Clint.

"No, no, really. I think that's wonderful!" Aunt Bette said, standing up from the chair, "Tell you what! I'll even spring for popcorn!"

Bette reached into her back pocket and pulled out a Velcro wallet, took out a hundred-dollar bill, and waved it a moment before tucking it next to Lucille's right breast like she was a stripper. It was clear Bette tried to belittle the pretty young lady.

"Uh, that won't be necessary, Aunt Bette. Lucy won't need to pay her way."

Neither Clint nor Aunt Bette realized Lucille had already walked across the living area to the front door. As she stood next to it, holding it wide open, she said, "Clint, we'd better go. The midnight shows are always packed."

"You know you're right, honey. We'd better get going. It was a pleasure to…" Clint said before stopping and watching Aunt Bette lick the bottom of the glass she held. He lowered his hand, turned his back to the liquored-up old dame, and moved toward the door.

After Bette got the last drop out of the crystal iced tea glass, she looked up as though interrupted and hollered after Clint,

"Okie-dokie, smmokey! You kiddzz have a faboo time at the beejoo!"

Clint began toward her because he feared she was about to nose-dive into the floor, but Lucille stopped him.

"She'll be fine. Just let her go," Lucille said, "she's way stronger than she looks."

***

"Baby, don't," Lucille whispered, "it's just the Coming Attractions."

But it was too late. Someone had already triggered Franken-Christ, the God-fearing automaton, and he leaned forward and tapped the young man seated in front of him and Lucille on the shoulder.

"Sir, I've already asked you twice to lower your voice and not to use language like that. I'm with a young lady, and the stuff you're saying is just so inappropriate."

Jawan partially turned his head and spoke this time, whereas he hadn't even acknowledged Clint before.

"Maannn fuck you."

Clint eased back into his seat and began scratching his left cheek. He told himself that he had to keep it together, and he managed to do that—for a moment.

Then, as Jawan turned toward the screen again and continued talking as loudly and explicitly as before, he felt a sharp sting on the back of his head. Clint had leaned over and thumped him.

Jawan leaped up and tried to come at Clint over the seatback, but his girl held on tightly to him by his jeans. So Jawan grabbed the paper tub from its coaster and doused Clint and Lucille in buttered popcorn. Clint gritted his teeth and rose, realizing he had to throttle the guy to calm him down. But as he stood, he noticed the popcorn that had gotten in Lucille's hair and the frightened, surprised look on her face.

It was then that Clint left Clint behind, and he left Lucille sitting there, too. He turned down the volume of the DBX sound system that roared in the theater. He zeroed in on the glaring threat in front of him. And in the blackness, he saw only one person among the dozens in the theater, several of whom seated around both parties had started to take notice of the altercation as it unfolded.

But all Clint saw was Jawan. He couldn't see anything but Jawan. He couldn't feel Lucille's futile attempts to tug him back into his seat. He couldn't hear the gruff Marine that was about his size except decked out in his uniform barking, "Take it outside, fellas! Take it outside!"

It was Jawan. That's it. Clint Wallace was on the Earth with only one other living soul. And that soul was Jawan Pettway.

Lightning flashed, the wind in front of him separated like a spear was cutting through it, and Clint's giant fist smashed into the center of Jawan's face, snapping his nose and splattering blood everywhere.

Finally, someone became visible in the place Clint had gone, and it was the only other person in the theater with a ticket to that place. In his thirty-eight-year-old life, the Marine had been on several tours of that world before. And he'd excused several young men, who were just like Clint, from that world whenever they'd stumbled into it. He was shaking his head and snarling at Clint, equally unaware of his surroundings.

"I said to take it outside! Now get your ass outta here, boah! Move! Move! Move!"

"Yes, sir!" Clint barked back, amazed that the man was reaching him in that place.

Clint followed the man's orders, taking Lucille's hand and guiding her down the aisle toward the exit. By the time they reached it, he'd almost forgotten everything that had happened to him in the moments before.

Almost.

Clint burst from the theater, nearly dragging Lucille by her wrist. He stopped suddenly, beeped his Ford Raptor, and handed her the keys.

"Go wait for me in the truck," he said calmly.

"Baby, please, no," Lucille started but was shut down immediately.

"Go to the truck," Clint repeated.

Lucille grasped the keys and looked at the savage a final time while caressing his cheek. Clint turned her on so much, and she wanted to stay near him to see what he was about to do. But after taking the first timid steps backward, still staring at Clint, she turned and did as he instructed.

Clint watched her climb safely into the truck. Then, he was slightly confused when she started it while looking at him. Maybe she wanted the AC on.

Clint swiveled around and began to pace back and forth in front of the theatre. He'd calmed down a bit, but it wasn't enough to keep him from finishing what Jawan had started inside. He walked back and forth, looking at the asphalt and intermittently looking up at the front door of the building.

Then, when Jawan's entourage flew out from the door, Clint started readying himself and falling into the mode he was in only ninety seconds earlier. So much had happened in those ninety seconds, though.

Jawan had sauntered to the theater's exit, praying he wouldn't find Clint when he came outside. The theater manager, Sammy Rose, had called the police. And someone who knew Jawan had filed out behind his party after they walked past his aisle seat. He wasn't tight with Jawan or anything. But he knew him. He knew Clint, too.

Realizing he'd have to make good on all his bravado, Jawan marched toward Clint and began shouting. He hoped it would scare Clint enough for him to jump in whatever car he'd come in and drive away.

No such luck, though. Clint positioned himself squarely and started to sway slightly from side to side. He was subconsciously counting the steps Jawan took in his direction, and when they reached a certain number, his brain would direct him into action. An action that might just be lethal.

But, as if God intervened, sending one of his angels to diffuse the situation, Marcos Griffin hustled in front of Jawan's crew, positioning himself between the young men, throwing his arms out to his sides, and walking backward toward Clint.

"Uh, uh, baby. Uh, uh," he said to Jawan, "you ain't want none of the dis, baby. You ain't want none of this man here."

Jawan recognized Marcos from fifth grade at Larose, but he couldn't imagine what he was doing there now or why he pled with him not to beat this white boy's ass. Yeah, the white dude had gotten a shot in on him, but that was in the dark. He'd had time to recover, and his denial that a white boy could do him any harm had started to regenerate his courage. So, he kept on toward Clint. But he stopped cold with Marcos' next words.

"Baby, dat Ofay!"

Nobody in Jawan's and Marcos' circles paid any mind to academy ball. To them, that would be like cheering on your favorite tee-ball or flag football team. It just wasn't the same game. The game they loved could make millionaires out of miscreants and thespians out of thugs. It was an obsession, especially around that time of year. It was the time when the admonition for their failing grades stopped. The teachers and principals tread lightly around them, even paying them respect on a good day. But absolutely none of that had anything to do with puzzyazz, slow, ra-ra, go-team-go, white boy football.

But one white boy stood out among the pantheon of all-star athletes in Memphis. And it didn't matter that his team didn't play anybody worth a damn or that they didn't win any titles. Hell, he *was* the team, and just as had happened tonight, he was the only reason they ever managed to win a game.

Young men like Jawan and Marcos were experts in assessing talent. They knew how fast, strong, and agile everyone that mattered to the game was. And Clinton William Wallace, colloquially known as "Ofay," was a sure-enough beast. He outran scatbacks, wide receivers, quarterbacks—it didn't matter who. He lifted three-hundred and fifty-pound left offensive tackles from the ground and tossed them aside like ragdolls. And the boy hit like a locomotive crashing through a brick wall. And when Ofay put it on somebody hard enough, they just didn't get back up. Some of them never wanted to play football again.

Suddenly, the pain in Jawan's nose and the power he'd felt behind the blow delivered to his face made a whole lot more sense to him. Because if it was like his homie from Miss Jenkins' homeroom was telling him and that it was Ofay who leered at him from behind Marcos, then he absolutely didn't want any of him.

Jawan looked over at his girl Princess, who was clueless about who "Ofay" was. She didn't give a damn. But she didn't want her man to go to jail, either. She hadn't told him yet, but he would be a father again in the spring. And she didn't mean to spend time rippin'-an-runnin' between McDonald's and school just to put money on his books. So, she gave both young men an out.

"Come on, baby. Let's just go. You would kill this man, and I would never see you again. Let's just go. It looks like your nose broke anyway 'cause he hit you when you wasn't lookin'. We can just go to my Ain-tee's house and put some ice on it."

Jawan would be eternally grateful to Princess and Marcos for their intervention that night. So, he turned and hurried with Princess toward his car because he realized the police would be there soon. He wouldn't go to the hospital until the following day when he'd become the second person in twenty-four hours admitted to the ER because they had gotten in the way of "Ofay" Wallace.

***

"It's just some racist term old black men use when they're talking about white men. I don't know why they call me that, either. All my friends are black. My first girlfriend was black. Shoot, I don't even like being around white people as much as I like being around them. Kinda' mean if you ask me. But you know what? I prayed about it, and I'm no longer angry that they call me that."

Clint was blathering to Lucille, who had asked him what "Ofay" meant. She hadn't anticipated such a hearty, emotional answer. She reached over, placed her hand on his, and squeezed.

Clint was everything a girl like Lucille wanted in a man. He was strong, good-looking, and sensitive. He was the man she'd needed her entire life but hadn't even known he was missing.

By the time they pulled into the driveway of her aunt's house, Lucille had reached a boiling point. Clint had stirred the animal within her. She wasn't sure she'd be satisfied with a peck on the cheek, although that was how she envisioned things ending.

So, Lucille was shocked and a little scared when she felt Clint's hand come from nowhere and tug her by the center of her bra, dragging her over the truck's console. She let out a whimper as though she were afraid of what he'd do to her, and maybe she was.

Lucille had never seen a man move like Clint did that night. When the situation warranted it, he moved fast, effortlessly, and mortally. It was as though the same primordial urges that plagued her also dogged him. She imagined she was on the verge of falling victim to his urgency and brutality. Still, she submitted to them instead of protecting herself or resisting his advances.

But her desire to become his willing slave was decimated when he stopped in mid-passion and slumped back into his seat. She knew he was, regrettably, trying to bring himself under control. It was clear to her that he had trouble doing that based on how he'd behaved earlier. She was just sorry all that passionate energy had been wasted on violence—at least violence on someone else.

"I'm sorry, I'm sorry," Clint started, still gasping, "I don't know how I could let that happen. I just lost control."

"Oh baby," Lucille said, reaching down and taking his hand again, "Oh baby, no. It's not your fault. It's my fault. You got all worked up because of that guy, and then I know you had that game tonight. It's just what men do, honey. It's what they do. Never apologize for being a man, baby. You're going to have me one day. And I'm going to have you. But I want it to be special, just like you do. I want it to mean something. And it will."

Lucille knew exactly what to say to Clint. With a few words, she'd absolved him and removed his regrets and doubts. And more importantly than anything, she dangled the prospect of them having sex, but only under circumstances he was willing to accept. Clint was a project. He was an enigma. But he was someone she would exercise the patience required to figure out.

"I've got to go," Clint said.

"I know you do, baby. But it's probably for the best. Next time, I'll cover these up a little better," Lucille flirted, cupping her breasts together, delicately juggling them for a moment.

It was one last pass, one final dig to keep Clint intrigued about how naughty she could be if she wanted to. Lucille was a temptress.

After seeing her into the house, Clint pulled away.

***

"Hello??" Lucille called into the darkness, but no one answered.

Walking toward the kitchen for a Pelligrino, Lucille noticed the lights were on out back on the patio. She knew what that meant, but she walked in that direction anyway. As she stepped outside, she didn't see anything at first. But then she realized her drunken Aunt Bette was under the giant pillows of the patio furniture. Bette's old "boom box" rested on the glass of the end table as it blared "Wind Beneath My Wings" across the lawn.

Lucille stepped over and turned the music down before plopping next to Bette. Without opening her eyes, the lush crawled into Lucille's lap like a child, not wanting to be awakened.

Lucille felt so sorry for her. She knew everything she'd been through, so she took compassion and stroked her hair.

"It's okay. It's okay. I'm home now," Lucille said.

The pathetic woman took her hand and gave it a delicate squeeze. But that squeeze was a type of communication that they'd established. The message varied depending on how insistent the squeeze was.

Sometimes, it asked for water and three Aleve caplets. Other times, it said to keep it down and that you were making too much noise.

Tonight, though, the squeeze was verbose. It said, I love you, I'm glad you're home, and I know you didn't misbehave with that old boy because you know how I would feel about that. It said that she realized she was wasted but that she'd be fine tomorrow and not to worry. And it closed by saying I love you. Please stay here with me and watch over me while I sleep. Please?

As it turned out, however, the hand may not have even realized to whom it was speaking. The wretched little woman who could drink more than men twice her size came to for a moment, still with her eyes closed, just long enough to say, "I love you, Roe."

And that's when Lacy Knight stared up at the ceiling fan, holding the miserable woman's hand and begrudgingly, but still tenderly said, "I love you too, Prissy."

CHAPTER EIGHT

"Did you go to Kroger?" Liza asked as she whizzed past Josh, who was sitting on the living room couch.

She was in a mood that afternoon. She'd been in a mood all day, scrutinizing everything he did and trying to find something else to get mad about.

First, it was the trash he'd forgotten to roll to the street the day before. Then it was because he left the range on all night. When she tripped over his workout bag in the mudroom, Josh thought he'd be checking into a hotel like Michelle had forced Gil to do.

And now, their prescriptions were at issue.

"I did," Josh said, watching the last few seconds of the Birmingham Bowl tick off.

He didn't give a damn about either team, but anything was better than listening to Liza piss and moan. Steering clear of her also gave her fewer opportunities to launch into him about something—anything, it seemed.

The side of Josh's face grew warm, and he felt like he was being stared at. When he turned to his left, he saw Liza glaring at him.

"What? What is it?"

Liza didn't answer him, though. Instead, she huffed and walked back toward the kitchen.

Josh knew what the real problem was. Liza didn't want to go to Gil's cookout that afternoon. Hell, Josh didn't want to go either. He felt obligated, though, especially after the lengths to which Gil had gone to apologize to him the week before.

Josh hadn't returned Gil's calls or responded to his texts since their set-to in Madeline's the week before Thanksgiving. So, Gil made an appointment with him online using a co-worker's credentials. The only box he checked on the automated assessment form was "Excessive Guilt," which was a clever way to prelude his visit. After the initial shock, Gil told Josh what he wanted to hear and what he'd kidded himself into believing. Liza had never carried on with Brad Lawrence behind his back. In other words, Gil lied to Josh.

"Where are they?" Liza called to Josh from behind the island in the kitchen.

"I didn't leave them on the counter?" Josh asked.

"No, you didn't leave them on the counter," Liza grumbled.

"Do you have your contacts in?" Josh asked, knowing he shouldn't have because he knew how Liza would react.

He didn't even wait for her to get started, though.

"Okay, let me run out to my car when the game's over," he whined.

"Game over," Liza said, pointing at the screen.

Josh sighed, forced himself up, and headed toward the garage to get Liza's medicine. He kept a store of "emergency" Advair and albuterol inhalers in his Model X's console for those occasions when he hadn't made it by the pharmacy. He got samples from a drug rep whenever the guy brought him food or they went to lunch. He left Josh all kinds of samples, including the anti-anxiety drugs he took as a much younger, less confident physician.

Liza insisted that Josh still take his meds, which Josh thought was just another attempt to assert control. So, he played along, updating his prescriptions and even going so far as to dump them out and leave the empty bottles at the top of the trash can between refills.

***

"I don't understand what this is going to prove," Liza said as the Model X flew down the two-way Mississippi country road.

"Slow down!" were about the only other words she uttered, which she said several times during the trip. And those, of course, were a directive.

"You know, you didn't even confirm this with me. You didn't even ask," Liza groaned as the car turned when the nav told them they were five miles from their destination.

"I did too, Liza," Josh replied, "I asked you about it Thursday when you got back from HIIT."

"Yeah, whatever, dude. *'Liza, we're going to Gil's Saturday. I want you to dress hot.'* That's not what I consider being asked to do something. It's being told what to do." Liza said.

Josh smiled at her, took her hand, and kissed it.

"Well. If it's any consolation, you follow orders well."

She shifted her eyes toward him without turning and smiled briefly. Then, she pulled down the vanity mirror and checked her appearance as Josh started to talk.

"Listen, there's something else I want to tell you," Josh started, "but I don't want you to freak out about it, okay?"

"What? Freak out about what? Why would I freak out about anything?" Liza asked.

"Well, it's complicated. Um, the reason Gil invited us over is to meet his new love interest. He's already kinda' sort of half-filled me in, but it might come as a shock to everyone else there."

"Kinda-sorta-half? What the hell does that even mean, Joshua?" Liza quizzed.

Josh nodded as he devised a better explanation.

"Like I said, it's complicated, and I know that sounds like a Facebook relationship status, but, in this case, I feel like it's pretty accurate."

"If you don't start telling me what's going on…" Liza began.

"Okay, okay. Well. Gil is involved with this girl now, but he could get in trouble if anyone finds out. I think it shows incredible recklessness on his part to have this little shindig, but that's another reason I wanted to come today. I wanted to make sure Gil doesn't do Gil things and screw up his whole life in the process."

"A *girl*? Did you say he was dating a *girl*?" Liza asked.

"Yes. And I mean that like it sounds. She is, in fact, a girl. She's only eighteen."

"Are you *sure*, Joshua? Is that what he told you? That he's dating a *girl*?"

"Yes! A girl! Why do you keep saying it that way? I'm quite certain it's a girl for reasons I can't go into. Damn, Liza. What's with you?"

Liza was relieved.

"Oh. Well, look. I'm sorry. I didn't mean to be any kind of way. I just. I don't know. It kinda' sorta' halfway surprised me, that's all."

"Are you being a smart ass? " Josh asked.

Liza leaned over and kissed him on the cheek in an about-face from how she'd acted all day.

"No," Liza whispered, massaging his thigh, "you're being a dumbass."

"Duh, hey!" Josh kidded.

Liza continued her overture, leaning over and nibbling at his ear.

"Stop, Liza. Quit doing that. I don't want to walk around the cookout all afternoon with a woody."

Liza slumped back into her seat.

"Don't worry, Joshua. I don't think anyone would notice."

"Oh, ho, ho, is that right?" Josh said, laughing as he turned onto the long shell driveway.

At the end of that driveway was a ranch-style house with a wing that formed a half-courtyard out back. The cars pulled onto the grass out front seemed out of place, giving it a strange likening to a very expensive car lot on a rural highway. Mercedes, Audis, BMWs, and a muscle-bound Bentely graced the front lawn. And that was before considering all the less exotic but still extravagant four-by-fours with mud splashed up on the fenders as though their drivers had just come in from hunting.

A similarity among them all, though, was a giant Yale-blue "M" with a Harvard crimson shell conveying their owners' statuses as Ole Miss Alumni. Almost every car had that decal because that's who Gil's reference group was: extraordinarily but unlikely wealthy socialites who may have once hailed from all over the country. But after attending Ole Miss, they never lived outside a 100-mile radius of "The University." The greater Memphis area had always been home to a large contingent of Ole Miss alumni.

***

Stephen was laughing when he opened the door but abruptly stopped when he came face to face with Liza, whom he'd seen at Gil's hotel a month before. He recovered magnificently and started smiling again as he extended his hand toward Josh.

"Hi, there," Josh said, "we're here for the cookout. I'm Dr. Joshua Odom, and this is my wife, Liza."

"Oh, yes, I've heard about you two. I'm Stephen. Stephen McCullough. Gil's been talking about you all week," he said but quickly revised his statement.

"Today! I meant today!" he assured them.

"Well, I hope it was all good things," Josh laughed.

"Always! Always!" Stephen continued, "Liza, it's a pleasure meeting you."

This guy is smooth, Liza thought to herself.

"Oh, absolutely, Stephen, the pleasure is mine," she said.

Meanwhile, Josh prepared to act aloof when Gil introduced Lacy. He hoped Gil had groomed her for the cookout without saying too much about anything else. Still, he hated being in on the whole charade.

But, really, what choice did Josh have? He didn't want to abandon his friend. He was more concerned about Gil's ability to pull things off. Josh also had to trust that Gil hadn't disclosed to Lacy that he was aware of Josh's being her psychiatrist. It was all such a hot mess. Josh was cautiously entertained by it all, though.

"Joshkoshb'gosh!" Gil hollered from the grill as Stephen led the couple onto the back lawn.

Gil tried to project light-heartedness because he was going to have to suck up to Liza after ratting her out to Josh. Her denial to Josh that she'd ever screwed around helped Gil slightly. It enabled him to cover his tracks with Josh, saying it was something he'd made up in frustration. But Gil still hadn't dared to tell Josh about his lover. Stephen, before that day.

"The one and only!" Josh hollered back as he started toward the grill.

"Liza Ngyuen-Odom! You get your pretty little self over here right now, girl! Do you hear me?" a blonde woman wearing gaudy jewelry and black sunglasses with enormous lenses yelled.

Liza thought she looked like a giant insect luring her toward itself, and that was somewhat accurate because Liza had indeed walked straight into a WASP nest.

"Look at you, girl! Just look at you! Just as pretty as a St. Kitts sunset, you aw-er!"

Said woman was Bonnie Dupree of the Roy City Duprees. She was an erstwhile nobody who grew up in Dallas but attended Ole Miss. Her husband's family had more money than God and insisted on living in the quaint Mississippi town forever. Hers was the Bentley out front.

The remaining people were the same ones Josh had seen at similar functions. He didn't know them as well as Gil, but he was familiar enough that most knew Liza and him by name.

Besides the Duprees, there were Simpson and Bitsy Winslow, Rayford and Suzy Cox, Darren and Darlene Whitehurst, and Roger and Eileen Meadows. The only thing missing, Liza thought, was Gil's wife Michelle. Liza liked Michelle because she always treated her like one of the girls. But they'd usually visit privately, away from the sorority sisters' chattering.

When Josh reached the grill, all the men held neat cocktails or pretentiously crafted beers in bottles. He caught the tail end of W.C. Dupree, or "Dubya," as everyone referred to him, saying, "…if they split the stock, I can easily dump half of it and cover my losses cause these millennials are gonna jump. Then I can hold onto the other half and just see what happens with the whole green energy thing, y'know?"

Josh greeted the gathering of wealthy men, extending his hand toward Dubya. He started to say *it's good to see you again*, but the man spoke first, introducing himself. Gil quickly came to Dubya's rescue, talking in a thick Southern drawl.

"Naw, man, you remember Josh, Dubya! He's the one that give y'all his week at the camp last year when you was on the Coast?"

"Aw, yeah, yeah. 'Course I do. Hey, Josh. It's good to see you, man."

Josh was always astounded by Gil's rapid adaptation to his surroundings, whether it was his accent or the deterioration of his grammar. And once again, he thought maybe Gil suffered from borderline personality disorder.

Josh looked around for Liza, wanting to assure her with his eyes that they wouldn't stay longer than was necessary. Then he saw her sitting alone with Stephen. Predictably, she'd meandered away from the discussions about shopping, vacations, and jewelry. But she and the Stephen guy were chatting it up as Josh watched from a distance.

"Listen, honey," Stephen said softly, "I don't know, and I don't care. You don't need to worry about that or make anything up. Lord knows Gil and I have done our share of sneaking around. And it's one hundred percent none of my business why you were at the Comfort Inn, okay? "

Josh saw Liza smile and put her hand on Stephen's knee, and he got a little jealous. But he calmed down when she got up shortly afterward and showed no lingering interest in the dandy, who appeared to be in his late twenties or early thirties.

After Gil forked the last steak off the grill, he carried an enormous tin of them to the long outdoor dining table where everyone had adjourned.

The conversation at dinner was just as dry as the steaks were. Gil had either gotten too ambitious with the sear or, more likely, was distracted by what remained for the afternoon.

But everyone loosened up as dinner went on, and they began visiting more freely. The alcohol helped.

"More Vin Santo, yawl?" Bitsy offered the table, lifting a giant decanter.

"Oh, yes! Right here!" Bonnie said, holding her glass out toward Bitsy.

"Ohhh no," Dubya said, "she's alraght, Bitsy. She doesn't need anymore."

"Dubya Cotten Dupree! You don't cut me off now, you here?" Bonnie whined.

"Alraght, Bonnie rabbit. But you ain't drivin'off in that damned Bentley if you get shitfaced," warned Dubya.

"I will draav wherever the hell I wawnt to! Now you just go on with your silly little self!" Bonnie snapped.

Even though Dubya meant what he'd said, he and Bonnie weren't actually into it with each other. People like Dubya and Bonnie never really fought. Or if they did, they didn't carry on in front of people. It was just cutsy banter that most of those present had witnessed from them since college.

After a couple of hours, when everyone got to the point they were adequately buzzed or, as Dubya had prophesied Bonnie would be, shitfaced, Gil tapped his glass with his steak knife.

This is it, Liza thought to herself. *He's about to blow this whole lawn bash open.*

At the same time, Josh thought, *what in the hell is he about to do or say? Is Lacy going to come bouncing in and table dance or something?*

Stephen, invisible throughout the meal, sat up straighter in his seat and rested his elbows on the table.

"I tell you, it's great to be here with friends, my true friends today," Gil began.

"Hear! Hear!" Bitsy said as everyone joined her and raised their glasses.

"No, no. We're getting to that," Gil continued, "Listen, folks, I know you've only ever known me as the better half of a loveless marriage, but I mean what I said. You're my friends. Each one of you, in some way or another, is very close to me. And each of y'all knows what I'm talking about, and we'll just leave it at that."

After a moment, Gil continued somberly.

"I've been alone, y'all. I've been married for a lot of years, but I've been alone for the past ten. And it's nobody's fault but my own. I was just kidding about Michelle a second ago. Because what's a guy like me going to do but disguise his emotions with humor? Am I right, Josh?"

Josh stayed quiet but nodded uneasily before Gil went on.

"Michelle is a beautiful person. And I love her very much. She's given me everything an ordinary man could want. Two beautiful daughters, a boy that would make any Daddy proud, and we had a whole lotta good years together. But our time together has passed and gone off somewhere. And it's not coming back. And the God's truth of it is, neither one of us wants it to. It was a beautiful thing for more years than it wadn't. But it's time to move on, and I hope she'll do the same and find somebody else like I have."

Josh was the only person not bored. Liza and Stephen were the only ones that weren't in the dark. And Bonnie took the title of drunkest Ole Miss slut, one which she'd held uncontested for a long, long time. Everybody else just kind of blended into the ether.

Gil proceeded along the precise path Liza had thought he would. He went delicately, calculating every move. But as with all commitments, there was an eventual point of no return.

"Stephen is going to help me find my way from here on out," Gil said, reaching over and grasping his beau's slender hand.

Immediately after that, the lone discussion at the table was a private ventriloquist number in which a pitifully naïve Darren Whitehurst leaned over and muttered, "Wht'deejussay?" to the more streetwise Dubya, whose closed-mouthed response was, "Heszuhfaggert."

It was Mississippi. Men killed the food, and women cooked it. You waited for your old man to kick off before you assumed the reins. In the meantime, you had children you hoped would aspire to the same goal of being a wealthy Southerner.

So, anybody could've guessed what would come next. Gasps would christen everyone's response. That would be followed by declarations of outrage and cries of disbelief, all building to an inevitable shunning of Headmaster Gilbert Wallace.

That ain't what happened, though. That ain't what happened a'tall.

Bonnie Dupree slowly rose from the table and just as meekly started to clap. Eileen Meadows joined her, but she shot up much quicker and fluttered her hands together, giving an enormous, toothy smile. Before it was all over, the collection of classic liberal nouveau riche stood on either side of the table, and 'Oh my gawahds' and 'Bless yore hearts' abounded. Even Dubya smiled reassuringly as Darren Whitehurst searched everyone else's expressions to ensure everything was kosher.

CHAPTER NINE

"Really? And you're under the impression that a relationship predicated with lies has even a remote possibility of lasting?"

Josh was frustrated. He was still hung over from the New Year's Eve gala with Liza at The Peabody a few days before. Gil's boyfriend, Stephen, had gotten them VIP passes because he and Liza had become fast friends since Gil's lawn party.

Josh drank so much tequila that he wound up in the emergency room on an I.V. He wasn't a big drinker, so after he left the ER, he'd spent the last several days in bed, slurping bone broth and binge-watching *Frasier*. He wasn't in the mood for another episode in Lacy Knight's ongoing saga of sexual conquests that, this time, she'd reconditioned into what she thought was love.

Love? What in the hell did she know about love? As far as Josh could tell, she had never experienced love in her life, and her "this time it's different" assurances didn't sway him.

Nonetheless, Lacy told Josh she was involved with someone new and that while their introduction had been contrived, she'd fallen hard for the young man. However, she said she couldn't go into much detail because Josh might be judgmental if he knew all the circumstances. That pissed him off even worse.

"Do you think I'm lying to you?" Lacy asked, sensing Josh's aggravation and becoming a little fussy herself.

That's when Josh thought maybe he shouldn't have kicked off his return from sick days with Lacy Knight.

"Lacy," Josh began.

"No! Do you think I'm lying to you? Do you think I can't fall in love? Do you think I'm not capable or something?" Lacy snapped.

Over the previous few weeks, Lacy had showcased her dexterity in interpreting people's thoughts and emotions. Josh didn't know how she did it, but she seemed to predict all the questions he asked and what motivated him to ask them. It affronted his ego because her tactics were the same ones he used. Analysis was supposed to be *his* job, though.

Josh still found himself in awe of Lacy at times. But who wouldn't be? She was only eighteen, which made her prowess incredible to Josh. He and Liza had Taco Bell sauce packets floating around the damned house that were older than Lacy Knight.

"Well, I don't know, Lacy. You tell me everything again, but this time, tell me without describing his physique, eyes, or how he vanquished someone who dishonored you. Don't mention the urges you felt or any of the details of how you either acted upon or suppressed them. Forgo comparing him to others you've slept with, especially since you haven't slept with him yet. Don't tell me any of that, and then I'll give you my answer."

Lacy's lips started to tremble, and she teared up. She looked like a frightened, distraught, and very troubled little girl.

"Maybe I don't know what love is then. If it's not any of those things you're beating me up about, then I guess you could be right. Because when I look at him, I feel all the stuff I thought girls were supposed to feel about boys. But his eyes *are* beautiful, Dr. Odom.

And when I'm with him, I *do* feel safe. I feel like nobody in the world can get to me because he won't let them. And I want to have sex with him, too, but I want to have a baby with him. I don't know if any of that stuff is love. But I haven't ever felt like this before. I know you think I'm just a slut, Dr. Odom. Everybody does. But you're the only person I have to tell all this shit. And everything I'm telling you is the truth."

Game. Set. And match. Lacy had defeated Josh again. Not only did she pulverize his implication that she was a lovesick child with unrealistic expectations and hormone-fueled dysphoria, but she reconfigured his argument and used it against him. She portrayed herself as a victim of circumstance before saying exactly what love means in the context of how a woman views a man. She'd passive-aggressively eviscerated Josh.

And what did Josh do?

"Lacy, I have to end our session now. I'm not in the right mind frame to unpack everything you've just touched on."

Lacy looked over her shoulder at the clock in another flagrant display of intellectual superiority. Josh had always been sure no one had noticed the clock. Then Lacy turned back and looked at him as though she deserved an explanation, so Josh had to acknowledge he was ending things early.

"I realize we have five or so minutes left, but I'm feeling puny because of the weather change. And the things I'd like to say can't be left open-ended. We'd only be visiting new issues that we couldn't redress."

Damn, Lacy made him nervous. She made him feel stupid, too. Josh worried he was losing his touch because a few months before, he'd have bet the house that Gil Wallace was the dark horse she was pining for. But that was blown out of the water just before Christmas when Gil announced he was in love with Stephen.

"That's fine," Lacy said indifferently, "I've got to be somewhere in a little while anyway."

As they both rose, Josh snidely asked, "Big date?"

"Yeah," Lacy said cooly, "something like that."

A black pickup with a crucifix decal and The Punisher logo on its windshield chugged up, and its passenger side door flung open. Lacy climbed in and said, "What's up, babycakes?"

Then Lacy leaned over and pecked Clint on the cheek. Afterward, the truck roared a moment before it pulled out onto Poplar Avenue.

***

"Lucy, I've been asking God what to do about Aunt Bette," Clint said.

"What do you mean?" Lacy asked.

"I mean, I've been praying and asking God what he wants me to do about your Aunt Bette," Clint continued, "because it's just not right. I don't think you need to be exposed to her lifestyle anymore."

"Clint," Lacy started.

"No, listen. Just listen to me, will you? I don't believe it's God's will for you to be around her anymore, which is why he brought you to me. I'm sure of it."

Lacy sat quietly, staring forward and refusing to look at Clint. She wanted to be a good person, decent and respectable, but Clint made things so difficult.

Lacy's plans were working out perfectly, but Clint said something that frightened her each time she thought she'd made headway toward salvation. She didn't know everything he was capable of, but she had an idea based on how he'd dismantled that other boy at the theater. So, she shuddered to think about what he'd do to Prissy if he knew the whole story.

Clint was so powerful. He marched like a protective soldier whenever they walked somewhere together. And Lacy could feel it in his hands when he took her wrist if the couple happened upon any other males. His dragging her around like a kewpie doll embarrassed her sometimes.

But it also thrilled Lacy. It made her feel special, like somebody's prize, and she'd never been made to feel that way before. At least, not outside of being ravished by a man, but that always dissipated immediately following. And she was left feeling more used and worthless afterward.

Things were so different with Clint because Lacy knew he wanted to do all the same things those other men did to her. He wanted it badly, and even if he'd wanted to, he couldn't conceal it.

What distinguished Clint was that he didn't act. He made no foray into physicality beyond a certain point. He always held back, which Lacy found just as frustrating as flattering. And that was the essence of Clint she found so alluring. He didn't just give in to his urges. He fought them. He showed more restraint than she knew men could because no one had ever exercised any with her.

"Clint, she's pitiful," Lacy finally responded, "and she doesn't have anyone in the world except me. And you think God wants you to take me away from her? Doesn't God want us to be stewards of his word? And doesn't God's word tell us in Matthew to love everyone, even our enemies?"

Lacy had been memorizing Bible verses since she got going with Clint. But she didn't know whom she was messing with about scripture. Clint had been at the Bible since he was knee-high. Vacation Bible School, Sunday School, Royal Ambassadors. Clint was a Centurion in the Army of God. The scriptures were his direct orders, and he always followed orders.

"Psalm fifty-eight. *The righteous will rejoice when he sees the vengeance. He will wash his feet in the blood of the wicked.* It goes on in fifty-nine. *Do not be gracious to any who are treacherous in iniquity. Selah.* Lucille, Aunt Bette shows no will to change in her heart, and that's evil in God's eyes. She has no desire to put the bottle down, and she's using that to keep you in her life. Haven't you ever wondered why she doesn't have a man? It's because she doesn't take care of herself. You told me she was thirty, but she looks way older than that to me, Lucy. And she's not the type of woman a man wants to be with. Can't you see that?"

Lacy started to feel uneasy. She didn't want to lock horns with Clint. Not like that, anyway. So, she directed attention away from the conflict by pointing through the windshield and shouting, "Gracie Bleu! Gracie Bleu!"

Lacy wanted to diffuse any heady, philosophical discussion about scripture, so she changed the rules mid-game, just as she did with everyone else she played with. But she also love-love-loved Gracie Bleu frozen yogurt.

"Pleeaase," Lacy said with a cutesy frown, poking out her lower lip.

Clint couldn't resist his Lucy when she looked like that.

"The little girl says Gracie Bleu, the little girl gets Gracie Bleu," he said, smiling as he whipped the wheel into an illegal U-turn.

But Clint hadn't noticed the Germantown police officer behind them. And he hadn't noticed him when he dropped Lacy off, either. He also didn't notice the officer who followed him to Orangetheory Fitness, a block away, where he worked out during Lacy's session. So, he was startled by the siren chirp and the blue lights in his rearview.

"License, registration, proof of insurance," the officer asked after Clint pulled over. The policeman stared at Lacy the whole time, but she refused to make eye contact with him.

"I'm sorry about that, officer," Clint said, "I was in a hurry to get this young lady some yogurt, and I got stuck in the left lane. It was stupid, and I know that."

"The left lane is for passing," the young officer said before continuing.

"Are there any weapons or illegal substances in the vehicle, sir?"

"Uh, no," Clint said, clearly aggravated, "there aren't."

Meanwhile, Lacy nudged her purse between the door and her seat. That didn't go over well because she hadn't been nearly as stealthy as she'd thought.

"Ma'am, don't move like that again!" the officer barked.

Clint was oblivious that the officer knew Lacy. He knew her in the capacity of his service as a law enforcement officer and personally as well. And the cop was willing to wager that her purse was just full of goodies. There'd be paraphernalia, a freebase mod or two. She might even be holding if he were lucky.

The reason the officer knew all those things as he stared at Lacy's supple breasts was that he'd snorted several lines of cocaine off of them before.

"Calm down," Clint said when the officer touched his firearm.

It was all for the show, though. Officer Ruston knew Lacy wouldn't have a firearm, not as long as she was with Terminator psycho Jesus anyway. But he wanted to flex. He wanted to show that little whore that while, yes, he was a bad boy sometimes, he was also an officer of the law. And people had to do what he said.

He wanted her to know he had just as much dominion over her now as when he tied her to the headboard face down.

Then, incredibly, Lacy threw herself into the discussion. Clint had never heard her use the tone she used nor seen her behave the way she did.

"Are we being detained?" she demanded, leaning over and leering at Billy Ray Ruston.

Ruston's seemed like he was taken off-guard. He looked between Lacy and Clint several times, gauging whether he'd lost face in front of the hulking athlete who glared right back at him.

Ruston had no choice but to pull back from his scheme to humiliate and emasculate the boy he knew would kill him in hand-to-hand combat. Part of his brain had played out fantasies all morning, though. Fantasies in which he'd pistol whip Clint in front of Lacy, take the boy to jail, and then take Lacy back home with him to dominate all over again.

But Billy Ray Ruston had picked the wrong day and circumstances to mess with Lacy Knight. She didn't seem worried about him, his badge, or anything he might divulge about her to Clint. She seemed to think it would be the other way around and that she held all the cards. Like she would expose him as the drug-swiping, child-molesting, opportunistic thug they both knew he was.

"Let's all just back up a second, okay?" Ruston said with his tail between his legs. "Let's start from the beginning, alright?"

Lacy relented, but she seemed as though she hadn't wanted to. She wanted to pull the pin just to spite the stupid cop. She eased back into her seat and didn't say another word. She just let Billy Ray continue with his good-guy façade and issue his Nerf traffic warning to Clint.

She may have been damaged goods and undeniably came with a ton of baggage. But Lacy Knight was something else and might even have been an unbelievable mother one day. Because, just like her mother, you didn't mess with her or hers lest you pay dire consequences for doing so.

Lacy had begun the next leg of her journey to normalcy. It would be a long and arduous one with a lot more deception. But she'd shed all that just as a butterfly sheds its cocoon before becoming a beautiful creature, admired and adored by everyone. Lacy was on her way to eternal life in heaven, and though she didn't know it yet, her approach to that destination had been hastened months before.

CHAPTER TEN

Gil and Josh sat at the bar at Forest Hill Grill, having lunch. Josh had agreed to meet with him because Gil said he needed to clear the air.

"You wouldn't let me tell you this before, but I never touched the Knight girl, Josh. I swear to God I never laid a hand on her."

Josh didn't know what to believe. He knew what he *wanted* to believe. He wanted to believe Gil was telling the truth. But his doubts lingered, even though Gil had professed his love for another man. After all, Gil was still Gil.

"She was molested, and I guess I'm sort of guilty in that sense because she had sex with Terry Marvin, who's on my staff. But I wasn't involved. I was a voyeur for five seconds, but that's about it."

There was no way Josh was letting Gil slip that in without a full explanation. His expression said as much, so Gil continued.

"I didn't intend to be, you understand, but I walked in on them while he was going to town on her. It was the weirdest thing I've ever seen. Terry is wailing away with his eyes shut tight, but the girl looks at me and freakin' smiles, dude. It was like she thought it was funny or something. Her head's bouncing forward because he's really goin' at it, but she never stops looking in my eyes. Then she bounces her eyebrows like, *Look at me, you wanna be next?* Then I heard glass break from the showers behind them, so I snapped out of it and started hauling ass to see what the noise was because I didn't want anybody else to see what was happening in that office, right? Terry hears me and starts zipping up, but I keep going, and I'm totally saving this guy's ass, you know? But I had to make sure I was the only person who saw what I saw, or it's over for him, man. And I'm thinkin' it might be over for me too because I'm the one that hired him."

At that point, Josh was glad he'd met with Gil. For starters, it gave him insights into Lacy Knight, provided that Gil's words were true—insights uncompromised by either her perspective or her lies, which Josh knew weighed into every statement the girl made. It also allowed Gil to redeem himself, and he made remarkable strides at doing so.

It was difficult to picture Gil as a sympathetic character in a story so rife with opportunities for him to be the opposite, but his tale grew more compelling as the story progressed.

Then, it also turned Josh on. It may have been morally reprehensible, but it did.

"When I walk in the showers, the window up near the ceiling is busted, but there's nobody around. So, I ran back through the office and told them to stay put. But by the time I leave the office, run through the gym, and head out to the field behind the building, I don't see anybody. But let me tell you, that meant they had to run at least a hundred yards in like ten, twelve seconds. And they had to be bleeding, too, because there's glass all over the place in the showers. And it's that old single-plate stuff. Man, that shit will cut you *up*. No way that guy didn't shred his fist."

Josh spoke for the first time since Gil got started.

"You say, 'that guy'. Does that mean you have some suspicion about who it might've been?"

Gil shrugged as he rolled his eyes before continuing.

"Well, that's just it. I don't know *who* it was. But it had to be another dude, you know? I just don't see a girl, one of my students, breaking glass like that, climbing up through the window, and moving that fast to get away. Naw, man. This was an athlete. This was somebody strong and fast. Like, Usain Bolt fast. And agile as fuck. That window's gotta be, I don't know, eight feet from the floor?"

Gil took a more likely turn as he continued the story.

"And you know what else? I think whoever it was? They probably like to watch. Which, hey, I understand, right? I mean, far be it from me to stand in judgment about that because you know how I've always been. But they can't do that shit with my students. I don't know if it was a man or a kid or what. It just made me so damned mad."

Josh was relieved. Gil appeared to be sincerely troubled about what happened. And if that were the case, he would let him go on. And he felt justified in doing so because, technically, he was getting information about someone who clearly needed psychiatric counseling, notwithstanding all the other stuff Lacy had told him. What Gil related confirmed what a whore she'd bragged about being, but it also—tentatively, at least—exonerated Gil Wallace. In some twisted way, it was all good news for Josh.

But Josh still had questions. Things didn't quite compute. If Gil was so concerned about Lacy, why wasn't this Terry guy in jail as they spoke? And why weren't Lacy's parents involved? Hadn't Lacy suggested her mom was very protective? No, Gil would have to keep talking before he was off the hook.

"What did you say to this guy, Gil? You said you told them to hang tight. Well, what did you say when you came back to the office? What did *they* say?"

"Oh, shit. Here we go," Gil said, dreading the explanation he was about to offer. He let out a long sigh and then looked directly into Josh's eyes.

"She threatened me. She threatened me, and that prick Terry just let her do it. I guess he was trying to protect himself and whoever his buddy was that ran away. But how fucked up is that? First of all, you're banging a teenager and letting someone watch. Then you hear her threaten your boss, who found you doing it? Totally complicit. I didn't expect the guy to fall to his knees and pray to God for forgiveness or anything. But I sure as hell didn't expect him to take sides with Lacy and whoever they were protecting, either."

"Threaten. What, threaten? How did she threaten you, Gil? What does that mean?" Josh asked.

Gil continued with a leery expression.

"It's such a hard thing to talk about, Josh. Because I'm guilty of a lot of the stuff I just said Terry was. Well, almost. I never touched Lacy Knight. But I've watched her have sex before," Gil managed sheepishly.

Yep. There it was. Gil was an asshole, and Josh was a sucker. He knew it. Goddamn it. He knew it all along.

But then the story took an even sharper and more captivating turn than it had been up to that point. It had everything so far. Lurid sex among the wealthy or at least their offspring, making it even juicier. Violence. Somebody destroying property whose identity and motivations for being there remained at large. Yet their desire had been so great that they'd broken a dozen laws, then their desire to leave had been even greater. Then there was the intrigue about Gil's actual role in everything. Still, Josh was put off by Gil's delivery.

"Damn it, Gil. You've always done this, man. You've always baited people when you tell a damned story. You always divert the focus from being on you while you draw a lot of other people into it, and then you finally fess up to whatever it is you're trying to avoid the penalty for. It was the same in school, man. Same damned shit. Remember when you bottomed my car out and busted the catalytic converter? When you finally told me about it, though, you said you were in the car with a bunch of drunk girls down in Oxford, and Bonnie Dupree grabbed your crank. That was what you said, but who in the hell knows if that was even true? I mean, why didn't you just say, 'Josh, I'm sorry, but I bottomed out in your car?' No, you had to implicate everyone else and everything they were doing wrong at the time. Jesus, Gil. Grow up, will you? Grow the fuck up."

Gil had already begun shaking his head before Josh stopped talking, though, and shook it more intently as Josh went along. He looked like his heart was breaking, but he also looked like he was warning Josh, foreboding him not to do or say anything else.

"No, man. No. It ain't like that, alright? That's not what this is at all," Gil assured.

"What in the hell are you talking about, Gil?" Josh asked.

It was another obstacle to climb for Gil. Gil felt like he was guiding Josh up a steep mountainside, but he was the only one who knew their destination or how much further they had to go. Nonetheless, he spoke as though he were taking the hand of an emotionally exhausted Josh and helping him up the craggy slope.

"Stephen and I are both in this group, Josh. A bunch of us are. It's called the Qadeshian Society, but I'm sure you've never heard of it."

No. Josh had never heard of it.

"It's swingers, Josh, okay? It's swingers. There. I said it."

It was a peculiar element to add to the story, even if it was a predictable one as far as Gil's involvement was concerned. Josh could see Gil getting drawn into something sordid like a secret sex society, which is whatever he'd called it sounded like to him. Josh thought it was a little strange for such to exist in a place like Memphis, but it certainly wasn't beyond the realm of possibility. He'd treated some pretty sick tickets in town, and they'd seemed to have gotten sicker with the proliferation of social media.

Then Josh got a little put-off. If Gil had been searching for something he never knew he'd wanted, that being another man, and that was supposedly his path to love and contentment, then where did sex come into play? Promiscuous, perverse sex at that? That's not how things worked. Not in Josh's professional estimate, anyway. If Gil loved Stephen and Stephen loved Gil so much as they'd said, then why were they pursuing immoral sexual activities instead of a nurturing, loving, and mutually respectful relationship?

Then, as he watched Josh's gears turning and struggling to come up with a question, Gil slapped his sensibilities on the other cheek.

"Stephen is bisexual, just like me."

Oh, man. It didn't get any richer than this. You just didn't see things like this. It was like a sitcom shot through a smut director's lens. Except it was feature-length with an unlikely cast. But almost as fast as Gil turned the wheel of his tale, Josh's thoughts quickly fell onto Liza.

It hadn't bothered Josh before because, in his arrogance, he'd not viewed Stephen as a danger. Stephen liked men, so he posed no challenge or competitive threat to Josh. That was changing, though.

Was Gil telling him that this guy, Stephen, the one who Liza had befriended, liked to screw women as much as he did men? And he did it for sport, just like Gil always had?

Josh was so preoccupied with that prospect that he almost couldn't concentrate when Gil continued the story. But his paranoia and sudden insecurity about Stephen kept him tethered to Gil's words.

"We meet up every couple of months, and, well, we swing. Guys bring their wives and girlfriends or boyfriends, and we just let it all hang out for a while, doing what swingers do. But it's not hurting anybody, and nobody is there that doesn't want to be there."

"Yeah," Josh asked impatiently, "and?"

"Well, a little over a year ago, when Stephen and I first started seeing each other, Lucas Millard—you know Lucas, don't you? That trial attorney? He's that *'You crash, I dash'* guy with all the billboards and those cheesy commercials?"

"Yes. I know Luke," Josh confirmed, "but he's marr…Nevermind. Go on."

"Yeah, right? And his wife is a member of Qadeshians, too, believe it or not. She just wasn't there that night for some reason. Maybe he was slipping around, or maybe she just didn't care, I don't know."

"Caroline?" Josh asked in disbelief.

Liza knew Caroline well, too. They were the only wives in the circles that both Josh and Gil moved who weren't also mothers. They played tennis together. They were both administrators of a Gen-X group on Facebook. And at least a few times a year, they went out for a "ladies' night."

This was becoming worrisome. Josh didn't like it at all. Moreover, he *hated* it.

"I know, right?" Gil said while nodding and offering an uneasy smile.

"Anyway, Lucas shows up with this hot-ass woman. She has tits til tomorrow and a nice ass. She's dressed up and made up like Nefertiti, too. At least, that's who she said she was supposed to be. I mean, who knows what Nefertiti looks like?"

"You're doing it again," Josh said.

"Right, right. Okay. Sorry. Well, the point is, she looked unreal, this woman. Every dude there was watering at the mouth, and they couldn't wait for them to bang the gong. You see, they have this gong that…"

"Gil," Josh said.

"Alright, alright. Anyhow, this woman walks up to me with Lucas, except when he introduces us, she takes my hand and licks my damned fingers. Then she rubs my index finger on her lips like she's putting on lipstick or something. Josh, I don't think I've ever been that hard before in my life, man. I mean, I was so hard that it hurt! But the more I got to looking at her…"

"It was Lacy," Josh interrupted, "the woman you're talking about was Lacy, wasn't it?"

Josh hadn't needed Gil to confirm it, even though he ended up doing so. Josh felt like he'd always known where the discussion was headed. He was just trying to envision whatever it could've been that led to Gil watching her have sex.

"Yep," Gil said, "and I figured it out when she said 'Hi, Mr. Wallace.' She said it just like every other damned girl I pass in the hallway. It was, I don't know, gross or something. And I was instantly turned off."

Josh felt like he had to warn his foolish buddy.

"Gil, you do realize that doesn't matter, don't you? Even though she was there, presumably of her own accord, there's no way she could have legally participated in any of that because she was beneath the age of consent. I can't believe Luke could be so stupid. He's a damned lawyer, Chrissake. But I also can't believe he could do something like that anyway."

Gil responded as though trying to defend himself and convey to Josh that he knew exactly how illegal everything that had taken place was.

"Look, I'm telling you exactly what happened. And she may not have been at the age of consent, but let me just tell you, she consented. She consented a bunch of times. She probably consented with all the men in there and about half of the women. I know that still doesn't make it okay. But what choice did I have? What was I supposed to do? Blast an airhorn, get everybody's attention, and ask them to stop climbing all over each other long enough for me to tell them there was a kid in the room? Yeah. Right."

Josh looked at Gil and shrugged as if to say, *Should that matter?*

"I know. I know," Gil said, "and I've been trying to cope with the fact I didn't stop it. But she had me dead to rights on two counts, Josh. First of all, because I was even there, which is huge. But I was also there with another man. Very apparently with another man because Stephen and I had been kissing when they came in the room. She could take my job and destroy my family, such as it is, if she wanted to."

"Where in the hell did all this take place, Gil?" Josh asked.

He wanted to get as much information as he could and for as long as Gil wanted to talk because he imagined Gil would reach a point where he didn't want to say anything else.

Stephen being involved bothered Josh, too. Stephen, with whom Liza had fostered such a kinship in such a very short time. What was that about?

"Y'know that old hotel outside of town, just off 55 when you're driving south? Looks like it's been shut down for years? Well, it hasn't. It's still open, even though it doesn't look like it. The owner leases us the whole left wing whenever we go out there. He doesn't know what's going on, or if he does, he pretends like he doesn't. He's glad to get the business, and we're glad to have a place to go. And he lets us use the ballroom, too, pardon the pun."

"It has a damned ballroom? That place??" Josh begged.

"Yep. The only other business he does is with workmen and people like that, but they're never there on the weekends. So once every couple of months, I'd say, we all drive out there and party. Pretty swanky, too. Open bar. Catering. And it's not my thing, but there's probably more coke there than everything they cut with Ajax or whatever and sell in Memphis in a year. Mad, crazy cocaine, and Stephen told me it's pure. He'll take a hit or two, but I never got into that."

Damn it. Stephen increasingly sounded like someone Josh didn't want on the same planet as Liza, let alone trading recipes or any of the other things she'd been doing with him. What else had she done, or was she contemplating doing with him? With Gil, even?

Josh dismissed the thought, though. He didn't think it was likely that Gil would do anything like that or let anyone else do it, either. And although it had been because of Gil's suggestion, his paranoia had gotten him in really hot water with Liza back before Thanksgiving.

"I guess you can just add contributing to the delinquency of a minor to my rap sheet," Gil said.

Josh wondered if Gil expected him to console him or feel any sympathy for him. Because he wasn't going to. He didn't feel much sympathy for people who got burned when they didn't keep their libido in check or when they developed unsavory habits like illicit drug use.

Whether you liked it or not, and no matter how unfair or unpleasant you found it, society had rules. And if you wanted to participate in that society, you had to follow them. Holding a job, having a home, driving a car. They were all dependent on following those rules. And it seemed the more adherent you were to them, the better your lot in life would be. In Josh's mind, allowances had already been made to accommodate virtually any lifestyle—within reason. Were that not true, Gil would never have been able to have his little "coming out" soiree as he did.

So, Josh didn't have the patience to sit there and coddle Gil about going to a swinger party where his boyfriend snorted lines of coke as everyone else ravaged a child in some twisted, fantastical Romper Room.

"I don't pass judgment on anyone, Gil. But I just have to ask you. Are you honestly surprised you find yourself in this situation? What did you expect? Be friends with and love whoever you want to, man. Just know that whenever you do, they become part of what defines you in others' eyes, whether you want them to or not. And with something like this, it's definitely a big responsibility to do that. It didn't matter that Luke was okay with using Lacy like he did. It really doesn't matter whether you said anything or tried to stop it, either. It was over the first time you went to one of their parties. Something like this was bound to happen. Do you even know who any of these people are? How they live their lives? For all you know, you've joined some cult. And they might be planning to sacrifice you and serve you up."

Gil sniggered a little.

"I know all of them. I don't know what that says about me to you, but I know all of them. You know some of them too, Josh. Maybe better than you think."

Okay, what did that mean? Josh started thinking about Liza again. Surely not, though. No way did she slip around behind his back and participate in anything this lewd or immoral. That just wasn't her. She was a wildcat for sure, and they'd done some role-playing and light bondage in the past. But this? No way.

Then again, Liza did seem unhappy at times. Lately, she got fussy with him at the drop of a hat, and it was always over some stupid shit, too. He thought she was just dissatisfied with her own life and not with anything about him. He'd been a devoted husband, and he'd also showered her in luxury the whole time they'd been together. They didn't need their large home, and she didn't need to drive a top-of-the-line Mercedes SUV. Those were all things that women with families had. Like all of her friends had. Since she had all the other stuff, did she covet their lifestyle instead?

And with that thought, Josh's anxiety peaked. Was Liza regretful they hadn't had children, after all? Because they'd covered that point even before they got married. They agreed that children would take away from all they wanted to go and do in life. They'd aspired to intercontinental destinations and meeting personal achievement goals that were distinct from kids' soccer or baseball or toiling over their homework with them. And they'd never step foot in Disneyworld because they hated crowds and lines, and they were both afraid of heights.

But they hadn't done any of that. They didn't travel the world. They didn't hike up Mt. Fuji or kayak in the Snake River. Liza hadn't started a public relations firm or, really, anything at all. They seldom left Memphis. Josh had a career and went to the office every day, but Liza stayed at home. She was always trying to find projects or hobbies or causes on which to expend energy. But had that been enough?

Thankfully, though, Gil clarified to whom he'd been referring.

"Bonnie and Dubya are Quadeshians. So are Simpson and Bitsy Winslow. Darren and Darlene Whitehurst aren't Quadeshians, but they swing, too."

Josh wasn't shocked. A little surprised, maybe, but people made such revelations to him all the time. Seeing that his disclosure hadn't been the surprise he thought it might've otherwise been, and because he was anxious to return to the burger that had drained juices all over his plate, Gil moved toward wrapping things up. He'd said what he wanted to say, and he wasn't looking for Josh to absolve him of anything. He just hadn't wanted his old friend to believe any of the lies that little bitch had told him.

"Well, I wanted you to know that I wasn't the kind of person that would do anything like Lacy Knight may have suggested to you. I hope you know I'm telling you the truth because I had to give you a lot of delicate information to get to it. But it's important to me that you know that for both practical and philosophical reasons. And I appreciate you letting me talk."

Josh wished he got half as much gratitude from his patients. Then he supposed they also wished he didn't charge thousands of dollars to listen to them. So, it all worked out.

"Can I ask you something else that has nothing to do with Lacy Knight, then, Gil?"

Gil stopped just as he was about to take another bite of his burger. Then he set it on his plate, sat back in the chair, and smiled at Josh. He seemed confident. It was like he'd already gotten everything off his chest that he needed to, so he needn't lie or mince words anymore.

"You can ask me anything. Anything you want to. I'm all ears." Gil assured.

"Does Michelle know about you and Stephen?" Josh asked.

His question took all the gumption out of Gil, who slumped his shoulders and sighed. Then, Gil's answer was curt, as though he wanted to lock the door leading to any further discussion on the matter.

"Yes."

Realizing Gil didn't want to talk about it but being incapable of checking his curiosity, Josh asked another question.

"Does Clint?"

As though he'd known Josh would ultimately go there, and wanting to end any further inquiry, Gil replied,

"No. No, I haven't told him yet. I will. But I haven't."

***

"Oh, I meant to ask you," Stephen said over his shoulder from the bathroom as he brushed his teeth, "how'd everything go with Josh today?"

Gil was lying on the bed a few feet away, thinking deeply about that very thing.

"Fine," he said, still staring at the ceiling, "I guess."

Stephen continued brushing while staring at himself in the mirror.

"I guess as in '*he understands and isn't going to say anything to anyone*' or as in '*I guess he's not surprised, but I still don't know if he'll stay quiet*'? Those are different answers, you know."

Gil didn't look over at Stephen. He just kept staring upward blankly, but he raised his tone as though annoyed.

"I guess as in, I guess I don't really care anymore, Stephen. If I'd have cared, I suppose I wouldn't have told him anything in the first place."

That brought the tooth brushing to a halt. Stephen spit a mouthful of suds into the sink, then leaned on the doorframe leading into the newly remodeled bathroom.

"And the little bitch? What did he say about her? Did she bare her soul to him, or what?" Stephen asked.

Gil lay quietly for a moment before answering.

"I guess."

CHAPTER ELEVEN

Coach Terry Marvin set the four-pack of Keystone tall boys on the counter before noticing Brim's Cheese Puffs on the wire rack beside him. He grabbed two bags and set them on top of the beer, and his mind was elsewhere when Manosh, the store owner, said, "Eeet-twin-dee."

Terry yanked the bag and walked to his truck in the Star-Mart parking lot. As he walked along, he replayed the events of that afternoon, trying to figure out how to tell his old man that he'd probably lost his job. Again.

Terry thought he'd been out of the woods for a while by that time. So, he was stunned when Gil Wallace came into his office earlier that afternoon and told him he was indefinitely suspended, pending board approval of his dismissal. Then the bastard had gone on to threaten him, but he did it like he was doing him a favor.

"Look, Terry. I'm trying to keep it so you can get another job somewhere instead of going to jail. Is that what you want?" Gil said, "Because if it is, I can ensure that happens, and I will."

Terry's immediate response had been a threat of his own, informing Gil that he'd not only tell the board that Gil was a swinger. He'd also tell them he was a homosexual philanderer who went to parties where little girls were part of the entertainment.

That one had gotten under Gil's skin. He'd turned, locked the door, and walked back and leaned forward, placing both hands on Terry's desk.

"Tell me something, you backwoods, slack-jawed, repugnant, hillbilly piece of Appalachian white trash. Of all the times you were checking in to that motel in Mississippi with Lacy, did it never occur to you that you'd be under surveillance? And no, stupid. I don't mean like somebody was spying on your stubby ass. Who would ever want to do that? I sure as hell wouldn't. I'm talking about security cameras, you listless, worthless, child-molesting pile of shit. A security camera that could very easily capture you checking in while another got a good look at who was in your car? Not to mention the one that recorded your license plate when you pulled into the parking lot or the one with you going into a room with a minor and a bag of weed."

Although bluffing, Gil had come into his own that day. He was shoring up his defenses and righting the ship and had been doing so for a while. He couldn't get away with what Marvin might claim he was guilty of—that being a swinger. But if it were known he was gay, he'd sure as hell use that as a defense and claim the little toad had been blackmailing him and that he'd never heard of any 'Qadeshian society.'

The only remaining leverage someone might have over Gil was his family—his son, Clint, specifically. And he'd have to cross that bridge when he came to it. Something he wasn't aware of yet but that would be revealed in good time was that Lacy Knight had already built that bridge for him.

***

Terry cranked up the old F-150 his dad bought for himself in 1992 when he retired but gave Terry to drive throughout high school a decade afterward. It was nice back then. Fancy even. CD, extended cab, bed liner.

It was a piece of shit now, though. The liner was splattered with paint and had gouges from back when trucks were used as work vehicles. It didn't have a stereo anymore, and no one could roll down the passenger's side window, which was even worse because the AC hadn't worked in years.

It still cranked, though. Cranked right up—even in cold weather. And that's nearly all Terry Marvin had been reduced to caring about.

Terry pulled out of the parking lot after he put the envelope addressed to the Restoration Academy Board of Regents in the glove box. After having more time to plan, he'd decide whether to send that letter certified the next day.

If he was going down, he was taking absolutely everybody with him.

***

Terry hoped his father would be asleep when he got to his trailer out on Destry Ridge. That's where he lived. With his father. In a trailer. On Destry Ridge.

As Terry turned onto the property's driveway and cracked across the shells leading to its free-standing, metal carport, Terry noticed something in the dark. It was only for a moment, and he'd barely had time for it to register, but it was a streak of white that appeared and disappeared just as rapidly.

Terry's pulse raced because he was a hunter. So, instantly, he entertained the idea of running in the house and getting his shotgun because he'd bet anything it was a whitetail deer. Probably the same doe that had eaten all his dad's pole beans that year. Deer season had been over for months, and even though he was on his father's property, at law, the deer belonged to the State of Tennessee. And you couldn't just go bagging deer, even if you were at home and even if they were a nuisance. It was such bullshit.

Thinking better of it, Terry turned the truck off, grabbed the plastic sack with his beer, and walked into the trailer. When he got inside, the TV on the wall was on, and two plates of food were on the coffee table. One was partially eaten, and the other had a paper towel over it.

It seemed that Terry's dad had expected him home earlier but got tired of waiting on him, so he'd covered Terry's plate, trying to keep it warm. That had been a couple of hours ago because the paper towel had soaked up juice from the crowder peas and swabbed grease off the country-fried steak.

Terry knew he'd be hungry after he drank all the beer and what remained of the fifth of Jack Daniels he kept over the fridge. And the steak, peas, mashed potatoes with gravy, and combination salad looked inviting, even if they were cold.

Terry wouldn't eat right away, though. No, that made it impossible to get drunk, which was his ultimate goal that evening since he didn't have to be up the next day. Or the day after that. Or the one that followed. As he thought about that, he hissed, "Shit!"

Things just couldn't get any worse than they were. Terry was thirty-two years old, lived at home, and his last paycheck would come after he and that perverted sissy-Mary met with the board, which he imagined would be in a very short time from then. He was already unemployed, but by then, he'd be flat broke, too.

Terry took the beer to the fridge and tore one off before putting the rest inside. Then he reached over it and grabbed his whisky and an opened, days-old, flat bottle of Dr. Thunder.

Terry's M.O. would be to nurse beer until he ran out, then start hard on the whisky before gradually reducing his shots until he ran out of that, too.

He streamed "The Handmaid's Tale" to the television. But it could have been anything because he wasn't watching it. Instead, he wondered how he'd pay for the internet in a few more weeks. His dad didn't care about things like that. How would he pay for his auto insurance? For gas? For booze? He wondered if his dad cared about those things, too.

Nonetheless, Terry would have to ask Daddy for it, just like he'd had to ask him for everything else. But that always came with a detailed accounting of what he was spending money for because Terry Sr. didn't have a credit or debit card. His cell phone was one he'd gotten through the AARP, and it was without data or a smart screen, so he didn't know what the hell "Cash App," "Apple Pay," or "PayPal" were. His dad used checks for everything from groceries to utility bills, and he still wrote what they were for in the memo section. That made it embarrassing for Terry when he had to go to the bank and deposit a check that was donned as "Terry Jr.'s insurance," "Groceries for Terry Jr.," or anything else for which his dad gave him money during his multiple runs of unemployment.

It looked like that was about to start up again, and Terry was tired of his dad. But what worried him most was that his dad might be tired of him, too.

***

Something roused Terry from his sleep. When he woke up, he realized he must've dozed off because the beer he'd opened when he got home was beaded with condensation on the coffee table. It was also full and warm to the touch. And via the Hulu app running on its screen, the TV was asking him, *"Still there?"*

Terry's head pounded, and he was disoriented. He wondered why because he'd hardly had anything to drink. But he was frazzled for sure, and the pain in his temples was as though he'd drunk all night. He had to catch himself from falling when he rose to exchange his warm beer for a fresh one and fill his mini-cooler with ice to return to proper drinking.

Then he remembered something. He had some weed left over from New Year's, and it was in the bathroom under the sink. Whenever he smoked, that was a surefire cure for a headache. It was also the best preemptive hangover remedy he'd ever discovered, although expensive. His head hurt so badly that he didn't care, though. His dad was asleep, so he'd burn one until it went away, then he'd get back to drinking.

After pulling the joint out of the bag, Terry slid down on the floor with his back to the lavatory, put the roach to his mouth, and lit up.

Terry Marvin would've died anyway. The truth of the matter was that he was already dying, and his father, Terry Senior, was already dead in his bedroom a few feet away. But when Terry activated the pen lighter he kept on his keychain, the trailer on Destry Ridge exploded.

The last thing that occurred to Terry before he was overtaken by a blinding flash and the brutal force of the air spontaneously igniting in a chain reaction was: "*The damned gas line is rusted th...*"

Were it not for the explosion, no one would've known Terry Marvin Junior. and his father were gone. No one paid the Marvin boys much attention, so the explosion in the middle of the night that heralded their exodus from this life into the next may have been the best thing to have happened.

The mailman might've gotten suspicious when the odor got putrid enough to reach their mailbox a hundred yards away. Or maybe a coon or a coyote would've dragged a hand or some other limb out in the open to where someone might have seen it. Other than that, their bodies would've rotted for weeks, perhaps months, before anyone noticed.

Alice Marvin died seven years before, and when that happened, Terry Sr. withdrew. He sold the house, bought land with a trailer at a county auction, and planned on wrapping things up in the country where he'd be left alone.

Alice's passing affected Terry almost as severely. During that period, and only because his depression kept him grounded, he'd somehow managed to get an education degree, though.

Before landing at Restoration Academy, he'd only held temp jobs as a substitute teacher. The job at Restoration had been a coup for him, and it was the longest tenure he'd had until that day.

It would seem tragic to the uninformed onlooker. A double funeral service was attended by a lone priest who'd use very little of the funeral insurance proceeds he'd receive because they were better utilized in the coffers of the Diocese and Little Flower Catholic Church. Then, a salvage company was rummaging through what remained of the half of the mobile home that wasn't blown to smithereens, finding only Terry's rusty tools, some lady's shoes, and the rest of Alice's wardrobe.

It was the closure of two miserable lives, with the only thing to show for them being a dugout plot of land and a few pathways, which were seldom traveled by anyone.

Apart from Terry, no one either came or left from the Destry Ridge trailer, whose skirt was shrouded in weeds and wild climbing vines, some of which had begun to crawl through its rotted floor. The beaten path between the back of the trailer, the garden, and the woods surrounding the property had scarcely been walked on for months. Terry Senior had retired as a gardener after the deer ate up his beans. And all Terry Jr. ever did was come home and get drunk.

However, someone else had recently been along those paths. Always in the darkness of night and never too close to the home. They covered all those trails thoroughly and macheted through one that was overgrown and had once led out to Highway 76. That's where they'd parked their car each time they rehearsed. After returning that trail to function, they performed several dry runs before their grand performance. But that performance was only their opening night.

CHAPTER TWELVE

"Okay, dudes! I'm about to head out in a minute here!"

Fab Knight called out as he stood at the foot of the marble staircase that wound to a landing on the second story of three in the enormous home that sat back from Poplar Avenue in a wooded area.

The mansion's lawn and columns were hidden from the road. No one could tell it was there until they traveled the driveway that disappeared into the glade of the six-acre forest where it was nestled. And, at the moment, so were all the machinations and ulterior motives of the hot dog that called up the stairs to his kids.

Lannie "Fab" Knight was no ordinary father. He wasn't a career man who came home after work each day before playing catch in the yard with his son and helping his little girl with her math homework. Although technically his address, he seldom appeared at the family's Germantown home, where the children lived alone since he and his wife had separated years before and his older child had reached majority age. He was only in town that week because he'd had to meet with the shareholders of a Memphis-based startup he'd helped get off the ground.

Most of Fab's days were spent galivanting around the globe, jet-setting to places like Necker Island or Lake Como, usually in the company of three or four young women, ranging in age from their mid-twenties down to his daughter's age.

He was unquestionably wealthy. But he didn't consort with the rabble of pretentious macho men who joined country clubs, smoked cigars, or went deep-sea fishing in the Gulf. He didn't sit in the stands and cheer on his son at baseball or football games. He had never endured a piano recital or watched his daughter move across a stage in a pink taffeta ballerina outfit in the Galleria for a beauty pageant.

He was too sophisticated for all that. He spoke five languages to the extent that he needed to eat fine cuisine properly, exchange pleasantries with dignitaries, or dress down servants in the exotic locales to which he ventured. He was easy on the eyes, and he was brilliant. He was also refined up to a point. But despite all his fanciful grooming, cosmopolitan bearing, and financial successes, he was still just a drunken, coked-out himbo.

And as the private plane waiting for him at Memphis International reached cruising altitude, moving toward an exclusive Caribbean destination that evening, he would, after some insistent goading and a few lines of cocaine, have sex with the beautiful blonde female pilot.

Why? Because he wanted to. And that's all Fab ever did. He did whatever humored him at any moment because he could. He had become independently wealthy as a younger man by busting his ass during the first tech boom and creating an employment agency for graphic artists who specialized in everything from font design to web content. He sold that agency for a healthy nine figures, emerging from the era as an estranged husband and custodial father of two children.

But those days were far gone. And now, he was just what he had always wanted to be without the headache of worrying over small children, but he still had to go through the motions sometimes.

His kids, a young man in his mid-twenties and a beautiful girl a few years younger, made their way down to the landing. Both looked like their father. They had long, pretty eyelashes and regal bone structure. The son wore a skull cap, baggy jeans, and a Battlestar Galactica tee, and he held a game controller in his hand. The voluptuous and very comely young lady appeared dressed for a night out.

"Where are you going today, father?" Lacy said down from the landing.

Fab smirked while shaking his head, "You wouldn't know if I told you. Then again, you wouldn't know where it was if I told you I was going to Belize, Martinique, or any of those other redneck hotspots. Would you?"

Lacy's brother, Tristan, fielded the question on her behalf, "Belize is a tropical nation on the Eastern coast of Central America, and it borders Guatemala, Mexico, and the Caribbean Sea. It's…"

But Lacy interrupted him, "Thank you, Rain Man. That'll do for now."

With that, Lannie got aggressive with his daughter.

"Hey! You don't talk to him like that? You understand me, missy? Do you?!"

Tristan was pitiful. Ironically, he was much like his mother in some ways but not so much in more outwardly displayed social aspects. He was very intelligent and could perform calculus in his head. But he couldn't carry on a normal conversation, and he sometimes got lost between downstairs and the third floor, which was almost exclusively his.

Tristan's space in the home had taken on different decors and themes over the years that were ideal expressions of then-current pop culture. It started as a giant nursery, a place attended to by nursemaids and nannies. Then, it became a Toys R Us satellite store in the zeros. Its current configuration had been adopted when he was in his mid-teens. It became an enormous game room with several wall-sized flat screens, various gaming stations, and CPU towers during that era. It even had a recording studio where Tristan could capture his "bussin" lyrics and edit them later in Adobe Audition.

Tristan had the demeanor of a once playful puppy that got left at home by itself while the family went on vacation. Except in his case, it had been a very long vacation that had, so far, lasted his entire life.

Tristan's mother, Olivia-Addison-Knight, was a wildly successful workaholic who'd been out of the picture for some time. She still loved him and his sister. But as vexing as Tristan found things like changing light bulbs or opening mail, so did Olivia consider dealing with emotions. They were foreign currency to her. She didn't know how to use them or what to do when they were conveyed to her.

Men were just as confounding to the vulgarly wealthy technology baroness. She was attracted to them, and she understood all the physiology behind her desire for them. And all her parts worked fine as she'd produced two children in short order after marrying Fab in the nineties. But emotional intimacy got lost somewhere in the mix. It was easiest to say that Olivia loved her children. But she didn't know why, and she didn't know how to express it, either.

So, as part of their legal separation agreement, Fab wound up with a special-needs Tristan, which he agreed to only because he was a boy of whom Fab was very protective. Unfortunately, custody of Lacy was part of that brokered package.

"Anybody want to come give their Dad a hug goodbye?"

"No," Lacy said curtly before turning and leaving her brother alone on the landing.

Tristan seemed nervous, as if unsure of what to do. He looked to his left and right for a moment, then glanced in his father's direction, although he didn't make eye contact. He looked like a child lost in a shopping mall.

"Go on, buddy. Get back to your game. Your Dad loves you," Fab said solemnly.

Tristan didn't move at first. He just stood there, looking from side to side.

"Go on, champion. It's alright," Fab reassured him.

Then, Tristan turned and disappeared into the long hallway leading to an elevator shaft. After he was gone, Fab raised his custom gold Apple Watch to his mouth and said, "I'm ready."

Shortly afterward, the front door opened, and a Senegalese woman in a chauffeur's uniform entered the house. Her getup looked more like a sexy costume as it was unbuttoned to reveal her chest line as she stood, holding the door open for Fab. He sauntered toward her, attempting to swagger the entire way, but the nineteen-year-old, Khady, was terrified to even make eye contact with Fab Knight despite his leering.

That was alright, though. Because Fab would have her pull over on the way to the airport, and he'd pressure her into having sex with him, too.

***

"So, where was Jim Dandy headed tonight?" Prissy asked as she flipped on her blinker and turned onto Poplar Avenue, "I saw the limo pulling out as I was coming in. But why was he sitting in the front seat with the limo driver?"

Lacy sighed from the passenger side of Prissy's Subaru and hung her head before mumbling, "Jesus Christ."

"Oh," Prissy said apologetically, "sorry."

As they went along, Lacy started thinking about Clint because she wanted to be with him every moment she could. It wasn't possible for now, but she knew she would get there eventually. It was just going to take a little longer. She had to be patient.

Lacy's goals were, for the most part, wholesome. She wanted to change her course before it was too late. She didn't know if Clint would wind up playing in the NFL or if he'd be a middle school football coach in Sequatchie County, and she didn't care. She'd have her house. She'd have their son. And they'd all go to church together and on vacations to Disneyworld and the Grand Canyon.

But before all that, she'd have Clint. She'd put it on Clint like no other woman could. They'd get married and go on their honeymoon to Niagara Falls. And when they returned, they'd unload all their family and friends' wedding presents in the house they'd built together.

Lacy's fantasy was interrupted by that thought. How was she going to protect Clint from his father's horrible secrets about her? Did they even have to see anybody else once Clint proposed, but before he took her away to paradise? Couldn't they just elope?

Lacy was afraid she knew the disappointing answer to that question, but she still wasn't discouraged. She'd figure it out. If she had to entrap Clint until she could show him the kind of person she was capable of being, then she would. Nothing was beneath Lacy Knight once she decided she wanted something.

"Oh, my God," Lacy said when she noticed the bottles of Chardonnay and old DVDs on the back seat as she turned to look at Prissy.

"What? What's wrong?" Prissy asked.

"Are you serious? Again??" Lacy demanded.

Prissy began shaking her head as if suggesting Lacy already knew what was planned. But she rapidly switched gears and became visibly annoyed that she had to explain things to her.

"Lacy, I'm sorry we're no longer into the same things. And maybe we need to start talking about that and deciding if we even need to be together. You seem to want this button-down existence, and that's fine. What worries me is that I don't know if you want to have that with me. You know me. You know everything about me. And even though spending the night with me isn't like spending it with that freak, at least you know what you're getting. That crazy bastard could wind up killing someone if they look at you wrong. Or he could even end up killing you. I don't know why you don't see that."

"Oh, mah'God, get real. He's not going to kill anybody, Prissy."

Prissy snapped backward with both hands at the wheel and looked back and forth between Lacy and the road.

"How do you know if he will or not, Lacy?"

"Because I *know*, alright? I *know* he won't," Lacy insisted.

Prissy lost it.

"Okay. How about I drop you off with him then? Is that where you want to go tonight?!"

Lacy teared up, but instead of responding, she looked straight ahead after flinging her hair back over her shoulder. Her lips were pouty, and she briefly shook her head before falling completely silent. She stayed that way until Prissy spoke up again.

"Look, our Friday nights have always been our Friday nights. You used to love them, too. It used to be something we did together."

Lacy looked over at her as though Prissy's suggestion was insulting. It didn't faze Prissy, though. She continued to be aggressive.

"But I guess that was before Mr. Momoa came along, huh? That was back when girls were beating you up in the shower and following you home to finish the job. You had nowhere else to go but Prissy's, right?"

"Oh, mah'God, it's not like that. It's not like that, and you know it, Prissy," Lacy blurted.

This time, Prissy was the one who went radio-silent, and she sulked even more than Lacy had. She sped up and changed lanes several times, jerking Lacy and the bottles of Chardonnay in the backseat around as they clanged together with each turn. She'd calmed down by the time they reached the first stoplight.

"Can't you just be the way you used to be? You were such a different person then. You had a fun time, and it was wonderful. I want that happy young lady back in my life. I know it's getting tiresome, and I promise to work that out. But could you just pretend like you're having a good time? Okay?"

Prissy struck a chord with Lacy because what she said was true. She had always enjoyed Friday nights at Prissy's. At Prissy's, she was free from judgment. She wasn't made fun of or made to feel bad about her body or how she wore her hair or makeup. Contrastingly, she was worshipped for all those things. Adored. It was a safe place to let herself go and be Lacy. She knew these days were rapidly coming to a close, and thankfully, it sounded like Prissy did, too. So maybe she could do as Prissy suggested and pretend to enjoy herself the whole time.

But in reality, Lacy was kidding herself just as much as Prissy. Because Lacy Knight did enjoy it. She enjoyed it very much.

***

"I'm going to go take a shower," Lacy said when they pulled up the driveway to Prissy's house.

"Okay," Prissy replied, "I'll unload all this stuff, and maybe we can order a pizza or something unhealthy later."

Lacy smiled, bounced her eyebrows, and said, "Ooo, pizza!" before hurrying into the house.

Once in Prissy's bedroom upstairs, Lacy stepped out of the beautiful, short-skirted dinner dress she had on. She'd worn it as a distractor for her father, although she didn't know why she bothered. Fab never even noticed what she had on unless he felt it was too tight or unflattering. Even then, he didn't give a damn. But in some way, he thought he was doing his daughter a favor by giving her critiques.

"That fat ass of yours is going to bust right out of those jeans."

Or, drunkenly,

"Lacy, you remind me so much of your mother in that dress. You look like a Goddamned slut."

Lacy sat in front of the seldom-used vanity next to the bathroom door. She opened one of its drawers and pulled out a small cellophane baggie containing a pinkish powder. She kept stashes like it all over Prissy's house.

But based solely on the color, it wasn't going to do. No, ma'am, Lacy would have to clean that stuff up tonight because she imagined she would need it once she went downstairs again.

Lacy retrieved a tiny stainless steel Gerber baby food spoon from the drawer along with a lighter, a small syringe with a 27-

gauge needle, and a rubber strap she'd taken from one of Tristan's old wrist rockets. Then, she got to work.

By the time Lacy finished, she'd reduced the powder to a formidable ninety percent concentration. She didn't have lab equipment or anything. It was experience that told her she'd achieved that purity. After wrapping the rubber strap beneath her bicep, she tweaked her arm with the syringe a few times until the blue vein she liked to use presented itself. She always waited on that one because it was shaped like a horseshoe. And within moments, it was on. She was on. The world was on.

The euphoria Lacy felt within that world was overwhelming. It was like awakening into a beautiful garden, and the further she moved through it, the more beautiful things became.

**

Lacy came downstairs an hour later, dressed in her school uniform, except she'd modified it by wearing one of Prissy's larger white dress shirts, cinched in a knot around her midriff. Gobs of mascara darkened her gaze, and her cheekbones had rosy circles on them. Another twist she'd added was that she had dotted her face with large cartoonish freckles using the same mascara.

Prissy wasn't visible, but the TV was on, and the first DVD of the night was playing. Lacy had seen it before. She'd seen them all before, and Prissy's selections always seemed to follow a theme.

The four men sitting around the coffee table who had been watching the movie for the past hour rose. The first one who stood began unbuckling his pants and was immediately followed by the others. That's when Lacy started toward them, staring into each of their eyes and behaving as though Prissy wasn't around, just as Prissy had instructed her to behave in the past.

After Lacy walked among the men, they all stood for a moment, encircling the buxom girl who was reaching up and placing her hand on their chests and faces one at a time. They were several inches taller than Lacy and looked like wolves preparing to pounce on a little white bunny rabbit in the woods. The pornography of a gangbang had stirred them into a frenzy, and they'd barely been able to control themselves, longing for Lacy to join them.

Abruptly, Prissy's voice rang out from the darkness on the far side of the room as she said, "Take her."

The men immediately responded, as did Lacy, dropping to her knees in submission.

Prissy watched as they overtook Lacy. She watched their hands cupping her flesh and caressing her fair skin. She looked on as Lacy surrendered herself to the men. And whenever Prissy squinted her lashes over her eyes, she could almost see her old flame Roe having the same thing done to her as had been rumored to have happened in college. There'd never been any discussion about it between them because Prissy didn't have the confidence to bring it up or the resilience to cope if all that had been said was true.

But the mere suggestion it had happened took a battering ram to what remained of Prissy's self-esteem and left her a miserable, demented, and very perverse young woman. She was no longer capable of commingling love and sex. Life had chiseled those things apart as distinct entities in her psyche. The remnants of what love once was to her devolved into an instinctual longing for sex to take place, but it weaponized sex to elicit the strongest emotions possible. And that type of sex was the only thing that happened for the next three hours.

CHAPTER THIRTEEN

"Lacy, you'll never get better. You'll never find love because no man will ever have you with everything you've done and how you've behaved."

"What? Why are you saying this to me? You're supposed to be my psychiatrist, Dr. O! But you're just going to abandon me? What kind of doctor does that make you? What kind of *man* does that make you? You're not a man. You're not a man at all. If you were a man, your wife wouldn't be servicing half of Shelby County while you're sitting here talking to me!"

"Sit down, Lacy…I said sit down!"

"No, you sit down, Dr. O. You think I'm a liar? You think I don't tell the truth? You're the one that doesn't tell the truth! You lie! You've been lying to me all this time?! Josh? Josh?! Joshua!!"

Josh opened his eyes to Liza, looking down at him on the sofa. She held a large Ziplock bag at her waist, and the fist she'd bopped him on top of the head with was still clenched. She thrust the bag up like she was waiting for an answer. All he could do was look between her and the bag several times because he still hadn't figured out what was happening. It made sense when he saw the amber plastic bottles bouncing and clattering in the bag. He reached for it, but she pulled it away.

"The fucks wrong with you, Josh?" Liza demanded.

Then she dodged another of his attempts to get the bag as he rose and lunged for it. Finally, she slammed it into his chest and walked toward the kitchen.

"Where did you find these?" Josh called after her.

Liza stopped, slowly turned and said, "I found them where you stashed them, Joshua. I also looked at the bag. Some of those bottles are over two years old! I can't find anything newer than 2022, Joshua!"

Liza had him on that one. She had the evidence. She'd caught him in a lie, perhaps the only unforgivable thing to Liza Ngyuen-Odom. *Just don't lie to me.* Josh felt he could do or say anything else in a moment of anger or the heat of passion and that she'd forgive him. But, ironically, she couldn't abide a liar.

Josh knew he'd better open his mouth and turn loose with anything by way of a defense, or else he'd be sleeping on that sofa that had so handily lulled him into a power nap that afternoon.

But Liza beat him to the punch.

"Joshua, I can't be with the person you were in med school. I can't."

Her tone had mellowed, but her expression and message remained dark.

"You take your meds for a reason, honey. You aren't the same person when you don't. And you may not believe this, but I've wondered for a while if you stopped taking them. It sure as hell would explain a lot."

Liza was right, and the truth hurt him. But Josh continued to hedge.

"Listen," he began, "I know I get a little weird sometimes, okay? And, no, I have *not* been taking my meds like I'm supposed to. But this isn't what it looks like, Liza. Alright? Yes, these are my scrips, and you can see where Randy has been filling them for me. But I use these as a backup, baby. I swear to you. You know what an idiot I am! I don't remember to eat sometimes, Chrissakes! I keep those in the car in case I forget to take them before I leave. Almost every bottle in this bag has been opened if you'd bothered to notice. And I know you didn't count pills or anything, but if you had, you'd see some are missing from every one of them. I goof up sometimes. But not like that, man. I haven't just stopped taking them."

Liza looked at him suspiciously and went back on the offensive. She wasn't letting him off that easily.

"Okay, then what's with you and alcohol, Joshua? Huh? And what about New Year's? Do you even *remember* everything you said and did at New Year's?"

No. Josh didn't remember. He'd tried to block out whatever had happened. He recalled looking around at laughing faces. And they were all laughing at *him*. What were they laughing at? What had he said? What had he done?

That wasn't all, either. Josh had been drinking a lot more over the past several months. Whenever he and Liza had wine with dinner, he always stopped off and got another bottle on the way home. She was a lightweight and would only have a half-glass before she went to bed. He stayed up and finished the rest, though. Every time. And his beer drinking didn't end at the close of college football season as in the past. Moreover, he'd started finishing each day with a few bourbons before turning in.

Truth was, Josh had been spiraling out of control since Gil had plowed his way back into his life. And he brought a lot of unsettling memories with him. With those came feelings Josh hadn't had in decades, but at the root of them all was inadequacy. Gil made Josh feel like less of a man, even with his revelation that he was queer or bisexual or however he viewed himself.

Josh's fundamental approach to treating his patients revolved around honesty. He frequently quoted Polonius, 'To thine own self be true.' But he'd strayed from following that and several other pieces of wisdom he'd given over the years. He was quickly becoming a failure and beginning to realize it. He'd failed everybody of late.

Josh was guilty about believing every morsel of intel Lacy Knight gave him about her affiliation—whatever that was—with Gil. He hadn't even given Gil a chance, whereas that's all Gil had ever done for him.

With the same mindset, Josh had been dismissive about Prissy Tillman, and although she'd seemed receptive to his treatment, she'd never darkened his door since that first day.

Josh wondered if that had to do with something she picked up on in his behavior. She may not have even been aware she was having that perception, either, because people who'd been as punished by life as she had developed an acute defense mechanism for separating themselves from the danger posed by others. Is that what her subconscious had suggested to her? That he posed some sort of threat to her? He sure hoped not.

The possibility of that gave Josh concern over all his other patients. Had his life become so unraveled that they were picking up on how unstable the foundations for all he said and suggested were? How many people had his slide-rule, off-the-cuff advice impacted to their detriment?

Finally, there was Liza. The person he wanted to satisfy and protect more than anyone. She could be a pissy little bitch sometimes. But her spunk was a lot of what attracted him to her.

It was clear that Josh had embarrassed her and that something ate away at her. It couldn't just be his stupid pills. Was it the bedroom? Did he not satisfy her there? He'd always tried, and he felt like they had a healthy sexual relationship that was bold enough to push limits without tarnishing the sanctity of their marriage.

Josh believed he'd been everything he could to her on virtually every front. But the question that lingered with him was whether that was good enough.

As Josh considered all the issues haunting him, he realized he was postponing the "best" for last. And that was the beautiful, buxom, perhaps nymphomaniac, perhaps not girl he'd grown protective of throughout her treatment.

"I…I've got an issue at work, alright?" Josh said.

"What kind of an issue? What are you talking about?" Liza asked.

"It's this patient. They're really out of control, but I don't know what to do for the first time in my career. They're difficult to read, and honestly, I think they're that way on purpose. I find myself preoccupied with their circumstances. It's getting to where they're all I think about, and I truly believe that's by their design because they do that to everyone. They redirect every road in people's lives back to them somehow."

"It's the little bitch, isn't it, Josh?" Liza snapped shortly after he finished speaking.

That's when Josh knew all he described was yesterday's news to Liza. It was chewed meat. And that made him feel colossally naïve. Because it was apparent that Gil had told Stephen everything.

Stephen, in turn, told Liza. They all acted like it was junior high while he was left to contend with the grown-up responsibility of treating Lacy Knight. So, it was Josh's turn to be outraged.

"Huh? What did you just say?" he asked.

Liza relaxed her shoulders and slumped a little. She knew she'd messed up.

"To what little bitch are you referring, Liza?" Josh insisted.

"I," she started.

"No! What little bitch is that you're talking about, Liza?" Josh thundered.

Things abruptly changed. And all the chaos that followed Lacy Knight wherever she went exploded into the room and took hold of Josh as though he were a chess piece. The game was underway.

Having gained her composure, Liza started up again.

"Oh, come on, Josh. Don't give me that. I understand that you're trying to protect a patient, but could you just get real for a minute? You're not even supposed to talk about your sessions, but you just did! And don't you think other people talk about their discussions with you with the people in their lives who care the most about them?"

Josh wasn't sure what world he was in when he returned to Liza in a rage.

"What in the *fuck* are you talking about, Liza? Just listen to yourself! How dare you? How *dare* you?!"

Liza realized she'd gone too far a couple of sentences back. But she maintained her indignant posturing, which made Josh even more livid.

"You think a patient's situation is open for discussion in the peanut gallery? That you and Gil and his fucking boyfriend are at privilege to discuss someone else's life just because they did something to Gil Wallace? Or, excuse me! Because Gil Wallace *claims* they did something to him? What are you, in the eighth Goddamned grade?"

Both of them stayed quiet for a moment. Liza struggled to come up with something else to say, and Josh waited eagerly to pounce on whatever that would be. After thinking another moment, she fired back.

"No, I'm not in the eighth grade. I'm not in the eighth grade because if I were, you'd probably be making excuses for me to your wife! Even if I was a little nymphomaniac slut! And why is that, Josh? Why are you making excuses for a little nymphomaniac slut?"

Was Liza saying what Josh thought she was saying? Did she have the brass cojones to suggest what he thought she did?

"Oh, man," Josh said, "Oh, man, oh, man."

Josh darted his eyes back and forth as though he were planning an escape route, which he was. He couldn't take any more. He couldn't bear it. His wife was turning on him. His best friend—his only friend—was talking about one of his patients behind her back. Even worse, Gil may or may not have been a party to defiling the girl so badly that she sought psychiatric treatment.

No. He couldn't do this anymore. He had to get out of there. Or at least away from Liza.

Josh charged toward the stairs, and Liza said, "Where are you going?"

"I don't know yet," he barked back, "away from you, though."

"Chickenshit!" Liza hollered at him up the stairs.

"Catty bitch!" Josh hollered over his shoulder, continuing toward his home office.

Josh couldn't even remember the last time he'd walked through its door. But when he did, he slammed it and plodded over to the futon folded in the seating position. He pulled the handle, laid it flat, and plopped onto it facing down.

Josh couldn't believe Liza had the gall to discuss his work performance with others. Then he was even more hurt that she'd suggested what she had about him and Lacy. Is that all she thought of him? Is that all she thought of his professionalism? In a BOGO swipe at his self-esteem, she'd simultaneously insulted him as a husband and as a psychiatrist. And clearly, she intended it to have the effect it was having on him. That hurt worst of all.

After an hour, Josh sat up and decided he no longer needed to lie down. He had a ton of energy. He was going to draw a line in the sand that night. He was going to be a better person, and he was going to start by cleaning out his office and turning it into a workout room.

Josh believed the room's condition was symptomatic of his postponement of addressing all the disarray in his life. It may only have been symbolic, but the room was filled with things he no longer needed or had procrastinated fixing. It all had to go.

Josh got up and started with the Christmas tree bagged up in the corner. He and Liza hadn't used it in years because she always went to her parents' home for Christmas, so he unzipped the bag and pulled the tree out. Then he emptied boxes of old journals, magazine subscriptions, and paperbacks he'd read over the years and started cramming them into the bag.

While Josh had never been fat, he'd been a few sizes larger, and all his "fat clothes" hung in his office closet. He yanked them from hangers and stuffed them into the bag, too. By then, the bag was getting full, but he remembered they had U-Haul boxes on the top shelf in the closet, so he took them down and began assembling them. He filled four boxes total, being mindful that he would have to get all of them down the stairs, so he was careful not to overfill them.

Josh looked around the room once he'd emptied the closet, gathered all the loose things, and boxed them away. He noticed his old Compaq laptop sitting closed atop the desk and wondered if it still worked. He could use it to make notes or download journals at home instead of at the office.

He slid a drawer open, following the computer's cord into a power strip that still fed a bunch of antiquated devices via a tangle of cables. As it opened all the way, he saw his face looking back at himself, but it was a much younger face than the one he looked at in the mirror daily. He moved the intertwined USB cables and the collection of old phones and PDAs that covered half of the photograph. Then he saw that it was the picture he'd taken at the Fellowship of Christian Athletes state summit when he was fifteen.

Josh remembered those days and the kind of person he used to be. He was kind to others and helped them whenever he could. He cared for other people, and he wanted them to care about him.

What had happened? How had he gone from being that child to becoming so cold?

He didn't know, and it bothered him. But damn it, he intended to do something about it.

Josh had only felt inner peace during that era of his life. He attributed that peace to the nurturing environment he experienced at church as a Christian. It may have been a lot of nonsense, but who was he to say that? Who was he to question what God thought or how God's mind worked? It was, after all, God.

Having exhausted all practical measures to perform a self-analysis, Josh did something he hadn't done in over thirty years. He prayed.

Josh prayed for God to save his marriage and deliver him from the impure thoughts that had invaded his mind ever since that cretin, Gil Wallace, came back onto the scene. But he prayed for Gil, too, carefully being ambiguous with God about Gil's present life choices. Instead, he merely prayed for Gil to find happiness however God saw fit for him to find it.

Josh prayed for all the patients he had been remiss in treating and promised God he would do a better job.

Josh prayed for Liza, and he told God that he knew she had been raised Christian, so she knew better than to meddle in others' affairs, especially those who were lost, infirm children who couldn't defend themselves.

And the last person Josh prayed for was Lacy Knight. She was an innocent who had taken up residence in a world of sin and debauchery, and Josh lobbied that her decision to do so had been beyond her control. She was too young and too uninformed to make such decisions and to be on the path she was. And he feared that path was a dangerous one. He promised God that he would do everything he could to deliver her to mental health because he believed with all his heart that she was in imminent danger. The kind of danger anyone should have anticipated and done something about, but he was the only one who seemed willing. And he told God he knew if he didn't act, Lacy Knight might find herself in horrifyingly dire straits.

"In your precious son, Jesus' name, Amen."

CHAPTER FOURTEEN

Josh's next session with Lacy had been grueling, and he felt like he was babysitting a spoiled teenager instead of counseling a young woman back to good mental health.

Then, in the middle of everything, she started acting like she was taking ownership of her misdeeds, thereby accepting responsibility for their outcomes. She also gave him a glimpse at what she was afraid of regarding the consequences of her actions. While it didn't make up for anything, it was a more hopeful direction for the session.

"Maybe things are already like you warned me they could get. Maybe I'm too lost to find my way back, Dr. Odom. Or maybe I don't deserve to be given a chance at anything I want. The chance to be happy. God, that's stupid. I know I don't deserve it, is what I meant. But I'm tired of fighting to make up for things I can't undo, you know? It's like there's no way to make up for my sleeping around or screwing married men. Because no matter what I do, that will always be there. The only thing I'd get out of telling anyone about it would be losing them. I just… I've been so bad, Dr. Odom. I didn't care before now, though, you know? I didn't give a damn. It was fun, and I know that sounds awful to you, but it was. It was fun, and it felt good."

They were getting somewhere now. Culpability. Remorse. All the while recognizing the importance of honesty, which was key. Those were the rudiments of recovery for nearly anything wrong with someone. Alcoholism or other chemical addictions. Intermittent explosive disorder. Hell, even depression and generalized anxiety disorder could be combatted if those things were accounted for.

"It felt good. I understand that, Lacy. Sex feels good because it's supposed to feel good. Any denial about that, whether to others or yourself, is just folly. However—and I don't make the rules, mind you—as we've developed and society has developed around us, having that society has come at a cost. We've had to give up acting on our urges and instincts, or at least, we've had to refine how we act on them. Otherwise, you'd have people killing other people for no other reason than they made them mad. Or having sex with people, as you said, just because they wanted to, and it felt good. And while the practical considerations of not doing those things are apparent, there's an underlying order. Some people believe that it's a manifestation of good and evil or God and Satan. Then Buddhists believe everything that is of benefit to both you and others is what's right, while those things that are harmful to both are wrong. For the scientifically minded, it's the difference between order and chaos. But no matter what someone's beliefs are, the universe has basic, observable, and testable principles. A scientist named Newton developed the laws of motion, and the third of those laws is that for every action, there is an equal and opposite reaction. Then there are the laws of thermodynamics, the first two of which..."

"Hooookay. Thank you very much, Dr. Science. But I wasn't tryin' to hear all that," Lacy interrupted.

"Sorry," Josh said smugly, "I get going sometimes, and I can't turn it off. But what I'm telling you, and the part I want you to remember when you leave here today, is that everything you do matters. And everything you don't do matters. I hear you saying things like, 'I want to be with this person' and 'I don't want to lose this person,' and I understand. But I can't stress enough that satisfying your needs comes at a cost. If it didn't, that would make you God, and you certainly wouldn't be sitting here talking to me. You have fundamental needs as a mortal human being and a member of a society that can only be satisfied through an energy exchange. We're constantly aggressing and yielding as human beings, and for every ounce of take, there's a commensurate ounce of give. Does that make sense, Lacy?"

Lacy's response would've been more convincing if she hadn't yawned before giving it, but she said, "Well, yeah. I guess so."

"Tell you what," Josh began, "why don't we return to the young man you're seeing? You haven't told me much about him, and you seem hesitant to do so."

Lacy instantly perked up. Her eyes twinkled, and she smiled. She looked like a child whose parents had just pinned her kindergarten artwork on the refrigerator.

"Gah, I mean, I don't know what to say other than what I already told you. He's strong and brave. And he's got a good heart, Dr. Odom. A really good heart."

Lacy had continued to smile as she began telling Josh about her man. But she stopped smiling and took a quizzical look when he interrupted her.

"Lacy, I don't want to seem like I'm questioning your judgment of character. But, may I ask, how do you know he has a good heart? How do you know what kind of a person he is?"

Lacy started with the first thing that came to mind.

"Well, he's tender-hearted, for one thing."

"How so? What makes you say that?" Josh asked.

"He just is. He's very sweet."

"Really?" Josh asked to indicate she'd have to give him more than that.

"Yes. Really," Lacy said, as though aggravated.

"And what makes you say those things, Lacy? Tender-hearted. Sweet. Again, I don't doubt you. I'd just like to know."

This time, Josh pressed the wrong button because Lacy drifted back into cynicism and resentment.

"Of course you'd like to know. How could stupid Lacy not get tricked by somebody trying to get into her pants, right? She needs someone else to make sure nobody catfishes her or lies to get what they want. After all, she's just a ho, and I've got to look out for the little ho. Well, get over yourself, Dr. Odom. You're not my father, and I don't need you to tell me who's right or wrong for me, okay?"

"Uh, Lacy. I guarantee you that I didn't mean that the way you're interpreting it. I'm sorry if I touched on a sensitive area you're uncomfortable discussing. Let's just move on."

Lacy wouldn't let that insinuation go, and Josh knew it. He just sat and waited for her to take the bait. It didn't take long, either.

"You didn't touch on *anything*. Gah! I'll tell you why I said that. It just takes me a minute. I'm not used to expressing myself that way and telling someone why I think something. Jesus. I feel like I'm talking to a cop or something."

There it was again. That rebellious, delinquent side of Lacy. The one that always seemed to ooze out during every session. She talked like a member of the Legion of Doom, referring to one of the Super Friends when she said the word "cop." Josh could picture several potential reasons for that, too. He let all of them go, though, and listened to her story.

"A coupla' of weeks ago, he was taking me back home. Just before we turned into my driveway, I saw something moving on the side of the road. I thought it was a cat, a puppy, or something that was too scared to cross the road. But I knew when it did, it was gonna get ran over."

The whole session was new ground for Lacy. It was the first time she had indicated concern for anyone other than herself.

"I told him to stop 'cause I was afraid he was gonna hit it. Then he slammed on his brakes and asked me where it was. I told him it was next to us in the road but that somebody was gonna run it over if we didn't do anything."

Lacy fell silent for several moments. Then her eyes got watery until a teardrop trickled down her left cheek, but she quickly wiped it away with the back of her hand. She was trying but failing miserably to keep it together. She eventually gave up, though, and started to cry.

"What's wrong, Lacy? Why are you so upset? What happened?"

Lacy composed herself, but her voice sounded nasal, and she sniffed as she began speaking again.

"When we got to it, it wasn't a cat or nothing like that. It was a raccoon. And it looked like...like,"

Josh grabbed a tissue box from the table and held it toward Lacy. She grabbed a handful of squares and dobbed her eyes and nose with them.

"It looked like somebody had already ran over it. But they didn't stop. They didn't stop. I mean, who doesn't stop for an animal? And then when they hit it, why wouldn't they try to see if was okay before they just drove off?"

Lacy was approaching a complete meltdown. She became infantile again, begging in earnest confusion, how or why something was the way it was in the world.

"Whew. I can't answer that one for you," Josh said, "but I will say that it's people who are devoid of compassion. People who are so self-involved they can't relate to anyone else's pain. They view everyone as objects to employ for their purposes. My profession calls them narcissists."

Josh had feared all along that Lacy fell into that category. That she was a manipulative, calculating whore, just like he envisioned her mother being, especially since she seldom mentioned her. He was beginning to wonder if that had been an incredibly poor call, though, regarding Lacy. She always threw him off kilter like that. Every time he thought he had her figured out, she transformed into a different person. Presently, she was a wounded and very compassionate child. He wondered what all the transformative impetuses were that moved her from state to state. Lacy Knight fascinated him from a clinical standpoint.

"Yeah, well. Clint's not. He's not like that at all, Dr. Odom. He got an axe handle from behind the seat of his truck. And he pushed that raccoon until it was off the road and on the curb. Then he went back to his truck and grabbed his workout shoes out of a box and put the raccoon in it. He said his dad had a new place out in the country and that he'd take care of it all week until he could get it to Mississippi. And he did, Dr. Odom. He took it to his dad's, and it's still alive. And…"

Josh didn't hear anything after that. He didn't hear another word of the story about a triumphant raccoon who had overcome despairing odds to retire to an estate in the country. He didn't find out that it had gained ten pounds and was so big that he'd had to move out of his size 14 shoebox and into a much larger Amazon box where he enjoyed things like table scraps, peanut butter, and

Skittles. "Coony" loved Skittles. They were his favorite. And though Lacy hadn't seen Coony since Clint dropped her off and drove away with him that night, he assured her that Coony lived a life of splendor, wanting for nothing in the world.

Josh didn't hear that, though. He didn't hear it because, with only a word, he'd been triggered. And that word was "Clint." Then, all the other pieces of the puzzle came tumbling down and locked tabs until they rendered a horrifying depiction that formed a backdrop to the patient sitting across from him.

No.

Just. No.

What was the likelihood of what he was thinking? Was it possible? Could the "Clint" she referred to be the same baby boy Josh had visited at Le Bonheur shortly after his birth? The one whose mother, Michelle Wallace, a liberal centrist, had named after Bill Clinton in a pathetic homage to the ex-President? Clint was a weird name. Clint was a Gen Xer's name. Among the hundreds of men he'd treated in recent years, mostly millennials and zoomers with a few exceptions, he'd never heard of another "Clint,' besides Gil's kid.

And hadn't Gil told him that Clint was some kind of a football prodigy? Didn't he have scholarship offers from all over the country to come and play football? Because that's what Lacy had told Josh about her beau. They'd even made plans to elope and for her to get an apartment in Los Angeles where he'd play for the USC Trojans.

"Excuse me a second, Lacy. Did you say 'Clint?'" Josh asked.

Lacy stopped talking, then said, "Yeah. Why?"

Josh had to move quickly. He had to devise a reason for being so distracted by someone's name that he'd interrupted a patient to confirm it. Think, Josh. Think.

"I...I just wasn't sure. I've got to remind myself who Clint is when I review our session notes, and I wanted to establish that clearly in my mind before you went any further. We've never touched on his name before, and I know that for a fact. You've never mentioned it."

Now Josh needed to shut up. Just as fast as he'd needed to explain himself, he needed to shut the hell up.

"Oh. Okay. Well, yeah. It's, it's Clint. That's his name," Lacy said, gathering her hair and casually pulling it back over her shoulders before going on.

But Josh had already tuned back out as he began evaluating all the implications of Lacy's latest Earth-shattering revelation. So, he didn't hear a thing she said.

Josh's mind spun out of control before it settled into paranoia.

Josh wondered how much Lacy knew—or was letting on to know—about her boyfriend's family. Because if she knew anything at all, that would mean she had even more cunning than he'd already credited to her. Frightfully more. If she knew who Clint's father was, she was taking everyone on a ride for reasons he simply couldn't discern. Had she purposefully established a relationship with Clint to shield herself and Prissy from the power Gil wielded over them? Hadn't that been a self-contained explosion because of her seeing him at that sex party? Wasn't that enough?

Then, the hair raised on his neck when he contemplated further. Had Lacy somehow discovered that he and Gil were friends and purposefully sought his treatment to give credence to a cock-and-bull story about her principal, which she'd use to destroy a man instead of getting kicked out of school again? Was Josh just another clueless slob in her scheme? A useful idiot?

But how could she have done that? How could she have known they were friends? That would've required a lot of research on her part, and that didn't seem likely to Josh for someone who confused algebra with trigonometry.

The last person for whom Josh's paranoia accounted was Gil. Was Gil the one who'd been lying the whole time? Was Gil the aggressor and Lacy an innocent party, someone he tried to intimidate, all because he couldn't keep it in his pants? Had Gil made up the orgy story after Josh busted him? He'd certainly had enough time to come up with something after he stormed out of Madeline's that day.

Josh looked at Lacy intently as her lips moved, although he wasn't hearing what she said. She spoke with a lot of emotion. She'd just been crying, for God's sake, and the things she told him before that point were things that could potentially make a person of conscience cry. He didn't think she was intelligent or experienced in life enough to use what he knew about human behavior against him that way.

No. Lacy was innocent on that count. She was guilty of most of what was wrong in her life, but Josh didn't believe pulling the wool over his eyes was a part of a scheme. While greatly respecting her intelligence, he didn't think she was smart enough to bamboozle him that way.

Lacy said little more and wrapped up her discussion about her boyfriend, "Clint," shortly after Josh confirmed the boy's name.

"Nobody, no guy, at least, that I know would've done something like that, Dr. Odom. Clint's different, and he's sweet. And I want to be with him so bad," she cried.

Josh presented her with the tissues again, straining to come up with something to say. He weighed confirming Clint's identity against determining why the boy meant so much to Lacy.

But his Apple watch brought their session to a close as its "By the Seaside" alarm tone sounded. He no longer paced his sessions with the clock Lacy had busted him for using at their first meeting. The clock was still there, but he'd completely obscured it with a few volumes of *Frontiers in Psychiatry*.

"Oh ma'God, that ringtone is *sooo gay*, Dr. Odom!" Lacy said, giggling.

Another transformation. Lacy reverted to being a carefree teenage girl who made fun of things like people's ringtones or how they dressed. She always morphed that way at the close of her visits. It was as though she wanted to take all the dark, troublesome aspects of her life, which she'd shared with Josh during the hour, and leave them there so she could return to being a fun-loving gal who had a lot to live for. It seemed like she couldn't face them by herself.

Josh's reaction that day was a little different, though. All the Lacy bombs he'd endured during their session had taken a particularly expensive toll on him. Whenever that happened, he knew he'd spend much more time than the usual fifteen minutes per patient he allotted after each session.

Josh settled on believing she was just a mischievous kid with an unfortunate penchant for finding trouble, whether she'd been looking for it or not. That she was the victim in a world that didn't make allowances for age or naivety. That wasn't true for most of his patients, but he believed it was for Lacy.

But that's exactly what Lacy had wanted him to believe.

Because Lacy was in control.

And she'd let Josh know everything she believed he needed to know when the time was right, but not a moment before that.

CHAPTER FIFTEEN

October 30th, 2007

"Well, this isn't really about you, though, is it?" Olivia Knight asked.

She was getting to that point again. The one where she'd blow up and walk away because idiots and simpletons interfered with the way she wanted to do something. She'd reached that point many times since her company's stock had gone public a few years before.

Despite her military service to the country abroad, as well as being the youngest woman ever to own a Forbes 500 company while being on the Forbes 400 list simultaneously, she felt like she still didn't garner the respect that was due to her. She was right.

Olivia's life could sometimes be insufferable because it was filled with detractors, people like the undersecretary of Defense who called her a snake oil salesman and a "total bitch." What an idiot that guy had been. Then, there was that arrogant Senator Radley from California who'd allowed his ego to cost the State of California thousands of jobs. It seemed like those people were everywhere, though. And they only mattered to Olivia when they dared to get in her way.

But the person she spoke with now had posed the most persistent problem to her because he'd fathered and was the custodial parent of her two children.

"Dooon't give me that shit, Liv! It's easy for you to sit back on your ass while I'm trying to raise YOUR fucking daughter, who, by the way, acts just like you do!" Fab Knight growled at his ex-wife through the phone.

Olivia pulled her iPhone away from her ear and stared at it. She would've eaten it if she could have. And she would've devoured Lannie "Fab" Knight, too, ignoring his squeals and pleas for mercy like a rodent in a reptile's mouth just before swallowing his flesh and his protests along with it. Instead, she put the device on speaker as Fab continued because putting it close to her ear gave her the sensation of moving him closer to herself.

"The most pathetic part is that you think you can scare me with all your cloak and dagger bullshit! I made my bones a looong time before you did, honey! You always say you're the one that carried these children for nine months! Why don't you start acting like it? Be more like a mother and do something for someone else instead of yourself for a change! You're not GI Jane! Jesus Christ, that was the stupidest fucking movie ever made!"

Once Fab stopped cutting into her, Olivia said,

"I already have, you whiny little bitch."

***

Lacy stood behind her brother in the condominium with sweeping views of New Orleans and the Mississippi River. Neither appreciated that view because most of the walls in their lives had been just like it. Breathtaking landscapes and soul-inspiring vistas were commonplace in the children's experience, so they weren't impressed by anything that went on in the distance or immediately beneath them from hundreds of feet overhead.

Their backs were turned to all of that because, at the moment, their foremost concern was what was on the 55-inch screen on the opposite wall. Tristan sat Indian style, holding a game controller, while Lacy stood next to him with her arms crossed and her lips poking out.

"Dora is lame," Tristan told his sister after she'd informed him his playtime was over and that it was time to put her DVD in.

"No, she's not!" Lacy insisted, hugging a blue backpack to her chest and stroking it like a kitten.

"Lame," Tristan coolly reassured Lacy, which prompted a quivering lower lip and tears from his little sister.

Blanca Garcia, the Ecuadorian ninera who attended to the children whenever they were in New Orleans—mostly around Mardi Gras—had slipped up behind them unnoticed. She placed her hand on Lacy's shoulder.

"Que pasa?" she asked with her head cocked to one side as she stared down and stroked Lacy's beautiful blonde hair.

Startled but delighted to suddenly have an ally, Lacy said, "Tristan is being mean!"

"Don't worry, Miss Lacy. Come conmingo. We see Dora en la television de tu padre. On your Papa's TV!" Blanca urged.

Lacy loved Blanca. She didn't understand that Blanca was paid to do everything she did. In fairness, though, Blanca lost sight of that, too, at times. Because she adored the fair-skinned little girl with such beautiful hair who, Blanca believed, was mistreated by her parents. Blanca didn't have an opinion of her mother because she'd never met the woman. She may have felt differently about all of them if she could've looked into the little girl's future and seen how she'd impact the lives of Blanca and her family. There were things Blanca didn't know, though. Things she'd never know.

Blanca kissed Lacy's head, took her hand, and started to walk the dispirited child toward the staircase leading up to Fab Knight's bedroom. Halfway there, Lacy twisted around and returned to where her brother sat. She reached down and grabbed her Dora the Explorer DVD from the floor, but before rejoining Blanca, she yanked the HDMI cable from the back of Tristan's PS3, causing Drake from *Uncharted* to fall to his death.

In any other household or with any other boy Tristan's age, that may have resulted in an explosive, potentially violent response. Instead, Tristan looked at his sister with the same expression he'd been studying the display on the wall and waited. That hadn't been the response Lacy wanted, so she raised her bookbag to thrash Tristan with it, but she was interrupted by Blanca.

"Muchacha, comportate! Come!"

Lacy looked back at her brother, who was still staring at her. She didn't know why he had to be so mean. He was her brother. But he acted like he didn't care about her at all. He wasn't like all the big brothers on TV.

Nobody in her family was like the people on TV, though. There was something wrong with her family, especially through the eyes of an innocent little girl.

Lacy relented and walked over to Blanca, taking her hand.

***

Olivia regretted not being able to be in New Orleans that day, but it would've been impossible to pull off. That morning, she was to be at NASA in Washington, DC. From there, she'd fly to Vienna to meet with representatives of OPEC before jetting on to Riyadh and donning a battoulah for a sit-down with the king.

In her stead, however, she'd arranged for a very special person to be in New Orleans to celebrate Lacy's birthday. The person's real name was Luna Alvarez, and she was an acclaimed Peruvian child actress who had landed roles in motion pictures watched all over Latin America. But that day, she would play the part of Dora the Explorer. Lacy would launch into the air on a hot-air balloon and travel east until she arrived at the magical Chandeleur Islands off the Coast of Gulfport, Mississippi, where she'd rendezvous with Dora and Bookbag.

A guide would be waiting to take them by "ship" to her mother's palatial Ocean Springs home. They'd be entertained there by the Ancient King Bellicose and his silly queen, Lulabell. The actors would immerse themselves into their roles, with King Bellicose, clad in a purple cloak, holding his scepter and hollering at his Cuckoo Court to allow passage to Dora and the beautiful Princess Lacy.

Though potentially spectacular, the event was not heralded as such. Nobody knew about it because that's the way Olivia wanted it. She'd wanted Lacy to believe she was spending the day with Dora and that the ship they boarded traveled through time, puffing purple smoke to its destination in the secret city of Ocean Springs.

In keeping with the other things in Lacy's life, though, it all turned out to be one big disappointment.

***

"Look, I know, okay? I know! But do you have any idea whose kid I'm waiting for? Because if you did, I think you'd change your tune!"

Lance Duplantier didn't have time for Lacy's birthday either. He had to be in Loxley, Alabama, early the next morning, which meant he'd had to arrange for transporting a whole crew to reoutfit his balloon with a different envelope after exchanging the ridiculous one that he'd travel to Mississippi with. There was no way he was landing in Alabama on a Dora balloon.

Lance had already had to go through the vetting process with the Department of Defense. And while he thought it'd be cool that he'd been the only aeronaut—maybe in the country—with a Top-Secret Clearance, he was over all of it by that time.

And then those damned helicopters. He didn't care what anybody said or how far away from him they stayed as they escorted the balloon. They would affect air displacement. And the last thing he needed was to wind up on Ship Island instead of the Chandeleurs or somewhere else in BFE Mississippi.

One of the Orleans Parish deputies spoke up, clearly unimpressed. He couldn't count the number of times somebody asked him if he knew for whom they worked, but it was a lot.

"I don't give a damn if it's Drew Brees' kid! I still want you to pack all this shit up and leave! Do you understand? You had an hour to get it done! That's what it says right here on the damned documents! An hour! And that comes from the FAA and Homeland Security? You ever heard of them?"

"Maaan, it's just a baby's birthday party," the other Deputy said, "why don't you just chill, Grady? Nobody's gonna care. They already rerouted everything. It's a little girl, Grady. You've got a little girl, man. So do I. And she loves her some Dora the Explorer! She'd kill to have a Momma or a Daddy that did something like this for her instead of one that ain't ever around and comes home mad all the time. Just chill, Grady."

"Shut the fuck up, Cedric. I didn't ask you a damned thing." the first deputy, Grady Miller, snapped.

Cedric sighed, knowing Grady wouldn't yield to the balloon guy

"Man, why you always gotta be so damned mean?" Cedric asked before Lance broke into the discussion.

"Look, that's it! Okay? That's it because I don't give a shit anymore! Will you at least let me fly the hell outta' here? My chase crew is halfway to Ocean Springs by now! And I gotta get this thing to Alabama in the morning!"

"Get!" was all Grady said back to Lance, leaving him to wonder whether he was okaying the flight or telling him to get the hell out of Orleans Parish some other way.

But Lance didn't care anymore. So, he rambled over to the balloon, climbed in the basket, and prepared for departure moments later.

***

"I already told you! I can't! I can't do all that stupid shit because I don't have time! What don't you understand, Liv? I am the *King* of the Krewe of Mystics this year! I'm taking pictures with the mayor and Senator Fourcade and I'm supposed to be at Emeril's for brunch! So, go throw one of your weird temper tantrums! Go make somebody disappear! I don't give a shit what you do! Just go do it and leave me the hell alone!"

That was it. Olivia couldn't go any further. She didn't have time. She had to be in other places and do other important things. And just as Fab Knight had insisted, he didn't have time either. No one had time for little Lacy Knight.

"Shiiiiiiit!" Fab hissed as Dora and Blanca watched him throw the Garmin satellite phone into the wall as hard as he could.

"What? What? What now? What is it?!"

Blanca didn't say anything but stared at Fab in terror. She wanted to make sure he didn't have anything left to throw at anyone before she spoke. Instinctively, she took Lacy's shoulders and corralled her behind her back while the unhinged gringo caught his breath.

"Que?" Fab panted in Spanish as he calmed, "What is it, Senora Garcia?"

When Blanca was confident that Fab could communicate without hurling something or shouting, she continued.

"Senor Knight, would be okay if I take Senorita Lacy to see Senorita Dora? Ees on my way home. Ees no prah-lens. I can breeng her back to joo when chore pardee eess ober."

Fab sighed. That beaner had a pretty good idea, he thought to himself.

"Maaan, Dora—I mean Blanca —that would be such a big help to me! Such a big help! Es muy bueno!"

"Si senor," Blanca replied, smiling.

Both were relieved, and Lacy didn't realize how much Blanca's selflessness had averted a tragedy. It had never crossed Lacy's mind that she wouldn't make her magical trip to Mississippi. She thought that was up to Dora, not any grownups.

That made it particularly stinging when Blanca turned south on 190, nearing the launch site using the coordinates Senora Knight texted into the Escalade. Just as Blanca turned off the Interstate toward the rural White Kitchen community, a pastel balloon with the image of Dora drifted above the tree line.

"Dora!!!" Lacy squealed from her booster seat.

It looked to Lacy like Dora stared directly at her, arms making a "V" and smiling brightly. It was exhilarating for the little girl who believed Dora was her only friend. That wasn't too far-fetched because Dora was the only person who spoke directly to Lacy when she broke the fourth wall, saying things like, "Can you say muy delicioso?"

Blanca was almost as astounded as Lacy, and the little girl inside of her immediately started blowing the horn in her elation that these people she worked for actually made dreams like this come true.

However, it was the cynical little girl in her who was the first to notice that the balloon was drifting farther and farther away as it climbed rather than descending toward the coordinates displayed on the nav's console. Blanca sat at the stoplight after it had turned green, just to make sure her suspicions were correct. She didn't move until the car behind her honked. Then she realized that Dora was indeed going away.

Blanca sped up, hoping the road would wind back toward the balloon at some point, but she was scorned by Lacy once their backs were to its heading.

"You're going the wrong way! You're going the wrong way! Turn around, Blanca! Turn around!"

Blanca pulled to the shoulder of the road and called Fab Knight from her cell phone. She didn't want to speak to him over OnStar because Tristan, who was riding shotgun, and Lacy in the back seat might hear it, and Blanca feared the worst coming from Senor Knight.

"Si. Si. Okay. Si, Senor Knight," she said before turning back to look at Lacy, whose eyes had already begun to tear.

Lacy knew the drill, though. And she started to come up with reasons that she was culpable for everything that had gone wrong. Lacy had been misbehaving recently, and Dora had probably known about it. She'd likely seen her push the stool to the counter and nab several Oreos after everyone else had gone to sleep the night before. Dora probably watched as Lacy carved her initials into the back of Tristan's game discs using nail clippers. And she'd almost assuredly seen her rip the cord from the back of his PS3 earlier that morning. Lacy imagined Dora didn't want to hang around a girl like her, one who always misbehaved.

But instead of throwing a temper tantrum or lashing out at Blanca, Lacy settled into her car seat and looked toward the floor. The gesture broke Blanca's heart because it was such a sad thing to behold, even if she'd seen it dozens of times before.

Immediately, Blanca called Senor Knight back. It wasn't over yet.

The next day would be Halloween, and all the children in Slidell, where Blanca's elderly parents operated a Mexican restaurant, would flood the streets, trick or treating. Blanca's children, Sevi and Conchita, would be among their numbers. Sevi, the same age as Tristan, would go as Buzz Lightyear, while Conchita, a year younger than Lacy, would dress up as Ariel. Since Lacy was already dressed as Dora, she'd be fine. Then Blanca could either piece a costume together for Tristan using something from Sevi's old costumes, or she could pick something up for him at Walmart.

The day after that was El Dia de los Muertos, the Day of the Dead. Traditionally, families in Ecuador would visit their deceased loved one's graves, bringing fresh flowers. And while that wasn't possible in America, they still cooked those relatives' favorite dishes and made a day of it. They'd prepare Colada Marada, a tropical drink, to accompany those dishes. They also made "Guagua de pan," which was a bread baked to symbolize a baby in deference to the babies whom King Herod ordered decapitated following the birth of Christ.

By the time that festival was over, it would be the weekend. Blanca could take the kids to the Audubon Zoo or the Mississippi Coast to the IMAX theater while her husband, Hector, played blackjack at the Beau Rivage.

Lacy would have the most wholesome time she'd ever have. She and Conchita would ride bikes through the neighborhood and eat Tex-Mex at Conchita's grandparents' restaurant. Tristan and Sevi would play PS3 together until Sevi couldn't bear to lose anymore or be around the weird kid who never spoke as he soundly whipped Sevi in every game genre they played.

It was the most fun and carefree time Lacy would remember from her short life. Unfortunately, it also laid the framework for a horrible scene to unfold a decade following.

Conchita and Lacy would remain friends throughout their preadolescent and teen years. And as soon as Lacy got her driver's license, she would make the six-hour haul to New Orleans several times yearly. They'd coordinate their visits through chats, emails, and DMs.

But instead of bringing hopes for a hale and hearty family outing, Lacy would bring cocaine. Lots of it. And the two jaw-droppingly beautiful girls would take New Orleans by storm. It would start with underaged drinking in the quarter before elevating to raves, late nights, and hit houses in places you'd never expect to see a beautiful, wealthy white girl or her equally as ravishing Latina compatriot. Lacy always dressed in jet black and Conchita fire-engine red as they laughed and danced, sometimes with strange men, at others with each other, while raising the bar for entertainment the later it got.

At the zenith of the last of those raunchy excursions, one that would take place while Conchita's parents were in Ecuador, Lacy would walk away from the ladies' room of a Slidell gas station, leaving Conchita in a stall as she freebased. Lacy wouldn't remember why she'd left or how she'd gotten back to Memphis. She'd remember pieces of it where a stranger was driving her car. Had that been a hitchhiker? She wouldn't remember, but the boy would seem nice in her recollection.

When Conchita didn't respond to her DMs or phone calls, Lacy grew concerned. And then she became a mixture of heartbroken and terrified when she discovered a week afterward that Conchita had died of a cardiac arrest in that Shell gas station bathroom.

Lacy's life would implode upon discovering the news about her friend. But instead of swearing off drugs for the rest of her life, Lacy quadrupled her frequency and dosages. She stayed that way for two weeks. And when she came out of it, she agreed to go to some fuck party with that lawyer who'd gotten her out of a possession charge. He was gross, but he was connected, and he always had cocaine.

Such was the course of Lacy Knight's life. The die had been cast a long time ago, and her fate seemed to be on an inescapable trajectory toward doom with intermittent emprises of ecstasy and indulgence, all hurtling her toward her final destination.

In just a few words, Lacy Knight was lost. She was alone. And she was afraid. So terribly afraid.

CHAPTER SIXTEEN

"Oh, my God, with the *Frasier*! Why don't you watch something with a little more…I don't know…substance? Something, maybe, that doesn't have a laugh track? Like *Stranger Things* or *Game of Thrones?*"

Liza had stopped on her way to the kitchen when she noticed Jane Leeves arguing with John Mahoney on the screen, which meant that Josh was watching *Frasier* for the thousandth time. It annoyed her for some reason. But tension had festered in the Odom household of late, and Liza's constant complaining was just a symptom of their mutual frustration.

Liza had always been a bit abrasive, but the things she got upset about seemed to become less significant. First, it was Josh's meds. Then, it was his friendship with Gil. The only thing Josh felt that might have been warranted was Liza's resentment of Lacy Knight. His behavior changed after she came along, and even he was aware of it.

However, Lacy Knight was like no other patient Josh had treated. He spent far too much time thinking about her, waffling between being concerned and detesting her because of her behavior.

The icing on the cake was the latest issue of her involvement with Gil's son.

Josh didn't look at Liza when he replied. He continued staring at the screen, but he did pause the stream so that she could hear him.

"I don't watch *Stranger Things* because I'm not one of those pathetic Gen-Xers that can't get it through their heads that Reagan is dead or that there's no way Duran Duran is making a comeback in this lifetime. And I don't watch *Game of Thrones* because, well, I'm not a dork. And *Frasier* was recorded live, by the way, so there was no laugh track. Either one of those pieces of shit you mentioned could use one, in my opinion, though, because they're both so Goddamned silly that they make me nauseous."

Liza realized then that Josh was in no mood for her needling.

"Jesus, what's up your ass?" she asked, "And you're totally wrong, Joshua. You're a tremendous dork."

Although he wasn't humored, Josh smiled. But he still refused to look at Liza.

"Well done, Liza."

He could smell Liza's favorite fragrance, Tuberose Gardenia because she'd bathed herself in it. And when he finally looked at her, he noticed how she dressed. She must've been planning to go out.

"Where are you going?" Josh asked.

"Oh. Stephen and I are going to a party in Memphis. I don't know anybody there, but everybody loves Stephen, so I'm sure we'll have a blast. Why?" Liza responded.

Everybody loves Stephen. That was such a loaded observation. Josh wondered if Liza knew just how much and how many people had "loved" Stephen.

And then why had Liza asked, 'Why?' Was it abnormal for a guy to ask where his wife was going in a short skirt, jewelry, and smelling like an Estee Lauder factory?

"Who's going with y'all?"

"Nobody. Why?" Liza quickly came back.

There it was again: 'Why?'

"What kind of a party?" he continued.

"Jesus! What kind of a party? Well, gosh, let's see. I assume it's just alcohol and catering, but I didn't ask. Why? Are you trying to land an invite? I can ask Stephen if it'd be alright if you joined us?"

At face value, Liza was being facetious and trying to shut Josh down. But a part of her was also aroused. Aroused by the thought of Josh joining her and Stephen and having his mind blown by all that would happen at the party they were going to.

Her relationship with Stephen had changed the rules. He had introduced her to a world she never believed existed but whose depictions she devoured through her novel selections. She loved to read about different women's sexual vantages. It made her feel normal enough to entertain fantasies of her own. Not so much that they became stolid or predictable, though. That would've killed the whole thing for her. And there had to be some satisfaction along the way—even if it was measured.

So, to that point, Liza had just been a cautious observer at Qadeshians parties in the past, laughing and cheering on others.

But if Josh went, her role would change. They'd become a part of the scene. Liza would even look the other way if Josh wanted to participate in all the fun. Then she kind of laughed to herself. Who was she kidding? She wouldn't look the other way. She'd pull up a chair and watch him. Then she'd put Josh in that same chair and make him watch her do all the same things with another man. Or maybe two. Maybe three.

Josh deflated the depraved balloon that was inflating inside Liza's mind.

"I just don't get it, Liza. None of it makes sense. First of all, you're way older than Stephen. You could be…"

"Watch out," Liza warned.

"I was going to say older sister or cousin or something. Even though Tuan is only twelve years younger than your mother. I mean, how did that even happen?"

Liza got mad but didn't let her anger destroy her hope for something that could be life-altering for the couple—*if* she could lure Josh into going with her and Stephen.

"You know what? Instead of being an asshole and insulting my political-refugee family, why don't you get up, get dressed and go with us? Come on. It'll be fun, baby. I promise."

Even though she was serious, Liza's goading made Josh think there was nothing to worry about if she invited him along. That's when he pictured it being Liza and a bunch of queer dudes laughing and dancing the night away. They'd giggle and start sentences with things like, "Girrrrl!"

What else could it have been? Liza screwing Stephen in front of him or something? Yeah, right.

As Josh mulled that over and Liza saw that he wouldn't make her dirty little dream come true, she said, "Alright, then. Have it your way. Don't wait up."

Just like that, she was gone. Her perfume lingered, as did the image of her twitching her hips through the kitchen, into the mud room, and ultimately to the garage. A few seconds later, Josh heard her drive away. He thought she could've at least asked to drive his Tesla.

Sure, honey. You can take my car. Just go. Go on out with your gay model boyfriend and the other dudettes. Take my AMEX. I'll be waiting right here for you, precious.

In truth, Josh was sort of glad she took his car. Because that meant she was going to drink and force it to drive her home. And while he wasn't thrilled by that prospect, it was better than her riding with some Uber driver or getting in the car with someone who had the outward appearance of being sober but would get everyone killed.

Josh reserved the right to feel any sort of way that night because he was a psychiatrist in conflict with himself. That happened a lot in his profession. There was a constant tug of war between a psychiatrist's morality and the doctrines of their structured education. The cheering and jeering onlookers included all their patients' sins and misconduct, as well as whatever moral code with which they presented.

Whichever side won out depended on a host of factors. Clinically speaking, a psychiatrist's moral judgments should never have come into play when dealing with their patients. There were limits to that credo and even to their Hippocratic oaths in some ways. Not to mention the legal implications of deciding whether to involve others. Like law-enforcement.

Lacy Knight had brought virtually all that to the table when he'd taken her on as a patient. And now, everything had intensified upon his discovery that it was Gil's son with whom Lacy was involved. The stakes of the internal conflict would rise due to his action or inaction, and it wasn't just the people around Lacy who would be affected anymore. She had metastasized to his inner circle of friends and family, which was incredible to him.

What Josh wasn't aware of yet is that none of it mattered. And that was because Lacy Knight and all her bullshit were about to be taken off the table. The spunky little girl who stood her ground when dealing with her older brother. The salacious siren that lured everyone—not just men—into her world and held them captive until they cared about her, shortly before she cast them aside. The hopeful, repentant young "Lucy"—who may have started maliciously and with other intentions but had fallen victim to a passionate love for a man she believed was pure of heart.

Each version of her was about to go away. And except for a few glimpses under horrifying conditions, no one would ever see Lacy Knight again.

***

Josh awakened into darkness. He'd fallen asleep with his brain in overdrive. He'd overexerted himself the past several hours and was spent.

After sitting still for a moment, his iPhone began to vibrate on the arm of the sofa. He raised it and looked at its screen, which read "UNKOWN CALLER." Whenever he received such calls, he ignored them because they were either automated or someone was trying to sell him term life insurance. He was about to put his phone on Do Not Disturb when he noticed that he'd received a stream of calls over the past several minutes. 1:43 AM. 1:47 AM. 1:55 AM. Holy shit, what time was it?

That's when Josh got scared. It was past two in the morning. What horror could be waiting for him on the other end of that call? And then it stopped, and he realized his phone had been vibrating longer than he'd been awake and that it was probably what woke him up in the first place. Someone wanted to talk to him urgently.

But there was no way to call a number back. He'd have to wait and pray that whoever it was called back.

"Liza! Liza!!" Josh hollered across the house as he shot up from the sofa.

Liza had left early—before seven. Why in the hell wasn't she back home yet? Had that been her calling? Was she stranded somewhere? They had roadside assistance with their cars, so was she calling him for another reason? Was somebody else calling on Liza's behalf because she could not call?

"Liza!!!" Josh screamed, terrified.

Then, he was relieved when Liza walked out of the butler's pantry, wearing Air Pods, and headed toward the microwave with a plate of nachos.

When she noticed him, she pulled one of the headphones from her ear and said, "What? Were you calling me? What's wrong?"

Josh exhaled as the pounding in his chest peaked. The hairs of his neck stood on end, and then that tingly feeling of an adrenaline rush that felt like an all-at-once acupuncture rolled over his scalp.

"Yes! I was calling you!" he shouted in frustration.

"What? I'm sorry, okay? I didn't hear you! Jesus, Josh!"

Josh's phone began vibrating again. Who in the hell would be calling him at two in the morning? He didn't know, but he didn't want Liza to find out, because no matter who it was, she'd put her two cents in about it.

"It's okay, Liza. I'm sorry, I'm sorry. I just woke up weird. You weren't here, and I...I'm sorry."

Liza smiled and said, "No, I'm here babe. I'm here. Calm down."

Josh smiled back at her and chuckled, saying, "I'm going to go upstairs for a while and unwind. Maybe read a little or something."

"Josh?" Liza asked as though talking to a child.

He knew what she was about to say, so he nipped it in the bud.

"Yes, Liza. Yes, I took my anxiety meds. And no, Liza. No, I'm not going to stay up all night again. I just have a lot on my mind, and I feel like I've bottomed out, alright? I've got to chill out a little before I put my head on the pillow."

"Okay, hon. That's all I wanted to know. Are you hungry? You want some nachos? I was about to nuke'em, but I can put more on here."

Josh looked down at the plate Liza held, and he'd be damned if it didn't look delicious. He hadn't realized it until then, but he was ravenous. Whether or not he ate nachos was up in the air, but if he didn't, he would gorge himself on whatever he could find. Screw his diet. He was making a profound life change Monday when he began the "75 Hard" lifestyle regimen. So, tonight and the next day could be his last indulgences.

Liza had gotten creative with those damned nachos. She and Josh always used the big cheapo Santita chips. On top of them, it looked like she'd emptied the butler pantry fridge's "takeout" section, which shelved their Taco Bell from the night before. She dumped everything on top of the tortilla chips. Taco meat, refried beans, rice, jalapenos—she'd even crumpled the remaining Doritos Locos shells atop the mound as a finishing touch.

Realizing he couldn't do any better than that, Josh started nodding.

"Hell, yeah. Put some more on there. Is there anything left?"

Liza smiled sweetly, reaffixing her headphones with one hand, then returning to the pantry to load up. And just as she did, Josh's damned phone began vibrating again. He looked at it and got the same notification: "UKNOWN CALLER."

Josh decided that the smartest and safest thing he could do would be to ignore whomever it was calling him. Liza was home safe, so he couldn't think of any other reason to answer the phone. So, he just slid his thumb up to the red "Decline" circle and tapped it. Then he said, "Hey, Siri, put my phone on Do Not Disturb."

***

Just as Josh had, Lacy Knight awakened into darkness. But there was no plate full of nachos. Josh was greeted by a loving wife and comfortable surroundings in which he'd stuff himself full of food and then have unbelievable sex. Lacy Knight woke up alone. And the only thing she felt was terror.

They'd come back to her. She knew that much about them. The only question remaining was, what would they do when they arrived? Is this the way things would wind up? No husband. No house behind which to garden or kitchen to cook dinner. No chubby little blonde-haired Stuart to cuddle between her and the husband she'd never have. Was the life she'd led up to then all that was intended for her? Was she that meaningless?

Lacy knew she couldn't overpower them. No way. They'd proven to be very strong and heavy-handed with her, something she'd not thought they were capable of.

Then, when it seemed there was no hope, and everything she'd tried to change about herself had been for naught, Lacy felt something resting on her ankle.

It felt cold and metallic.

And it had heft.

It was dense.

Glass, maybe?

When she wriggled her toes across its surface, she felt the unmistakable nibs of a keyboard. She ran her big toes across its surface several times to confirm it before deciding that, yes, it was indeed a keyboard.

Lacy felt a surge of hope. She almost didn't want to find out, even if it was not a keyboard. She grabbed whatever it was between her bound feet and began the difficult task of moving the object toward her midriff.

She didn't know where she was because she hadn't been conscious when they'd brought her there. So, she knew nothing about her surroundings except that they were quiet. She didn't hear cars, voices, or anything else. She wouldn't hear anything for several more hours until they returned. But for the time being, it was hell.

But what was this thing she'd now managed to get between her ankles? It would take hours before another significant advance because one misstep and it would flop away from her, beyond anything on her body that she could grapple or undulate with. And with it would tumble any hope she'd had to escape.

Could it be one of those old-timey texters or some weird cellphone without a touch screen?

She didn't know. But she'd make it her life's final mission to get to whatever it was, take it in hand, and use it against her captor. And use it she would, to surprising and unanticipated effect.

***

"Would you believe I'm still hungry?" Josh said as he stood a few feet away and looked at Liza, who had just sat up in bed and was immediately taken to tapping on her phone.

"Jahhhsh," Liza whined, "I can't! I'm too tired! Why don't you just eat some damned cereal or something."

He laughed and said, "Relax! I was just telling you that because I'm craving Cracker Barrel. You don't want to come with?"

"Oh. Golly. Let me see, uhhh, redneck food…a bunch of hillbillies…and you gotta walk through a flea market to get there? Hmm. I think I'll pass, thank you very much."

"They have tomatoes!" Josh reasoned before breaking into a chuckle.

"No, no. You go on with ya bad self. Liza is staying in the hizzy this morning."

"Oooo," Josh said, unbuckling his pants, "ghetto talk! You know that turns me on, homegirl!"

"Josh! No!" Liza said, "No way! What is wrong with you? Wasn't that enough for you last night?"

Josh stopped tugging at his belt before refastening the buckle and saying, "I was just kidding, Liza. Jeee-zum, lighten up, will ya?"

As he turned to fetch a mid-afternoon helping of a Sunrise Sampler, he stopped and said, "I knew you wouldn't want breakfast. I was just kidding around. But I've got to get all those boxes down to my office to go through them. I'm finishing my gym project today!"

"Just in time, fatass," Liza said as she texted with somebody.

"Who's that?" Josh asked, even though he felt like he already knew.

Liza looked up at him, puzzled, and he knew she hadn't heard what he'd asked. It annoyed him that she paid more attention to texts than she did him talking—especially if they were from Stephen.

"On the phone," Josh said, "who are you texting? Hello? Anybody home?"

Liza held her phone up for him to see, although she knew he was too far away.

"My mom, ok? We're talking about Tuan."

"Really?" Josh asked, "Wow. Minh is texting now? This is becoming a strange world, isn't it?"

"Shut up," Liza whined again, "Go eat your damned grits and hog jowls."

"Ouch! That hurt!" Josh said playfully before turning and going toward the stairs.

The thought of lugging everything he had to carry down the stairs suddenly occurred to him. Then he wondered if he had enough room in his car to put it all—even with the under-hood storage. So, he turned around and went back into the bedroom.

"Can I take your G?" he asked Liza, who still fumbled with her phone.

She looked up and said, "Sure, go ahead," before returning to her texts.

Boy, that was easy, Josh thought. Liza didn't like anybody driving her SUV. But he didn't want to question her generosity, so he walked over to the nightstand and grabbed her keys.

***

Josh was fussy about his things. He'd carved out little safe spaces for himself all over the house, places he could retreat to and exist without all the clutter of the areas he shared with Liza. She took over everything, stacking her clothes, perfumes, and bath products everywhere. So, he got angry as he put the last box on top of the stack in her cargo hold and noticed the mud streaks splattered on his Tesla's fender wells in the garage. Where in the hell had she driven his baby? She didn't have respect for a damned thing, he thought to himself.

Josh pulled out his phone and started to let her know about it. He couldn't decide if he wanted to get into it with her as he stood in the driveway because his neighbors would probably hear him. So, he opted to text her instead.

The Tesla looks GREAT BTW!

Josh stared at his phone, eager to hear her excuse. The little indicator dots started to ripple in a speech bubble, so he knew she was typing. Then they stopped. Then they started again before coming to another halt. At last, they started up again and were sustained for several seconds.

"This oughta be good," Josh said aloud, standing in the driveway and peering down at his phone until a bigger speech bubble blooped up.

Srry bout that. Stphn wnt thru puddle in pknglt we cdnt see. X ddnt say anything wrng so we kep going. Meant tell earlier. You wnt me take to carwash whl u gone?

Josh shook his head and sighed. So now Stephen was driving the X? He texted back a pointed jab. He knew it was passive-aggressive as he typed, but he didn't have the energy to enter a debate. Not with that one.

You know, you text just like your mother sounds when she talks. Thought I was talking to Minh for a second there.

He could almost hear the text indicator clattering as though Liza sat at a keyboard. And just as before, it started and stopped several times.

ROFLMMFAO!!!

CHAPTER SEVENTEEN

Prissy lay on the couch, still drunk and falling deeper into depression, but the Chardonnay made everything worse.

Her dilemma was the same as it had always been. It was merely the person from which it originated that had changed. But the heartbreaking theme was unwavering from one point in her life to the next. She was going to be alone again. Her beautiful muse, her wildflower, didn't love her anymore. She was losing her, and she was losing her to a man.

Nobody else she loved wanted to talk to Prissy either, though. Roe had stopped answering her calls and texts years before, but Prissy realized why she'd chosen to ignore her. Who wanted to answer the phone and listen to a blubbering, self-pitying drunk, which is what she'd become?

Roe didn't have time for such silliness because she had a man now. And Prissy thought that real men didn't behave that way. Men were strong and hard, like Prissy's father. They didn't twist in the wind or shy away from confrontation as she did. They were forthright and fearless.

And she hated every Goddamned one of them.

Back when Prissy first began losing control, she tried to stop herself. She tried to get help. She just couldn't find anyone to give it to her. In a last-ditch effort, she even attempted to reach out to that arrogant little doctor Lacy had so mercilessly duped. But he hadn't answered his phone, and part of Prissy thought that was, perhaps, poetic justice because she might be getting just what she deserved.

If nobody wanted Prissy anymore, though, she sure as hell didn't want them either. And she was prepared to make that abundantly clear to all of them. She might not be able to stand toe-to-toe with someone or shout over them. She couldn't frighten anyone or intimidate them because that just wasn't in her.

She'd still tear it apart, though. She'd burn it all to the ground, just as she had in the past.

Prissy was always willing to accept her share of the blame. Even though she couldn't help the way she felt, she could still assign outcomes to actions, and her actions had been loathsome. Detestable. But most resulted from her meeting, consorting with, and falling hopelessly for Lacy Knight. And that's where the lines between her culpability and victimization began to gray.

Lacy had seemed different to Prissy. She was just as passive and skittish as the other little rich girls on the court, but she appeared to have her heart in the right place. She tried. She worked hard and paid attention to Prissy's coaching. So, as time progressed, Prissy began to develop feelings for her.

Prissy's feelings began innocently. But then they moved on to a questionable fondness before alighting on inappropriate. The little games they'd play. The sexually charged comments they'd make to one another, even during volleyball sets. Prissy would call a time-out, and after breaking from the huddle, she'd hold Lacy back, and they'd talk about everything Prissy wanted her to do, both with her and with other people, always men. They did this in front of a gym full of other students and parents. It was thrilling.

Their relationship was more than just sex, though. Prissy became Lacy's refuge and Lacy hers. They confided in one another. They began spending time away from Restoration Academy with each other. Lacy was the first, if not only, person who had ever listened, truly listened to Prissy, and she knew everything about her.

However, even beyond the relationship's forbidden nature, Prissy's insecurity gave it little chance of survival. How could this beautiful girl be in love with her? Lacy didn't love her, she thought. Lacy only ran to her for protection, like when that McCormick girl beat her up. Then, when the other girls cornered her in the gym after school, held her down, and threatened to cut off all her hair.

Nonetheless, Prissy held on tightly, believing she could protect Lacy. Worse still, Prissy would've assumed any role Lacy would've given her—if only Lacy would stay.

Please. Please stay with me. Don't go away.

Prissy certainly had chances in the past to do what would've been best: to leave Lacy Knight alone. They hadn't been courting long before Prissy got the first inkling that Lacy was a manipulative liar. She should have left Lacy to flounder then.

Toward the beginning of their ill-fated courtship, Lacy was upfront about her then-involvement with an attorney—some guy named Luke. It began when she went to the man for help after being arrested for possession. He'd helped her alright. And just like any other appreciative innocent, Prissy was sure Lacy wasn't sophisticated enough to realize that his kindness and interest in her stopped immediately beyond the stunning curves of her physique and the mesmerizing lines of her beautiful face.

Later, Lacy gladly accepted his offer to take her out on his boat with his "family." What that devolved into, however, was a bunch of other attorneys and their mistresses getting drunk before snorting coke off the passenger side's helm. Lacy was much more beautiful than the other girls, so she found herself in the same quandary as always: adored by the men and shunned by the women.

After Lacy related that story to her, it hurt Prissy to think about her baby girl having been mistreated by that coven of whores who wouldn't talk to Lacy and made fun of everything from her over-the-top makeover for the outing to the size of her butt. Once Lacy told her about everything they'd said and how they'd made her feel, Prissy even thought about doing something to all those people. One at a time. Away from everyone else. At a distance.

Things continued with Luke for a time, but then that relationship turned peculiar, too. At his insistence, Lacy accompanied Luke to a few parties at a hotel just south of Memphis. They were themed parties, Lacy said. Something to do with honoring an ancient Egyptian goddess. However, what they were, she told Prissy, was an excuse for the attendees to have orgies. The parties were long, drawn-out affairs, sometimes lasting for hours, where everyone got crocked and crunk. Then, once the members were sufficiently inebriated, someone banged a gong, and the festivities descended into hedonistic, indulgent sex. Some men had their wives with them, while others brought their mistresses, but for everyone there, the entertainment became an unfettered, unabashed flesh festival.

Prissy was decimated when Lacy shared those things about her past. But she was also willing to forgive Lacy because she attributed her sins to her naivety and the opportunistic abuse of others. Prissy allowed herself to believe that everyone had victimized Lacy. Those evil, arrogant, pompous bastards had befouled Lacy and lured her into their demented circle. They gave her drugs and then used her like a whore. She never thought Lacy had willingly gone to a swinger's party or joined some twisted, sexual, social order.

Even after learning about her association with that freak society, Prissy remained under Lacy's spell. Her cherishing of Lacy only intensified. She became obsessive and, ultimately, lethal.

Prissy didn't emerge unscathed by all the depravity, though. Moreover, she was subconsciously inspired by it.

One day, as Prissy was about to leave school late after running laps around the track, she caught Terrence Marvin, the basketball coach, in a compromising, unflattering act as he watched something on the computer at his desk. He hadn't noticed her walk in to lock the equipment room. But as she tried to creep away backward, her tennis shoe squeaked on the concrete floor, sending her boss into a tizzy. He'd thought he was the only person left on campus.

As Prissy assured him that it was okay and that she knew he'd thought nobody had been around, she noticed what he'd been looking at on the screen over his shoulder. What he'd been watching was Lacy. He stared at a video of her in the showers that he'd surreptitiously recorded early one morning when, for some reason, Lacy came to school to change.

After discovering what Marvin was looking at, Prissy became more aggressive, but not for the reasons one might assume. Yes, there'd been outrage and resentment. Jealousy made its usual appearance, as well. But all of that gave way to Prissy's libido. Seeing Lacy in the context she was seeing her heightened the perverse, burning urges she'd developed at Princeton while chasing after Roe.

Someone wanted what Prissy had. But instead of triggering a defense mechanism or a desire to protect what was hers, it turned Prissy on because of all the psychological trauma she'd been through in the past. Lacy was beautiful and sensual whenever she did something as innocent as walking across a room. So, standing in the shower like some Rubenesque statue with water cascading down her body as someone else watched romanticized Prissy's askew lust.

Prissy did the routine, though. She told Marvin how wrong it was and that he shouldn't look at her players or any other Restoration girls that way. In tears, the coach acknowledged what she said, and he swore up and down that he'd only done it because he'd been under a lot of stress.

"Coach Priss, you gotta understand now. I'm just a man."

Prissy eyed him up and down, seeing the pathetic fool he was, and responded,

"Oh, I know. You're certainly right about that."

Even though he'd eventually find out, at the time, Terrence Marvin had no idea of the danger he'd clumsily tumbled into as he spoke. But Prissy did. And the power it gave her to lord over him made her giddy.

Terrence didn't stop pining for Lacy, though. Prissy caught him watching Lacy several times as her girls practiced. He always managed to sneak a little gander as he passed by volleyball practice.

Prissy caught him a final time, staring through the one-way glass between the coaches' common area and the gymnasium. He was undoubtedly gawking at Lacy because apart from her, the only other person on the gym floor was a heavyset, less athletic team member that Lacy was helping with her serve.

Prissy gathered enough courage to approach Terrence in the middle of his filthy ponderance.

"Are you turned on?" she'd asked him, startling the hell out of him.

But after looking at her for only a moment, Terrence could tell Prissy wasn't angry, and something else was in play. As he stared at her, attempting to determine her next move, he subconsciously became aware of the familiar glint in her eye. Terrence was too stupid to draw such a conclusion on his own. But he was on instinctual autopilot and sensed that Prissy was aroused. However, he mistook her interest as being oriented toward him. Nevertheless, he was intrigued when she told him to return after everyone left that day and that she'd ensure his every need was satisfied.

By that time in his life, Terrence didn't care. Shoot. Prissy was good-looking enough. And if she wanted to play, he was willing to play with her. She may have been a little spindly and leathery, but she was fit. Had a perfect little ass on her, too.

Then, it was as if every perverted dream Coach Marvin ever had came true when he returned to his office that night to find Lacy naked and positioned just so in front of his desk and Prissy seated in the corner of the room. Initially confused, he came around when Lacy started walking toward him like a cheetah moving through high grass, closing in on its prey.

Those interludes continued for several weeks, with and without Prissy's knowledge or attendance. Marvin and Prissy would sometimes get together without her because he could snag blow for her from the South side much easier than her going alone. Then she'd go to motels with him, and they'd party for hours, all building to him getting everything he wanted out of Lacy.

The last fantasy involving Prissy played out much differently than she had planned it. It was the one where she'd intended to become an active participant. She'd materialize in the middle of Lacy and Terrence's encounter, and then she and the coach would have their way with Lacy.

But that idiot, Gil Wallace, had wandered into the room as Prissy waited around the corner in the showers as scripted. Ironically, that was the only good fortune she'd had because it would've been over for her, too, had Gil found her there, caught up in the middle of everything. So, she leaped from the showers where she'd hidden, scrambled to the window, broke its glass, and ran faster than she'd ever run before. The world seemed to fly past Prissy like she wasn't exerting effort.

After Lacy came home that evening, Prissy was relieved, if a little confused, by how things had ended with the headmaster. Prissy had feared that she and Terrence Marvin were going to jail, just like all those other teachers she'd seen get arrested on the news for carrying on with their students.

"I don't think so," Lacy said, "I don't think that's going to happen."

That's when Lacy disclosed a few more details about her past and her involvement with other people that she'd intentionally left out before. It was also another chance for Prissy to break from Lacy. To leave her behind in her world of deceit and treachery and move forward with her life. But for reasons she'd curse for the rest of her days, Prissy refused to abandon her. Those details, however, were life-changing for Prissy.

Lacy told her that Gil Wallace had been present with his boyfriend at the final Qadeshian party she'd attended. That's right, Lacy said. The Headmaster of Restoration Academy was bisexual. And he was also a swinger.

The information was surprising, but what Lacy went on to tell Prissy destroyed her.

Lacy said Mr. Wallace had cornered her during that party when everyone else was distracted. Luke had been with two other women while Lacy sat at a table, taking hits of nitrous oxide from a tank that a dentist had brought to the soiree. Lacy said Wallace didn't acknowledge their association but started caressing her face and running his fingers through her hair. And then he told her to lick his fingers. Lacy said she was so stunned that, before she realized it, he'd taken her by the arm and guided her to an area of the room where he started molesting her.

"I didn't know what to do. He wouldn't let me up. He's so big and strong, and I guess everyone there thought I was into it when I was begging them for help. A lot of other men got in a circle around us. And they started calling me names and asking how I liked it."

By the time Lacy finished her account of what happened that night, Prissy Tillman was clinically insane.

She already couldn't stand Gil Wallace, but the thought of him touching Lacy was too much for Prissy to withstand. She would get Gill Wallace. She'd take him down whichever way she had to.

As Lacy watched the craziness overtake Prissy's expression, she began reassuring her psychologically abused puppet.

"He's not going to say anything to anyone," Lacy said, "Just the fact that he was at the party will probably keep him quiet. He'll lose his job. But if he does, he'll go to jail, too. Because I'll tell everyone what he did to me at that party."

Though mired in pain, Prissy kept her wits about her and offered her take on everything.

"Honey, you don't know how things work, but I do. Even if you told them about him…the way he…all the things that…what you told me he did to you, they won't believe you. Not only will people be doubtful about anything you say, but they'll *want* to believe someone like him instead. They put that son-of-a-bitch in a position where he was responsible for young women, so they have almost as much to lose as he does. Wallace will destroy you because of what you know, and they'll help him. He's probably been trying to figure out how to do it, and we just offered him the way on a silver platter. He'll nail Marvin, who'll throw me to the wolves, and then they'll take you away from me before I go to jail."

That's when Lacy came clean about yet another person she'd been involved with and the reasoning behind it. After her rendezvous with Mr. Wallace at Qadeshians, Lacy was paranoid that he would eventually find a way to get her drummed out of school. She had the summer to devise a plan to get at Mr. Wallace another way. She hadn't known how, but she'd tried to get close enough to him to figure it out.

***

Despite casting herself as a babe in the woods, Lacy wasn't helpless after her interlude with Mr. Wallace. She'd gone immediately to work. Like a spider slapped from its netting, she'd quickly moved on and spun another tacky web into which she'd drawn someone innocent and unassuming. Unlike a spider's, though, her selection had been very discriminating. Cherry-picked.

A few weeks after the party, Lacy followed Gil around, taking her brother with her as a cover and for protection. Tristan didn't know what was happening and remained politely disinterested the whole time, instead playing Cult of the Lamb on his Steam Deck. He diverted his interest when Lacy followed Gil to the Best Buy parking lot and into the store. After walking alongside her, he broke from his sister and headed directly to the high-dollar acoustics aisle. Tristan needed a new mic.

While inside, Lacy noticed a strikingly handsome young man. She was immediately drawn to him and started following him instead of Mr. Wallace. She was sneaky about it, stealthily keeping her distance while evaluating him. He was big and muscular, yet somehow graceful. He had rigid facial features that were simultaneously pretty. She couldn't stop watching him while thinking how beautiful her children would be with a man like that.

The young man stopped momentarily in the audio equipment section, raising a set of red Beats headphones and pressing the button to listen to them. But he quickly yanked them off his head and left them dangling from the display. It looked as though whatever he'd heard through the headphones had disgusted him.

He moved from there to the store's back wall, unaware that he had a buxom, beautiful admirer in tow. Meanwhile, Lacy dodged, dashed, scurried, and paused, her eyes never leaving Clint. She liked the way he walked. It turned her on. She liked the way he looked around as he moved, as though ensuring nothing around him posed a threat. His stern expression conveyed so much to her along the way.

But her lust was interrupted, and she returned her focus when the man made it to the flat-screen section at the back of the store. The person who had been waiting for him there was Gil Wallace.

Mr. Wallace tried to embrace the young man, but he resisted by placing his hand in the center of Mr. Wallace's chest and pushing him back a little. They had an intense discussion for a moment before Mr. Wallace presented the young man with a credit card. Then the young man reached over, picked up a giant box under one arm, turned his back to Mr. Wallace, and walked back toward the front of the store. He grumbled as he moved past Lacy, who quickly faked interest in the headphones he'd been playing with. Keeping her distracted was the fact that they smelled like cologne. Expensive cologne. They smelled like the handsome young man.

When he walked past her, Lacy noticed something else about him. He looked just like her principal, Gil Wallace. His eyes, nose, and even the shape of his face were identical. That made Lacy feel less disgusted about the hour and a half spent being assaulted by Mr. Wallace at Qadeshians. Instead, it made her recall it fondly, fantasizing about the boy doing all those things to her rather than her principal doing them.

Lacy had begun her espionage that day without a specific goal. She was only gathering information—as much as she could about the headmaster's habits, affiliations, and places he frequented. But she had an epiphany upon seeing Mr. Wallace's son standing beside him. Everything fell into place, and the path she'd take moving forward was charted neatly ahead of her.

It was a sham that would lead Lacy to join a church, posing as a good Christian gal from out-of-town who was spending the summer with her Aunt Bette. On the outside chance they ran into anyone who knew her and spoke to her, Lacy became "Lucy" in that world, which made provision for explaining it away as a mispronunciation. Her real name might arouse suspicion at Clint's home. A beautiful blonde named Lacy, who was high school aged? She needed more time. Time to invest herself fully in Clint and for him to do the same with her. Their relationship had to have some substance before she revealed herself to Mr. Wallace. Otherwise, Clint would just walk away.

After leading her to church, her scheme directed Lacy to Camp Redemption. Lacy decided her partial penance along the way would be studying and memorizing scripture, which she'd have to recite at camp. She'd also have to endure all that horrible music they all listened to. Christian gangsta rap? Who did they think they were kidding?

Camp Redemption gave Lacy passage directly into the adoring arms of Clint Wallace, the inhumanly strong, potentially violent, and acutely possessive boy that Prissy would have to accept at first.

***

Lacy provided all those details for Prissy, leaving her more wounded than she'd been from all the other tragedies she'd endured combined. Yet she still hadn't told her everything. She couldn't. And she'd hoped she'd never have to.

There was a lot of shouting after that. Prissy and Lacy blamed each other for their circumstances. Prissy called Lacy every name from the book of misogyny, while Lacy insisted it was Prissy's twisted sexual fantasies that were the culprit. When they realized it didn't matter who was more at fault, they began to assess things as a team. They had to determine the potential threats and how to act on them.

Prissy maintained that Lacy didn't have enough credibility to accuse Gil Wallace of anything publicly.

"No one is going to believe you, Lacy. And Terry Marvin isn't going to vouch for anything because it will serve him best to keep his mouth shut. We need someone else, unbiased, who'll corroborate everything you say. Someone who would believe you. Someone that would have to believe you."

That made sense to Lacy. She had to make damned sure that her story was watertight. To do that, she'd have to have assistance. She'd have to enlist someone to attest to everything she claimed, and they'd do it obediently. Passionately.

At first, she considered going to a priest. Priests were respected, and people believed them. But the unspoken fear of God she'd developed from being around Clint made her think differently about doing that. It had to be someone else, someone not involved in any church. She briefly thought about going to her school counselor, Mrs. Fogel.

"What about Mrs. Fogel, my guidance counselor?" Lacy suggested.

"Are you kidding me? Hell no. That bitch loves Wallace. It'd be like telling him directly what you were up to."

Yep, Prissy was right again. But that's when Lacy decided she'd go to someone completely removed from the situation. And in a horrible twist of both their fates, she decided to go to a psychiatrist. She'd lay out everything for them. It wouldn't be as grand as the media circus that would happen if she detonated a bomb in the open. Her weapon would be more like a land mine. It might explode. Or it may lie undisturbed for the rest of her life. But in either case, she would move on. She thought she'd transform into the person God always wanted her to be.

"Okay, then what about a psychiatrist? People tell them everything, and they're not allowed to say anything to anyone. But if the shit hits the fan, they'll support whatever it is I've told them. And I can say that it was Mr. Wallace I was having sex with, not Coach Marvin. Or, hell, I could say it was both of them. And I wouldn't even be lying, technically."

"A psychiatrist?" Prissy asked, mulling over the suggestion.

A psychiatrist. Yes. Prissy thought that was a brilliant maneuver. A psychiatrist's credentials would be impeccable. They were doctors. They'd gone to medical school and were often called by courts to offer their opinions on what they knew. But whatever a psychiatrist would know about Lacy would be whatever she told them about herself. They'd be forced to listen to everything she said and do so without passing judgment or notifying anyone about what she'd tell them. Of course, they'd have to believe whatever Lacy said. But Prissy felt that would be no problem for her girlfriend, who'd masterfully played everyone else.

Prissy reviewed the list of preferred providers in the Memphis area under Lacy's Empowered Youth coverage, which was key. And she blindly settled on one of only a handful of psychiatrists practicing in Germantown. His name was Dr. Joshua Odom.

Soon after that, Lacy's disease would infect the innocent doctor, too, causing upheavals in both his professional and private lives. He'd fall victim to Lacy just as everyone who'd ever cared for her had.

And so, it all began. Lacy's conniving gave birth to the involvement of someone who would change everything.

However, the plan had a critical flaw. Neither Prissy nor Lacy knew that the psychiatrist they had settled on also happened to be friends with Gilbert Wallace. This was detrimental to everything, yet it couldn't have been foreseen.

Through it all, though, the only thing Lacy could see was opportunity. Opportunity to protect herself from Mr. Wallace. The chance to break from the drug-fueled drudgery and hopelessness her life had become. No more Friday nights at Prissy's. No more messing around with Terrence Marvin in exchange for drugs, which she needed to be able to endure those horrible Friday nights. No more dealing with that simple brother of hers or being debased by her father, who hated her. Lacy began seeing an opportunity to eliminate everyone except the people she wanted from her life, and the only person she wanted in it was Clint Wallace.

***

It was all as plain as day to Prissy now, though. The story's moral was that everything that came out of Lacy Knight's mouth was a carefully structured, elaborate, self-serving lie. Lacy drew everyone to herself like a magnet, aligning them with her objectives. She was a temptress of the highest order. She had no mercy or compassion for anyone because Lacy Knight was a narcissist.

After considering everything, Prissy reached a resolution that day, although she'd had to be soused to arrive at it. Even in her stupor, the glaring fact remained: it was over. She would quit her job, sell the house, move away somewhere else, and try in vain to forget all about Lacy Knight. But before leaving, she would take as much away from Lacy as possible. She'd already gotten the ball rolling, but it was time to take it farther.

Prissy stared out the back window at the toolshed Lacy had helped her decorate. Lacy made it look like a cottage one might happen upon in a magical forest. Its façade had shuttered windows beneath which hung boxes filled with impatiens, and there was a stoop with a doormat branded with the words "She Shed." It even had a doorbell camera that Lacy suggested, and Prissy didn't protest because she saw it as added security for the house.

As she stood staring into the backyard, Prissy looked at the cottage and all its little details, which were as fake as everything else about their relationship. Maybe she'd burn the son-of-bitch down once everything was over. She stood in the window, gawking at the little building and pondering all it held inside. It was a tragic metaphor for her relationship with Lacy. And it made her feel ridiculous as she looked on.

Prissy woke Lacy's iPhone and went to its "Favorites" on the Contacts screen. If she hadn't been committed before, she became so when she saw that she wasn't on that list anymore. Clint's was, though. His picture looked like Lacy would have taken it from the passenger's side of that redneck-mobile he drove. The psycho hated posing and had an annoyed expression on his face. But she could still sense the adoration of whoever had taken that picture.

Prissy pressed her finger on Clint's big, beefy face, and her heart, simultaneously broken and under tremendous strain from all the alcohol, began pounding.

"Hello, Clint? This is Lacy's Aunt Bette. Yes. No, she's not here right now. But that's why I'm calling you. I want to speak to you about a few things you need to know. Huh? No. No, I didn't. Listen, I'd like you to come over here to chat for a little while. That doesn't matter…no. No, that really doesn't matter, but what matters are the things I need to tell you, okay? So, are you coming or what? Yes, that's fine. I'll be here. Okay, I'll see you then."

CHAPTER EIGHTEEN

A man walked into the Germantown Police Department one afternoon with flesh gouged from his arms. It seemed he'd inflicted the damage himself, but the police couldn't be sure. They assumed it was drug-related, though. Probably synthetic cathinone, considering his age and how he was dressed, but they didn't have much else to go on.

He acted like a lunatic, maniacally quoting scriptures at some points and then breaking down at others.

The EMTs came in to take his blood pressure, and after they got him to open his shirt to examine him, they discovered that he'd etched a cross into his chest. It was crude and caked in blood, but it was undoubtedly a crucifix. The police were baffled.

Making matters worse, the man was immovable. He was like pieces of iron welded together, and they could hardly get him to stand or do anything. Because of the man's size and state of mind, they cautiously started flooding the room and the hallway outside with officers.

He was huge. Probably six-five or six-six. And he looked to be about two-forty, maybe two-hundred-fifty pounds. Blood gushed from his densely muscled arms because of the vascularity webbed over them. They had to fetch cleaning rags and rolls of paper towels from the custodian to wick all of it because they were frightened that he'd bleed out.

Then, everyone put their hands on their weapons, and the EMT shuffled back when the monster stood up and looked around the room. They all wondered what in the hell the crazy son-of-a-bitch thought he was seeing. He looked like someone who had just been beamed down to a strange planet, as though he suddenly became aware that his surroundings had changed.

It got even stranger when he broke into tears and began reciting the beatitudes, hiccupping and wheezing them out in a stream. And when he reached the eighth one, everything exploded.

"Blessed are those who suffer persecution for righteousness' sake! For theirs is the kingdom of heaven!"

Then, the Goliath leaped forward and took hold of Captain Lewis' .357 before anyone realized what was happening, and he went through three men to do it. Remarkably, Captain Lewis grabbed the barrel and twisted it out of his hand just as the man reached his mouth with it. Had Lewis not done so, everyone standing behind the man would've taken a brain-shower. But the maniac wasn't done yet.

He grunted and kneed Captain Lewis in the stomach before tossing him to the side like a paper cup. A herd of officers attacked the man's flank but ended up crushed between him and the wall when he raced backward as they kicked and pushed with everything they had. After that, the situation deteriorated into what looked like a Three Stooges routine.

Officer Fremont was on the man's back, holding his chin with his left hand and gouging at his eyes with the right. Two other officers grabbed at the man's legs and knees, trying to topple him, but that's when he started staggering around the room and swinging his fists. He dropped one officer. Then another. And just as he felled the third cop, Captain Lewis fired his taser, hitting the center of the crucifix. But that only lasted for a second or two as the man ripped the dart from his chest and screeched.

"Stop it! Stop it! You're going to kill him!" Captain Lewis yelled at the two other police officers who'd inadvertently fired their tasers simultaneously. But even though things had gotten out of hand, their waylay achieved the intended effect as the man collapsed.

The EMT, Larry Bush, rushed up and began performing CPR on the man, terrified he might wake up as he did. He'd seen what could happen when someone was on something like flakka or ozone and had been abruptly placed in a hostile environment, even if the threat was only perceived. They ceased being human. They had supernatural strength, and if they got ahold of you, it was over. Even if you lived, you'd probably lose an eye or your nose or whatever else the hallucinations scared them into biting off. But a guy like this? As big and as strong as he was? Larry feared he'd kill everyone in the police station before they could stop him.

As Larry performed chest compressions, he looked at his partner and yelled, "Hit Methodist! One forty-six! Get the AED!"

Several officers excused from the room by Captain Lewis earlier looked on, taking turns peering through the door's little window. Roderick Hester took a particularly long look, squinting his eyes as though puzzled.

"Man, you know who that is?" he finally said.

"Who?" an officer asked.

"That's Ofay," Hester informed everyone.

"Look out, now, lemme see, lemme see," Detective Michaels said as he pushed his face to the tiny square, "Gahh-ahd dayum. That is Ofay!"

"Who is Ofay?" another officer asked before whispering to the officer next to him, "Who in the hell is Ofay? What, is he Irish or something?"

Inside the room, Captain Lewis knelt and began talking to the man, hopeful he could reach him in whatever place he'd gone to. He patted his leg and spoke tenderly like a father talking to a child going into the deep end for the first time.

"It's alright, son. Hold on. Hold on to me, do you hear me? Nobody's trying to hurt you. I won't let them. I won't let them hurt you. Do you hear me?"

Lewis noticed an iPhone that had spilled out of the assailant's shirt pocket when he hit the floor. He quickly scooped it up and tucked it away, hoping the EMT hadn't noticed. He looked too concerned with saving the man at the moment, but you just never knew.

***

Only a mile away, another EMT, who'd just missed responding to the call to the police station a few minutes earlier, set his coffee in his coaster and nudged his partner.

"You wanna do Picadilly?" Darius asked after Jimmy sprang awake and shot forward in his seat.

"Picadilly? Man, that's denture food, bruh," Jimmy complained before rubbing his eyes and yawning.

"Denture food?" Darius asked as though his feelings were hurt, "Maaan, you don't know what the hell you talking about, boy. Chuckwagon steak. Fried chicken. Limas…"

Jimmy interrupted, "Yeah, with blenders and straws available upon request."

"Bwahahaha!" Darius cackled as he bounced back and forth in the driver's seat.

Then, he was interrupted again by dispatch.

"848 Country Club Woods, female, 40 years old, non-responsive, possible 217, severe head trauma, breathing status unknown, female, 84 years is outside location."

Darius grabbed the microphone and said, "Medic 5, copy, 901K."

"Man, these folks is hard at it today, ain't they?" he said to Jimmy, turning on the siren as the ambulance eased into traffic before flashing away toward the call.

When Darius and Jimmy arrived at the address, an elderly woman wearing a house coat rushed toward the ambulance, waving her arms. She was crying and shouting, and her elbows were badly bruised. A little dog seemed to try and protect her, hunching in front of her with his front legs spread and his head bucking with every yip.

* **

Theresa Collier had been looking out her kitchen window, emptying her coffee cup, when she noticed that big truck that had been parked in her neighbor's driveway squeal out and race away. She hadn't seen who got into it, but she presumed it was that man who dated her neighbor's daughter. She didn't think anything about it at first, apart from being a little put out by the man's reckless driving. But as she walked back toward the patio to water her daylilies, her mind began replaying things to make sense of what she'd just witnessed.

The first thing Theresa recalled was that the only vehicles in the driveway had been the man's truck and her neighbor's Subaru. The daughter's Mercedes wasn't there. So why was the young man at the house if she wasn't? Theresa never saw that truck if the Mercedes wasn't there.

Next, she remembered that the front door had been open as the pickup shimmied back into the street before tearing away. Maybe the daughter had broken up with him. Who knew? Theresa didn't care either. She kept to herself, and her dachshund, Ralph, was nearly the only living thing she talked to anymore. Ralph and her daylilies.

But when Theresa returned to the sink to refill her watering can, the door was *still* open, and it remained open on her third trip back.

It was rude to leave the door of someone's home open when you left, even if they had done something mean to you. Whatever it was couldn't have been her neighbor's fault. That poor gal always stayed at home and had very few visitors. Theresa wondered how she'd even managed to have a daughter and privately believed the little woman must be gay. The only other time Theresa saw people coming or going at that house was Friday night every month or so when she imagined the daughter was out with the man somewhere in town. On those nights, three or four men showed up after dark.

Theresa wasn't sure how many, but they all came in different cars. While they were still there when she went to bed, they were gone when she got up in the mornings. She wondered if they were family or something. She couldn't see them very well from a distance, but she didn't think they were the same men each time, which was odd. But maybe the woman had a bridge club or a movie night or something.

Poor little thing, Theresa thought. If the woman had been raised better, she might not be alone now. Maybe she wouldn't be "one of the fellas" playing cards or watching movies on a Friday night if her parents had taken the time to show her how to dress and act pretty so she could fetch a man. 'Cause throwing on jogging britches, tennis shoes, and running every morning before sunrise wasn't a recipe for romance. That might be something men did, but it wasn't anything that would make them want a woman. You couldn't be tougher or stronger than they were, or they wouldn't have anything to do with you.

Theresa believed a lady should be soft and feminine. And she should put up with all of a man's mood swings and temper tantrums. She should make him feel like he's right, and it doesn't matter if he takes the wrong exit and ends up lost in the bad section of town. You should never tell a man he's doing anything wrong if he's fixing something. You just wait until he breaks it and gets a new one, or figure it out yourself when he gets mad and storms away from whatever he's tinkering with. Then you tell him later that he'd fixed it after all—unless you *do* want a new refrigerator or a coffee pot or any of the other things that he has no business taking apart and trying to fix.

"Ralph!" Theresa chirped, "Ralph, you hush up, now! You stop behavin' that way!"

Ralph stared up at Theresa and growled, but he wasn't wiggling his butt and wagging his tail like he did when he wanted her to feed him. And his barks were repetitive and a lot more urgent.

To calm him down, Theresa opened a can of Alpo Prime Cuts and forked some of it into his breakfast bowl. He'd already eaten that morning, but when he got like that, sometimes it was the only way to make him shut up. It didn't work, though. Ralph continued to bark and charge forward on his front paws each time, and it became clear to Theresa that something else bothered him.

"What is it? What is it, smoochie? Wass is wrong? Huh? Wass is wrong with hims?"

But Ralph tore into a new wave of insistent yipping and hopping from his front paws, which he could hold up a half an inch and only for a moment because of his natural shape and his fatness.

Theresa walked toward the kitchen sink with his bowl. If Ralph was going to behave like that, he could just wait until dinner, and he could eat dry food, which was all his little fat butt needed anyway.

As Theresa stood angrily tapping the bowl over the sink drain, she looked up at the lesbian gal's house again. That door being open sure was ominous to her. A house that size would warm up fast in the spring with the front door wide open. Not to mention the gnats and fruit flies it would welcome in. Why wasn't the lady closing her door?

If she could remember the lady's name, Theresa considered looking up her number to call her. But then it occurred to her that she didn't get phone books anymore. Nobody had a damned house telephone, anyway. And she still struggled to recall the woman's name. What was it, damn it?

Maybe she could leave Ralph at home, slip over, and close the front door herself. If anyone saw her, they'd know she wasn't a burglar, and she knew the young gal would appreciate it later in case she'd been out somewhere the whole time.

***

"Hello? Helloo?" Theresa called through the front door when she reached the threshold and leaned her head inside.

"Honey, did you know your door was open?" she asked while squinting and trying to make out anything she could inside the dark house.

The front door opened into a cavernous living area, so Theresa's voice echoed as the frigid air blew over her face.

"Young lady?" she asked again, but there was no response.

Sensing that no one was home, Theresa took the front door handle and began creaking it shut. She was terrified an alarm would go off or that she would be on camera as she went. But right before the door closed completely, she heard something, so she stopped.

"Hello?" Theresa called again, "Hello? It's Mrs. Collier. Your neighbor? I'm just closing your door, sugar! I hope I didn't disturb you!"

The noise came again. It sounded awful. It sounded vulgar. Theresa was worried that maybe her neighbor was sitting in the bathroom with an upset stomach and didn't want to come to the door because she was embarrassed.

"Sugar? Sugar, are you alright?" she asked, working up the nerve to push the door back open and step halfway into the house.

The first thing that hit her was the smell of alcohol. It was strong, too. It smelled the way Albert used to smell after he'd played cards all night and shuffled in drunk. At least, that's where he always said he'd been. She had an idea he'd been at that little hussy's house the whole time, though. And that remembrance put Theresa into the worst frame of mind.

If her neighbor was stumblebum somewhere in the house with the vapors, she was getting what she deserved, and Theresa wasn't worried about closing her door anymore. Instead, she was angry she'd even bothered to come over, trying to be neighborly.

As Theresa moved to leave the house forever, her thoughts fell on her own daughter, Lorene. So, she stopped and stood for just another moment.

Lorene would've turned fifty the week before. Fifty years old. Dear Lord, where did the time go? She would probably have been married and given Theresa a houseful of grandchildren, too. But that had not been what the Lord wanted for whatever reason. 'Course, the Lord hadn't put that bottle of whisky in Lorene's hand either. And he hadn't wanted her to be friends with all those other little girls at Ole Miss, the ones who drank until they couldn't walk straight and went home with boys.

And that was fine, and that was their business. But why had they left Lorene at that apartment in Oxford? Couldn't they have just taken her to her dorm room instead of leaving her drunk and alone? So drunk that she'd fall in the bathroom and hit her head on the tub? Why? Why, God? Why didn't they do your will? Why didn't you make them do your will? Why did you let them leave my baby alone to stagger around vomiting until she hit her head and died?

Theresa muted all those memories and feelings, just as she'd done dozens of times a day for the past thirty years. And she thought about what she could do now to prevent something like that from happening to another woman's little girl. So, she pushed the door back open and marched into the house.

Prissy! That was it! The lesbian's name was Prissy! She wanted to say it was Lacy or Sissy or something like that, but she just couldn't remember. No, it was definitely 'Prissy.'

"Miss Prissy? Miss Prissy? Are you alright, sugar? Are you sick?"

Nothing.

"Honey, why don't you come to my house and…"

Theresa gasped because the noise she'd heard a moment before was from Prissy Tillman lying on the floor, struggling to breathe. It was a terrible noise that sounded like a sustained snort or a snore.

Prissy had been traumatized, beaten within an inch of her life. Ironically, her being drunk may have been what saved her because she had also vomited, which amplified the odor permeating the living room where she lay. That stench was what lured Theresa further into the house, forcing her to contemplate, yet another time, how her daughter had passed.

All of Prissy's teeth were missing, but before they'd been pounded out of her head, they'd punctured her lips and the skin surrounding her mouth, which looked like a trembling, twisted, bloody chasm. She lay in a pool of blood originating from the back of her head, but that had since splayed out in several directions. Blood was splattered all over everything else, too, as though someone had stomped on her face until it exploded like a water balloon.

It wasn't just a beating. To Theresa, it looked like the pictures she'd seen of that zookeeper the chimpanzee had gotten ahold of while feeding him. Prissy didn't look like a woman to Theresa. She looked like a monster. A monster emitting a horrifying groaning sound as though it were in extreme pain, and it begged for someone to put it out of its misery.

Theresa turned away, then twisted back toward Prissy before turning in the opposite direction again. She babbled while treading in a circle the whole time, "I…let me…just wait…I'll…I'll…house…house…house phone!!"

That's when Theresa charged out of the home as fast as she could, raced to her house, and tumbled inside, falling flat on her face. Rather than trying to push herself up, she crawled out of the foyer, down the hallway, and toward the kitchen. When she arrived, she struggled on her elbows toward the princess phone on the wall beside the refrigerator. She yanked the receiver down and pressed 9-1-1 following several missed attempts. After crying and squealing to the dispatcher, who insisted Theresa stay on the line, she dropped the receiver. She lay sobbing on the floor, shaking her head back and forth, once again imploring the Lord to reveal why something so horrible had happened to someone.

Theresa began thinking about what she'd considered all morning. It was something dozens, then hundreds of others would contemplate for several days to come. And that was: where was that girl?

Where was Lacy Knight?

CHAPTER NINETEEN

When Michelle Wallace finally reached Gil on the phone, he went from mildly annoyed to shocked, just as she'd done. She had nothing more than a timeline to offer him because she hadn't known much else. The police had called. Then they called back. And by that time, she was on her way to the hospital.

After Michelle arrived, one of the ER docs accompanied her to a room where two police officers waited. She demanded someone tell her where her child was, but they only quizzed her. The doctor asked if Clint was on any medications and if he had any allergies that she knew of. Did he have a history of mental illness?

What the hell was he talking about? No, her son wasn't mentally ill! He was healthy and strong and an honor student! How dare he ask her something like that? Worse still, *why* was he asking her something like that?

The policemen were nearly as obtuse as the doctor, but they'd been instructed to limit their questions and leave diagnostics to the detectives. They wanted to know if Clint had ever been arrested for anything before—harassment, assault, maybe?

Michelle was in a tailspin after that, struggling at each turn to get answers. What had Clint done that was so bad that it had resulted in him being arrested? Had he gotten into a fight with someone? Had someone hurt him? Is that why they'd taken him to the hospital? Shouldn't they have taken him to the hospital *before* arresting him?

Gil's arrival made things worse. He was boorish and even more demanding than Michelle had been. He wanted to know what was going on, and he wanted to know immediately.

Mr. Wallace was so aggressive that Officer Brown, who'd witnessed everything at the police station, became frightened. The Wallace guy was big, like his kid. And if he were even half as strong as the boy, Brown would have no choice but to tase him just like the guys at the station had tased the assailant.

Michelle got Gil under control just in time to find out that their son had been rushed to surgery. They both fell to pieces after that. It was like getting punched in the face, only to swivel around and get walloped in the opposite direction. And still, nobody would explain what was happening.

Things finally settled down that evening when another doctor arrived and told Gil and Michelle that their son was stable in the ICU. He said that Clint suffered a heart attack during an altercation and that EMTs had revived him and brought him to the hospital. Clint's bigger problem, he explained, was that he'd fallen and hit his head. The fall resulted in a brain hemorrhage, which they'd had to operate on immediately. They were uncertain about any brain damage, and they'd just have to wait until they could perform a CT scan. Until then, they placed Clint in a medically induced coma.

***

Michelle and her mother, Cecelia, sat in the room with Gil, not speaking because they didn't know what to say. In the past, her estranged husband would've tried to console her and assure her that everything would be alright. But he wasn't worth a damn at that moment.

Given all that had happened, Gil was understandably alarmed when three men wearing badges on their hips walked into the private waiting area. They were also in suits, which heightened his concern because the suits meant they were detectives.

"Hi, folks. I'm glad we're catching you here. I know you're dealing with a lot right now, but I need to ask everyone some questions. My name is Captain Tony Lewis. I'm with the Germantown Police Department, and these are Detectives Hester and Michaels."

All the men shook hands as Gil stared back at the detectives blankly before Captain Lewis quickly moved on.

"We know you're frightened, and we know you have questions. But to be frank, we do too. We're here to piece all of this together, hopefully, but we need your help."

"What's goin' on, man? What's happening? Nobody is saying anything," Gil interrupted.

Captain Lewis looked toward Gil compassionately and said, "I know you're confused, Mr. Wallace. Here, why don't we sit down for a few minutes and talk about everything."

"Sit down? Hell no! I'm not sitting down! Why won't anybody tell us what's happening? What's going on with my boy?" Gil shouted.

"Mr. Wallace, please calm down. Let me finish speaking."

Captain Lewis tried to be firm yet mindful that he was dealing with a terrified parent who seemed just as confounded as the police were. But at that point, he didn't have enough information to tell the Wallaces anything that would make sense to them. Nothing made sense to him either, so far. But in similar situations, he'd learned when emotions ran high, and confusion prevailed, a good detective remained calm. They sat back and watched things develop rather than become part of them. It was in that foggy window that they tried to discern things from the haze.

"We don't have to sit down if you don't want to. So, let me just tell you what we know so far," Lewis offered.

Captain Lewis began relating the story, careful not to disclose too much. He didn't want to lead the Wallaces in any particular direction. He wanted to use them to see where he might've made a misstep during his preliminary analysis. He spoke to them like he was reporting the news rather than orienting their focus.

"Your son came into the station this afternoon and asked to speak to a police officer. He was very upset, Mr. Wallace. And he was bleeding."

Michelle gasped and started to cry at the thought of Clint being alone in a police station, injured and asking for help. Why were they being so cavalier about that?

"I don't understand," Gil said, "What do you mean bleeding? Was he cut? Did someone stab him?"

"No. No. Now, let's not get ahead of ourselves, okay? Just let me continue, and I'll explain everything that I know. Your son's wounds appear to have been self-inflicted. Now, hold on just a minute. Hold on. I only tell you that because he didn't say anyone had done anything to him and because of his subsequent behavior. He seemed to be experiencing what I'd describe as an internal conflict. It was like he wanted to tell us something but couldn't bring himself to."

Michelle couldn't take any more.

"Why didn't you help him? He's just a child! Who doesn't call an ambulance for a child?"

That got under Lewis' skin a bit. He was sparing their feelings by not telling them that Clint had assaulted several officers and wrangled his pistol away before attempting to kill himself. He'd personally saved their son's life, and all his other officers had shown remarkable restraint by not killing the boy. They may have excessively tased him, but even that was a curbed action compared to what they would've been well within their rights to do.

"Mrs. Wallace, your son may be your child, but he is, by no one's measure, a little boy. It was all we could do to keep him from hurting one of us. Maybe even himself."

"What in the hell are you talking about?" Gil asked.

"Mr. Wallace, your son became aggressive. We think it was because he was frightened, but I assure you it wasn't because of anything we'd done to him. You see, we don't know how he got into the mental or physical state he was in. I'm not going to ask you if he's on any medication because you've already informed our officers that he's not. He's apparently not a drug user either, is that correct?"

Gil took on a predictable air of indignance.

"Absolutely not. My son doesn't even drink. He's the president of his Fellowship of Christian Athletes chapter and a captain on his football team, for cryin' out loud. He's never used drugs in his life, and I would know. I can promise you that."

It was difficult to be a police officer. You had to bite your tongue and swallow your pride, not only at the expense of your ego but also to enable yourself to carry out justice and protect the public, sometimes from themselves.

"I understand, Mr. Wallace. I just wanted to confirm. And your son is also a very religious young man? Is that right?"

"Yes," Gil said, gritting his teeth before Clint's grandmother, Cecelia, stood up and spoke for the first time.

"Clint is a good boy! He's a Christian, and he's a good boy! That doesn't make him a religious weirdo, though!" she insisted.

"Ma'am, may I ask who you are?" Captain Lewis asked.

He wondered why the woman had taken her description that far if the boy wasn't exactly what she described.

"I'm his mamaw! His grandmother!" Cecelia declared.

"Ma'am, I didn't mean anything by that. I'm also a person of faith. I'm asking that because of some of the things your grandson said. That's all."

Captain Lewis wondered if Grandma would change her tune if she saw that kid stretch his shirt open like Superman to reveal the crucifix he'd carved into his chest.

"Anyway, he reached a point where it seemed he'd tell us what happened to him, but then he just exploded. He became violent and had to be restrained. My officers did their best, but again, Mr. Wallace, your boy is very strong."

Lewis refrained from asking about steroids because he realized that even if the Wallaces knew if he used them, they'd say no. He'd been through this so many times with so many different parents. It was always, 'My son is a good boy,' or 'My son couldn't hurt anyone if he wanted to.' If only these people could've seen what he'd seen. Along with everyone else in that questioning room, Lewis had feared for his life because of the 'good boy' who abstained from drugs and captained the football team.

"And he had an unanticipated reaction to being tased, so the EMTs we'd called to treat his wounds brought him here, and that's where we are now."

"You *tased* him?" Gil railed over Michelle's blubbering, "You tased my son?"

"Mr. Wallace, your son gave us no choice, do you understand? We wanted to talk to him and have him tell us what was wrong. Can you imagine trying to help someone like that who was in the mental state your son was in, and then they attacked you? I know you love your son, Mr. Wallace, but my officers have families and children, too. And unlike most jobs, they could potentially lose everything if they slip up."

When Lewis was sure he wouldn't have to defend what his officers had done, he continued the story.

"Your son, uh, began quoting scripture shortly after he started talking. And that seemed odd to us. He acted like he was obsessed at times. Then, at others, he showed remorse. He repeatedly said he was sorry. I have to ask, is your son romantically involved with anyone, Mr. Wallace? Does he have a girlfriend or anything like that?"

Gil could easily answer that one. He doubted his son had ever even kissed a girl. He was too religious for anything that might lead to romance.

"No, my son's only focus has been…" Gil managed before Michelle interrupted him.

"Yes. Yes, he does. Why?" she asked as her pulse rose along with her concern.

"What?" Gil asked. That was news to him.

"He's been seeing a girl for the past several months. Maybe even a year. Why are you asking that?" Michelle continued with Captain Lewis.

Lewis had presumed the father would be the one who came clean about something like a girlfriend when he'd started questioning the Wallaces. But now, it seemed his mother would be the one from whom he'd glean anything along those lines.

"Is that Lucy? Is that the girl's name?" Lewis asked.

"Yes, that's her name," Michelle said.

"When did this happen, Michelle? He hasn't said a damned thing to me about it," Gil whined.

Michelle only had to look at Gil for a moment to give him an answer. Her expression said everything.

This surprises you? When would he have told you that or anything else? Your son doesn't want to have a damned thing to do with you, Gil.

"Well, do you know if he's been with her today or the last time he was with her?" Lewis continued

Michelle acted as though she'd said more than she intended. Like she regretted having spoken at all, nevertheless, she answered hesitantly.

"I have no idea, sir. And I don't understand why you're asking about her. I don't think they're serious enough for her to be a part of this."

Michelle lied her ass off. Clint always told his momma everything. He also went strong on everything he ever devoted his attention to. And he'd gone extraordinarily strong on Lucy Kent, the girl he went on about endlessly. Michelle hadn't met the girl yet, but apparently, she'd fallen as deeply as her son had. Michelle knew kids didn't always think straight when they were in love. Combining that with her son's temper, a whole ocean of possibilities flooded her mind after Lewis asked about Lucy.

"Please understand, Mr. and Mrs. Wallace, that we're not trying to gather evidence against your son. We'd like to learn more about the 'why' this happened than focusing on any charges against him. And right now, we haven't got the first clue."

Lewis didn't think he was making any headway. He imagined the setting and the circumstances were too much for the Wallaces and that if he went too aggressively, he might cause them to hunker down.

"Listen, I'm probably guilty of poor timing, and I'm sorry if that's the case. I know you're tired, and I know you have a long night ahead of you. But could we speak to either or both of you tomorrow? We could do it away from the hospital if you'd prefer that. I promise we won't keep you, and I'll make sure my detectives are brief. Is there somewhere we could meet? Maybe at your home?"

Gil and Michelle looked at one another. Her expression said 'absolutely not' while Gil seemed to want to accommodate the officers. Michelle didn't realize it, but he was particularly concerned about detectives being involved.

"Okay, how about my office?" Gil asked.

"Gil, no!" Michelle insisted.

Gil gently took her arm and walked her to the corner of the room, where they began whispering.

"Michelle, please. We both know this has to happen. I won't say anything that could hurt Clint, though. You know that. I'm sure they realize I won't incriminate my son. And they're the only ones close to knowing what's happened to Clint. And if we lawyer up before talking to them, we might not get all the information they have. I don't know what's going on any more than you do. But stop and think for a minute. Okay?"

Michelle looked across the room at Captain Lewis staring at her. Something told her it was a bad idea. The man just seemed smug to her. Like he already knew more than he was letting on. Why didn't Gil see that?

"Gil, you don't know Clint like I do. You don't understand how his mind works. But I carried him inside of my body. He was once a part of me. He still is. He's my baby. He's my little boy. And these men…"

"No, Michelle. No, I don't know Clint as well as you do. But he's my baby, too. Goddamnit, Shelly, he's the only reason I keep living, honey. My life is about nothing else but him. Can't you see that?"

Gil was becoming as emotional as Michelle was, and he knew that wouldn't help anything. But even though her entire world was collapsing, Gil had reached Michelle. She was touched.

"Okay. Okay, Gil. Go ahead. Talk to them."

***

The meeting at Restoration Academy the following morning never took place. Captain Lewis had someone from protocol contact Gil to tell him they'd have to reschedule. He didn't make the call personally because he didn't want to arouse any suspicion.

That morning, Detective Michaels had come into Lewis' office and asked if he'd checked his email. When he said no, Michaels told him he'd better look at it before they went anywhere.

"What's going on, Michaels?"

"Well, you'd better look at it, Captain," Michaels answered.

"Listen, we've got a lot of ground to cover," Lewis started.

"Captain, please just take a look," Michaels repeated.

Lewis didn't like intrigue or suspense because he'd had enough of them over the years with his job. He'd become so cynical that he was nearly incapable of being surprised. But he swiveled around in his chair and opened the file attached to his email.

It was a police report, and he started rattling off its content before scrolling down the page to the report's vitals.

"Caucasian female, thirty-eight, assault...Jesus," Lewis said before going on more slowly, reading only half the particulars aloud as he came to them.

The violence he read about was impressive. Dislocated mandible. Fractured skull. Luxated eyeball. Partially degloved face. It read more like a traffic accident than an assault. He hadn't even seen shit like that when he was in Memphis. But this happened in Germantown?

"Look at her bio, Captain," Michaels instructed.

Captain Lewis looked at Michaels, squinting and trying to read his expression before he turned back around and continued perusing the report.

"Single, no family, occupation school teacher..."

Captain Lewis halted. His lips moved momentarily, but then they stopped, too. He looked back at Michaels, who nodded.

Just when Lewis thought he'd heard everything, Michaels said, "There's more."

Lewis looked at him and asked, "What more?"

"Somebody put this in my hands this morning, Captain. A salvage company discovered it in a truck on that property where the trailer exploded on Destry Ridge. Do you remember that? I didn't want to scan it into evidence until you looked at it yourself. That, and I wanted to be here when you read it," Michaels said.

Michaels handed Lewis a manila envelope with the handwritten words "Germantown PD." When he opened it, a Certified Letter addressed to Restoration Academy was inside. Atop the return address was the name "Terrence Marvin."

CHAPTER TWENTY

Restoration Academy – Board of Regence
300 Redeemer Lane
Germantown, TN 38138

To whom it may concern:

I am writing to tell you about something I discovered about Mr. Gil Wallace that I think is important and that you should know I had went to my office on or about Tuesday, February 25th at approximately 4PM to obtain my truck keys that I had left in my desk by mistake that day. I was approached by Mr. Gil Wallace and told I was no longer an employee of our wonderful school and I asked him why and all he did was act mysterious and told me to pack up my desk and leave off the campus. He used profanatie and called me a hillbilly and basically just said that I was fired but I kept asking him why and he wouldn't say anything about it that would make me try to understand what he was talking about so I basically just got my stuff and left. I arrived home at approximately 7:00 PM that night and had started working through my mind about what this could be all be about per se and I thought then that it had it figured out. I would like to formally report that Mr. Wallace os involved in a sex ring in town called the Kardashians. It's not just that thought. He is in on it with Coach Prissy Tillman to and they are both in the group that is nothing more but a sex group where people go and have sex with each other while using illegal narcotics and other drugs. I discovered this after I caught MR. Wallace having sex with one of our students and I think it wasn't the first time he had did that when she told me everything he had done. I asked the student how she knew about all this and she said that Mr. Wallace was president of the Kardashians and that Coach Tillman is also guilty of having sex with this student who shall remain nameless at this time. But it is my belief that they singled me out because I found out about there little game and I wanted to tell you about it but I did not want to get fired over it because times are hard and I really need this job because of the economy. I have more information that I can provide at such time that you would like to meet with me so that we can go over everything about Coach Tillman and Mr. Wallace. But I felt like it was my civic duty to inform you about this and can be reached on my phone if you would like to find out more about everything.

Respectfully,

Terrance D. Marvin

CHAPTER TWENTY-ONE

"Police-dispatch-what's-the-nature-of-your-emergency?"

<Hello?>

"Police dispatch, what is the nature of your emergency? Why are you calling?"

<Hello?>

"Sir, this is the police department. Why are you calling us?"

<I need to talk to the police>

"Okay, sir. What do you…why do you need to talk to the police?"

<My sister hasn't come home, and I'm hungry.>

"Sir, why are you calling?"

< I'm very hungry, and my sister hasn't come home. I don't have any more Takis.>

It was the first time anyone had acknowledged that Lacy Knight was missing. The first time anyone expressed any interest at all, and even then, it was due to concern for themselves. For something Lacy could do for them.

That's all Lacy was to anyone else: the fulfillment of their needs, which always seemed to fall to those most basic. She was a literal conduit for the satisfaction of urges and immediate wants, no matter how they manifested. It's who she was. It's what she was. But she was missing.

Juanita Ochoa executed the dispatch, and the police arrived at the enormous home from where the call had been placed. The only thing that had been clarified to Juanita was that a person at that address was hungry, and their sister was missing.

***

Detective Fuller was assigned to the case because, technically, the girl the police were called about had been missing for a good while—even if that was by the reckoning of someone who was mentally disadvantaged. After talking to the person who'd called, Fuller got the girl's name, and then the boy led him and the other officers upstairs.

The room he took them to was strange and not in keeping with the girl's age or how the young man had described her. Everything, from its furniture to the color selections, made it seem like a little girl's bedroom. All the furniture was lacquered white, and the walls were painted pink. The canopied poster bed seemed too small to accommodate a teenage female. Some of the stuffed animals that lay at the head of the bed were also featured on the room's walls as Fathead decals. Among those decals were a little girl, a monkey, and a purple bookbag with eyes. The young detective immediately recognized them as Dora, Boots, and Backpack because his younger sister had been a Dora the Explorer fanatic.

Fuller had been dismissive and a little agitated before that. Why didn't he get assigned to the bigger cases? Like the one earlier that week where they arrested that principal and his son for killing a teacher. At least he'd gotten to watch some of those pornos the other detectives got a hold of in that case.

Man, the girl in those videos had it all. The body, the eyes, the hair. She would've otherwise looked like a goddess to him, but he didn't suppose goddesses got down like that chick did. She was unbelievable.

But seeing Dora and her crew made Fuller think back to his teen years when his sister couldn't be peeled away from the television, and he had to fight her to use his PS2 because she was always watching Dora DVDs. And he felt like a heel, both for being mean to his baby sis back then and for lusting over this girl who must've been around his sister's age. It made him consider that this person missing was somebody else's sister and that she could potentially be in harm's way.

However, Fuller's compassion for Lacy Knight was as fleeting as everyone else's when he opened her closet door to see a life-sized depiction of the girl from the videos staring back at him. It was so large and vivid that he jumped back for a moment, thinking she'd been standing in the closet the whole time, aware of all the dirty thoughts that raced through his head.

At first, Fuller thought he was imagining things as he surveyed the Fathead sticker on the wall. The only ones he'd ever seen like that were for athletes, either in action poses or standing menacingly, but always in uniform. The longer he looked at it, though, the more convinced he became that he was looking at the star of every sexual fantasy he'd had over the past few days.

At that time, Fuller didn't know about the girl's involvement with the teacher or the alarming nature of those videos beyond the obvious because he didn't have any particulars about the other case. He wasn't worried about anything but getting to watch all those flicks. He knew the teacher had died, though. And from what he'd heard, that was a good thing. That guy's son had beaten her so badly that she looked like a monster. Who would've wanted to live like that, anyway?

A little while later, Captain Lewis stood in the same closet staring at the beautiful young woman who'd dominated his thoughts since he'd seen her in action. There she was, as voluptuous and inviting as ever. She was bent at the waist in a schoolgirl's uniform with her hands on her knees, staring to the side and looking at the detective through sultry eyes with her lips pooched out as if blowing a kiss.

Lewis exited Lacy's closet and said, "Oh, yeah. That's her."

"Holy shit," Detective Michaels said as he and Detective Hester looked wide-eyed at one another.

Captain Lewis was as much of an expert as one could be about Lacy Knight. And though it was for different reasons from everyone else's, he'd viewed the videos of her in action more than anyone else in the Department. He was older and much more mature.   But he was still a man. Yet he'd managed to restrain the thoughts that rushed into his head while he watched the young lady be overtaken by several men, sometimes in succession, sometimes en masse.

Lewis had come to view the girl in a different light. He had compassion for her. He pitied her circumstances and struggled to find answers for whatever brought them about. All he knew before paled compared to what he learned about her that morning. She wasn't some Only Fans model or escort that made house calls. She didn't need to peddle her ass online or in-person to pay the light bill. She had money—a lot of money. The real estate beneath his feet told him that much. Then, there was the staggering opulence of the home sitting atop it. It was like a castle. A castle monitored twenty-four hours a day by a private security company he'd combat over any footage they could provide him in the coming hours.

The old maxim came to mind and made Captain Lewis think that it was assuredly true: money can't buy happiness.

It was a fairly simple deduction Captain Lewis made that morning. A freshman detective could've figured out that someone as violent as Clint Wallace was involved, and he'd probably killed Lacy Knight. That was likely the reason she was missing, especially since the boy fearlessly marched into the police station after pummeling that coach into permanent disfigurement. The guy was a nut case.

However, they'd amassed even more evidence supporting that first crime in the past few days. And while it may have been a horrible thing to behold, they all watched the video of Prissy Tillman's beating captured from afar by the Ring doorbell on her "She-Shed." The savagery it showed Clint Wallace was capable of could've landed the Dalai Lama on death row. It was sickening.

In the footage, the house's patio door suddenly burst open and leaned, hanging only by its lower hinge. Clint Wallace had the teacher in a one-armed stranglehold while she clawed and gnashed her teeth. Then, when she realized there'd be no overpowering him, she slid his sleeve up and frantically scratched into his arm until it caused him to release her. She fought like hell. They could see the tissue under her nails, making her look like she'd clawed into a roasted turkey. She ran back toward the house, seemingly to get anywhere so long as it was away from the Wallace kid. But he halted her escape by diving and tackling her under the full weight of his body.

Taking a handful of her hair, the Wallace boy began to pound her face so hard into the corner of the patio that everyone watching the video for the first time gasped.

It no longer looked like an assault on anything alive. It looked like a primate trying to crack a coconut on the concrete, growing frustrated with each sequential blow.

Even though the boy was obviously and supremely fit, he became exhausted from pounding the coach's head into the pavement what had to have been twenty times. No one had the stomach to stare long enough to count them because the assault was so brutal.

After catching his breath, Clint Wallace grabbed the coach by her left ankle and raised her from the ground as though he had just delivered a baby. Then, continuing with her in one arm, he dragged her back into the house, ostensibly to do more damage without anyone hearing it.

The footage was blurry after that because the camera focused on squirrels, birds, the wind blowing through plants—just anything except what was happening inside that house. It was as though even the camera didn't want to document the horrific brutality.

Prissy stayed alive in the hospital for a little while with stitches holding her face together and her eyeball in her head. Of course, the doctors said she'd never see again, anyway. The right eye had been reset, and the torn muscles that formerly held it in place had been repaired. But the damage to the retina was inoperable. And if she managed to hang on somehow, the other eye was useless because of the damage done to her ophthalmic nerve. That woman couldn't see, smell, or probably even ever taste anything again because of how badly she was injured.

Yet Prissy hung in there for several hours, responding with squeezes when the doctors and nurses communicated with her. She even managed to answer a few yes-no questions that Detective Hester asked her about her affiliation with Gil Wallace and their mutual association with Lacy Knight.

Prissy's answers to those questions would become a catalyst for welding the pieces of everything together. And while they were paper thin from the standpoint of evidence sufficient to convict, they still pointed them in the right direction. She'd never be able to testify for the prosecution anyway. She didn't have a prayer against a defense attorney. They wouldn't hold her hand and gently walk her through a delicate Q&A. They, too, would beat the hell out of her.

That didn't matter, though, because sometime between 1:00 and 1:04 AM on the fifth morning of her redefined existence, Prissy Tillman coded. And no one among the doctors and nurses was in a great hurry to "save" her because it wasn't right. You didn't keep someone alive with the sole hope being that they'd regain awareness of a world where they were no longer human as anyone knew human to be. You just let them go. And that seemed a fitting punctuation at life's end for a little girl who'd slowly transformed into a monster over its course. Before Clint laid a hand on her, the world had already done to Prissy Tillman's soul what Clint Wallace had done to her body.

***

"Her name is DeLasi Marigold Knight. She's twenty years old, but her school records indicate she's only eighteen. She's a senior in high school, but according to her transcripts, she's about two years short of having enough credits to graduate in Tennessee. That doesn't matter, though, because the young lady has a trust fund worth eleven billion dollars, which, in perpetuity, has increased in value about twenty percent annually for the past five years. The reason is that in addition to all the real estate, cash, and other assets in her portfolio, it's tied to stock in her mother's company," John Barrett informed the roomful of detectives.

The detectives were having a powwow now that Lacy's identity had been established.

"What the hell kind of company is that?" Detective Michaels asked, unsure if he'd heard 'millions' or 'billions.'

"Just hold on a second. I'm getting to that, but you'd better sit down first," Barrett warned.

"Her mother—Jesus, I don't know why we didn't figure this out before. Her mother is Olivia Addison-Knight, and the answer is yes before you ask. *That* Olivia Addison-Knight. The OAK." he finished.

Sadness. Loneliness. Wealth. Power. Captain Lewis had seen so much during his careers in Baltimore, Memphis, and now, Germantown, Tennessee. And all those things seemed to exist in life inalienably. And the worst things appeared to happen to the people with the most to lose at the hands of those with the least. It made it seem like everything he struggled to protect and serve was meaningless.

Lewis hated to think that way because it made his life harder. Dealing with humanity's absolute sludge and filth was bad enough, but to consider that it was all done in vain was despairing.

Lewis considered himself moral. He couldn't be bought or sold. He knew that was pointless because making it to where you didn't have to worry about money anymore was a step closer to inevitable faltering. And the farther you ascended, the farther you'd fall.

Oh, hell. Maybe there was a way, though. Maybe if you got wealthy enough, you could protect yourself from anything. Maybe this gal Olivia Addison-Knight, whom the media referred to as "The OAK," hadn't tried to do that with her daughter. Maybe there was something else entirely going on with her husband and her family.

Then, there was that bunch of pervs from Memphis. After making several inquiries, Lewis eventually realized that Coach Marvin's letter should have read "Qadeshians" instead of "Kardashians." Then he googled it and discovered what "Qadeshian" meant. It was a reference to Qadesh, a supposed Egyptian Goddess of ecstasy and sensual pleasure.

The letter about the student's identity had been vague, so Lewis did a little exploration. He already knew that Lacy or someone like her existed. He just didn't know who she was at the time. But he knew who some of the others in that Qadeshians group were. They were all prominent Memphians and wealthy Mississippians, and the only reason he knew that was because of cocaine busts. It was rumored that more than one penny-ante dealer had historically tried to rat out some of Qadeshian's members in exchange for reduced charges, but nobody had ever believed them.

Lewis believed it when he heard about it, though. He believed all of it. So did Detective Hester.

When they talked about Qadeshians the day before—all the group did, and who all was involved—Hester looked at him and said, "Man. They really are just a bunch of devils, ain't they?"

Lewis dressed his old friend down for his little racist remark. But at the time, he wondered if Hester wasn't right. He continued to contemplate that as Barrett went on with his briefing.

"She drives a 2021 Mercedes Benz AMG Stealth Convertible, which is yet to be impounded, but it's not missing. It's been parked outside of damned Gracie Bleu Frozen Yogurt for the past four days. But apparently, that wasn't enough for anybody to pick up the shittin' phone and tell somebody about it. What the hell is wrong with people, man? Are you kidding me? Just pick up the damned phone and call."

"Alright, Vince, what do you have?" Lewis asked his IT officer.

"Well, I guess that explains her phone being unable to be ID'd. I finally got a call from the Department of Defense this morning, and it turns out the phone is part of a fleet account belonging to, guess who? Dark Knight Industries, which is…yep. It's owned by Olivia Knight. We're still working on the coach's hard drive and trying to pick up the men from the videos, but that one's hard to do. Because of the lighting and the cameraman—or excuse me— camerawoman's focal points, FAC-ID will be tough. We did identify one of them because of his tattoos, but he's already in County. Shit, if anybody believes him, he'll be a legend in there because of the way he put it on that girl," Vince said as everyone started chuckling.

Lewis rose quickly from his chair and pounded his hand on the table beside him.

"That's enough!" he snapped, "We've got a dead girl here, do you understand me? And I don't care what she did or *who* she did! She was still just a baby! So, if I hear another one of my officers make comments like that, or if I see where anyone else downloads those videos, that person is going to be pulled off this case, suspended, and I may even try to get your damned badge!"

There was a long pause where those officers who'd been cutting up remained quiet. Eventually, Vince spoke up, "I'm sorry, Captain. I was outta line, sir. And if you suspend or fire anyone, it should be me. I'm the one who circulated those videos. I guess you already figured that out, but I am sorry, boss. I mean it."

Captain Lewis looked around at the room of officers, and most of them weren't much older than Lacy Knight. They were just babies, too. But they all had five o'clock shadows. They were in flagrant violation of the Germantown Police Department's dress code for detectives as their collars were unbuttoned, their ties pulled loose, and some even had untucked shirts. But they weren't being disobedient. They were that way because most had put in twice as many hours as they normally would—even during a busy week. So, Lewis took mercy on them and followed up in a different tone.

"Look, I know you're all tired, and I know you've been working hard. And, yes, that girl is beautiful, and I'd be lying if I told you my mind didn't wander while I watched her in action. But then all I think about is that same gal lying in the hospital or a bog somewhere because that little bastard did the same thing to her that he did to Prissy Tillman. And that's enough to kill any hard-on my guys, and that's no cap."

Everyone stayed quiet for another moment before Vince addressed the group again.

"I love it when Cap'n says words like 'cap' and 'my guys,' don't y'all? I think it makes him sound cool, don't you? He's still out here bussin moves and living his best life. I think it's wholesome, man."

"Alright, that'll do, Sergeant," Captain Lewis said while the officers laughed at Vince's comment.

As they all continued laughing, nobody noticed Lewis motion to Detectives Hester and Michales to come and talk to him in the hallway.`

"Alright, we're going to have to protect this kid. We'll have to surround him at the hospital, do you hear? Michaels? Assign an officer detail to stand outside the ICU, twenty-four-seven. Hester, you get some fellas to…"

"Wait a minute, Tony. Why? What're you talking about?" Hester interrupted.

Lewis got annoyed again and cut loose on his detectives.

"You'd think you all would figure things out on your own sometimes. Why don't you use some of that cynicism you've built up to open your eyes and realize how the world works? You don't just kidnap or kill people like these and walk away. But you *really* don't kill or harm their kids and walk away. They're too powerful. They can get to anyone. Does the name Jeffery Epstein ring any bells? Well, we're not going to take any chances here. We're going to put that kid on lockdown. If that girl is dead, it doesn't matter why he killed her. And before they get to him—and they will—we gotta get the media involved. Hell, it might not even matter then.

But when these people do what they'll inevitably do to this kid, everything we need to know about why he killed Lacy is going to die with him, along with whoever he did it for, whether that's just himself or his old man, too. The little son-of-a-bitch is close to death anyway. And we don't even know if the girl's parents have found out about it yet, so somebody needs to get in touch with the Knights. It may not do any good, but they've got to be drawn into the public eye just until we can either implicate the headmaster or rule him out."

Hester and Michaels leaped into action while Captain Lewis remained in the hall. He peered in the conference room window and saw an officer making a motion as if juggling his breasts while he bounced. The young joker was stopped when Vince walked up and wagged a finger in his face. Afterward, all the men became serious.

Man, I'm gonna have a hard time keeping these guys focused, Captain Lewis thought.

Lewis was right, though. If the girl had been homely or obese and a plumber's kid, he didn't imagine much humor would be shared among his officers and detectives. They'd likely be more serious-minded and professional about the matter. It would strike closer to home for many of them.

But DeLasi Marigold Knight wasn't just anyone's kid. And she was the furthest thing in the world from homely. She was stunning. The kind of pretty that made you stare at a woman the whole time you sat across a crowded room from her somewhere.

Ironically, Lewis thought, she'd probably used that beauty her entire life to manipulate others, ensuring she was paid the most attention possible. But now, that God-given gift worked against her. And that made Captain Lewis pity her even more.

CHAPTER TWENTY-TWO

Josh was drunk again. He'd stopped off on the way home and picked up a fifth of Jim Beam to drink himself into a stupor with before he'd go to bed. Recently, those were the only waking states Josh floated between. Sleep and drunkenness. He experienced much malaise during both, but the isolation was the killer.

Despite all his degrees and beliefs to the contrary, over the past year, Josh had adopted the mindset of a man from a much older generation. He became more like his father. Josh had never had anyone besides Liza to confide in or express his fears.

But you didn't share much about your fears with your wife. If you were too forthcoming with them, you became weak in their eyes. As a man, you stifled your fears. You pretended they were only imagined. Women wanted men who could protect them and make them feel safe.

For people like Josh's best friend—his only friend—his outlet had been sex. It'd always been the pressure valve that kept Gil from exploding and going off the deep end. Where had that gotten him, though? What had that resulted in? He wound up putting himself in league with people whose asses he kissed—sometimes literally—or following them down pathways and corridors that led to places from which someone couldn't return.

But Gil had recently been scrammed out of one of those places and into the light of public opinion, where the police waited for him with handcuffs. In addition to his own life, those people and places had laid claim to Gil's son's life and the lives of his wife and their daughters. Even as bad as things had been in the past, they were absent tragedy on a scale like they were dealing with and would deal with from now on.

The only question remaining was how much that tragedy would pillage their lives. Would it leave anything at all? Or would Gil, having already lost his wife and the esteem of his children, lose his son, too, either to death or a life sentence in jail? Would he go right alongside him?

Josh blamed Gil for most of that. Gil would soon be a grandfather, for God's sake. Why had he been playing at things that any fool could see would backfire? Why had he put himself in the position to risk answering for so much that would lay waste to everything in his vicinity, including, to an extent, Josh? He'd placed Josh in an impossible predicament and left him waffling over how to behave or what to do next.

Yep. It was Gil's fault. It sure as hell was. And the boyfriend? That was total bullshit. It was merely a symptom of how lonely Gil was. Hell, Gil wasn't gay, although it was remarkable he'd convinced himself that he was.

But Josh thought Gil had simply latched on to Stephen because he'd paid attention to him. It was difficult for a middle-aged man who'd backed himself into a corner to find anyone to give a damn about him.

That raised questions about Stephen's motivations. He could've done a hell of a lot better than a clod like Gil. Was he just toying with him? What kind of a sadistic son-of-a-bitch could do something like that? They'd have to be a narcissistic sociopath.

In fairness to Gil, Michelle had always been sort of a bitch, so she had some culpability, too. She was a spoiled brat whose father was, himself, a drunken brat. She'd never worked for anything, but she remained a materialistic daddy's girl, running to her father to foot the bill for everything. That had to have been emasculating for Gil.

The drunker Josh got, though, the more introspective he became. You had to be drunk or on something to look at yourself for who you truly were. With that came all the emotions and regrets that mounted until the only thing you could do was drink a little more.

Josh wouldn't allow himself to stay the way he was for much longer. He had his anxiety meds if he needed them, but you had to split time between those two things. It was one or the other, but for the time being, he opted to get shit-faced because it was quicker. It also allowed him to be himself, as painful as that might be.

The real issue Josh faced hit closer to home, though. The situation threatened his professional standing and licensure, and it had also begun to migrate to his married life. Presently, he'd had a bit role in all that was happening. But that role forced him to evaluate everything, not only through the eyes of a physician but as a friend and a husband, and all those elements of his life were at varying risk.

Just as sure he was that Gil wasn't gay, he was positive he hadn't harmed nor allowed anyone to be harmed. Gil was too stupid for that. But Josh believed it was his responsibility to share that fact and all the others he possessed with the police. It wasn't anything he'd do haphazardly. He'd suffered over it ever since Gil called him and told him he'd been arrested as a suspect in Prissy Tillman's murder. He'd also told Josh that he believed they were trying to implicate him in the abduction and likely murder of Lacy Knight.

That angered Josh and puzzled him at the same time. How incompetent were these police? Did they settle for indictments based on someone's private sex life and their fear of it being discovered rather than putting the time and effort into finding the person who was responsible? Everything pointed to Clint. That may have been good for Gil in a sense, but it also meant he would lose his son forever.

The only person who could bring things to a close, Josh realized, was Josh. He had information about everyone involved that he believed could resolve everything or, at minimum, exonerate Gil. If they were going to arrest someone based solely on their presumed dalliance with Lacy night, that list was long. It should at least give them pause before they bet the house on Gil being guilty.

And beyond those she'd bedded down, there were others. Josh wasn't so sure that if he were the police, he wouldn't look into some of the girls who'd been so cruel to her. Either them or their boyfriends. Or their brothers. Or their boyfriend's brothers. They had no idea how much Lacy Knight had alley-catted around, but her catalog of conquests was extraordinary.

And justice? Would justice ever honestly be served? Would they ever link Clint to Lacy's disappearance definitively enough to get a conviction? Josh didn't see how. Or did they already have intelligence about something exonerating Clint? And were they just toying with Gil to coerce him into admitting to something, whether he did it or not, because they knew he'd protect his son?

That wouldn't surprise Josh. Nothing surprised him anymore. He believed his heart was in the right place, but he had virtually no confidence that anyone else's was. He'd done his best so far, but he had one step left. He needed to go to the police station the next morning, find whoever oversaw the investigation, and lay everything out on the table.

"Again, Josh? You're drinking again?"

Liza interrupted Josh's train of thought as he sat in the darkness, grappling with his conscience and overwhelming loneliness. He'd purposely distanced himself from Liza but was disappointed she didn't try to involve herself in his dilemma more. He'd ordinarily loath her input, but lately, he longed for it so he wouldn't feel so alone.

Not only was Liza distant, but she also seemed preoccupied with other things. She didn't acknowledge that her husband was at the most crucial juncture he'd ever been. Instead, she was more concerned with trivial things like whether he'd eaten anything or if he remembered it was his turn to take Scout for a walk.

Liza didn't pull any punches when it came to that damned dog. She didn't like her, she didn't want to feed her, and she sure as hell didn't like picking up her shit with a plastic glove. That's why Scout stayed in her kennel most of the time, suffering the same loneliness Josh did of late, and both were the result of Liza's indifference. Whether she tried to be or not, Liza could be so cruel sometimes.

"Yes, Liza. I'm drinking again. I've been drinking for a while, and I'm about to drink some more. Can I pour you one?"

When Josh spoke, he realized he'd already caught a buzz. He slurred, and his voice was gravelly from drinking alone in the dark.

"No, thank you, Josh. It doesn't look like you have enough there for me," Liza quipped.

Josh strained his head toward her, realizing she was being sarcastic. Then he looked at the bottle before whipping back and saying, "Yeah. I think you're right."

"Why don't you turn the TV on or something?" Liza asked.

Josh looked at her as though she should have known better.

"Because if I turn the TV on, it'll be the news. If I watch the news, I'll get updates on all the reasons I'm sitting here getting shitty in the first place. And then my getting shitty won't be about escaping things anymore. It'll be about Gil Wallace. It'll be about Gil, and it will be about..."

"The little nymphomaniac bitch?" Liza cut in.

Josh snorted a laugh through his nose and slurred, "Precisely. It'll be about that little nymphomaniac bitch."

Liza frowned and shook her head.

"I can't stand to see you like this, baby. Why don't you stream a movie or something? I'll grab Green China, and we can hang out here, eat, and just chill. How does that sound?"

Although surprised by Liza's sudden compassion for his plight, Josh refused to respond. He forwent the crystal lowball he'd been drinking from, lifted the bottle of bourbon instead, and took a swig.

"Okay. Okay. I get it. I know you're hurting. A lot of people are hurting," Liza offered back.

Josh looked over with a puzzled, incredulous expression, making her feel she'd better explain herself. But what she said made things worse.

"Just imagine what Stephen's going through. He's going to lose Gil no matter what, and it looks like Gil doesn't even care. That asshole hasn't even called him since he got arrested."

Josh looked away from her, facing straight ahead, and said,

"Ya know what? The last person in the whole gahdamnn world I'm worried about right now is Stephen. Fuck that sissy."

Liza knew she'd get nowhere then. Josh was too drunk. Reasoning became impossible whenever he started being mean. She either had to get some food for him or simply abandon him.

"Honey, I'm going to grab Green China, okay? I'll get some Beef Mai Fun, some Teriyaki sticks, fried rice. How 'bout that? We can eat and hang out. I haven't seen the *Frasier* reboot yet. Is it any good?"

Josh fell silent again. He stared straight ahead in the darkness, with the only light cast over him coming from the island in the kitchen. His eyes were glossy, but Liza couldn't tell if it was because he was drunk or because he was about to start crying.

Liza felt sorry for him and had remorse for everything she'd done, but it wasn't her actions that troubled her. It was their impact on Josh because they were the opposite of what she'd wanted. She wanted him to be free, not just from Lacy Knight, but from all of those nutjobs he had to talk to every day. They'd changed him over the years.

Josh needed a release and freedom, and Liza wanted to give it to him—the freedom to explore other things, just as she had.

However, she realized that he needed her to be someone else at the moment. The cute, sweet girl he'd fallen in love with in college. She had to direct all her energy into being that Liza of ago who might be able to give her husband some hope.

"Babe, I love you. Do you hear me? And I'd do anything for you. Anything in the world. I know I'm a bitch sometimes, but I don't ever want you to think that's honestly me because I love you, and I can't stand seeing you hurt. This will all be over soon, and we won't have to deal with Gil, Stephen, or any of them again. They'll charge Gil's son with whatever happened to that girl if they ever find her. And Gil's life won't be worth anything, but we can't worry about that. Okay? We need to start living for us for a change, and I mean us as a couple."

Josh didn't say anything. But the welling in his eyes grew, and a tear eked out from the corner of one of them, which he immediately wiped away. Liza was losing this one fast. She had to stay positive and fight for her man.

"We could visit my parent's village like we said years ago! Or we could go to the Himalayas! We could hire one of those sherpa guys and camp and hike and all that stuff. Wouldn't that be awesome?"

Josh still refused to speak. He looked down, and she thought he would say something, but he didn't. He just sat there. Then, Liza would come at him from a final angle before she'd just give up.

"I want you to stop working so hard because it's killing you. You're going to wind up having a heart attack, and you're going to leave me here alone. Do you want to do that? Do you want me to be alone in the world?"

Josh laughed a little again. He didn't look over at her, but he finally spoke.

"You won't be alone. You've got Stephen."

Game over. That was it. Liza couldn't be sure, but she imagined then that Josh had somehow figured out everything about her and Stephen. How she'd carried on with him and all the other things she'd done. It was hopeless. And there wasn't anything she could do anymore. So, she humored Josh for the time being.

"That's so stupid, baby. That's so, so stupid, and you know it is."

Liza waited for a moment. One last time. She wished he'd say anything back to her, even if it were just to argue or, better still, to tell her that he was sorry, drunk, and that he'd be better the next day.

But he didn't.

"Listen. I'm going to get Green China. And if you don't want any, that's fine. I'll eat it all by myself. But at least get out of that damned chair and stretch your legs. Here, give me that."

As Liza took hold of the bottle, Josh grabbed her wrist and glared at her. He looked like Scout whenever Liza went for her bowl before she was done eating. Liza knew she didn't want to engage whatever emotions were behind those eyes, so she let go of the bottle.

Reassuming her peppy, upbeat attitude, Liza walked over to the patio doors and pulled up their blinds.

They'd spent a fortune on the seating area out there. Liza had decorated its walls and tables with Vietnamese heirlooms her mother had given her. They'd planted palm trees, fatsias, and other such vegetation. During the day, it looked like a tropical paradise, and at night, the accent lighting made it look like a Vietnamese riverside village. It was breathtaking no matter what time of day you sat out there.

"Look. Get up, take your bottle out there. I'll bring you some ice, but promise me you'll eat when I get back. Okay? Will you do that for me?"

At last, Josh spoke, but he didn't acknowledge Liza's suggestion, which hurt her feelings.

"I'm gonna go walk the damned dog," he grumbled. Any more expression than that would've been slurred.

Then Josh slogged toward the utility room where they kenneled Scout most evenings. Liza heard him wrestle with the cage door and the dog's collar jingling as it wiggled its butt and ears, undoubtedly happy that someone finally paid attention to her that day.

After Liza heard Josh go outside with the dog, she walked over to the patio door and looked out at the beautiful lighting that came on automatically whenever someone opened the blinds. It looked so calm and peaceful outside. She could hear the water's delicate gush and splash onto the river rocks a few feet below the fountain. It was beautiful, and it took her back several years when they'd planned it all out. She'd stayed after the contractors along the way, ensuring things were exactly how she wanted them.

Liza stared at everything momentarily before reaching up and turning off the lights, completely darkening the beautiful landscape.

A few moments later, a person stepped from that darkness and came close enough to the glass door to look into the house, yet far enough away so they wouldn't be seen. They'd been there the whole time as Liza and Josh argued. They stood and watched, wondering if Liza could see them as she picked up Josh's glass and wiped the table where he hadn't bothered to put a coaster. She looked into the darkness briefly, but the person couldn't tell if she was looking at or past them. Then she walked away toward the kitchen, carrying Josh's glass.

The person looking on was indulgent, but what fed that indulgence was fear—other people's fear. It turned them on. It clarified their self-perception. It made the person feel alive and powerful. Because they knew they could take the lives of other people if they wanted to. But taking that person's life wasn't enough. They wanted the person to know they were about to die. They wanted them to feel hopeless. Abandoned. They wanted them to experience utter despair.

The person looking into the house was industrious, highly motivated, and ambitious.

The person looking into the house was Lacy Knight's killer.

***

Josh staggered up the driveway toward the back of the house. He had to be careful on the delicate slope because it was dark outside. It would only take one slip, and he'd tumble forward, and he knew that in his condition, he might not react fast enough to raise his arms and protect himself from falling flat on his face.

When Josh reached the back of the driveway, he took out his phone and opened the garage door. Just as the clattering of the door rolling up ceased, he heard a noise from the back of the house. It sounded like something had vaulted from the shrubs lining the back walkway. It was big, whatever it was because it sounded like several of the aspidistras leaves lining the back walkway had separated with its exit. But whatever it was moved rapidly because the rustling stopped immediately after it began.

Scout went nuts. She barked, growled, and tugged Josh forward, making him afraid he'd splat.

"Whoa! Whoa! Easy! Easy, girl! Calm down, would you?" Josh scolded.

Josh was glad Scout was there, though. Stupid dog. If that was a coon or a possum or something, they'd already hauled ass. But what if it was something else? What if it wasn't an animal at all? What if it were a burglar? They'd have to be pretty stupid because everybody had cameras these days.

But then Josh thought that if they were that friggin' stupid, they were the kind of person that would become desperate. They'd kill you just to get away. There was no telling what someone with that mindset would do if they felt threatened.

Josh lifted his phone to look at the cameras, but just before he opened his security app, he was relieved to see a cat running along the fence separating his backyard from his neighbors'.

"Damnit, Dusty! You scared the shit out of me!" Josh hollered at the lard-assed cat, who stopped, sneered at him, arched its back, and hissed at Scout.

That cat and Scout were established combatants in the territorial war between their owners' homes. Scout started to lurch harder and harder, trying to get Dusty. Realizing the dog couldn't break away, Dusty stopped, sat on the fence, and stared, sending Scout into hysterics.

"Come on, Scout! Stop it! Let's go to bed, girl!" Josh ordered the dog.

Dusty got the last word in, letting out a long, sustained mew and staring at the stupid assed dog that still barked at him. Dusty's groan continued until the rolling garage door obscured their views of each other.

The walk with Scout and all the fresh air had done Josh some good. He was renewed from that and the exhilaration he'd just felt. He breathed deeply and smelled the distinct aroma of garlic. That made him realize how hungry he was.

When he entered the kitchen, Liza stood at the stove, stirring something in a skillet while whatever it was sizzled.

Josh decided he'd be the one to end the spat because he'd been the only one acting contrary in the first place.

"What happened to Green China?" he asked.

When Liza looked at him, she seemed surprised, and it appeared she'd start to complain. But when she saw him smiling, she closed her mouth and smiled back at him.

"I'm sorry, baby," Josh said, "I don't know what's wrong with me. I mean, I do, but just like you say, I shouldn't make that our problem."

"Oh, honey," Liza said, crumpling her face and tearing up, "I'm so happy you said that. You have no idea how happy that makes me."

Josh looked puzzled and hurried over to Liza.

"Whoa, baby, what's wrong? Why are you crying? I said I was sorry."

"I don't know why I'm crying, Josh. I just hurt so much when you hurt, I guess. That's all, baby," Liza said, resting her head on Josh's shoulder.

Josh stroked her hair for a moment before he resurrected Liza's original plan.

"Come on! I'll ride with you to Green China! We can roll the windows down! The spring air is so refreshing! It'll make us both feel better!"

Liza brightened, wiped the tears away, and said, "Okay, baby. Let me go pee first."

Then she disappeared around the corner, entering the master bedroom as Josh called after her.

"You gotta drive, though!"

CHAPTER TWENTY-THREE

The amount of money and the origins of the power Olivia Addison-Knight wielded were unprecedented for a defense contractor—especially a woman. However, Olivia was an aberration in many ways, including her appearance. She cut a fearsome stance at a bit over six feet tall, and as impressive as her physical stature was, so was her womanly appeal. She was raven-haired with large blue eyes, full lips, and a flawless complexion. Olivia Addison-Knight was beautiful.

While Olivia founded one of the world's most prolific defense industry service corporations, the road she took to get there was extraordinary and complex, beginning with her military service. It was an unlikely trajectory for a woman's career when she began her journey.

Olivia enlisted in the Army and was among the first women to enter the Special Operations Aviation Regiment's Night Stalker training in her early twenties. And even though she loved aviation, she dropped out because the analytically-minded young woman's passion was computer science. She eventually earned a Bachelor's Degree from Carnegie Mellon before a brief career working for the Crystal City, Virginia-based Miramar-Hawley in their robotics division.

By then, Olivia had married and had her first child, Tristan, with a young Lannie Knight, whose highly specialized employment agency was absorbed by Microsoft for a princely sum in 1998. During those years, Lannie's nickname, "Fab," was picked up by the media, and he became a bit of a celebrity. That was a boon to Olivia launching her company, and Fab frequently reminded her of it in later years when her achievements eclipsed his.

Nevertheless, Olivia started her first company using Fab's connections in the Human Resources world, and just like Fab, her business snowballed into a gargantuan endeavor because of its degree of specialization. Jockeying off her ties to the Army, she invested herself in the military-industrial complex and was rewarded handsomely for her decisions and efforts.

Apart from the U.S., the company she established conducted business throughout the European Union and across democratic regimes in the Middle East, judiciously tight-roping the International Traffic in Arms Regulations to get things done.

In tandem with the Defense Advanced Research Projects Agency and the Missile Defense Agency, her company engineered innovations in vital segments of defense computer design technology, including surveillance, unmanned aircraft, threat detection, and intelligence-gathering. Because of the staggering amounts of money involved, her company, Dark Knight Industries, made her name synonymous with wealth, prestige, and power.

In addition to her military enterprises, Olivia diversified into other technologies, such as sustainable and clean energy initiatives. Her EV company, Oasis, produced and supplied buses to mainland China, North Korea, and other fledgling markets in the US and abroad. Afterward, Oasis began manufacturing EV automobiles, which took the market by storm, and the company went public in 2008. And though she divested much of her defense contracting firm and its subsidiaries for over a billion dollars, she continued to be a principal shareholder and serve on its Board of Directors, remaining close with industry insiders on the government and private sector sides.

Very early on, when enormous amounts of money had begun to roll in almost overnight, Olivia was forced to reach a decision. She could either devote herself to her business and leave the child-rearing entirely to Fab, or she could give everything up and return to watch him deteriorate into a drug-addled alcoholic who spent as many nights away as he did at home. She opted for the former and assembled a staff of people to which she delegated parental responsibilities while furthering her career. She knew Fab would be a non-entity in the equation and allowed him to flounder, permanently separating a year after her daughter, Lacy, was born.

When she looked back and was honest with herself, Olivia regretted that she'd married Lannie and was even more repentant about her decision to have children with him. She always knew there wasn't much substance to Fab and that he'd eventually succumb to his proclivities for alcohol, drugs, and pretty young women. She'd only found herself in that dilemma because she'd thought that's what women did. They got married. They had children. And they subordinated their aspirations to those of their husbands for the sake of their families. She resisted her preternatural longing to achieve, to dominate. To conquer.

Her greatest regret, however, was not being motherly and more available to her children. It was something she'd regret for the rest of her life.

***

The black 747 glided across the Memphis skyline, arousing curiosity and fear among the Memphians, who stared up as it remained in a holding pattern. It looked like a bird of prey, hovering and peering down from overheard, waiting to strike from the air, cup its mark in its talons, and fly away again.

The plane was black because being black made it faster than it would've been if Boeing had coated it in the heavier white enamel aircraft finish, like most passenger versions of the model. However, this was no passenger plane. This was a moveable sky fortress whose telecommunications capabilities were rivaled only by its armaments.

The plane had flown into and out of war zones in the middle of the night so that its master could conduct business and participate in decisions that affected economies and political institutions worldwide. It had refueled in skies over all the Earth's oceans, flying at altitudes whose heights and depths were unorthodox and unfathomable. It had airports and waypoints across the globe, from Bangladesh to Burkina Faso. But its current destination was Memphis, Tennessee, and its ETA was imminent.

Aboard the plane, a woman sat on a perch, staring at the dozens of people who scurried around the fuselage beneath her. The hoard of men and women included professionals from every business and financial profession imaginable. CPAs, Chartered Financial Analysts, Commodities Brokers, a band of attorneys, and other technical and professional wizards. And they were all prepared to jump upon command, just as the plane was whenever it was directed to do so.

"Rotarran, turn right one three zero heading, move to ground point 65, runway 4, proceeding to Gatemouth."

"Copy, tower, Rotarron, right one three zero."

After dozens of men on either side of a hangar hurried toward one another to enclose the plane in darkness, dozens more raced to begin its stringent maintenance so that it would stand prepared to launch all over again with little notice.

As the woman rode down the elevator toward the conveyor that would take her to a concealed exit at the plane's rear, she wasn't distracted by any of the tasks or assignments frantically being carried out around her. Her thoughts were solely about her little girl. Like her mother, the girl was beautiful, and as far as the woman knew, she was an innocent child, a captive in the chaos between her mother's iron and stone world and the superficial, hollow one in which her father had raised her.

So much about the girl had changed since the last time the woman laid eyes on her, though. And just as with most of the information she received daily, she'd discover what many of those changes had been through the clinical relation of strangers.

The woman knew so much. She had information about places, policies, and actions that qualified her to discuss nearly any topic and make crucial decisions. But the information she already had pieces of and that she would acquire more of very soon would be actioned over the next several days, mostly by the Federal Bureau of Investigations, the Shelby County Sheriff's Office, the Memphis Police Department's Sexual Victims Unit, and the Germantown police.

She had others at her beck and call, though. They analyzed, excised, reconfigured, and patched the infrastructure of the woman's world continuously. Many of those were from her cleaning and maintenance department and originally hailed from the United States military's regiments seldom spoken about, some of whose existence was only known to decision-makers like her.

The woman who set down in Memphis that day was powerful, nearly impervious to any other man or woman. But she was currently compromised by a wounded spirit and was soon to suffer from a broken heart.

The OAK was in town, though. And, as usual, she was in town on business. And Olivia Addison Knight was the most formidable, astute businesswoman in the world.

***

"Holy shit," Liza said while staring at the TV and standing behind Josh, who sat on the couch but, though perplexed, hadn't managed to speak yet.

They both gawked at the set, as everyone else in the viewing area did, waiting to find out why a mysterious plane was circling Memphis. The folks with the news capitalized on all the intrigue as things transpired despite being just as in the dark as everyone else.

<Coming up: Who touched down in Memphis this afternoon? Find out that and more on News Channel 3, your leading source for Memphis news and weather.>

"Is that the President?" Liza quizzed Josh.

Josh stayed quiet for several moments before saying, "No. That's not Air Force One, Liza. Not unless he tried to make some political statement by painting it black."

The TV went to a commercial.

<At Tillman Tires, we know what matters to you most. And we've dedicated ourselves to bringing it to you comfortably and safely.>

Josh continued watching the television as a young mother strapped a blonde-haired little girl into a car seat before tousling her hair as a modernized cover of Sam Cook's "Bring it On Home to Me" played in the background. The tyke was beautiful, with pudgy cheeks and a giant green bow resting atop her head as she thrust her arms forward and kissed her momma on the nose.

As he'd done for several days, Josh was trying to muster the courage to get up and drive to the police station. But what would he say when he got there? Who would he ask for, and how would he ask for them without causing a stir? Or getting tackled by a squad of Germantown Police officers and hauled off to jail himself because they wouldn't believe him?

"Uhh, yeah. I need to talk to somebody about the guy they think had something to do with the kidnapping or murder of that girl. No, no, no y'see, they've got it all wrong. I'm the guy's best friend, and I treated that lady coach who got killed. I also treated the girl who's missing who went around saying she screwed him, but you got that wrong, too. If I could just talk to somebody in charge, I think I can straighten all this out for everybody, and my friend can get out of jail, y'all can start looking for who nabbed the girl, and everybody will be happy. How's that sound?"

That exchange wasn't too different from how things rolled out after another hour, when he became bold enough to get in his Tesla and say, "Navigate to the Germantown Police Department."

Josh didn't even know where to go. Despite Gil pleading with him over the phone, he hadn't cultivated the nerve to go and comfort his friend. He was too scared, and that made him feel like a coward. So, this trip to the station would serve as a kind of self-administered therapy for Josh, who feared he was hurtling toward agoraphobia. He hadn't wanted to see other people. He hadn't wanted them to see him. All he wanted to do was to come home from work and drink. And he imagined he'd have difficulty resisting that compulsion when he was done bearing his soul that afternoon.

***

"Dr. Odom, I've taken all this information down. Is there a number where we can reach you once we've had time to review all of it?" a uniformed officer asked.

Was this lady kidding? Hadn't she listened to a word he'd said? Josh thought the police officer was blowing him off, but that couldn't be right. Everyone in Memphis was tuned in to what was happening in its elite satellite community, whose citizenry had among the highest per capita incomes in the Southeast. And Josh had information that should've been Earth-shattering to the stupid cop sitting across from him, deigning to break away from her busy schedule as a Germantown policewoman. Instead, this gal acted like Josh provided very little added value to her day, as though he were wasting the Germantown Police Department's time.

Josh wondered how they'd react if he told them about one of their own, chaining the missing girl down and abusing her after loading her up with cocaine and God knew what else. But he didn't give in to that temptation because it would only confuse matters.

Josh was risking everything by going down there. He stood to lose his career by moving into the limelight, a place he rarely and only selectively enjoyed. But he was willing to come forward, just so that justice could be served. And then his friend could be at his wife's side with their son, who Josh feared would be in a vegetative state for the rest of his life.

The truth was that the Germantown Police and others were learning everything about Lacy Knight. They would eventually discover places she'd been, things happening around her, and words exchanged between her and her captor or, perhaps, captors. But none of those discoveries had been made just yet.

Meanwhile, Olivia Knight was relating the information she'd obtained from sources one couldn't imagine within quarters concealed deep inside the military-industrial complex. Her initial instincts had been wrong, leading to an awful lot of mayhem and impulsive behavior on her part. All of that had gotten started a few days before.

***

Down around New Orleans, at a house on pylons that was visible from where Dora's magical balloon had landed over a decade before, two men were hunkered down in its driveway behind a 1987

Dodge Minivan. Moments later, as Stevie Guice went to open his refrigerator door, one of those men, a former Navy SEAL, slipped up behind him, placed a cylinder to his throat, and pressed a button. A spring then propelled a cyanide-laced shank into Mr. Guice's internal carotid artery, and he died before either hitting the ground or realizing what was happening. The other SEAL was doing the same thing to Mr. Guice's brother, Lennie, in a similar fashion as he lay asleep in a recliner. Afterward, the first SEAL walked to the back corner of the home, where he knew three teenage girls were sleeping. He knew a fourth one to be in the shower.

The SEAL kicked the door open and tossed an isoflurane charge into the room, where it detonated and rendered all the sleeping teenagers unconscious. When the African American girl walked from the bathroom, the other SEAL muzzled her with his hand, placed an Ontario MK3 knife against her cheek, and whispered into her ear, "Shhhhhhhhhh."

The first SEAL went to the other girls, all Caucasians, and moved systematically, opening each of their right lids and scanning their eyes with another cylinder.

As though talking to no one, but in actuality speaking to somebody far, far away, the SEAL said, "Bruno. LZ-HVT negative."

The other SEAL carefully released the young black girl like someone letting go of a child learning to ride a bike, waiting to see what would happen. She didn't move, though. She stood like a beautiful onyx statue, with the whites of her eyes fully exposed. And then she felt dread as the first SEAL walked toward her with a look in his eyes like she'd never seen before.

He looked angry. Vengeful. He looked disgusted. It was then the girl realized that he was the Devil and he was going to kill her before taking her back to hell with him.

But the blue-eyed white man stopped short of her by about three feet. He stood and stared into her eyes again with that bone-chilling gaze and cocked his head to one side. Then he reached into a small duffle around his waist, rifling through it with one hand while maintaining his stare. He pulled out a tightly bound money clip, which the girl would later learn held ten thousand dollars.

"I don't care where you go, but get the fuck out of here. And no matter what else you do, don't call your momma. Do you understand me? I know all about her, honey. I know everything."

The fourteen-year-old black girl grasped the money clip, looked at it, and began crying as she nodded and staggered out of the room backward before she hauled ass down the road in her terry Walmart bathrobe.

Afterward, at a command center that was high and hidden in the Sierra Mountains, a woman posing as a dispatch officer called out from over a thousand miles away, *"10-29V, Dodge Caravan, maroon late-model, Chef Menteur Highway at Lake Catherine,"* to which a police officer responded, *"Uh, copy that, dispatch, 10-20?"* before confirming the address and tearing toward the house, which the former SEALs had already abandoned.

Operations similar to that were carried out throughout the Southeastern United States, with particular concentrations in US-Mexican border towns and multiple other sites in satellite communities of Atlanta, Miami, and Houston. They also took place in dozens of other locations across the U.S., all minimally secure, yet every one of them a known safe harbor for human sex trafficking.

***

The woman responsible for such clandestine efforts across the nation sat in a conference room in Germantown, Tennessee, talking to the police. Three agents from the Federal Bureau of Investigation had joined them, but the Germantown Police Department was not receiving them well at that moment.

"Could I ask why you guys are here, Glen?" Captain Lewis asked the Federal agent, who was about his age.

But Glen didn't get a chance to answer before Olivia Knight interrupted, saying, "Because I told them to be here."

Strangely, nobody said a damned thing. Because every last one of them knew that what Olivia Knight said went, but you'd better make damn sure you needed to before you asked her 'why.'

Finally, Glen Fields, the senior agent, spoke up, saying, "Mrs. Knight, it's my understanding that you have some information about your daughter's disappearance. Is it something you'd like to discuss with the Federal government in private, ma'am?"

Olivia didn't immediately answer the Special Agent; rather, she stared forward, seemingly preoccupied. As though everything being said around her would remain nonsense until she clarified things for everyone. Agent Fields left her alone and addressed Captain Lewis instead.

"Look, Tony. I'm doing what I'm told for reasons I'm sure you've figured out by now. And I swear to God we didn't know either, Tony. I swear to God."

Olivia was calm when she spoke again.

"Yes, Special Agent Fields. I would like to speak to you alone in just a moment. But first, I'd like to have a private discussion with Captain Lewis. If everyone would oblige me, I'd certainly appreciate it."

The officers, agents, and detectives started to move as though they were being called to dinner or as if the final bell of the school day rang. The sound of chairs sliding across the floor resonated in the conference room, and the only people who didn't rise to leave were Captain Lewis and Olivia Knight.

Puzzled but just as anxious to find out why he was the one the mega-billionaire held back, Captain Lewis cleared his throat and spoke.

"Mrs. Knight, if I can do anything related to this case for you, I assure you I'll do it. But I'm afraid you're going to be disappointed because I know very little about your daughter's disappearance. I may be the least informed person on the subject. So, why don't you let me call two of my detectives back to sit in on our discussion? I'm just a liaison between those guys and the Chief. And he only knows what I tell him. You'll need to move further down the chain of command to get to this case's mechanics. But to be as frank as possible, I can tell you that unless something else has happened that I don't know about, everything we discussed before the Bureau got here is everything we know."

Olivia didn't appear surprised or disappointed. She sat quietly and listened to Lewis' protest, waiting for him to finish. Then, she gave him a few details that confused Captain Lewis even more.

"No. I'm quite sure I have the right person, Captain Lewis. I've done a great deal of research before I arrived here today," Olivia said, causing Lewis to gulp and squirm a little in his chair.

Olivia was a stunning specimen—tall and lean, wearing a completely black business suit with black framed glasses. She exuded alpha and scarcely spoke, making anyone listening to her anxious to hear her next words and do her bidding. She imparted that visage to Captain Lewis as she continued to speak.

The gist of the information Knight provided was simple. Because despite all her resources and the army of people who answered to her, Knight knew she'd eventually need Lewis. There'd come a time when the police detective would be an integral part of the investigation, serving in a far more important capacity than he presently served. He might have been nothing more than he said, which was simply a facilitator and communicator. However, Lewis also had authority at the precise level Olivia Knight needed to wield an instrument. She planned on Captain Lewis being that instrument.

***

After an hour, Captain Lewis opened the conference room door and walked into the hallway alone. He looked horrified like he'd just been told the date of his death. He wasn't the ordinarily composed, bristly, demanding Captain as he'd come to be known by everyone. He acted confused. Dismayed. He acted like a gelding.

"You fellas, come with me, will you?" Lewis asked the two detectives before continuing, "Glen, she wants to speak with you alone."

"Me?" Agent Fields asked with the same confusion and fear Lewis had shown earlier.

"Yep," is all Lewis said back before he motioned for his detectives to follow him, and they left the agents standing by themselves.

Agent Fields looked back at the other agents like he didn't know what was happening. He looked embarrassed, but more than that, he looked afraid. Realizing he wouldn't get an answer to all the questions racing through his mind from anyone standing there, he timidly walked into the conference room and closed the door.

CHAPTER TWENTY-FOUR

Lacy Knight's wealth was not her defining characteristic but rather a tool she used to navigate her path of self-discovery. Her deep yearning for affection and love, a void she was desperate to fill, guided her actions and shaped her identity. The absence of love in her life, and her subsequent discovery of it with Cint Wallace, was a transformative experience greater than money's influence.

Captain Lewis, Olivia Knight, and all the other people tasked with finding Lacy witnessed firsthand the manifestations of what motivated the person or persons responsible for Lacy's disappearance. While other possibilities remained, at the end of it all, it seemed Lacy Knight was victimized by someone who wanted money. The passion, the envy, the depravity—all of it. It was just background noise.

Olivia Knight's everyday life included being bombarded with a deluge of data from all corners of the globe: schematics, engineering diagrams, and cost projections. This flood of information was then painstakingly dissected and reviewed as Olivia meticulously examined every article that could become part of one of the thousands of contracts her companies landed with the Federal government.

One day, a photograph spurted from the vortex of information Olivia was to review and settled on the surface. It was a picture of a young woman. The picture was in black and white, just like many others within the current that it flowed. But it was distinctive because the young lady in the picture was so beautiful and caught the eyes of the lowest member of the chain of command at Dark Knight Industries. The intern stopped cold and stared into the young woman's eyes, captivated by her appearance.

Her dirty blonde hair was parted down the center and hung down the sides of her face, with its layered tips touching just beneath her neckline. Though the picture was black and white, one could easily discern that her complexion was immaculate, without so much as a blemish or a wrinkle. Her lips were supple, curved downward in their corners like she was contemplating a frown or a grimace, yet they still lent themselves to how stunning she was.

She wore a tee shirt that read, "Onward Christian Trojans" with the University of Southern California logo beneath that, and she might have otherwise looked like any pretty young girl who'd been photographed by surprise and without their consent.

But her eyes were her most enticing feature, partly because of their almond shape but more because of the seeming depth of the darkness in their centers. Those eyes demanded that someone look into them so that they could relate all the emotions and feelings that stirred within the young lady.

Her eyes' conveyance and the crude narrative accompanying the picture were in different languages, but their meaning was the same.

Look at me.

Love me.

Help me.

It didn't take long after that. The picture and the disturbing language accompanying it blazed upward through the Dark Knight Industries' ranks until arriving at Olivia Knight's Inbox.

By that evening, Olivia had boots on the ground in several major cities. While many of those soldiers were former U.S. military, they no longer served in that capacity. Instead, they'd adopted a new credo. They'd all pledged their service to The OAK and the Kingdom of Dark Knight Industries.

**

The days leading up to Lacy Knight's last on the Earth weren't anything extraordinary. On the contrary, they were dull by her standards. Clint wouldn't fly in from Los Angeles until late that night, so she wasn't clinging to him all day like usual.

At his suggestion, she tried to read scripture and have devotionals in the mornings and evenings, but she couldn't concentrate without him being there.

She had finally ended her and Prissy's liaisons with strangers, so she didn't need to call anyone or, worse, drive around Somerset Village by herself to snag any tweak, yayo, or any of the other treats she used to make those occasions either more intense or merely palatable, depending on whatever mood struck her.

Most of the time, Lacy sat on the patio, trying to get into the playlists Clint had shared on her iPhone. But without him being there, that was even worse. Those songs were only meaningful to her when they were blaring from the sound system of his pickup as they roared down the road to see a movie, visit his grandparents, or go to Sunday services.

Since Lacy couldn't find anything else to occupy her mind, the inactivity allowed her to reflect upon all the horrible decisions she'd made during her short life.

Lacy hadn't realized how wonderful things could be. She hadn't understood that sexual desire, when tempered, was intended to be experienced between people who loved one another. It wasn't for satisfaction upon a whim. You didn't use it to attain objectives or acquire others' affection. Or drugs.

Lacy had come to believe those impulses were for a purpose and that, even though they might manifest differently for different people, they were of Godly design.

Lacy felt guilty about toying with those same urges in Prissy. She realized that all Prissy had ever been to her was a safe harbor from the aggressions and judgments of others and that she'd taken that refuge in defiance of them all. She didn't love Prissy. Not in that way. Worse still, she had capitalized on Prissy's misguided but sincere feelings for her. She lied to Prissy.

Prissy wasn't evil. She was diseased. That disease made her fall victim to an unsavory lust for watching Lacy with other people, a longing which Lacy obliged, not only to keep Prissy satisfied but to satisfy herself along the way. Men had only ever been objects to Lacy in much the same way she'd been objectified by them. What had Dr. O called people like that? Narcissists? Yeah, that's what Lacy felt like she was—a narcissist.

However, amid her scheme to control Headmaster Wallace, Lacy had been struck by lightning. Without warning, she believed God had energized her with an unimaginably powerful feeling, one whose sensations she had never experienced.

Lacy had heard about it. She'd seen it in movies and on television. All her favorite artists sang or rapped about it. In school, she'd learned that nations and kingdoms had been built and forfeited because of it, and authors had written such beautiful prose and essays about it. However, love had remained an elusive concept for Lacy. It was burdensome and unwieldy. And the positions people took because of it were peculiar and indefensible in her mind.

But Clint had changed that. Through Clint, Lacy had experienced an unprecedented fondness and adoration for another human being. It was as though all the emotional unrest she'd had since she was a baby had been remedied. It felt good, and she couldn't imagine how much better it would feel when she finally gave herself to Clint as a woman and accepted him as a man. It would soothe her, at last comforting the little girl who'd reached out with desperate arms for her mother to hold her, only to be shunned or passed off to someone else.

That baby wanted someone, apart from a servant acting from a sense of duty, to care that she'd fallen and skinned both of her knees. She'd wanted someone to be in the hospital with her when she awoke from having her tonsils removed. She wanted someone she cared for to pay any attention at all to her.

Having Clint would cleanse Lacy's soul, though. It would redeem her, and things couldn't happen soon enough for her.

Unfortunately, that day would never come for Clint or Lacy— either with each other or anyone else. It simply wasn't in the cards for them. Her destiny lay elsewhere, as did Clint Wallace's. He'd die a few days afterward in a hospital bed, having had his heart torn to shreds and the imagery of the world he wanted to exist in with her obliterated. He'd die on his back, catatonic and not knowing his love's fate.

Lacy, however, would die on her hands and knees, fully awake and completely aware of what was about to happen to her.

***

Lacy received a call around eight o'clock that night while at Prissy's. After a brief discussion, she agreed to meet with the person who called her. She considered turning location services off on her phone, but Prissy had gotten crazily suspicious when she'd done that in the past. So, after deleting her call log and text messages, she left her phone in broad view, which Prissy could see when she crawled out of her latest binge.

The person calling her would be the one who'd take everything away from Lacy Knight. They'd take it all. Ironically, that person acted on the same urges Lacy lamented having yielded to for her entire life up to that point. Greed. Selfishness. Indulgence. And a particular, if queer, brand of avarice.

Lacy knew the person who called. At least, she thought she did. But they were just another of the artifacts from a life that she aspired to leave behind forever when she and Clint moved to Los Angeles in a few months. She would abandon every person and all those things that were reminders to her of the world she once lived in and the person she used to be.

As it turned out, though, the mass of her past was greater than that of her future, and it tipped her backward on the fulcrum, dragging her into hopelessness before finally relegating her to non-existence.

Lacy would meet the person who called her, in her hopes, for one of the last times and then for the rest of her life. She wanted to explain that she wasn't the person she'd been and was going away. She wasn't going to do any of the things she used to, and she didn't feel she should have to answer to them because she only answered to the highest of powers now. She told them she answered only to God.

Lacy met the person in Gracie Bleu, and as she spoke with them, they rambled incessantly and, at first, talked in several different directions on seemingly unrelated subjects. Then, once they settled down, there was a continuity of theme, but that theme was no longer applicable to her life.

They talked about sex. When Lacy told them she no longer cared about anything they were bringing up and that she was leaving that life and never returning to it or them, they scoffed at that. In their way, they told her she was making a terrific mistake. They even mocked her for her relationship with Clint and asked her if she believed she could exist in a life like the one she described to them.

Lacy couldn't believe the person seemed to know as much as they did about Clint. She didn't think people like them truly comprehended such things, even though they might otherwise seem very bright.

No, they said. She belonged in a different world. It was a world they shared and one that she simply couldn't leave and close the door behind. She would have to stay in that world, perhaps forever, but even if she did leave, it would only be via their authorization. They also wanted her to come with them that night. They wanted her to return to that world again so that they could reinforce its significance to her and make her understand that all these new rules she'd established for her life were meaningless.

Maybe they were right. Lacy didn't know. Maybe she couldn't change. Maybe the pleasures she felt in that world were the only ones she'd have. It just amazed her that the person had the wherewithal to come to such a conclusion. Why did they so desperately attempt to get her to embrace her past? What was their motive?

Lacy didn't know if it was the tenor of the discussion or the implications of everything the person said to her, but she grew tired. She didn't want to talk anymore. She didn't want to be around that person anymore, either.

Her eyelids became heavy. So heavy that it felt like they dragged her head down with them as they closed. It seemed almost impossible for her to keep them open. In a horrid irony, she tried to force them open and wished she could keep them that way for a long time.

The last time Lacy opened them, she was walking toward Gracie Bleu's exit. She could smell the coffee brewing and wanted very much to have a cup of it. Its aroma and the sweet scents of ice cream, yogurt, and waffle cones gave her a little perk. She began to ask the person behind the counter if she could have a cup, but then she realized again that she was moving. She was moving forward as she stared at the cashier of Gracie Bleu, who held a scoop and stared back at her with wide eyes.

In those few seconds, Lacy felt envious. She was jealous that the girl behind the counter could have as much coffee, ice cream, and whatever else she wanted. But she was also jealous that the girl could keep her eyes open like that. Lacy wanted to open her eyes that way and sit down and talk to the girl while they ate ice cream and drank coffee. At that moment, it was all Lacy wanted in the world.

Then Lacy remembered. She couldn't. She couldn't because she was moving. She was going away. When she left Gracie Bleu, she'd be back in that world if the person she'd met had anything to say about it. And when they pushed the front door to Gracie Bleu open, and the warm spring air and the scent of daffodils replaced those of the coffee and the cold, sugary treats she loved so much, Lacy Knight began to cry.

No. No. I don't want to go. I want to stay. I want to stay there, have ice cream, and talk to the girl. I want to stay and talk to Conchita. I want to tell her I'm sorry. I have to tell her I didn't want to leave her alone at the gas station. I'm so sorry, Dora. I'm so sorry. But it's okay. You stay here with Bookbag. You stay here and have ice cream. I'll be back. I'll be back tomorrow.

Lacy rested her eyes for another moment. And when she reopened them, the person was looking down at her. They were no longer at Gracie Bleu, although she remembered standing in its parking lot. Then she remembered hearing a car door close and then, once again, losing the battle to keep her eyes open.

But now, they were somewhere far away from Gracie Bleu. She could tell. She heard jazz music playing and people talking and laughing. Then, her fears about where the person had been taking her were confirmed when they took their clothes off and climbed on top of her. She realized the person had already undressed her, and she started going through the motions of satisfying them, and as foreign or peculiar as it was, there was nothing *too* strange for Lacy. The mechanics were all old hat for her. She'd seen and done it all before. And she realized now that the person had wanted to do those things to her all along.

In Lacy's mental state, she couldn't remember if she'd done these things with the person in the past, but she felt like she had. They were familiar to her, but she hadn't known if she'd just imagined being with them before or if it had happened. She'd been with so many people, but it was always while she was addled. Compromised.

A while later, Lacy roused to consciousness with another familiar feeling. She felt violated. And she was sore like she'd been whenever she was passed among several men and sometimes women. The first time she ever felt that way was horrible. She felt like a piece of meat that someone had chewed to their satisfaction and then spat on the floor. But she'd grown accustomed to it. Given the number and frequency of times she'd experienced the feeling, it was impossible not to.

Lacy couldn't remember where they'd taken her, though. She didn't think she was in the same place she'd been earlier, where she'd heard other people talking and laughing. And she couldn't see. She closed and opened her eyes several times but still couldn't see. She felt her lashes pressed backward on her eyelids, and it was difficult to breathe. She opened her mouth to take a deep breath, but her lips touched the surface of something that crackled. Then she realized something was resting over her face, like a veil or something.

But when Lacy went to touch whatever it was, she couldn't raise her hands any higher than her chest. She tried several times before determining that she couldn't separate her wrists from one another. And with every move she made, the crackling came again. When she tried to stand, she discovered that she could barely move her arms and that her ankle bones were pressed firmly together. Lacy stopped trying to move and, instead, attempted to relax. Panicking, she realized, would do her no good.

As Lacy calmed herself, she started thinking about the love of her life.

Oh, Clint. I'm so sorry I've done all these things with all these different people. You deserve so much better than me, baby.

Then, the realization that she was in danger returned. It didn't matter that she knew the person who had gotten her into this state because the mere fact that they'd done so overrode everything about her previous opinions of them.

Their relationship had always been one of distance. Separation. While they occupied the same space at times due to the commonality of their existences, that's the only thing that had defined their relationship before. They had very little in common with one another apart from that. She'd always been under the impression the person was just gay, but now it had been made clear that they were game for anything. The scariest part was being unsure of what would come next.

CHAPTER TWENTY-FIVE

When Josh heard the buzzer, he instinctively rose and waited for Gil to appear on the opposite side of the glass. His friend looked pitiful. His eyes were red. His longer hair, which he normally kept slicked flat on his scalp, frayed from the sides and back of his head. And even though he was a big man, his orange jumpsuit appeared to swallow him. He was pallid. He looked weak. And his shoulders were slumped to keep the tension between the handcuffs he wore at a minimum. But that gave him the air of being defeated.

Josh had seen Gil in jail before, wearing a surprisingly similar uniform. But that had been decades ago when he went to bail him out of Lafayette County lockdown. And though simple assault and disorderly conduct weren't anything to be dismissive about, they were nothing compared to the charges awaiting Gilbert Wallace now.

Gil had already been fired. And though he'd lost her years before, the partial rekindling of the relationship he had with his wife, Michelle, incident to their child being in the hospital, had been promptly extinguished with his arrest.

"Oh my God, Josh," Gil said shakily, "I'm so glad to see you. You have no idea, man."

Gil had always come across as indomitable in the past. As a younger man, he broke all the rules, availed himself of all his urges—no matter how animalistic—and did it with virtually no consequences. Gil slept with whomever he wanted to, ate whatever he wanted to, and drank just as damned much as he wanted to. And if any of those things met with the scorn of society or the law, he simply disregarded it and emerged even more defiant.

Not this time, though. Gil couldn't dodge or hustle his way out of things this time. He was cornered. It looked like life would hold court for Gil Wallace, simultaneously with the State of Tennessee. Both their sentences would play off one another and be ruinous for the broken-hearted, lonely, and estranged husband and father.

Josh swallowed and regained his composure, realizing his mouth was hanging open. He watched all six-foot-four-inches of his idol fold into the tiny chair even lower than where Josh sat after the detention officer barked, "Sit!"

That added another vantage of Gil's despair because, in addition to all the personal struggles he faced without the ability to impact them beyond cries and pleas over a jailhouse phone, he'd become an animal. He was a trained beast now. Josh inferred from everything he'd just witnessed that Gil Wallace did what he was told whenever he was told to.

"Gil?" was all Josh could say at first, as though he were clarifying with whom he spoke.

But he quickly adjusted his tone because he knew his behavior was probably making Gil feel even worse if that was possible.

"Gil, I, I just don't know, man. This is unbelievable. And it's so wrong."

Gil looked into his eyes before speaking, and it looked like he was trying to assess Josh's sincerity. Then he cut his eyes down and started shaking his head.

"I know it is, man. I'm so sorry," Gil continued with a defeated attitude.

"I don't know either, man. I don't know what to say, and I don't know who to say it to," Gil went on.

Josh realized they were potentially being recorded. He figured the only time they didn't record Gil was when he was talking to his lawyer, who, in this case, was a public defender and had only seen Gil once. But Josh had fixed that. He'd provided evidence that Gil was his patient, thereby giving them doctor-patient confidentiality, which trumped anything. He'd planned that out way before he'd even decided to come to the jail.

"You can tell me, Gil. You can tell me anything and everything. Do you understand? Because I'm not just your friend. I'm your physician. And these people better remember that, too."

Gil immediately started explaining himself.

"I swear I didn't have anything to do with this. Well, I mean, apart from catching that little whore…"

Josh held his hand up to cut Gil off because, even though he knew the police shouldn't be recording their discussion, that didn't mean they weren't. He wasn't afraid they'd use anything Gil said against him in court but was more concerned about Gil saying something that might make a lazy detective complacent and less likely to try and find the actual perpetrator.

"Gil, she's just a baby, man. And if I told you some of the things she'd been through, you might even feel sorry for her."

Gil looked up and sighed before looking down again. He felt he couldn't win and didn't even have the privilege of venting to his best friend. He looked back up and blinked a couple of times before moving on.

"I know, Josh. I swear to God, I don't hate her. It hurts me, too, thinking about a girl, one of my students, Goddamnit, getting caught up in life with the kind of people I've been messing with. It makes me almost feel like I'm partially guilty. And that makes it hard to fight back, you know? It's almost like I know I deserve this shit."

Then Gil snorted as though laughing, but that immediately turned into sobbing.

"But my boy, Josh. My sweet, innocent, fat little baby boy. Why? Why, man? Why'd she have to go after him, too? Why couldn't she just leave him alone?"

Realizing he was being too emotional and that if he got any more upset, the guard was liable to end things, Gil pulled it together.

"You'll never know what it's like, man, and I swear to you I'm not talking down to you now. But I won't ever see Clint as anything but the little boy who used to cup my finger in his hand and walk up to Vaught-Hemingway with me to see the Rebels play. He won't be anything but a baby to me, and I don't care what he did or didn't do to that girl! Do you understand me? I don't care! I don't give a straight Goddamn because he's my baby!"

"Quiet!" the corrections office shouted so loudly that Josh wanted to get up and run away.

But Gil immediately calmed down and drooped his head, falling back into a glum state. Josh could still see his eyes, but he wouldn't raise them to look directly back at Josh. Instead, he darted them back and forth nervously as though he anticipated a rap to the back of his head with a baton. Josh thought, *what in the hell do they do to these people in here?*

Gil's loud but brief display had been the first indication that the Gil Josh had always known was still alive inside the man sitting behind thick glass. But it also highlighted how hopeless his situation had become when the officer gave a command, and Gil yielded to it without resistance.

Growing bold, Josh started to speak again.

"Listen to me, Gil. I talked to the police about everything. I didn't just forget about you, but I couldn't do it before now. I had to do some research. I had to find out what your rights are and what my rights are. And I had to figure out how to disclose everything I knew to these guys. That took some doing, man."

Gil looked up and squinted his eyes while he held his mouth open. He seemed moved that he finally had someone in his corner.

"What did they say? What did you tell them? Did you tell them I'm not a kidnapper or a murderer? Come on, man! You can do that! You can tell them that if I had done something, I would've already told you about it because you're my psychiatrist! Can't you? I mean, my God, you've got to tell them that! I hadn't even thought about that angle before! Who'd you talk to? Which one? Was it Michaels? He seems like a pretty good guy. But that other one doesn't. Lester or Nester or something like that?"

Josh raised his hand and nodded a little to give Gil some assurance and signal him to shut the hell up. He didn't have the heart to tell Gil how things were received by the officer he spoke with because he didn't want Gil to lose hope. He worried about Gil taking his own life and believed that might have already happened were he not still concerned about his son.

"Yeah, yeah. I talked to both of those guys. At least, I think those were their names. That sounds kind of familiar. Anyway, yeah. I told them everything, and I think it will make a difference, too. They said it may take them a while to digest all of it. But I think once they do, they'll let you go."

Gil's eyes widened, making Josh feel like he'd been a little too emphatic about the possibility of the police releasing him. But he couldn't take it back, so he just let Gil roll.

"Oh, my God! Oh, my God! I love you, Josh! I love you so much, man! You just don't know! You don't know how much that means to me!"

Gil's elation under the circumstances was infectious, making Josh smile back at him and continue with his encouragement.

"Hey, man. It's what I'm here for. Where would you be every time you got locked up if you didn't have Josh-Kosh-B'gosh to come bail your ass out, huh?"

Gil managed to smile and nodded, saying, "Right! Where in the hell would I be without you, buddy? I love you, bro."

Josh backed off a little. He didn't want to make Gil think things were a done deal. But he believed he'd gone just far enough to give him the hope he needed.

"I love you too, brother. And I'm going to do everything I can so that you can get out of here and be with Michelle. And you can both work on getting Clint better. I aim to see him on Saturdays in LA instead of in some stupid hospital bed."

Josh briefly considered how lucky Clint would be to walk again, let alone run onto the field at Los Angeles Memorial Coliseum.

Josh also realized how ridiculous his cheery forecast had been on Gil's account, but he refused to completely back away from it because who knew? Maybe, somehow, God would see fit to heal Clint Wallace. Perhaps he'd gift that to the boy whose only transgressions had been being born to a hypersexual father and falling for a deceptive nymphomaniac. But it would still be nothing short of a miracle for any of the things to happen that he'd offered to Gil as hope.

The two old friends stopped talking, and Gil rose after the officer hollered, "Time!"

Gil raised his hands to the glass with his cuffed wrists, and it jogged Josh's memory of the cute little girl reaching for her momma in the Tillman tire commercial. Gil seemed every bit as helpless as the little girl as his eyes teared up, and he flattened his hands on the glass. Josh also touched the glass, and for a moment, they looked like toddlers who couldn't bear to be separated from one another. It was such a pitiful ode to an old friendship that had lasted since shortly after they'd gone off to school, where each of them had become a man.

"Come on, come on, Mr. Wallace," the formerly strident corrections officer said, moved by the show of affection between the two men as he gently nudged Gil backward with his baton.

Josh turned away because he thought he was about to lose it. The last thing he wanted Gil to see was him showing all the despair he felt by crying. So, he hustled toward the exit and waited to be buzzed out before wiping the tears that had begun to roll down his cheeks.

Gil swiveled around after waiting until Josh was gone. Then he headed back toward the steel door leading to his cellblock, where he planned on praying until he went to sleep that night.

However, just after the door buzzed open, a skinny tattooed arm flung it wider, and a scrawny, white female with a stud in her left nostril peered up at Gil. It was, of all people, one of his former students.

Trudy. That was the girl's name. She had large eyes and long eyelashes that didn't need the fake ones sheathing them now, and her face was cherubic. She looked like a Girl Scout or a bright-eyed cheerleader until she opened her mouth.

Throughout her tenure at Restoration, she'd desperately wanted to be ghetto. And when she spoke, she sounded like someone who should've been a resident of the cells she tended rather than anyone who should be administering corrections. She had a tattoo across her neck that said, "Juicy Booty," which was why she'd been dismissed from Restoration Academy a few years before.

Gil remembered her well. Ironically, he'd gone to bat for the racially confused girl, telling the Board of Regents that she was close to graduation and that she'd already punished herself enough by getting the tattoo. She'd pay for that one for years to come, he said. He may not have come to her defense, or, conversely, he might've even fought harder for her had he known that she'd be his jailer one day.

Trudy had different plans and an amended route for Mr. Wallace that evening, though.

"Hey, there! Member me, fuckface? Yeah, I'm Trudy! Giancaspro? Come on, fuckface! You remember me, dontcha? Look," she said, pulling her collar back to reveal the tattoo that had been joined by several others since her dismissal from Restoration.

"Shut up, Tee. Leave him alone. Just take him back to his cell, alright?" the other guard said.

"Oh, nooooo," Trudy said merrily, "Headmaster Fuckface ain't goin' back to his cushy Germantown crib. Uh-uhhnnn, baby. You goin' ta big boy jail, nah! You done made it to the big show! And don't worry, I told my homies on both side-a-da-bars 'bout you, baby! That's right! They aaall know 'bout you, fuckface! And they waitin fuh y'ass, too! And it ain't na'am anybody can do about it neither! Cause they gone grease that booty up real good fa you, fuckface! Das right! Now get'cho big Herman Munsta-lookin ass down the hallway! You goin' fo' a ride, byotch!"

Gil didn't know how much more he could take. He'd previously exhausted all hope before Josh's visit. Then Josh had restored that hope somewhat by letting him know he'd become involved in the case.

But now, it seemed as though God was preparing him for another round of punishment as he looked at the low-grade piece of white trash holding the door open for him. She looked like a demon to him. A minion of the Devil, waiting to chariot him to hell. And he suffered to think about all that awaited him after she transported him to the County lockdown. He couldn't believe how things had gotten so bad, so fast.

It all began when Clint went berserk and attacked Prissy Tillman. However, within hours, the police had established the connection between Clint and Prissy, which was Gil Wallace, the assailant's father.

Then, the letter from Terrence Marvin recovered by the salvage company further complicated matters. It alleged that Gil Wallace and Prissy Tillman were members of a swingers group and also that they had both molested a student. Through a dubious means of communication, Prissy denied she was a group member, but she corroborated Marvin's letter as it related to everything else. She also admitted to having a relationship with a student and that her boss had one as well.

While the evidence was shaky, they managed to get an arrest warrant for Gil because he lied to them about everything. He said he didn't know anything about a sex ring, and he cited all the reasons Terrence Marvin had been fired.

However, Gil admitted he'd lied during the grueling, hours-long interview. He said he'd feared losing his job and his family finding out about his lifestyle. But his lies had been enough to establish that he was a flight risk, so he remained in custody.

The identity of the student who'd been molested was unknown. But they firmly believed the girl in the videos taken from the phone was that student. And when a young man called saying his sister was missing, and they established her as the one from the videos, everything fell perfectly into place. They still didn't have all the answers. But they had enough to upgrade Gil's charges to kidnapping, believing they'd be elevated again after they found her body.

They still had a missing person, though. She was someone they'd wanted to talk to all along, but they couldn't find her. They knew who she was, and they'd give anything to talk to her, but she was nowhere to be seen. Besides her mother and brother, they couldn't even locate anyone else who knew the girl who wasn't dead or in a coma. However, that was about to change.

CHAPTER TWENTY-SIX

It had been a difficult week. Captain Lewis had to find a balance between heading up the investigation into Lacy Knight's disappearance and assuming the role of emissary between Olivia Knight and the cities of Memphis and Germantown. He'd had to leave his detectives to their own devices, staying abreast of everything they discovered along the way. All the while, he'd catered to Camp Knight, which included the Federal government and whoever all those other people were.

Lewis did a good job of keeping himself aware in whichever capacity he served. He listened to developments on all fronts and pieced them together for his sanity and, as fate had recently dictated to him, his integrity.

But Lewis was an envoy on this occasion, delivering and gathering information to and from his detectives. They'd scarved down wraps and sandwiches all afternoon as they convened in the outside seating area of Moondance Grill.

"You want to know something else?" Lewis said, moving toward closing out the discussion, "Knight bought that hotel where all those people had their orgies. Paid cash for it. And by cash, I mean someone walked into the lobby and handed the owner a suitcase with half of whatever Knight bought it for. Then, they wrote a check for the rest."

It was puzzling news for the detectives, who initially didn't know what to make of it.

"Damn, that's sort of ghoulish, right? Why do you suppose she did that?" Michaels asked.

Lewis shrugged his shoulders and continued.

"Glen said Knight was setting up a command center down there as we speak. He said it was the wildest shit you've ever seen. The Geek Squad is there running cables and stuff, caterers bringing in food for her crew. It's just nuts, fellas."

"But why? Why there?" Hester asked.

· "Who knows why a woman like that does anything?" Lewis started, "I guess because...what? She can? I didn't ask, and I'm sure Glen didn't either. But Glen also said there are specialists from all over the country."

While his detectives' interest was piqued, Lewis provided another troubling piece of information.

"You know, the other thing is, nobody had even told her about Qadeshians yet when she started that business. Glen was shocked when he heard that one. That means Knight already knew about that club and that her daughter had been a member. It's like she's the one running the damned investigation, and she thinks she's telling us things on a need-to-know basis. I don't even know why she's involving us if you want to know the truth about it."

Lewis' revelation was a brazen insult to men who'd devoted everything to finding Lacy Knight, and they hadn't done it because of who her mother was or how much money the family had. They did it because they wanted justice for Lacy. Nobody honestly believed she was still alive. But Captain Lewis' passion over the matter had rubbed off on his two best detectives. And they were as committed to discovering what happened to Lacy as he was.

Or so it seemed.

However, as Lewis shared this new information, the men felt like pawns or lackeys that someone was humoring to keep out of Olivia Knight's hair. After all, Knight was the one who had all the resources. So, maybe their captain was right. Maybe Knight felt like she was in charge and that everyone else was serving an auxiliary role, like some redundant apparatus that couldn't guide the investigation but was there merely to block traffic for her and go out on fact-finding missions.

Exhibiting some of the frustration he felt at Lewis' comments, Hester heatedly began offering his opinion.

"You know, forensics has never been my strong suit. But I've worked in homicide my whole career, and I'm a damned good detective. And I mean to tell you, it all seems pretty clear to me what happened to that girl, even if there's some shit we can't explain. She disappears the same day her boyfriend goes wacko and kills her lesbian lover. That part is weird, alright? I'll give you that one. But then we find out her lover works for the boyfriend's father. Somebody else who was doin' the girl ratted out the lover and the father because he worked for the father, too. Then, the rat got fired by the father."

"And now, the rat is dead," Michaels finished for his partner, "and so is the girl's lover. And it looks like the boy is gonna die pretty soon, too, but that one is on us."

Hester stared at Michaels while Captain Lewis began eyeing the dessert menu.

"Does anybody believe there's even a chance that girl is still alive? I sure as hell don't, Tony. Do you?" Hester asked, looking over at Lewis.

Lewis looked back and forth between his detectives for a second before he said, "No."

Lewis looked disturbed, like his mind was elsewhere, as though he were pondering something before speaking again.

"I don't know what I think anymore, fellas. I just don't know."

Hester leaned forward, putting his elbows on the table, and went on.

"Listen. When you've got a group of people like that, a powerful group of people, who are doing all kinds of filthy stuff on the down low, you can bet they want to keep it quiet. And the only thing I can think is that young Miss Lacy was about to blow the whistle on the whole damned thing. I have no idea why she'd want to do that. She obviously wasn't blackmailing anybody because she didn't need the money. But it's just what I think. Do I have any proof of any of that? No. But it's what my gut is telling me. Lacy Knight was going to rip the whole damned thing wide open, and somebody shut her up. That girl is as dead as dirt."

"So, you're saying it was probably somebody in the Qadeshians group that had her abducted or killed? Like, maybe somebody else is involved?" Michaels asked Hester.

"You're damned right I am! It was either Wallace or somebody else in that group of freaks! What else could it be, man? And I don't need the FBI or the Geek Squad to help me figure that out, either!" Hester declared.

Captain Lewis broke into the discussion, seemingly to put his restless detectives' minds at ease and look toward the future.

"Well, we got one of them, and he ain't going anywhere," Lewis said, "and I know this sounds stupid. But you want to know who I would give anything to talk to right now?"

"Who?" Michaels asked.

"Lacy Knight. That's who. It's like she's already talking to me, though, without words. Like she's trying to get my attention by pointing at different people and places and wants so badly for me to figure things out. I swear to you, fellas. It really feels like that to me, and that hurts. I wish we knew more about her. What she did in the days before this happened, and even before that. I'd love to be able to climb inside of her head."

Like a child knocking over a display in a grocery store, sending merchandise tumbling to the ground where it shattered and shocked the hell out of everyone nearby, Detective Michaels posed a straightforward yet loaded question.

"Well, what did her shrink say?" he asked.

Michaels was so matter-of-fact that he sounded like he was asking Lewis if he would have the double fudge brownie or the key lime pie for dessert.

"What did *who* say?" Lewis asked.

"The shrink. Her doctor. That email I sent you?" Michaels continued as his expression began changing to one of concern.

Lewis' demeanor changed just as suddenly, but he took on more of a perturbed air. His brow wrinkled, and his eyes squinted a little bit.

"Um. What email would that be, Detective Michaels?" he asked.

Michaels acted as though Lewis was being forgetful and that he was reminding his boss of something he'd already shared with him. Because Michaels had already demoted the information in his mind. He thought it was old news and that Lewis had just put it to rest like he had.

"Shit, Captain. The one with his statement. I sent you his statement like I said in the email. Sergeant Phillips interviewed her psychiatrist the other day," Michaels answered, becoming even more concerned and acting as though he was waiting for an explosion.

"Wha??" Hester interrupted, puzzled that his young partner hadn't mentioned the information to him either.

Michaels got defensive.

"Look, It didn't sound like much to me. He came in while everybody was in there with Knight and wanted to talk to somebody. Phillips took his statement because I was trying to…"

"Damn it, boy!" Hester roared, "Not everybody checks their email every five minutes! I don't care what the procedures say! If you get evidence like that, you put it in somebody's hands! Do you understand? What the hell is the matter with you? Have you lost your damned mind?"

"Look, I just…" Michaels started.

"No, no. It's alright. It's alright," Lewis said, coming to Michaels' rescue before addressing Detective Hester, "The young man made an honest mistake, Roderick. That's all."

Lewis was as miffed about the junior detective's cavalier attitude as Detective Hester was. But he wanted to keep the information flowing. So, it wasn't the time to dress Michaels down, turning the situation into a teachable moment. He wanted to hear what Michaels had to say.

"Could you please tell me what the man told Sergeant Phillips then, Detective Michaels?"

Michaels couldn't win for losing that afternoon. His subsequent question was very telling about the differences between him and his superiors. It represented a collision between generational worlds because the men were born decades apart.

"You've got your phone with you, don't you?" Michaels asked.

Michaels wasn't being a smart ass, although maybe a tad insensitive. He was being a millennial. He'd grown up presuming that the first thing everyone did when they got up in the morning was check their email, texts, and social media accounts. He didn't understand a world where any of those were secondary considerations. They were how people from his generation lived their lives. Connected. Everyone locked in on everything everyone else was doing at any given moment. You had a bad meal somewhere? You didn't casually mention it in passing to one of your friends or your brother at some later date. You shared it with the whole world seconds after it happened. You tweeted about it. Or you Insta'd pictures of the chicken that hadn't been cooked all the way through. You Yelp!'d about it, screenshot your review, and then posted that screenshot on your Facebook page.

Detective Hester was more like Captain Lewis—maybe a scosche more tech-savvy.

"Boy, you really have lost it today, haven't you?" he growled at Michaels.

Michaels began stammering, unsure whether to pull the message up on his phone or continue defending himself. But Captain Lewis had already retrieved it and stared at his phone as his detectives looked on. Whatever information that doctor had was something he needed. He needed it for his personal knowledge and to pass it on because he'd been lying to his partners the whole time.

***

"Like I told the uniformed officer," Josh said, highlighting that the detectives hadn't given him the time of day on his first trip to the police station, "I believe that Lacy Knight backed herself into a corner. I know what her intentions might have been. And I don't think she was malicious or trying to hurt anyone. But I believe her plan backfired for whatever reason."

Captain Lewis was happy that Josh had fallen out of the sky with all the details he seemed confident discussing. But he didn't want Josh to feel threatened or strong-armed, so he had to get something out of the way.

"Dr. Odom, sometimes I have to ask questions that upset people. But I have to ask them anyway. So, keeping that in mind as we go, I need to ask you something, but I don't want you to be offended or think it will…"

"I'm not a member of Qadeshians, sir," Josh said, heading the captain off, "I knew you were going to ask me that because I didn't say anything about it in my original statement. But, no, I am not a member of Qadeshians. I wasn't even aware it existed until Lacy Knight became my patient."

Josh put Lewis' mind at ease. Had Josh been involved in Qadeshians, the landscape would have changed dramatically. He was just surprised Josh had shown up alone and without an attorney. Lewis didn't want to look a gift horse in the mouth. But, based on some of the information Josh had given Sergeant Phillips, Lewis first had to clarify the nature of Josh's affiliation with the things and people he'd mentioned.

"Okay, well, you say you became aware of Qadeshians because Lacy Knight told you about it. If that's the case…"

"I didn't say that, Captain. I said I didn't know it existed until she became my patient."

Lewis felt that Josh could have explained things better initially instead of being so vague.

"Alright. Well, may I ask how you became aware of its existence? But before you answer, please feel free to give me all the information you believe is relevant to your answer. I think it would save us all a lot of time."

Josh appeared annoyed at the captain's suggestion that he hadn't explained himself well.

"Captain Lewis, you must understand, I'm not here trying to be a good citizen. I came forward because I believe you have the wrong person in custody. As I told you from the outset, the person you're holding happens to be a friend of mine, Captain Lewis. A dear friend of mine. I'm not saying he's a choir boy because he's not. And I want you to realize I know how stupid this sounds, but Gil Wallace is a good guy. I don't mean that because he's morally beyond reproach. But in the context of what we're talking about and considering the moral framework we're dealing with here, Gil Wallace is a pretty good guy—certainly not a kidnapper or a killer."

Lewis countered by clarifying what Josh was saying. He thought Josh was dodging his question.

"Then it was Mr. Wallace who told you about Qadeshians? Is that what I'm hearing you try to tell me?" Lewis asked.

Sensing Lewis' aggravation, Josh gave a definitive statement this time.

"Yes, Gil told me that it existed," Josh replied.

"Well, why didn't you disclose that in your statement to us, Dr. Odom? Why didn't you tell Sergeant Phillips what you're telling us now?" Lewis asked.

"Would it have mattered, Captain Wallace? Or wouldn't it still have taken you this long to speak with me?" Josh replied.

Josh had a point, Lewis thought. It was a little annoying to have someone else point out his mistakes. But what Josh didn't know was that they'd had ample reason for moving in the direction they'd headed.

"Dr. Odom, the person who gave us the little information we have about Qadeshians, gave it to us posthumously. But that little bit is what landed your friend in jail."

"Huh?" Josh asked.

Josh was confused. The only other person in the equation who'd been harmed by anyone other than the police was Prissy Tillman. Is that who Lewis was talking about? Gil's son, Clint, was responsible for killing Prissy. Like everyone else, Josh thought it made sense that Clint had done something to Lacy after discovering all the horrible things she'd done. So, what was this guy talking about?

But if Lewis now said that Prissy was involved with Qadeshians, that would add a brand-new vantage for evaluating Lacy Knight's deception. Had she lied about Prissy? Was Prissy not a victim of Lacy's manipulation but rather a sexual predator herself? Did she lure Lacy into Qadeshians? Josh's original fear about Lacy and Prissy duping him had not been so far-fetched if that was the case. He hadn't been paranoid. He'd been observant.

In any case, Josh no longer felt sorry for Prissy Tillman. Contemplating that reinforced his conviction to draw suspicion away from Gil. They had several other people they could focus on, and Josh still believed they were wasting their time.

"That's right, Dr. Odom. The person who told us that Gil Wallace was involved with Qadeshians is dead. They also told us that the person his son killed was involved with Qadeshians. That brings me to my next question. Does that, in any way, change your opinion of Gil Wallace moving forward?"

Wait a minute. What? *Another* dead person? Lewis hadn't been referring to Prissy after all? Who in the hell was he talking about, now?

Josh didn't know if Lewis was baiting or telling him the truth. Because Josh, like everyone else involved, had no interest in

Terrance Marvin. Didn't know he was dead. Didn't know anything about the man apart from the fact that he'd had sex with Lacy Knight—supposedly. So, Josh hadn't had a clue that the person Lewis was talking about was the one who told them about Qadeshians. However, he knew they'd found out somehow because Gil told him during one of his frantic calls from jail.

Josh would have to work through everything. And because he was hungover, he didn't have the energy to perform the mental gymnastics it would require. He wanted to stay the course and get his friend out of jail. But he also wanted to know who this extraneous person was that had tried to sabotage Gil. What were the circumstances surrounding their death?

Josh regained his composure and answered Lewis.

"It doesn't change things, Captain. It might lessen the value of what I've tried to be forthcoming about because you have a lot more information than I thought you did. You certainly have more than I do. And I may be going too far out on a limb here by telling you this, but if Gil Wallace had done anything to Lacy, I would probably have known about it."

And then Lewis became as confused as Josh had been. What did Josh mean by that?

"You think so?" Lewis asked.

"Absolutely. Gil and I are close. But he's also my patient, Captain. I know my records may be subpoenaed because of this case. So, I don't want you to think that's a lie because Gil Wallace won't appear in my patient logs, insurance claims, or anywhere else. I've treated him in an informal setting, and, yes, the context was usually as a friend. But being a psychiatrist isn't something you can just turn off. I tried to help Gil because of the state his personal life has been in. I know the wife. I know the kids. I know everything, which includes things you may or may not know. So, please, fire away any questions you have about Gil Wallace. And tell me everything you want to tell me about him and this case. But you'll see that my opinion regarding whether he could willfully harm someone will remain consistent throughout that discussion. Not only do I think he's incapable of killing someone, I don't think he could use anybody else to kill someone, either. Especially not his son. Clint is the only thing that man has going for him in his life. He sure as hell wouldn't sic the boy on somebody that had something on him. He's done his best to keep Clint in the dark about his lifestyle. And, let me tell you, some of that stuff is shocking. But nothing, in my professional opinion, points toward Gil Wallace as being responsible for Prissy Tillman's death or Lacy Knight's disappearance."

Detective Lewis remained skeptical.

"What about Clint, then? I don't suppose he was also your patient, was he?" he asked.

"No, he was not," Josh confirmed.

"Well, during your treatment of Mr. Wallace, did he comment on the mental condition of his son? Did he ever tell you anything that might lead you to believe Clint could be capable of what he did to Prissy Tillman? Because we know he's guilty of that, Dr. Odom. We have hard evidence that he curb-stomped that woman until her face blew up. Does that sound like someone who's mentally competent to you? Or does that sound like somebody who could be easily set off by, say, finding out his girlfriend wasn't the kind of person they'd thought she was?"

Now, they were fishing, Josh thought to himself. For whatever reason, they wanted his opinion of whether or not Clint was who abducted Lacy, and they were trying to get it by taking the next logical step—or having him take it for them. Out of loyalty to Gil, because Clint was his son, Josh would neither confirm nor deny that, but it made him feel better that they were at least moving in a direction that took them away from Gil Wallace.

"I don't know. And for the reasons I've stated, I'm not willing to speculate on that. I was at the kid's first birthday party, gentlemen. So, I'm sure you understand how troubling the prospect of him killing someone is to me. But there are things about Lacy that make that seem like a distinct possibility because she could drive anyone to murder. If you only knew all the things she's done. But just as I was, you might be heartbroken about what made her do them."

"Dr. Odom, let me just say that we're aware of many of the things you're, perhaps, referring to. We know the kind of young woman Lacy Knight is and has been. And, yes, that is heartbreaking, just as you said. But we don't have time to consider those things apart from how they relate to this case. They matter to us only to the extent they might have precipitated her disappearance. But it stops there. We're focused on finding her now. And so is her mother."

That was good news for Josh. They weren't referring to Lacy in the past tense as if she were dead. That told him they had hope for her still being alive, and that thrilled Josh. And, no matter how Gil had behaved or even whether he'd had sex with Lacy, it was a moot point. Deep down, Josh believed Gil hadn't abducted her. As he told the detectives, he didn't think Gil could harm anyone.

There were still others, however, that Josh thought they should be looking at. He felt it was a safe bet to assume it was Clint, but he didn't want them to rule out everyone else. Who knew? Maybe they'd get enough evidence to convict someone else. Provided he lived, Clint would still have to answer for Prissy's death if what Captain Lewis said was true and they had evidence to that effect. But it did no one any good if they continued to blame Gil for whatever happened to Lacy, especially whenever they found what increasingly started seeming like would be her corpse.

Josh continued to drive the bus away from Gil.

"Captain Lewis, there's something else you need to know about my being friends with Gil Wallace. It's kind of a gray area, but I'm not violating my oath by telling you this. I'm simply relating things that I observed myself. But this time, it's not me speaking as anyone's therapist. This time, I *am* talking as a concerned citizen because I think there's information that's potentially very important."

The officers remained quiet and anxiously waited for Josh to continue.

"While I'm not a member of Qadeshians, Captain Lewis, I do know several of their members. I don't know them as intimately as I know Gil, but I know them well enough to—that is to say, I have enough information to reveal their identities to you."

"Well, how did you discover this information, Dr. Odom? Given what you've said, I assume none of them are your patients. Is that right?" Lewis queried.

"No. I don't treat any of them. But telling you how I discovered this information is moving back into that zone where I'd be overstepping my bounds. I have met these people, though. I know who they are. They're mutual friends of mine and Mr. Wallace's. More his than mine, if that fills in any of those blanks for you. But there's even more than them, Captain Lewis. A lot more."

Josh sat in the conference room with the detectives for an additional three hours that afternoon. He had to call Liza to tell her he wouldn't be able to go to dinner as they'd planned, and he asked her to walk Scout. The meeting took so long because Josh disclosed every person of whom he had knowledge who'd slept with Lacy Knight. And there were a bunch of them.

Josh told it all. Perceived motives for the encounters ranged from the purely physical to the more manipulative seductions she'd crafted. But whether passionate or coldly devised, they were all objectionable. And he hoped that, in some small measure, it would bring to light the potential psychological impacts that could have on someone who cared anything for or about Lacy Knight.

There were classmates, team members, neighbors, and relative strangers. He even mentioned Lacy's brother, whom she'd caught watching her get dressed in the past. He didn't know if the brother had ever molested Lacy, but that didn't seem like an absurdity given all that had happened. He'd often wondered about the young man because Lacy became dark whenever discussing him.

There were casual interludes Lacy had, both locally and in other places. In addition to the dizzying potential those encounters brought, they were merely mathematical factors when one considered those people's acquaintances and family members. There were both jilted males and females. There were also loved ones affiliated with those same people.

Then Josh told them about the Qadeshians he knew of, which consisted of Bonnie and Dubya Dupree, as well as Simpson and Bitsy Winslow. But he told them if they probed deeper, they'd most certainly find others in the group that could be competent as suspects.

When Josh mentioned Luke Millard, it seemed to excite Detectives Hester and Michaels, whereas Captain Lewis stayed level throughout the discussion. He seemed neither fazed nor surprised by any of it.

Then again, Captain Lewis wasn't exchanging intelligence. He was only gathering what little of it remained. He knew many other things, yet he wasn't sharing all of those with everyone else. A particular piece of undisclosed evidence Captain Lewis had was that Lacy Knight was still alive.

CHAPTER TWENTY-SEVEN

A hobo scampered through the brush a few more paces before he dropped to his knees and lay on his side. His name was Clemmie, and it appeared the old guy was either too drunk or too tired to go further. As he lay on the ground, flat against the cold, wet mud and straw, he shielded his eyes from the sun and started mumbling. He behaved like a schizophrenic, as the words he spoke were nonsensical.

Clemmie's left ear was itching terribly, and he hoped it wasn't another ant like the one that had stung him several yards away about an hour earlier. He hated ants. He hated all bugs. But just as he often joked with the other hobos he occasionally communed with, they were an "occupational hazard."

Clemmie lay still and listened. Because whenever the bugs crawled in his ear, he knew the voices would soon follow. He knew it wasn't God talking to him, but he believed with all his heart that God oversaw those voices that sometimes came to him.

The voices told Clemmie to do things. Strange things that probably seemed eccentric and disturbing to anyone who caught sight of him doing them. But he yielded to the voices no matter what. And he did as he was instructed. He *always* did as he was instructed.

Because Robert Clemenceau was a former Green Beret.

"145, 1.4 meters," the voice said.

Clemmie hollered in case someone watched him, "You're not gonna take my lunch, buddy boy! Cause I already ate it!"

Then he whispered into the Alpha Tau Omega pledge pin affixed to his jacket, among others that were just as peculiar and unrelated but not nearly as functional, "HVT? Or are we going to the ant farm again?"

The female voice snickered, "No. No ant farms. HVT. HVT. Affirmative 100."

Clemmie rolled back over and belly-crawled before starting up with the lunacy again.

"Lizbeth! Lizbeth! I'm comin'ta join ya, honey!"

A young, handsome man in the control center Clemmie communicated with started laughing and announced to the room, "I mean to tell ya, that is one funny gahdamned snake eater."

Once he arrived at the coordinates, precise to everyone but him, Clemmie started patting around on the ground. It couldn't be underneath all this shit. It never was. Not unless they had buried the son-of-a-bitch, he thought to himself.

He stopped, exhaled, and was about to pull the spade from the back of his waistband, but his hand settled on something hard when he propped himself up. It was firm, cool, and metallic. And when he raised his hand and balanced himself in an upright seated position, he saw that it was what he'd been looking for the whole time, and it looked just like it had been described to him.

Clemmie's heart raced for a moment before he spoke in a much less excited tone, belying the exhilaration he felt.

"HVT acquired. RTB. Bruno out."

Clemmie thought about how far he'd have to walk and got agitated. But he took another deep breath, grabbed his prize, and started hobbling toward the bus stop.

"Mission accomplished," he jokingly said as he trudged back through the brush and wet Earth that sloshed beneath the shabby work boots that were a part of his disguise.

***

Oliva Knight sat in the ballroom of the Lamplighter Inn, studying its architecture.

The room's walls were papered with a raised-edge, gold paisley pattern. It was the kind her mother had always wanted in their living room at home but could never afford it.

Squared mahogany pillars reached up in intervals along the paneled wainscoting and the black and white tiled floors that spanned the room. The hall was divided by a single wooden arch into two sections, one for the tables where Knight sat while the other had once been designated for dancing and probably a band.

Knight imagined that, at one time, the large room hosted dances where nervous, sweaty hands touched for the first time as young gentlemen and young ladies were brought together away from school. Their arranged meetings resulted from wanting them to develop social sophistication in a society where men protected women who were chaste and unknown to other men.

Later, those gals would transform into young women as they were introduced to society as debutantes at their coming-out parties. She envisioned that after that, with every bit of hope, there would be grand wedding receptions, where hundreds of people mingled, and toasts would be raised to promising futures and all the wonderful things that life had in store for them.

My, but how things change, Olivia thought to herself.

Knight's misgivings about how that utopic society had deteriorated were not as much dissent as an indictment of herself. She, too, had prioritized things that should have been secondary instead. Rewards for pursuing and building a life with another person. A person that you loved and cherished and with whom, were you fortunate enough, you could share children and a family.

It was as if the consequences of her decisions were brusquely reminding Knight of her failures in life when a man carrying an iPad joined her and ripped her away from the imaginary world she'd fantasized about.

"Mrs. Knight, I need to share some news with you," the man began, "it's not definitive, but it points toward a troubling matter. Could you come with me?"

Knight didn't say anything. She stared back at the man and waited for a better explanation because she'd need one before she spoke or moved anywhere. After a couple of seconds passed, the man spoke again.

"Ma'am, my name is McAleer, and I'm a forensic pathologist. I should have introduced myself and the purpose of being here, but I was asked not to. I suppose that's understandable as we're all remaining hopeful that your daughter is found safe and can be returned to you," the young doctor said.

McAleer clammed up after that, too intimidated to say anything unless asked. Once he realized Knight was waiting on him, he started to speak again.

"Uh, ma'am. Ma'am, I've analyzed some data that has the potential…that is to say, it could…you might want to…"

"What…do you have to tell me, Dr. McAleer?" Knight said, curtailing her temper.

Dr. McAleer touched the back of a chair and began to slide it from beneath the table, then he stopped and asked, "May I?"

Knight nodded briefly, staring into the doctor's eyes as the man sat down and cautiously edged toward her.

"Mrs. Knight, I realize you've already looked at this picture more than you wanted to. And while there is a great deal of hope because of its setting, there are some things I believe we should stay mindful of as we go. As you saw, the picture was taken in an outdoor wooded area."

Dr. McAleer decided he couldn't proceed without some backup.

"Maybe I'd better get someone else to talk about that with you first," McAleer said, "Mike?! Could you come over here a minute, please?"

A gaunt, bespectacled man scampered to where Knight sat with Dr. McAleer. He was even more nervous than the doctor.

"Mrs. Knight, it's a great pleasure to meet you. I'm Dr. Michael Montfort, a forest botanist and Fellow in town at the University of Memphis." Mike offered.

Knight nodded again, extended her arm, and briefly shook hands with the anxious scientist.

"Mike, please brief Mrs. Knight on the information we covered earlier this morning," Dr. McAleer said.

"Sure. Okay. Why don't we step over here to the monitor so I can show you things as we speak," Mike said.

No one moved at first, waiting to see how Knight would respond. Then, when she rose from the table, all three walked to where a Geek Squad member was sitting in front of a computer.

Mike looked at the screen momentarily before looking back to ensure everyone was paying attention. Then, he began to speak in the most pleasant tone he could manage.

"Let's take a look here, shall we?" he asked.

The window he maximized was a photograph of Lacy, the subject of all the chaos in the ballroom. Knight could sense that, for some reason, something had caused a stir among all the specialists and experts who'd been gathered to work on her daughter's case.

Knight had trouble looking at Lacy, though. It was unsettling, and it made her feel nauseated. But Mike continued in a peppy, upbeat manner.

"Okay, after looking at the pretty girl, the first thing you notice in this image is the cluster of trees behind her. While that probably looks like any wooded area to the layman, we see a lot more when people like me look at it. It's like the old saying about being unable to see the forest for the trees. Well, people like me don't see the forest at first because we're so distracted by all those trees. We eventually see the forest, but we have a lot more information about that forest because of everything those trees tell us. Things such as its elevation. Where it would likely be located by state and region— even more localized than that in many cases."

Mike chugged ahead while trying to maintain his energetic posture. He was simultaneously terrified and compassionate.

"As I look at the images of where your daughter is seated, I can discern the family and species of those trees. I do this based on their leaf morphology, their bark, and their position relative to the ambient light at the time of day, which, this image appears to be taken as the sun is going down. It's getting dark, but I can still distinguish ten species of trees in the foreground, those closest to your daughter or the camera. The rest are just as obscure to me as they'd probably be to someone else."

Mike attempted to condense what he was saying.

"The point I'm trying to make is that of the ten species I can say with certainty are in the photograph, five of them are oak trees, and then the other half consists of sycamore, bald cypress, hemlock, and river birch. Further, I see the oak species of willow, Nuttall, Shumard, and white and chestnut swamp oaks. While that may not at once leap out at you as being relevant, I believe that would change if I went on to tell you that there is consistency here. It's something that all the trees I mentioned have in common."

"Why don't you tell her what you're thinking, Mike?" the pathologist said, fearing Knight might lose patience at any moment.

"Got it. Okay, there could have been any number of trees in the photograph, depending on where the young lady was at the time this picture was taken. But in this case, every tree species in the picture grows prolifically in the Gulf Coastal Plain of Tennessee, and they all grow near water in swampy or sandy soil. So, I believe this picture was taken near a stream, river, or somewhere like that. A lake, maybe? Even more importantly, though, those species indicate it's within the immediate vicinity of the Memphis statistical population area."

Mike then looked at Knight, smiled, and told her something far more hopeful than law enforcement's expectations.

"I believe she's close by, ma'am."

Dr. McAleer instantly started shaking his head as though saying. *Okay, you can shut up now.* He hadn't wanted to follow someone giving hopeful news, and he hadn't anticipated Mike's cheery forecast. He'd only wanted to delegate a portion of the let-down, making it easier for him to share the alarming discoveries he'd made that were left for him to discuss with Olivia Knight.

"Thanks," he told Mike, who looked back at Dr. McAleer with the concern that maybe he'd said too much.

"I'll take things from here," McAleer continued.

Then he raised his arm and gestured toward the table where he and Knight had been sitting.

"After you, ma'am," McAleer said before they returned to the table.

After they both sat, Dr. McAleer placed the iPad he'd been holding on the table and oriented it at an angle so that he could share what was on its screen.

"Mrs. Knight, a few other doctors and I have assayed your daughter's physical condition based on things we detected in the photo that you've been sent. Remember that this picture doesn't allow us to do that as handily as possible if it were a digital image. But I assure you, we're doing the best that we can."

Knight moved her eyes between the iPad and Dr. McAleer a few times because she was too frightened to look directly at its screen. But finally, she slid her chair forward, leaned over, and stared at the glass behind which her beautiful daughter sat. McAleer noticed Knight's left eye twitch as though she winced, perhaps from seeing Lacy staring back at whoever looked on from above the iPad.

"I'll try to be as forthcoming as possible. But I want you to stop me if I go too fast or say something that isn't clear," Dr. McAleer said before getting down to brass tacks.

"I hope you aren't bothered by this, but we requisitioned some additional pictures from your daughter's phone that were recovered after…well…once the young man…"

"Go on," Knight interrupted.

"Well, we did that to analyze her physical condition in the photo you received. In other words, we needed a baseline to gauge her health both before and following her abduction. The first consideration was none of our business. Still, given the information we had about her lifestyle, we were looking for certain indicators, if you will, about everything from the sleep and nutrition she was getting to the likelihood of using narcotics. We weren't making suppositions about your daughter's behavior, but we did have information in hand that I was told you were made aware of when you arrived in Memphis."

Knight nodded in disgrace because that's what it was: shameful. It was shameful that it required other people—strangers—to rattle off the events of Lacy's life when she knew she should have been intimately involved in it. McAleer went on.

"Well, it's positive in one sense, and that's that we saw no outward indications or markers that we believe pointed toward drug use. We had to go back for a good way in the photos before we were able to see that she had even used drugs at all, and I suppose that's the good news. I'm unable to give you a precise timeline, but I'm comfortable saying that she hadn't taken drugs for a considerable period before her disappearance."

"Fabulous," Knight said sarcastically.

"Allow me to turn the clock back and show you a few of the images we used to perform our analysis," McAleer suggested, trying to keep the gears greased so he could get things over with.

A slide show, Knight thought to herself. It was all she needed. A photo collage of the life that she left her daughter to live without her influence or input beyond the cyclic infusion of cash, and even that was done carelessly and with no interaction. At that moment, she realized she'd spent more time and exercised more care in dealing with Lacy's assets and investment portfolio than talking to or even thinking about her.

Once McAleer touched the screen and moved through the images, Knight noticed that Lacy was facing the camera in all of them, just as she'd been in the photo she received. Another continuity Knight noticed was that in all the pictures, Lacy's head took up comparable volumes of area on the screen, so it was clear that they had tried to catch her in the same position in space as the image she'd provided them.

Dr. McAleer's first image troubled Knight because it looked like a video still that someone had frozen. It was a headshot, but from what little could be seen of the rest of the image, it looked like Lacy was naked. At least she didn't have on a top because her bare shoulders were showing.

Knight wondered what was happening at that moment. What had she been doing? Why wasn't she dressed in the picture? Who had taken the picture or filmed the video or whatever was the case?

"This is the oldest image in our sample that was different from the rest of them, and without being too specific, we were able to determine that she was under the influence of some sort of CNS stimulant. We needn't dissect this one too much, and I hope you'll just take my word for it. I only included it because I wanted you to see that it appeared she had transitioned over time to be drug-free."

Mercifully, Dr. McAleer only pulled up three more images of Lacy, and she appeared happy in each of them.

She stood on an athletic field in one of them, and you could see other people in the background. It looked like everyone was wearing tee shirts that were one of two colors. Either fuchsia, like the one Lacy had on, or a fluorescent yellow. One couldn't make out the text on any other of the shirts from the blurred imagery in the background, but the one Lacy wore said "Camp Redemption '23' and beneath those words was the word 'Naphtali,' which Knight knew to be one of the twelve tribes of Israel. She deduced that it must've been a religious field day at a summer camp.

The next photo showed Lacy, once again happy, sitting at a table with an ice cream sundae in front of her. Even from the scant information she remembered about her little girl, Knight knew that Lacy always loved things cold and sweet.

Knight gently laughed but only momentarily because if she released any more emotion than that, she was afraid it might explode into weeping.

The third image was probably Knight's favorite—if she had to choose. In that picture, Lacy looked stunning. She wasn't one for a lot of makeup, anyway, but in this image, her beautiful complexion and the absence of lines or wrinkles on her face were most evident. She wore a blue chemise that perfectly matched the deep blue of her eyes, and while she displayed no overt emotion in the picture, anyone could tell she was content.

Lacy looked pacific. She appeared strangely and gut-wrenchingly wise. She looked like Olivia Knight's father, Rudolph.

As if rounding a corner and accelerating into a brick wall, McAleer brought up the final image of Lacy, which Knight had provided everyone with when she arrived in Memphis.

"This is the picture of your daughter you received, Mrs. Knight. I know it's hard to look at it, but…"

Knight looked down and stared hard into her little girl's eyes. She wanted to face her. She wanted to feel she was showing her that she was prepared to atone for everything she'd been and done in her life and everything she had not.

"Yeah? And?" Knight said as she started to become angry.

"Here, let me enlarge the image as best as I can. Again, please remember that this isn't a digital photograph, so there will be much more degradation as we go. But it will suffice for what I'm going to show you."

Knight eased back as the doctor unclosed his index finger and thumb, blowing up the picture of Lacy on the screen. Knight looked like her pain intensified as Lacy grew larger beneath the glass.

"Look at your daughter's pupils in this image, Mrs. Knight," Dr. McAleer began.

McAleer looked at Knight to confirm she was still watching before moving forward.

"Now, I'm going to zoom in a little more. Note the pupils' size and perimeter distance from the iris's margin."

Knight felt like she would hyperventilate if she had to look too much longer. She hadn't had a panic attack in years, but she believed she was vaulting toward one on a grand mal scale, so she did what she always did in those instances, and he shrouded herself in cynicism.

"Yeah?"

Feeling a little more confident, Dr. McAleer lowered his pitch and began speaking in a softer tone.

"That picture is the most recent one we have of your daughter. Now scroll backward and let me enlarge a couple of the other images for you."

Dr. McAleer wanted to keep Knight dialed in and feel she was participating rather than allowing her to succumb to emotion, so he had her scroll through the pictures herself.

"Okay, notice how the pupil moved mesially from the interior margin of the iris. Mesial means closer to the centerline of the human body."

"Okay?" Knight said in the way she spoke when she wanted someone to get the point, even though she dreaded it this time.

"Now look at the other one again. You see how it's moved?"

Knight flipped to the third picture, carelessly missing it the first time before getting it right the second time she touched the screen.

"And now, look at this most recent one again."

Olivia moved the screen a final time, seeing the picture of Lacy sitting in the woods again, and she tried to slide the screen to another frame as if wanting to move Lacy away from that horrible place and onward to the next chapter of her life. A place where she'd guard her even more and try, with everything, to be a better parent.

But the picture wouldn't move. Lacy bounced back to the center of the screen each time Knight tried to move her with her finger. It was like a crescendo of her life as her mother and Lacy's as her daughter.

There it is. Look at it. This is what you get, she thought to herself.

"Mrs. Knight, I'm sorry to tell you this, but it's my belief as the head forensics officer on this case that the movement of that pupil from mid-dilation to slight dilation, then becoming slightly constricted, suggests that the iris muscles are fully relaxed. And Mrs. Knight, that transition indicates to me that…"

It was the moment Dr. McAleer had feared. But he nailed his courage to the wall, closed his eyes briefly, and continued.

"That transition is consistent with the onset of rigor mortis, Mrs. Knight. Mrs. Knight, I am so sorry to tell you this, but I believe your daughter is deceased and that she was deceased before this picture was taken."

Knight didn't look at Dr. McAleer.

She couldn't.

Because if she looked at Dr. McAleer, she would become what thousands of powerful people who'd preceded her in history had, and she would do what they'd done: kill the messenger.

Instead, Olivia Knight continued to stare at Lacy. She rocked back and forth tersely, trying to search Lacy's expression to see if there was something she could find to refute what she'd been told. Then, she came up with something.

"Why are her eyes still open?" she asked, barely able to speak without crying.

It was a good question. It had puzzled those few involved in the case who were close enough to know everyone was looking for a cadaver instead of a young lady.

"We're not sure, Mrs. Knight," McAleer said, "We don't know because the quality of this image can only be analyzed so far. But we do notice two elevations on the peripheral margins of both eyelids as though something is tensed and holding them up."

Though he'd used jargon to describe it, Knight knew precisely what McAleer told her. It might have been sickening to ponder, but the answer was clear. Nevertheless, Knight wanted him to confirm it.

"They stapled her eyes open?" she asked, more in disgusted contemplation than posing a question.

"Mrs. Knight, I wouldn't have put it that way, but, in essence, yes. It appears that her eyes being open is not a biological event but rather an engineered presentation to make it appear as though she is alive."

Ta da! There you go, Mom! There you have it! And how could you possibly have imagined things ending any other way, you selfish bitch?! Did you think throwing money at something like raising a little girl was a surrogate for being a good mother? That a Mercedes for her birthday would make up for your being an egotistical, self-involved megalomaniac? Huh? Well, guess what, you autistic, arrogant, cold weirdo? It's just like Fab told you! If you fuck a whore, you beget a whore! That's right! Uh-huh! You brought a baby into this world with a self-centered fop because you thought your kids would be pretty! But that baby has checked out early, fuck-o! And you want to know why? Well, it's because things are just like these stupid, inbred, Tennessee-hillbilly keystone cops told you, too! She's a whore! She's a drug whore! And it was probably the easiest thing in the world for someone to get to her because you were never around! It could've been anybody, too! Mighta' been that fucking crazy partner of yours that you shafted! Or maybe those Goddamned Pakistanis whose brother you had killed! Point is, shit-for-brains, it ain't no telling who is trying to pump some cash out of your ass, and they're prolly doing it just to spite you!

Though no one could've attested to it because of her cool exterior, the damn had burst within Olivia Knight. And all the fearfulness and insecurity she'd felt comingled with anger, resentment, and despair, forming a heady brew. And that brew would intoxicate Olivia Knight. Moving forward, she'd not only be drunk with power but she'd be compromised by manic emotional states, all of which she'd keep to herself as they accrued atop each other.

Olivia Knight was going to find whoever had killed her baby. Her little girl. She was going to find them. And she was going to eat their face off. Whether she'd do that figuratively or literally remained to be seen, but she was then a resolved, inspired, and vigilant warrior who'd gone quite mad.

As she sat, no longer able to think about Lacy as anything but a dead girl, Knight mumbled something. Dr. McAleer couldn't make out what she was saying, and he wasn't trying that hard because he knew he was in for it from his superiors for jumping the gun.

"Mrs. Knight? I'm sorry, what was that? What are you saying?"

McAleer leaned forward, trying to hear what the billionairess was saying to herself, but he still couldn't make it out. Then, as he leaned in a little closer, he heard Knight close the quatrain.

"But all the king's horses and all the king's men…"

CHAPTER TWENTY-EIGHT

A technician in a clean-room data recovery lab aboard the IKS Rotarran plucked a small chip from a device and placed it into a cellophane baggie held by another technician. He used the same anti-static tweezers he'd used a moment before to transfer a tiny hard drive into a different baggie. The data on both those chips was of high priority to their boss.

Both baggies were delicately nestled into a titanium suitcase, which was locked and then loaded onto a minivan inside the Gatemouth hangar at Memphis International Airport. Moments later, the hangar doors slid open just wide enough for the van's passage before it tore across the tarmac and out of the airport gates. Four awaiting police motorcycles joined the van, turned on their sirens, and led it through the perilous stretch of rush hour traffic toward its destination: the Lamplighter Inn, just south of Memphis.

***

The file upload was instantaneous. After all, a Nokia N73 cellular telephone only had 64 MB of RAM, and even the mini-SD card accompanying it to the control center boasted a mere 2GB.

After the files were uploaded, they were segregated by file extensions. It included pictures, videos, and a couple of short text files, all of which would be deemed "fallow." That is, except for a few of the MP3 files. They were the newest files in the archive, with the rest dating back as far as fifteen years.

The audio from the files was atrocious at first. It would need rigorous enhancement because, they speculated, the cell phone's microphone had either been obscured by dust during its dormancy or, perhaps, even damaged.

With his first punch, Andy Romani yanked the headphones from his ears because the ambient sound from the MP3 file was a horrible crackling noise, as though someone had crumpled plastic or another thin, rigid material right next to the mic. Not helping matters was that he had inadvertently cranked the Yamaha AV receiver to MAX in the makeshift laboratory that the Geek Squad had set up for him.

"What? What is it? What's wrong?" Andy's partner, Matilde, asked anxiously.

He breathed heavily for a second, groaned, and said, "Nothing, Matty. It's nothing. But 'cause of that damned ghetto-blaster they've got me hooked up to, whatever it was sounded like the Big Bang. Jesus, I hate the Geek Squad. Stupid assed motherf..."

"Shhh! They're all over the place here!" Matilde insisted, looking nervously over both shoulders.

"Right, right," Andy said, returning to the seemingly impossible task of analyzing each of the seconds-long audio clips.

It would be a tedious endeavor, taking hours to complete. And as he worked, he wanted to beat whoever had recorded that sound file within an inch of their life, smacking them on the head a dozen or so times. He wanted to wallop the idiot good.

Andy didn't realize it then, but someone had already done that to the person recording. Except it was more like twenty or thirty times using a blunt instrument. With each blow, Andy would decipher that the recorder's assailant was growling and heaving in frustration because the person wouldn't fall unconscious. What's worse is that as the melee proceeded, Andy, using the DKI-2500 sound analyzer and predictive speech module he'd brought, could distinctly hear a female voice crying and sniveling after each strike.

That realization would make Andy shudder whenever he thought of it for the rest of his career. But it was the penultimate breakthrough of the session. The crowning discovery would come a few hours later. And as if the brutality had not been enough, the assailant had taunted who Andy and Matilde could only assume was the beautiful girl from that picture that had been on every monitor in the ballroom at some point or another since they'd arrived.

***

Olivia Knight hadn't moved from the table where she'd been sitting when the forensic pathologist shared his terrible hypothesis about Lacy. Several items littered the table, all tokens from federal agents, well-intentioned employees, and even a few Geek Squad members. One of those guys had brought her a bag of Fuego Taki's because he knew they were Knight's favorite from reading an article in *Sage X Q*, the weekly e-zine published by Dark Knight Industries.

There were several other tributes to the queen. All equally thoughtful parcels, delivered with either few or no words to bring even a modicum of solace to the most revered woman on the planet. A box of Twinkies, a sleeve of Pop Rocks, and a Van Holten's Garlic Joe pickle, to name a few.

While Knight loved all those things, they'd have little meaning to her for the rest of her days. They'd neither be as sweet nor savory, nor would any of the other modest pleasures she afforded to herself in life be as comforting or distracting as they once were.

Because her Lacy Girl had gone away.

Knight's grief that evening was the most profound emotion she'd ever experienced. But it competed with the remorse and dread she felt whenever she considered the kind of mother she'd been and all the things she should and should not have done.

She could've at least tried to make things work with Fab. She could've pretended to love him. She might have even gone through the motions by staying with them a week or two a year, if for nothing more than her little girl's sake.

But Fab was insufferable to her. She couldn't bear the thought of him, especially when there was such an abundance of guilt and culpability to be doled out among those who knew her daughter best. Certainly, much better than she did. The ones who could've potentially made a difference in her life rather than watch it run off the rails.

There were others besides Fab, though. Many others. That had been made clear to Knight once she landed in Memphis, and the police had clarified for her what she'd already labored with considering since the little girl was born. What chance at a normal life had she honestly had? Olivia had left her alone as a weeping babe in the woods, a glistening bounty for predators across an array of depraved walks of life. What could she have expected to have happened?

Lacy's affairs weren't like the daily problems in her life. She didn't have a team of people she could assign to serve as Lacy's mentor, encouraging her and reaffirming how beautiful and intelligent she was along the way. Instead, Lacy had to hear all those things from other people. Strangers. And that had empowered them to deliver those messages in whatever fashion they wanted to and with whatever motives they'd had.

They'd pay, though, Olivia thought. They'd all pay. Every last Goddamned one of them would pay for Lacy's delinquency and abuse.

As Knight steeped in the hateful, simmering broth she'd immersed herself in, two people approached her with information that would intensify her hatred even more. It was a Dark Knight audio engineer, Andy Romani, accompanied by his skittish assistant, Matilde.

"Mrs. Knight," the male engineer began, "I'm Andy, and this is Matty. We're from the Light and Sound Division of Dark Knight Interactive Entertainment. We're your employees, ma'am. We've been told to communicate our findings to our superiors, but nobody from DKIE is here. So, we wanted to come to you first with the results of one of our analytical procedures."

Though initially comforted that it was her people who'd approached Knight's table rather than someone from law enforcement bearing bad tidings, that comfort quickly gave way to apprehension. Since they'd come to her directly, they'd circumvented several protocols to get to her, which nobody ever dared to do in Dark Knight industries. Not unless the severity of what they were to tell her overrode those protocols.

Andy spoke again as Knight sat and considered the possible reasons for the engineers to have gone rogue as they had.

"Mrs. Knight, we extracted several sound files from the recovered device. The top of the waveform has been clipped and had to be enhanced, but we were able to pull them, analyze them, and save them in hundreds of different versions generated by the predictive speech module we used. A little over a hundred of those analyses deciphered comparable outcomes, so there's an extremely high confidence interval for the remainder of the population to bear the same conclusions. We felt you should listen to one of them because we've been told you may be able to clarify one of the voices on the enhanced files. Would you…could you please come with us to the sound pit so you can hear the audio and give us your take on it, ma'am?"

Olivia Knight rose from the table, signifying she was prepared to hear whatever they wanted. But she couldn't have been more wrong.

The groveling. The violence. And then the brief hopefulness followed ultimately by despair marked the emotions of both the victim and all the people who listened, after the fact, to the sounds of Lacy Knight being murdered.

Before the brutality commenced, four words were spoken to Lacy Knight. They were the last words she'd ever hear, and she responded with the last words she'd ever speak. But the four words spoken with such impudence and glibness before her last affirmation were the catalyst for all the tragedy and mayhem that would ensue.

Those four words were, "Are you afraid, Lacy?"

Beyond the torrent of anger those words elicited in Olivia Knight, they provided additional information to others.

They established for the first time that her killer was male. However, it was still indeterminate if he'd acted alone because a different woman's voice was captured in another file among the audio artifacts recovered.

The software analytics said the woman's voice calibrated as "insistent" and "directive." It was also determined that American English wasn't the female voice's first language because of its intonation with certain words. The possible origins of the female voice were also inconclusive. All the analytics could suggest was that the person hailed from either Southeast Asia or across the globe in Manchester, England, which made no sense. Because of the discrepancy between locations and the age of the recording device, the ancillary voice was also deemed "fallow."

They'd eventually identify who that female voice was, along with the person who had taunted Lacy before beating her to death.

They'd determine it was a golf club used to strike Lacy on the head repeatedly from behind as she knelt, facing in the opposite direction from them.

But that's not how Olivia Knight would find out who they were or anything else about how the event transpired. She'd confirm that information directly from the person who committed the crime.

An inadvertent benefit to law enforcement was that the sound file containing Lacy's murder made Olivia Knight realize there was no hope that her little girl was still alive. That meant they could scale back their operations as though they were looking for a hostage Whether or not whoever had committed the act would still try to collect a ransom remained to be seen.

But the federal government had taken the killer's option of walking away with a bag full of money off the table. None of the most astute agents believed it was a true ransom situation anyway. They thought it was someone merely trying to hurt Olivia Knight. But Knight, blinded by inextinguishable hope, had held on to the remote possibility that the person's motive was greed and that Lacy might still be alive. But that hope was gone now. And in its place festered something horrible.

The most shocking development, however, was the degree of emotion Knight expressed as she listened, which was negligible. And whether it was for her to shield her tears, after listening to the file, she turned her back on everyone huddled around the audio equipment in the sound pit.

After standing silently for a moment, Knight walked to the control center's central processing and data accumulation hub, about twenty yards away at the far end of the ballroom. A dozen flat-screen monitors were arrayed around the largest, configured to accept video signals from any processing station in the approximately ten-thousand-square-foot facility. Data ebbed and flowed on that screen, each time with the query "Expand?" appearing along its bottom margin.

"Yes," Knight said quietly, followed by, "Continue," a process which she repeated several times as the names and faces of all those people, those bastards who'd defiled her little girl, shuffled across the screen in sequence. They ranged from casual acquaintances to prominent figures in her life. Each image burned an imprint on Olivia Knight's soul, as did all of the data associated with each person.

As Knight's cathartic metamorphosis from heartbroken mother to vindictive, sub-human android took place, a federal agent joined her in the darkest section of the building. Knight wondered who he was as the man got close enough for his face to be illuminated by the monitors.

"Mrs. Knight?" the man started, "I know this is difficult. But I'd like to speak with you for a few minutes if I could, please."

A red and glossy-eyed Knight eventually turned around fully to look at the man who, unlike everyone else she'd dealt with from the government, hadn't flinched or acted afraid. On the contrary, everything about the man seemed forthright and deliberate as he spoke.

"Mrs. Knight, my name is Scott Pruitt, and I've been with the Drug Enforcement Agency for over twenty years."

Knight was compelled to send the man on his way because she believed he was just another well-wisher, sympathizer, or a redundant, incompetent nincompoop she'd foolishly enlisted to help find her daughter. But the agent seemed to realize the direction Knight's mind went, and he refused to miss his chance to speak.

"Mrs. Knight, I know you've spoken with many people like me and that they all tried to either make you feel better or give you false hope. And I'm sure you're not wanting to hear the same spiel, so I'll be brief. I'm also not going to try to tell you that there's a chance that Lacy is still alive because, as much as it hurts, a woman as smart and as worldly as you are realizes by now that's impossible."

After completing that monumental housekeeping chore and clearing the table for everything he was about to lay out, the DEA agent continued.

"Just as you are, but to a much lesser degree, I'm a person of influence, and I have a lot of pull, Mrs. Knight. I've got inroads with judges from courts beginning at the Federal District level down to state and po-dunk municipalities. I also have allies and operatives on both sides of the law."

Knight resolved that she didn't want to hear anymore, thinking the man had self-perceived delusions of grandeur, and she couldn't believe the unmitigated gall he showed by saying what he'd just said. Knight thought to herself: if he only knew to whom he was speaking.

But the DEA agent didn't give Knight a chance to dismiss him before he continued.

"Am I part of some clandestine arm of the government that operates without anyone's knowledge or assent? No. I'm not. What I am, Mrs. Knight, is a good old boy from Bell Buckle, Tennessee, whose Lord and Savior is Jesus Christ, and who knows how to say 'you're welcome,' and 'please' and 'thank you, kindly, sir or ma'am.' And that gets me a lot of my clout with these folks."

Sensational, Knight thought to herself. He's a Jesus freak, too.

"You don't have to say anything, Mrs. Knight. Fact is, I'd rather you didn't, ma'am. Just let me talk at you a little longer and tell you why all this is important to you right now."

Because of the scale of her suffering and her inability to get Lacy out of her mind, Knight settled in to hear what the man had to say, all the while thinking about her daughter when she was just a tot.

"Mrs. Knight, I'm sort of an anachronism within the DEA. Honestly, I don't believe many of my fellow agents' hearts are in their jobs anymore. I don't even think the DEA will exist in another ten or fifteen years. If it does, it won't be like it is now."

Knight thought the man spoke the truth. The DEA and men like the one talking to her were anachronisms. They were an antiquated institution dreamed up by people from the darkest of quarters who wanted to stay in power, and they used narcotics and controlled substances to do it. Knight's worldview related to drugs was quite different from the average person's. She knew how things worked. Drugs were used to control the masses, either directly or more subversively, through the rules of how they were dispensed. They had been weaponized to keep mankind in line.

The agent continued, but it was like a freshman student with a modicum of knowledge speaking to a tenured professor from an elite institution of higher learning—only the agent didn't realize it.

"There's a reason for that, though. Nowadays, everyone focuses on individual rights and personal freedoms, no matter how distasteful we older guys find that to be. Folks believe that if someone wants to waste their entire life away by shooting up or snorting their way through it, then that should be their business. They say we're the ones causing all the crime because if we'd just leave those people alone to do what they'd like, it would somehow magically end prostitution, violent crime, theft—hell, they even say tax evasion would be a thing of the past. Isn't that something?"

Pruitt showed signs of frustration as he spoke. He seemed embittered by what he was saying, but he managed to calm down and continue as Knight stayed quiet.

"I don't know if they're not right about that either, Mrs. Knight. I suppose it makes sense on a level. And I'm not saying that getting rid of the DEA wouldn't bring an end to drug dealers. But I am saying that it would redefine who they are and what that term means. It would give them credibility. It would sanction them to operate freely without prejudice. It may come as a surprise, but that's already starting to happen. And it scares the hell out of me, ma'am."

The agent made a tremendous stride with Knight by saying what he'd just said. At the very least, it showed that he'd considered that there might be a different vantage than the one generally accepted by most people in his position.

"For someone who's devoted their entire life to combatting the drug trade, let me just tell you that it's not always about locking people up to punish them for breaking the rules. If that were the end, then we wouldn't have received the funding we've received over the years. We wouldn't have had the endorsement and cooperation of every law enforcement agency in the country. And I'm not just talking about the feds either, Mrs. Knight. I'm talking about the foot soldiers—the fellas down in the trenches who witness firsthand what happens to people when they opt to live in an alternate reality rather than the one they were born into. What I'm trying to say is that there's a nobler cause here."

With that comment, the DEA agent appeared to drift into thought, likely remembrances that served as the foundation for the position he hawked.

"It's frightening, Mrs. Knight. You look at these people in the face, but there ain't nobody looking back at you. It's like they have no soul. Like they're just a hollowed-out piece of wood or something carved into a person."

Lacy's horrifying, ghostly visage appeared on the screen in the background as Pruitt spoke, but Knight couldn't bear to look at it.

However, it loomed over the Special Agent's shoulder as if imploring her to listen to the man.

"What makes that even worse is that some people profit from it. They reap those people's lives like harvesting a row of corn or something. And after their crop is dead and gone, they just replant the field and do the same damned thing, over and over."

Pruitt shifted emotions again. He seemed disgusted before taking an incredulous tone as he recounted what happened on his side of the law.

"My friends over at the Bureau know this, but they don't think it's any of their concern. Just like they don't think your daughter's abduction is any of *my* concern. They tell me that I need to stay in my lane and worry about busting any leads they give me for the people who were supplying your daughter with drugs."

Pruitt chuckled as he thought about that, but it was still clear that he was disgusted rather than humored.

"So, I say, 'Alright, Scottie. You heard the man. Get back to what you do best and leave the cotton picking to them.' I understand them. I honestly do. And maybe they're right," Pruitt offered before becoming dark again.

"But maybe they're not. Maybe it's just like anybody with some sense could see, and the people responsible for your daughter's death are right in front of us. It may be even worse than that, though. That's the part that scares me most, Mrs. Knight. Because maybe all these people with all this money have some of the same connections I do. And maybe I'm working against the clock to call in favors before they do."

The hair rose on the back of Knight's head, and her pulse quickened.

"Mrs. Knight, I don't know anything about your daughter other than what these folks have told me about her. I haven't studied Miss Lacy. I haven't done all the things I normally do yet. I'll do all of them, of course, because this case involves drugs. But I haven't yet. What I have done, though, is to make a preliminary inquiry into all those people you see on that screen over there. And while nothing surprises me, I believe that some of it might shock the hell out of you. But it's still information I believe should be available to you."

Pruitt began to restate some of his previous points, trying to keep Knight mindful of what had motivated him to come forward.

"Like I said, there's all this talk about protecting people's right to privacy, especially regarding the government. But not so long ago, if somebody did something to a man's daughter, the law would step aside and let that man take care of business. But it ain't like that anymore, Mrs. Knight. I'm telling you, it just ain't like that. Do you understand?"

Knight shared a moment with the agent where they met eyes and looked at each other honestly for the first time. As Knight looked into the agent's eyes, she saw a man doing his damndest to help her, although it was for reasons she couldn't understand. But those reasons resulted from what the agent saw when he looked back into Knight's eyes. And that was a heartbroken mother who'd never be the same again. A woman who'd never be at peace and one who'd awaken in the middle of the night, roused by nightmares about her daughter before becoming relieved, but only for a second. Then, that woman would once again reach the horrible conclusion that her daughter was gone forever.

"These folks with the Bureau are tunnel-visioned, Mrs. Knight. They've got in their minds, despite a mountain of evidence to the contrary, that your daughter's abduction doesn't have anything to do with all those demons you're looking at on that screen. They say that's too easy. They also say it doesn't make sense because the people I'm talking about wouldn't ask you for…what was it? Twenty-five million dollars? I was told that's a pittance to some of these people at the top, and the rest of 'em are doing well enough not to go to all the trouble. And based on the drug habits of a few of them, I'm inclined to agree."

It seemed that Special Agent Pruitt had been doing his homework despite downplaying all he'd done earlier.

"They fuel their lust with cocaine, Mrs. Knight. The expensive stuff, too. It's the kind of cocaine that gets diluted as it rolls down the hill and becomes something quite different that's ten times as addictive when it reaches the bottom. Not for these folks, though. No siree. The rules are different for them throughout the game."

Yes, Knight thought. This man did know a bit about how things worked. As that dawned on her, Pruitt mistook the expression on Knight's face as something else and became defensive.

"No, this isn't another shakedown. I don't want a damned thing from you, Mrs. Knight. Well, I suppose that's not entirely true. I'd like to see what every God-fearing man left in law enforcement would like to see. I'd like to see justice served. I'd like, for once, to see someone be punished for their sins without the ability to hide behind the law because when that starts happening, the law no longer works. Unfortunately, I don't think it's worked for a very long time."

The agent appeared to have a keen understanding of how things operated in reality. However, Pruitt's next move caught Knight off-guard.

"You know what we do when we want to get somebody? When we really want to get somebody? We break the law, Mrs. Knight. We don't break it ourselves, of course. We allow it to be broken by other people. But, you see, that's Bureau Policy, so it ain't against the rules."

No. This man was nothing like the person Knight thought she was when he'd sauntered up to her and began talking.

"I told you before that I had a lot of power, which I do," Pruitt said, "but it's not all because of my devilish good looks and incisive wit."

Pruitt smiled slightly, wanting to be light-hearted without sounding silly before continuing.

"Some of my power resides in the fact that I'm the Special Agent in Charge of this case as it relates to narcotics. I can pursue any information that comes to light throughout this investigation in any manner I want to pursue it, just so long as it has something to do with the laws governing controlled substances. I can confer some of that power on others because of my agency with the federal government and the powers bestowed upon me. All I need is a meeting of the minds with a judge, usually someone in the jurisdiction where infractions of the law have occurred."

The agent took a peculiar heading. It sounded to Knight as though he were trying to deputize her.

"That's where the good ol' boy part comes in. You see, I know all these judges around here. All of them. And if I tap the right one on the shoulder, I can utilize other people to obtain information about illegalities. The difference is that the person I choose can break the law, Mrs. Knight. They can do whatever they need if justice is served and if that's their only motive."

Pruitt paused to determine if Knight was buying anything he was saying because he wanted Knight to be clear that it was all true.

"That includes acts of violence, Mrs. Knight."

Knight's intrigue graduated to profound interest with those words from Pruitt. But she wanted to remain cautious to ensure she was hearing what she thought she was hearing. And Pruitt didn't waste any time confirming things for The OAK.

"We have a name for people like that. We call them 'OIAs' because their actions fall under the broad heading of 'Otherwise Illegal Activity.' And because I'm the SAC for narcotics in this case, I can make you an OIA, which would give you a permission slip to do just about anything you need or, in this case, see fit to do. It also means I can divulge information to you as you move down that road, all for your safety, of course."

Knight wasn't an idiot. Pruitt wasn't educating her on anything she didn't already know, and both knew it by then. Pruitt didn't realize, though, that Knight and her people had already served in the capacity Pruitt described to him, except she got paid billions to do it in places like Iraq and Afghanistan. She sure as hell didn't need the man's permission, either. But if the man telling her all these things thought he was acting on the side of justice and was privy to certain types of information, Knight believed he could be a powerful ally.

"Listen, Mrs. Knight. If these guys could do any better, they wouldn't be sitting here at your command center, and I can guarantee you that. But you must play by their rules as long as they're here. So, I suggest you tell them that the slumber party is over and it's time for them to go home. And you know what? They'll have to do it. They'll have to leave all these toys right here and go set up their own damned command center because they're here on your dime. They need to quit wasting your and other taxpayers' money and get back to work."

With that, Knight figured out she wouldn't have to work hard to recruit Scottie Pruitt to join team Knight—not like she'd had to do with others. This agent was already full on board and awaiting orders. More importantly, Knight believed Pruitt had intel that she urgently needed. As if affirming that notion, Pruitt ended his lobbying with a few heartfelt words.

"Then you can do as you will, Mrs. Knight. And in my heart, I hope that's the same as the will of the Lord."

An accord was reached that evening. And an alliance was formed. That alliance's intentions and course were directed toward Qadeshians. Just as Special Agent Pruitt implied, any fool could see that with that much evil going on, the death of a drug-addicted girl could certainly be among such an organization's watermarks. Qadeshians was a roost for the wealthy, powerful, beautiful, and simultaneously hideous group of monsters who had molested Lacy. They thought they could get away with it because their resources went beyond money. They had other weapons in their arsenal. Secrets. Information. Damning and damnable actions that were committed by those who gravitated to their organization. They believed all those resources made them infallible and beyond reproach.

But they were wrong.

Not all Qadeshians were power brokers, though. Some were simply perverse satellites of a demimonde that orbited the league of wealthy and beautiful miscreants. The league members used this fringe of people both for pleasure and to carry out their bidding.

Special Agent Pruitt had determined that fringe was where the answers they were looking for lay. And he was prepared to put as much information as he could in the hands of a woman who could do everything Pruitt was incapable of.

All the information Pruitt would provide Knight would prove unfortunate for myriad people within that depraved society of which he spoke.

While Agent Pruitt's hypothesis about Qadeshians was partially correct, it was the devil in the details that would bring the only opportunity to obtain justice for Lacy's death.

CHAPTER TWENTY-NINE

The motivations for murdering another person fall within only a few, albeit very broad, sometimes interrelated categories, as was the case in Lacy's murder. Most murders are also committed among the young, people within the range of adolescents to younger adults.

Anger, jealousy, vengeance, and personal gain are some of those motivations. Another such motivation is love, which, in one way or another, can be the spark for all the others.

On the night of her murder, Lacy's killer related several things to her. They did so in their own peculiar way, and the things they said were heavily prejudiced by a well-spring of their emotions regarding Lacy.

Her killer told Lacy there was no more room for her within Clint's life than there had been in anyone else's, including her parents. They claimed Clint was gay, and they showed her a Grindr account with his pictures and bio information. They'd say that Clint liked to get it on with men as much as she did. He wasn't visiting the USC campus because there was no reason for him to. He'd signed a scholarship months before, and whatever living arrangements for her they'd investigated together were a sham.

Her killer would awkwardly color Clint as a troubled, closeted young man who took every opportunity he had to be away from her so that he could indulge himself with other men. They told her that's what he'd been doing in Los Angeles.

Lacy's killer would insist that in an overdue and poetically just reversal of roles, Clint had used her like she used everyone else in her life. Making matters personal, they'd also challenge her to consider whether she'd used them just as she'd used all those other people.

They were all fabrications, and it hadn't been true. Clint wasn't gay. But for a moment, her killer caused Lacy to doubt herself, her relationship with Clint, and even Clint's sexual orientation.

Lacy's killer had a motive, but that motive hadn't been money. Not as they'd eventually suggest to Lacy's mother. Their true motive was purely self-indulgent. And though they attributed their actions to several other motivations, it was the power they enjoyed. The control. And the perfect storm for acquiring the ultimate power was the opportunity, the daring, and the facility to take another person's life.

After Lacy's killer presented their case to her a few more times, it became apparent to them that she was too far gone to accept the life they suggested she should lead, moving forward.

It angered the person. It made what they'd originally planned to do only as a failsafe that much easier. So much so that they were resolved long before their discussion with Lacy ended.

They were going to kill Lacy Knight.

Later on, Lacy awoke and realized the person had taken her to a place where no one was close enough to help her, so she began bargaining with her killer. She poured her heart out to them, pleading for them not to harm her. She told them they were wrong about her and that she had changed her life. She was no longer the person they'd claimed she was.

But her killer laughed at her. They told her she was foolish and insisted again that nobody loved her. And then her killer demanded that she have sex with them. She resisted at first, but then she gave in and did everything in her power to make it end as fast as possible, just as she'd learned to do in the past whenever sex wasn't to her liking. And after it was over, Lacy fell unconscious. She would sporadically fall into and out of consciousness for the rest of her life.

Though hurtful, Lacy reflected on everything her killer told her—that is, during the intervals she was awake because they kept Lacy drugged most of the time.

During those periods of introspection, Lacy realized she had no friends other than the types of affiliations she had in Qadeshians, and she felt foolish for having ever thought she could have sustained a relationship with Clint.

Then, pitifully grasping at straws, Lacy convinced herself that she did, too, have friends. She had Ardella and Jerome. They always encouraged her, telling her how pretty and smart she was and that she should live a better life than she did. She realized how positive and influential their wholesome existence together had been and that they were part of why she had changed.

After that, Lacy thought about Dr. O. He had been the main reason she'd changed, even if her relationship with him had started as part of another of her schemes. Through it all, she still believed he was her friend. She thought about how much he had helped her and made her identify all the wrong things in her life. Joshua Odom's influence over her had been the main reason she was different. She even confessed her love for the psychiatrist.

But when Lacy told all those things to her killer, they laughed long and hard about it. It was such a peculiar sight for her to see her killer express such an emotion that Lacy began to laugh, too.

However, the more Lacy looked into her killer's eyes as they laughed, she realized something was very wrong with them beyond the obvious. She realized they weren't laughing with her but *at* her. Her killer was mocking her, and she gave up hope after that.

But Lacy summoned the courage to make a final request. She told her killer that she wanted to sit and look out at the water one last time in the place she was able to find peace. She wanted to sit where she wouldn't rot away but that somebody would find her, and she wanted the people who found her to be her friends, Jerome and Ardella. She hoped they'd forgive her, but she hadn't wanted her body to be unrecoverable. She wanted a funeral. She wanted Clint to have a chance to tell her goodbye because no matter what the killer had told her, she said she knew that Clint loved her—even if he struggled with his identity.

Lacy begged and begged until her killer said they would grant her last wish.

Once they entered their final, solemn pact, her killer began their meticulously crafted plan. The segue to the final phase of that plan was to rape Lacy again, which they did several more times. Following that, they bathed Lacy. They placed her in a scalding hot bath, where she soaked for several hours. And though she wasn't aware of it, they drugged her again, just as they had drugged her in Gracie Bleu.

Lacy made a discovery during one of the intervals where her dosing had worn off. And that discovery potentially gave her the ability to be saved. But if she couldn't be saved, she was going to take her killer down with her. It was a last-ditch effort. A swing for the fences. But she made that desperate effort, and she took that final swing.

One of the last few times Lacy awakened, she was in a different place. She was bound again, though. So, she could move very little as she lay in silence most of the day. Night came and went a few times. She could discern that because of the way the light dispersed over the surface of whatever her killer had sheathed her in. And it was also clear that her killer continued drugging her intermittently throughout that period. Whatever they gave her, she imagined it was a mega-dose, for which she was thankful.

During those last hours and days of her life, Lacy had what she believed were visions. In those dreams, which were actually drug-induced euphoria, she spoke with several people in her life, both present and past.

The first person she spoke with was her father, Fab, who castigated her the entire time. He told Lacy what a foolish whore she'd been and that she was getting what she deserved. He said that she was worthless and had always been a burden to him, but also that he'd never loved her mother either and that she was wholly the product of lust on her mother's part.

Lacy spoke with Conchita and apologized again for abandoning her. Conchita didn't have the same voice she'd had in life. She sounded elderly. And she seemed afraid. She acted like something horrible awaited her and didn't want to get Lacy in trouble or expose her to whatever it was. Conchita ended their discussion by saying she couldn't stay any longer but wanted to comfort Lacy in her final hours. Conchita accepted Lacy's apology but told Lacy that she urgently had to be elsewhere. And then Conchita went away.

Lacy spoke with Prissy who was a much younger woman than she'd ever appeared before. She was also dressed femininely, wearing one of Lacy's short skirts and tops, and she was made over heavily with cosmetics, including deep, thick eyeliner. Prissy didn't say much, though. She didn't respond to any of Lacy's questions.

Instead, she just smiled and blew Lacy a kiss before walking up the stairwell of Lacy's home and disappearing into the hallway at the back of the landing.

Lacy spoke with Clint, who told her everything was alright, and he asked her if she was afraid. Then he told her that she shouldn't be afraid. He told her they'd be together soon. She begged him to stay with her in that place, but he told her he couldn't. He said it wouldn't be long before they were in paradise together for eternity.

The final person who communicated with Lacy was her mother. She was looking into the window of the place where she was, and she appeared angry. But Lacy didn't want to leave her that way, so she called out to her mother through the glass and asked her if she'd gotten the message she sent to her. Her mother couldn't speak for some reason, but she nodded. She also conveyed to Lacy through her expressions that she couldn't get into the building where she was, but she was trying to find a way in. She began to cry but assured Lacy she'd get to her.

Lacy could see helicopters flying in the background, and she saw soldiers marching in rows behind her mother. It made her feel safe and loved, but only for a moment. Because she had to tell her mother that she didn't have time. There was no more time to reach her, and she should go back to living her life and forget about her. She gestured toward a clock on the wall behind her and then looked back at her mother. Olivia placed her hand on the window and began to whimper before she broke down and sobbed.

Lacy cried, too. Then she tried to scream, but no one could hear her. Her mother was looking down at the ground outside and hadn't noticed that she'd begun to shriek. Fab came into the room and stood akimbo over Lacy as she lay on the floor.

As Lacy studied her father's expression, he slowly changed, as did the focus of his anger. It morphed into disdain for her. It was raw antipathy. And in that window of time, which was the final moments of her life, she watched as her father morphed into her killer. Except her killer was madder than they'd ever been. They pulled the shade to the window so that neither her mother nor the soldiers outside could see her anymore.

And that's when the pain came. But it wasn't pain as she'd known in the past. It was more as though her mind was letting her know that if she didn't act, her body was going to die. However, Lacy knew she couldn't do anything about it. It was impossible because she couldn't move. She couldn't move, and she couldn't shout, so the "pain" continued in several more waves until it stopped.

And then there was silence. And then there came blackness. And then DeLasi Marigold Knight was gone forever.

CHAPTER THIRTY

At nineteen years old, Jawan Pettway had done well for himself. And considering how the people around him usually got fat and all that had happened to them, it had been easy for him.

Those other folks sold everything from pills to powder, but if the streets didn't kill them, their bossman eventually would. That's how his brother, Dewayne, had died, even though part of that was his own damned fault. Dewayne had always come up short at the end of a week. But he became problematic when he started selling out in an hour with half as much to show for it. Dewayne wasn't around very long at all after that.

Jawan's job was simple, though. All he had to do was keep an eye on that white girl whenever she went places. He didn't have to do it all the time or every day or any shit like that. Just on the weekends. He had to make sure nothing happened to her and that she wasn't with anybody she shouldn't have been with.

Jawan thought the girl was just somebody's side ho. Somebody with a lot of money. Like, money to burn kinda' money. Because not only did she stay in Germantown, she drove a Mercedes and lived in a damned castle. You could barely see it from the road, and he didn't spend much time trying because those folks in Germantown didn't like people like Jawan around.

A redhead dude had come up to Jawan a year before and told him what the deal was. Jawan didn't even know if the girl was that man's ho, but he didn't think she was. He thought the redhead dude probably worked for some other dude and went back and told him whatever Jawan reported. And even though Jawan saw that ho do a whole lot of shit, he didn't share any of it. He kind of figured that if he told that redhead dude all she did, the other man would kill her, and he'd be out of a job. Shidd, he might kill Jawan, too, because she was something serious.

The girl bought all kinda' shit from people Jawan knew. He also knew that some of those dudes didn't even want her money as much as they wanted her. White girl built like that? No, man. They wanted something besides her money. They ended up getting both of them, anyway.

So, Jawan would just follow her, usually on the weekends or at other times once he'd learned her habits better. Besides, she didn't go too many places anyway. But Jawan wondered what that man that owned her would do if he knew how much powder she used or some of the other shit she was into.

Then she started seeing that boy. At the time, Jawan hadn't realized that boy was Ofay, though. Not until he found out at the movies that night. He thought he was just some goody-goody who always took that ho to church.

But once she got going with him, the redhead dude that paid Jawan stopped calling him as much. Jawan thought the other dude had probably figured shit out and that he was about to be done with her, and that pissed Jawan off. If he quit getting paid, he'd have to do what Dewayne did, and Jawan knew how that would end up. Either that, or he'd have to get on at McDonald's with Princess, and he sure as hell didn't want to do that shit, smelling like French fries every damned day.

That's when Jawan decided he was going to run that boy off. He was going to embarrass him in front of that ho, and then Jawan could go back to what he'd been doing, which was to keep a low profile. He was going to let her do what she did, too. She was going to be a chicken head for powder, and he was going to let her do laundry as much as she wanted to. Then he was going to keep getting that fat paycheck he got every week, and that would be the end of it.

But, again, Jawan hadn't known that boy was Ofay. Even though he hadn't known that, when that boy hit him, it wasn't even like getting punched. It was like that boy had lightning bolts for arms, and he shot one of them into Jawan's face before he'd even seen it coming.

It wasn't worth it. She wasn't worth it, and neither was the money he made if it would get him killed. So Jawan told the redhead dude he couldn't work for him anymore. He made up some shit about Princess being pregnant and moving to Mississippi and just let it go.

Jawan didn't hear from him for a while after that. Then the redhead dude started calling him again out of nowhere. Things were getting tight, so Jawan ended up answering the phone. After he met him at Princess' McDonald's, he hadn't been ready for what the redhead dude told him he wanted him to do, though. He didn't much know if he believed the guy at first, but the money he was talking about was phat money.

It turned out that the man had found out about everything the ho had done. At least, that's what Jawan figured had happened. Because the redhead dude told him he needed somebody gone that was inside. He didn't say it like that, but that's what he told him. A dude was inside, and it sounded like that man wanted him finished.

"What the hell you want me to do about that?" Jawan asked, "you want me to get locked up or some shit like that?"

Jawan laughed, but the redhead dude didn't. And he shocked the hell out of Jawan when he flatly told him, "Yeah. That's right."

Man, white folks were crazy. And when they wanted to kill somebody, they could do it some evil ass, weird ass ways, too. The guy they wanted dead had to be on his knees when it happened. And it had to be from behind with a shank. Redhead dude told him they'd wanted him to beat the fool to death, but he said they knew he wouldn't be able to do that for a lot of reasons.

"I'm going to show you how to incapacitate him first, Jawan. You're going to have to pay close attention to everything I tell you, though, because he's a big fella. Way bigger than even I am. And from what I understand, he's very strong too."

Jawan was told he'd be taken to the man's cell in the middle of the night. After they unracked the door, he'd have to move fast. It had to be get-and-go, and afterward, Jawan had to turn and walk expeditiously down the corridor.

But first, Jawan was going to have to be arrested. That had all been arranged, though. He would be pulled over in Germantown and detained for driving while suspended. At that time, they'd discover that he had outstanding warrants in Memphis for greater offenses, requiring him to be transported to the County. If he could do exactly as he was told in the way he was told to do it, he'd leave County the same night he finished doing what they wanted him to. Not only that, but he and Princess would be given new identities, a new place to live, and a shitload of money. They'd be able to move anywhere they wanted to, but they'd have to get out of Tennessee.

"Ok, den," Jawan told the redhead dude before slurping up the last bit of his McFlurry.

**

Simpson Winslow wasn't going to be able to last a whole lot longer. He was in too much pain. And he was exhausted from trying to push himself up from the floor. He'd never exerted any effort toward that end, but that's how his brain recounted things.

Nothing had hit right from the start. Simpson had dropped acid dozens of times before, but he'd never kicked things off by being nauseated like he had this time. That started a few minutes after he doused his tongue with the solution from the tiny Binaca bottle Jerry gave him, but it never let up.

Simpson hardly knew the guy, Jerry, but he should've known better when he saw Jerry's grimy fingernails as he handed him the LSD-infused tincture. Something Simpson would never know was that the solution had been saturated with 100 milligrams of strychnine along with the freehanded dose of acid. That was just enough to make him suffer mightily. And, when combined with the 150 microgram hit of lysergic diethylamide, it was as good as an ER doctor's signature on a death certificate or a psychiatrist's sign-off for the loony bin. Either way, Simpson Winslow was going away, and he wasn't returning.

The violence began shortly after they tied Simpson's wife, Bitsy, to the mattress under the guise of a bondage fetish, which is what Bitsy and Simpson had solicited the men for online. Then, once they finished with her, they started on Simpson—three against one. And even though it shouldn't have taken very long, they were slow about it on purpose.

Simpson could still see Bitsy's feet hanging off the bed. But they weren't moving anymore. He dreaded thinking about what her face must look like after taking that many blows to the head with a travel iron. He hoped they'd killed her for that reason. So, he just gave in and dropped his head back to the floor. And though he knew better, he held on with the hope that, whoever in the hell they were, they'd let him go when they got back.

That's not what was going to happen, though. And the more he thought about it, the more he realized they weren't returning. They'd left him and Bitsy in that motel room to die.

However, Simpson Winslow showed zero remorse even in the waning moments of his horrible, perpetually self-serving existence. That's because remorse for one's actions was Slave Morality. Simpson only ever observed Master's Morality. He believed he was an Overman, simultaneously imbued with privilege and absolved of any responsibility wherever his perverse leanings led him. Sometimes, it was to men. Sometimes, it was to women. Others still, it was little boys. Little boys dressed as Jack Horner in lacy pantaloons and long-plumed caps. What good little boys they'd been.

Evil. Just...evil.

After several hours passed, there was a shimmer of hope when the housekeeper rapped at the door. But by that time, Simpson could no longer move. He couldn't speak either. And the wave of spasms that rippled through his digestive tract made him want only to lie still and accept his fate—just whatever it took to make the pain stop.

God, kill me. Please, just kill me and be done with it.

But neither his pleas for death nor the hope of being rescued lasted long. Instead of entering the room, the maid moved on to the next one.

So, Simpson Winslow died that night, languishing in pain and having hallucinations that it was his father who had done all those horrible things to him and his wife. He called Simpson a sissy as he pounded the iron into Bitsy's face until his immaculate white tee was splattered with her blood. Then he and his two friends raped Simpson, just as had happened in the barn when he was a little boy. And when the last one finished and as his father looked on, they propped Simpson's head up so that he'd be able to watch Bitsy as she convulsed and eventually died.

***

Bonnie and Dubya were enjoying a traditional weekend for a change. No parties. No coke. No perverse, sacrosanct rituals. They'd decided to drive to their chalet in the Smokies for the weekend, and they listened to Nineties on Nine the whole way there in Dubya's Silverado.

It was so pretty outside that they'd thrown their bags in the truck bed because there was no chance of rain. The sky was a brilliant blue and clear as a glass countertop. And it was still cold that far north in Tennessee. All that meant was that they'd drink hot toddies instead of mint juleps while they looked out at the mountains.

Bonnie became restless as they sat on the deck, and she looked out at nature while Dubya stayed on his phone, using HuntStand to plot the map for his November whitetail excursion. So, she decided to take a little hit from the emergency sneeze she'd stashed in a tiny rolled-up sleeve in one of her prescription bottles. She'd known she'd eventually wind up bored, so she was glad she'd had the foresight to pack a little boost discretely.

"What? Huh?" Dubya asked, realizing that Bonnie was addressing him.

"G'on and put that damned phone down, Dubya. I told you we were g'on spend the weekend together, and you sittin' there playin' on that damned thing idn't what I had in mind when I did. That's not even fair, anyhow. How is tracking a deer down using an iPhone even huntin'? That ain't fair to the deer or turkeys or whatever y'all are huntin'," Bonnie complained.

"Alraght, Alraght, Bonnierabbit. Just let me—"

"No! Now, I'm not g'on tell you again to put that iPhone down, or I'll just make you take me to Knoxville, and I'll fly up to New York or down to Palm Beach while you sit here playin' Angry Birds or whatever!"

"Alraght, alraght. But just so you know, I hadn't played Angry Birds in, like, ten years or somethin'. Not since I was in line to pick up Holly at the schoolhouse. And I have an Android woman. It ain't no sissy-ass iPhone."

"Well...whatever," Bonnie acknowledged.

Bonnie sat quietly for a moment, trying to devise a way to make things peaceful again. It was best just to smooth things over with Dubya because when he went silent, he stayed that way for days. And she didn't want her whole damned trip ruined because she'd married a big baby. So, Bonnie brightened, took a pleasant tone, and made a suggestion.

"You want another buttered rum, sugar? I made a whole carafe full of 'em. I even used that God awful Captain Morgan's you like, so you g'on have to drink most of'em anyhow."

"Aw, shit, I reckon so. Here ya go," Dubya said, handing her the footed mug that remained steaming from his first drink.

Bonnie took the cup to the kitchen, where a carafe sat on the counter next to her Louis Vuitton travel purse. She'd take her first of three hits planned for the weekend and then pour Dubya his rum, hopefully making him more pliant as the day went on. She hoped the rum did the trick because he sure as hell wasn't getting any of her blow.

When she set his mug on the counter, she realized she hadn't brought hers. She'd just have to make another trip when she brought him his rum because she needed him to think the reason she was launched was because of booze. If he had any idea she'd brought cocaine with her, he would've pouted and sulked until she gave the rest of it to him.

Bonnie reached into her bag, and within moments, she'd unfurled the little envelope, set herself a line, and dragged it with the tiny, 24-karat bamboo chute that jingled among the other charms on the bracelet she wore.

That was some good stuff. That was Atlanta blow instead of that dirty shit from Memphis or New Orleans.

Bonnie looked at the beautiful porcelain slab backsplash that matched the island's countertop. She'd ordered the high-fired Jingdezhen surfaces from a company in China, and they cost more than anything else in the kitchen.

"For a damned cabin?" Dubya had protested at the time.

Bonnie felt vindicated now, looking at how beautiful the tile shone in her chalet's setting. The rest of the cabin was rustic, with wall-to-wall heart pine downstairs and Cedar in the loft. But the jaw-dropping galley was a miniature version of her magnificent kitchen back in Mississippi. It had all the same features and same-brand appliances, including Sub-Zero, Breville, and Miele.

Bonnie laughed, thinking about how she'd chastised Dubya for hunting with his phone because she was no better. She could prepare everything in their cabin, the only difference from home being that she didn't have to walk around as much because everything was almost within arm's reach.

Bonnie heard Dubya knock her mug off the rail before it cracked apart on the deck.

That was who she'd get to spend the weekend with. Cletus from The Dukes of Hazzard. She imagined Dubya would've been much more careful if he'd known what he'd dished out for that Baccarat

Harcourt coffee set. She stormed onto the deck to cut loose on Dubya for being such a klutz.

"Dubya Cotton Dupree! I just brought that set back with me from Paris at Christmas! And you can't even hold onto a Goddamned coffee cup because you're too busy…"

The pain that stabbed the side of Bonnie's head was so severe that she reached up to massage it with her left hand. In doing so, Bonnie finished off the second mug in the set she'd waited for months to arrive, and she heard it shatter, its shards mixing with the one Dubya had dropped.

Bonnie knew what it was. She'd felt the sensation before. It was "coke nose" from all the stuff she'd snorted over the years, but it had never been so acute. Then, Bonnie realized she was falling forward. She was plunging right toward Dubya, whose mouth hung open while his eyes looked glazed, staring out over the distant mountainsides. She got a good look at him before her head planted in the center of his chest. Then, the last thing she saw was the Rolex Submariner on his wrist and the blood that trickled down the back of his arm to his fingertips before falling, a drop at a time, onto the pressure-treated deck planks.

A tad more than two thousand meters away, Clemmie said, "Bruno, RTB. HVT acquired," before he stood up, dusted off his britches, and started walking to the 1998 Ford Ranger he'd driven to his location. Then, he, too, felt a sting on the side of his head, which sent him into hysterics. He frantically slapped at his face and head, saying, "Got-dang ants! I fahkin hate 'em!"

***

A full third of the Qadeshians of Memphis died in the following days and weeks. Two of them would be killed during a holdup at a rural gas station in Mississippi. There was a car accident, a bar fight, an accidental electrocution. Another of them would die in a

Brussels hospice seventeen days after ingesting a radioactive isotope that had been sleeved into his consommé. His wife hadn't traveled to where he was because she'd died in the throes of what they all loved doing so much. But the cocaine her suitor put on his Trojan Magnum wasn't the good stuff from Atlanta. It was some nasty God-awful shit cut with Palmolive crystals in South Memphis—that and a little cyanide. So, she'd gone into cardiac arrest as she gasped for air and experienced excruciating abdominal pain.

The fate of one of the Qadeshians who died had already been determined before the others checked out. Luke Millard was fumbling in the engine room of his Sea Ray Sundancer when it abruptly exploded behind his riverfront home. Unlike the other executions, that one had been courtesy of a wily, impish Prissy Tillman, who'd crawled into the engine compartment on a late winter night and tinkered, using the knowledge about engines she'd gleaned from her dear departed father. The only divergence from her plan was that Prissy could not watch from a distance as she'd done with that buffoon, Terrence Marvin.

Prissy loved to watch.

Several other Qadeshians were marked, hunted, and eliminated one at a time by either full-time employees of Olivia Knight or thugs who'd been paid handsomely for completing their assignments.

Qadeshians never held another event in Memphis. Instead, they promptly and predictably disbanded in the wake of what their members believed were acts of vengeance. The hotel would be razed, and a school would be erected in its place. It would be named the DeLasi Marigold Knight School for wayward girls, where children learned English literature and Algebra in Dora Hall and The Knight Building, respectively, before they'd end their day with a mandatory study hall in the library, affectionately known as the "Book Bag."

Law enforcement—all law enforcement—knew what had happened. A fool could've figured that one out. But they didn't do a damned thing about it. The FBI was already out of the picture. Still, every Memphis citizen who died under mysterious circumstances for over a year was checked against a list of names before a single resource was expended on investigations by anyone from a detective to the fire chief. It was a cleansing of sorts. A purge.

***

"Josh! Josh! Oh my God, Josh! Please answer your phone! Please, baby! Please! I'm going to hang up and call back! Please answer your Goddamned phone! Oh baby, oh baby, I'm in trouble. I'm in so much fucking trouble right now! I think they want me dead, baby! I can't tell you everything right now, but I swear to God I will! I'll tell you everything! They want me dead, too! They're going to kill me, Joshua! They killed Stephen! They killed him! And they're going to kill me! I'm…I'm…I'm near a cabin off Dantzler Road! It's way out here, baby! It's way out here by the creek! Just tell them it's at the end of a long road uh, gravel street, uh, pathway! Pppp-please! Please! Just look at 360 on my phone…at your phone…on your phone and ccc-call the police! Call the police, baby! I'm here! I'm here! Please send the police baby!!! I'm going to…Oh Fuck! Oh Fuck! Oh my God oh my God! He heard me! He heard me! He's coming! Oh my God nooooo!"

<To review your voicemail, press one. To erase and re-record, press two. To send a text message with your voicemail, press three. If you're satisfied with your message, press pound, or just hang up.>

CHAPTER THIRTY-ONE

It was a major decision, but Josh believed he'd reached the right one. It was time to stop putting others first and live for himself. Besides, if anyone was to blame for everything he'd been through, it was Gil Wallace. And though Josh's concern for Gil's family lingered, he couldn't change anything that had happened. Gil was stabbed to death in jail, and his son, Clint, had fallen prey to his anger to the point it cost him his life.

Josh still believed that justice had been served in some elaborate way. You just didn't do the things Gil had done without expecting consequences, and fate finally caught up with him. He'd paid the ultimate price because of his lifestyle.

Lacy Knight had wandered into the spotlight just long enough to be trapped, abused, and then discarded because of the dictates of an intolerant and hypocritical society. However, if Gil had not been the person he was, the girl might still be alive. Instead of molesting her, he could have mentored Lacy. She may have even found her way without Josh's assistance. Who knew?

As Josh turned into his parking spot at the office, he thought about Liza and how happy she'd been when he told her he was taking a sabbatical and selling his practice and the building. Then, just as he got out of his car, his phone started ringing. He looked down to see a still photo of Liza and Scout staring back at him from his phone.

"Speak of the Devil," Josh laughed as he strolled toward the building.

He declined Liza's call because this was *his* time. He knew how happy she was, which is all he imagined she was calling to say. So, Liza would have to leave him alone for a while as he finished packing before calling the realtor to let them know he was out of the building for good.

Josh inserted his key, thinking about it being the last time he'd enter his building. He was annoyed but not completely surprised to discover he'd absentmindedly left it unlocked.

"Dr. Odom," Josh heard a woman's voice say as he walked through the small vestibule leading to his office.

It startled Josh so much that he gasped and stumbled backward before seeing Olivia Knight sitting in his chair.

Once he got over the initial shock, Josh was agog. He'd already come to terms with the fact that his patient had been the daughter of one of the most influential people on the planet. That had happened a while back. But Josh was still starstruck when he saw the woman sitting only a few feet away.

Knight rose and moved toward him with her arm extended. She shook Josh's hand before sitting in the overstuffed chair where her daughter used to relate all her darkest secrets and noblest aspirations. The irony was chilling. considering the turn their discussion would eventually take.

"I'm sorry, Dr. Odom. I apologize for the unannounced visit, and I hope you don't mind, but I've wanted to talk to you for some time now. I suppose you realize I'm Olivia Knight."

Josh struggled, trying to find something to say, but Knight didn't allow him to speak before she continued.

"I realize that I invited myself in. But you left your front door unlocked. Besides, I can't afford to sit in public places for very long. I would've aroused a police officer's suspicion if I were loitering outside. And God help me. I've certainly seen enough of them over the past few months. I hope I'll never have to deal with a police officer again."

Josh was still unable to speak. He felt he was in the presence of someone like a President or a high-powered celebrity. In fairness, Olivia Knight's name was frequently on the tongues of Presidents and celebrities, so Josh was awed to have such a woman sitting in his office.

"Uh, Mrs. Knight...how did you...I mean, why are you, that is to say, what can I do for you, ma'am?" Josh finally babbled.

Knight flashed a pleasant smile before continuing.

"Please, Dr. Odom. Have a seat and entertain me for just a little while. I won't keep you long. I'm in town for the last time because I don't plan on ever returning to Memphis. I have a few things I'd like to tell you. But then I'll leave you alone forever. I assure you, Dr. Odom."

"Of course, Mrs. Knight! Please, make yourself at home, by all means!" Josh insisted.

Josh felt like a lackey, but he couldn't help himself. After all, Olivia Knight was sitting in his office. It was an opportunity he'd thought he'd never get. He wanted to tell Knight so many things about Lacy. He felt he owed it to her and that it might help the bereaved mother of his patient.

"I hate to seem forward, but would you mind terribly if I shared a drink with you, Dr. Odom? I'm not a big drinker at all. But I've found it can be a wonderful lubricant for awkward social interactions, which all of mine tend to be," Knight said with a delicate laugh.

You know what, Josh thought to himself, *why the hell not?*

"Mrs. Knight, I'd be honored to have a drink with you, ma'am," Josh said, "but I don't have anything here in my office."

Josh stopped talking, though, as he watched Knight remove a crystal flask from her inside coat pocket.

"Is scotch alright, Dr. Odom? It's from a Speyside distillery I own. It's quite luxuriant," Knight said.

"That's a beautiful piece, Mrs. Knight," Josh acknowledged, referring to the brilliant red crystal and pewter flask. "And, yes, scotch would be lovely. Thank you, ma'am. Let me get us both a glass," Josh added before scurrying to one of the open boxes he had left to tape shut.

Knight wasted no time filling both glasses before handing one to Josh, offering the ancient Scottish toast, "Slainte Mahth," and nodding.

Josh had promised Liza that he would quit drinking. And he'd made good on that promise since Gil's funeral, which was the longest stint he'd gone without drinking in years. But he took a healthy swig of the scotch to appease the commanding yet melancholy woman he pitied so much. As Josh swallowed, Knight began to speak.

"I suppose you're wondering why I've come to meet with you today. I know I'd be curious about such a thing."

It was a peculiar setting and an even stranger moment. Josh was talking to The Oak amid the packed boxes and tarpaulins the painters had brought in a few days before.

"I have to be honest, Mrs. Knight. I assumed you'd been informed about my role in Lacy's life as her psychiatrist. I was compelled to come forward and share with the police everything that I knew about her because of the relationship I had with her as her doctor. I believed they were moving in the wrong direction at the time."

Knight smiled at Josh again as though she appreciated what he told her as he went on.

"So, it doesn't come as a surprise that you've reached out to me. And I'm glad you have. It's a chance for me to share some of Lacy's feelings with you. It also allows me to give you what I hope will be some comforting news about her, even if comfort seems impossible right now."

Knight slowly blinked, and her smile disappeared for a moment before becoming brighter than before.

"You're a kind man, Dr. Odom. You're very kind and sensitive. And, yes, it would be a comfort to hear anything positive about Lacy right now."

Knight stalled for a moment, staring at the floor, and Josh quickly took up her slack, wanting to keep the conversation going.

"You know, Lacy loved you very much. I can't lie and tell you she wasn't a little resentful of your inability to be an active part of her life. But I don't stand in judgment of that. However, I want you to know she loved you. She just wished you were around more."

"Did she, Dr. Odom?" Knight asked as Josh detected a tinge of emotion in her voice, "did she honestly say that?"

Although Lacy hadn't said such things, Josh believed she felt them and would have said them had she been given the opportunity. So, he exercised an artful license when he answered Knight.

"She did, Mrs. Knight. I'd grown quite close to Lacy before we started down this horrible road we're on now. I dare say I was somewhat of a surrogate father figure to Lacy. I have so many insights and know so much about your daughter, Mrs. Knight. Perhaps even more than you know on certain subjects. I'm telling you that because there's a wealth of things to reveal about Lacy whenever you feel the time is right. I hope you'll let me give you my contact information when you leave today. I don't do the whole social media business. But I have an email address. I have a cell number. I even still have a home phone, if you can believe that or not," Josh said with an uneasy chuckle.

Knight laughed back a bit, and Josh interpreted that as an attempt to show her human side. Knight didn't immediately respond, so Josh continued, careful not to come across as edgy or nervous.

"I understand how you must feel, Mrs. Knight. All the anger and the emotion running through you now seem overwhelming."

"Truly?" Knight asked before Josh rapidly moved to expand on what he meant.

"I know of what I speak, ma'am. One of the negative aspects of being a psychiatrist is that you must train yourself to listen to others talk about their misfortune, which can be horrible at times. And when they do, that always has the potential to bring you down. But it also gives you valuable insights into human behavior. Incidentally, how they respond to things you've never experienced affords you the objectivity to see what's good about their approach to dealing with adversity and what's not so good. I believe that gives us, as psychiatrists, a distinct advantage in dealing with our own struggles."

Knight piped up with another compliment, which was something she seldom did.

"You're an insightful person, Dr. Odom. I can't think of a better word to describe you. Insightful."

"Thank you, Mrs. Knight. I appreciate that, and it means a lot to hear that, coming from a woman like you," Josh said before allowing Knight go on.

"But I must confess that I am angry, Dr. Odom. I've been an angry person my whole life. I've also been a very vengeful person at times. God said that 'vengeance is mine.' I suppose he said that for a reason. And I think it's because people don't employ vengeance very well. They tend to go overboard. They sometimes cut into the quick, so to speak. I've been guilty of that, too," Knight said.

Josh started feeling uncomfortable. He didn't know why, but the sensation that came over him was unpleasant as Knight continued.

"Sometimes, vengeance tears through the seams of justice. It takes more than its due, potentially harming the innocent."

Knight was speaking so bizarrely, and Josh didn't like her trajectory, whatever it was. Yet he waited patiently for her to finish.

"Some people believe the two concepts—vengeance and justice—should be distinct. But I believe those people are ideologues, and they're simply relinquishing something that is rightfully theirs to a supposed higher power. One that's wiser. More temperate. Saner."

Josh's uneasiness gave way to being impressed with Knight's reflection. She seemed genuinely contemplative as she spoke.

"I'm what I guess the kids would call 'old school.' You see, I believe more along the lines of what Moses offered in Leviticus. If someone harms you, you should be able to harm them the same way. They take from you, then you take from them. They strike you, and you strike them back. That's more in keeping with the physical principles of the universe. Don't you think, Dr. Odom?"

It made Josh ill to consider what a woman like Knight was capable of doing to the person who killed Lacy. And whatever those actions might be, the woman undoubtedly alluded to them as she spoke. Then Knight said something that clarified that for Josh.

"If you kill someone I love, I kill someone you love," Knight said before chuckling, "sounds a tad Machiavellian, doesn't it?"

Though Josh had been made uncomfortable and placed in the same curious predicament Knight's daughter had put him at their first meeting, he also felt challenged. He wanted to try and help Knight. But it nagged at him whether he would feel obligated to inform the police if harm should befall someone Knight had believed was responsible for Lacy's death. That outcome hadn't been ideal the last time he tried it. Nevertheless, he engaged Olivia Knight, attempting to answer her question.

"In psychological terms, we refer to that as catharsis, Mrs. Knight. Catharsis describes behaviors resulting from profound, negative emotional influences. Some believe it's a defense mechanism that relieves the mind from the effects of those emotions. It's also a means to discover repressed or hidden feelings. Clinically speaking, that can be true to some extent. However, the long-term effects of those behaviors are sometimes more adverse than whatever prompted the behaviors to begin with. That's the point at which morality enters the discussion. How moral is the person who exhibits those behaviors? Will they truly find refuge from those emotional impacts, or are they merely postponing dealing with them? A moral or decent person could be plagued by whatever retaliatory measures they take. A less moral or immoral person might act unfettered by any consideration of right or wrong. Those people tend to be indulgent people, Mrs. Knight."

Josh didn't think his intellectual posturing was doing much good. Still, he hoped it might give Knight pause before acting toward someone innocent of wrongdoing. It was the only reason he'd said anything back to Olivia Knight.

"Your education and your professionalism are inspirational, Dr. Odom. You truly know what makes people tick, to put it in layman's terms," Knight assured Josh.

"As we're communing here today, I'd love to have your counsel on some of what we're discussing and some of the decisions I'm facing as I move forward. I will pay you for that counsel, so I don't even want to hear any objections to that."

This woman didn't waste time with anything, Josh thought.

"Well, I hadn't anticipated that, Mrs. Knight. But I understand. I'm receptive to that if you think I can help you in any way. I'm also honored that you feel that way, having just met me. I'm fine with your paying me to listen, and I even think that might be the most prudent route for such a discussion. Sometimes, my patients mistake our relationship as being collegial when, in fact, it's nothing like that. I want them to get better, but I do so because it's my job. That doesn't mean I'm not a caring person because I am. But just like a surgeon, dentist, or any other medical professional, my duties as someone's physician have nothing to do with my feelings for them. So, if we predicate our discussion with acknowledging that..."

Knight interrupted Josh, and she seemed a little disturbed. It was as though she wasn't used to someone talking to her as much as Josh was.

"As strange as this statement sounds, money is worthless to me, Dr. Odom. If you'd like to know the truth, it holds no meaning to me, and it never really has. Money is a facilitator for me, that's all. I've amassed a lot of it. And that empowers me to do much of what

I do. But it doesn't motivate me to do anything. It's kind of like gasoline in a car. If you want to go across town, whatever is waiting for you over there is what motivates you. Not the want for gasoline—unless something is wrong with you!" Knight snickered.

Knight's ability to laugh under the circumstances was another positive sign for Josh. He briefly thought back to Prissy Tillman's first day when he'd made her laugh before Knight began talking again.

"But the more gasoline you have, the farther you can go, right? And the farther you can go, the more your ambitions to go to other places and do other things will be amplified. Some women ride around town all day, visiting their friends or running errands, and that's their only motivation. Others want to protect their families, but to do that, they must get up each day, work, and earn a living. That's what motivates them. Gasoline is just a part of what facilitates that. And using that analogy, I'd like you to understand that that's all money has ever been to me."

Knight's happiness appeared to subside throughout her statement.

"But I digress. And if I start to do that again, please pull me back on the road, Dr. Odom. I imagine you're good at doing that as you've had to listen to people ramble on the couch or in whatever position they rest as you speak with them."

Josh laughed, "No. As you can see, there's no couch. A lot of rambling, I'm afraid. But no couch!"

Josh made Knight laugh another time before allowing her to change topics.

"You know, I have a son that rambles a lot. He doesn't mean to, though. It's not within him to bleed on other people or blather about things when he gets afraid. He speaks his mind and only acts on his basic needs. While there's some variety within that range, it remains fundamental. He likes music, Dr. Odom. He likes rap music. And, like his mother, he loves Takis. In fact, if you put him in a big house and ensure he has an ample supply of Takis and plenty of equipment in a sound studio to record his rhymes, then he's pretty much alright. I only say that because that's essentially what I've done with him. You see, he suffers from a condition..."'"

Josh threw caution to the wind and stopped Knight before she said anything else.

"I don't mean to head you off, Mrs. Knight. But I already know a lot about Tristan. Lacy told me about him and her relationship with him."

Josh became distracted after interrupting Knight. His ethics had been challenged to their limits by his association with Lacy Knight, so he struggled with them to point Olivia Knight in a direction that Josh had considered the whole time. He didn't have anything to support it, but he still labored with whether to suggest what he was thinking as a possible scenario for what had happened to Lacy. He'd tacitly made that suggestion to the police, hoping they'd pursue it as a lead. Then, he just assumed they'd dead-ended on that likelihood and moved on.

But it seemed an opportune moment to reintroduce the idea that, perhaps, Tristan was responsible for Lacy's yet-to-be-solved murder. Maybe it was the right time to have that discussion except to make it meaningful. However, Olivia Knight closed the door to that option as quickly as it had opened.

"I already know where your thoughts have gone, Dr. Odom. I'm ashamed to admit that I considered the same thing for a time, and I'll share the reasons for this with you shortly. But I can say unequivocally that Tristan didn't have anything to do with Lacy's murder. And it still troubles me that I could've ever thought that about him. Especially since Tristan is my son."

Damn, Josh thought to himself. That would've made perfect sense to anyone. But if Olivia Knight said that wasn't the case, then Josh imagined she'd gone to great lengths to ensure it wasn't. Women like Olivia Knight didn't operate on assumptions because they didn't have to.

"Do you have a family, Dr. Odom?" Knight asked.

Josh was silent momentarily and took on a puzzled expression before answering.

"I have a wife. I don't have any children, but I have a wife. We'll have been together for twenty-five years this July," Josh said with a faint smile.

Josh figured that Knight probably noticed his wedding band and that she was simply making conversation. Or, worse, she might be building toward some banal nugget of wisdom that she wanted to share with Josh.

Josh was right. And Josh was wrong.

"I've only married one time, and that was to Lacy's and Tristan's father, Fab. I'm sure you've seen him somewhere in the media before. I'm sure you know all about him from talking to Lacy, for that matter—much more than you could glean from his public persona. Yet they're both probably accurate assessments of the kind of man he was. Excuse me. Is. The kind of man he is, I meant to say."

Josh wasn't necessarily alarmed by Knight's misstatement. However, it made him wonder whether Lacy's father could have been a suspect in what had happened to her. But he immediately dismissed that as illogical because he wouldn't have needed to ransom Lacy for anything. Not if, as Knight had offered, what the media said about him was true. He'd become a wealthy man in his own right. Then again, he'd also been depicted as a lecherous hound dog who'd squandered that fortune away on partying and as the result of poor decision-making. He'd taken Olivia to court several times over the years regarding palimony for their unspecified "young children," whose identities and even their genders and ages the Knights had managed to keep secret over the years. It hadn't appeared to have done them much good, though.

Still, Josh doubted Fab ever popped up on the police's radar once.

"I haven't had the experiences with my husband I imagine you've had with your wife. I couldn't trust him like I'm confident you trust your wife, right?" Knight asked.

Okay. Now that was weird, Josh thought. Why was Knight making presumptions—with confidence—about anything concerning the relationship he had with Liza?

"I really can't speak to that, Mrs. Knight. I don't know enough about your relationship with your husband, but I can't imagine it was ideal, or you'd probably still be with him, wouldn't you?

Knight laughed.

"Dr. Odom. You don't have to be diplomatic or spare my feelings. I know what you and everybody else think about Fab, and you're all correct. Lacy's father is a man whore. No, let me correct that. Lacy's father is a man slut. He used to be a whore, but now he's just a slut."

Josh grew uncomfortable, sensing the rage building in Knight. He wanted to steer her away from such feelings.

"I don't know what you'd like me to say about that, Mrs. Knight. Again, I never met the man."

Knight acted surprised.

"What? Lacy never said that about him to you before? She never told you about what a slut her father was?"

She said 'was' again, Josh thought briefly.

"No, it never came up. She did tell me that she didn't believe Mr. Knight was a very good father. She said that…"

Knight cut him off by raising her voice, lowering her pitch, and taking a vicious expression.

"Hold on a second there, Dr. Odom. Just hold on a second right there. He wasn't a bad father. The fact is, he wasn't a father at all! Do you understand? He positioned himself in the media as a victim because I was incapable of being there for my children, but that was something we'd accepted because of my career. And Fab didn't have a problem with it back then. No, he didn't. Remarkably, he didn't even have a problem when we began noticing that Tristan would be a special needs child. But on his second at-bat, when I agreed to have another baby with him, and it turned out to be a little girl, he suddenly became the put-upon, long-suffering dad who was asked to sacrifice his career—such as it was—to raise children. And I didn't even ask much of him then! But he made damned sure that I paid for it. Every step along the way!"

In milliseconds, Olivia Knight had undergone a transformation on Josh—or perhaps, 'succumbed' to one may have been more accurate. Josh believed it was a momentary glimpse into what kind of a woman Olivia Knight could be, and it scared him. Those eyes and the fire behind them. And the tone of voice she took at the drop of a hat. They were those of an entirely different person, and it was so severe and impressive that Josh squirmed in his seat momentarily.

You think of weird things when you're frightened. And at that moment, Josh remembered with crystalline precision that he *had* locked the front door to his office the last time he'd been there. That realization escalated his fear even more. Knight was changing right in front of Josh.

"Mrs. Knight, I..." Josh began.

"Nope. My bad. I'm sorry, Dr. Odom. You see? I told you I had a bad habit of getting off the subject. But let's just let sleeping dogs lie because I'm enjoying talking to you. It makes me feel good to get all these things off my chest. But we won't tarry over that subject any longer, okay? It's all in the record books now."

What in the hell did that mean?

"We were talking about your wife," Knight said, "I'd love to hear more about her, Dr. Odom. I'd like to do just as you said you've done, and maybe I can objectively learn from how you've handled things during your marriage. Tell me all of it, too. The good stuff. The bad stuff. I'd love to hear it all if you're comfortable talking about it. That's only fair, isn't it? I mean, Lacy has told you all about me, I imagine. So, I'd feel much more comfortable knowing more about you and your wife."

"Mrs. Knight, I'm not sure how healthy that exercise would be. I just don't..." Josh began nervously.

"Awww, come on, Dr. Odom. We're friends. And I guarantee you whatever you tell me won't leave this room."

Josh continued, but he remained ill at ease.

"It's just...I mean, I don't know where to start. That's a complicated subject to relate to someone."

Knight began nodding before Josh finished speaking.

"You're right. It is. So, why don't we do this as a Q&A? How does that sound? I can ask you questions about your wife, and you can answer them—but only to the extent that you feel comfortable doing so."

Knight almost seemed like she was mocking Josh and toying with him. Josh wanted to be patient, though. He realized the stress she must be under and how something like having a child murdered would affect a woman—particularly a woman like her. So maybe he'd been too quick to attribute her behavior to dissociative identity disorder.

Olivia was a winner. She stopped at nothing until she won. But someone had defeated her, and there was no remedy to them having done so. The spoils of the game they played with her was her daughter's life, so there'd be no rematch. And it might cost the woman her sanity, too, from what Josh could tell.

"Okay. I understand your hesitance in speaking on the matter. So, you don't want to answer any questions. Got it. Well, why don't I share a few things I know about Liza instead?" Knight said, widening her eyes and bouncing her eyebrows when she whispered Liza's name.

Knight saying Liza's name that way sent a chill up Josh's spine. Because it meant that she'd done much more by way of discovery than she'd let on to doing. Why hadn't she just said that, to begin with?

Josh was about to find that out. He was also about to find out a whole lot of terrible things about his wife. They would be things that would haunt him for the rest of his and things he'd never get over until he lay dying. Because Liza, as it turned out, wasn't who he thought she'd been.

Josh didn't know if she'd never been that person or if life had changed her into who she was. But what Josh was about to discover was that Liza was, without a doubt, a lying, manipulative, self-involved, and very greedy whore, just like Fab Knight. And Josh would curse himself for not having figured that out by himself.

Knight produced an iPad mini from her coat and placed it on Josh's desk, much the way the pathologist had done with her months before when he'd shared his terrifying hypothesis about Lacy with her.

From the moment Olivia Knight pressed play on the iPad mini until Josh reached the end of the video collage, he suffered greatly because of all he saw.

Josh first witnessed Liza in a compromised sexual position. She wore the garb and makeup of an Egyptian queen, complete with an elaborately embroidered corset and a gold headdress. As striking and beautiful as it made her, the acts she performed while dressed that way demoted her from a regal stature to that of a street whore.

Men groped her body as she seemed to go limp from whatever sensation she experienced. That is until one of the men took a handful of her hair and redirected her head towards his midriff.

Josh began noticing his pulse and the strength of his heart beating just before he had to acknowledge that he was losing control. He was going to that horrible place he went to sometimes, mainly when he'd been off his medication.

However, he was in for a lot more punishment—a whole lot more. He would never truly understand how or why Knight was making the disclosures she made to him that morning. But the band played on, and so did Liza.

In the subsequent clip, Liza wasn't dressed as an Egyptian princess. Instead, she wore the black blouse Josh had bought her from E-Luxury the previous Christmas. But instead of its neckline tantalizingly dipping just above her breasts as it was designed to be worn, it was unbuttoned. Either side of it feathered back as two masculine hands began cupping her breasts, and a man's head that dwarfed her own leaned down into the picture. She reached backward and caressed the side of the man's head with her right hand, turning her face a bit to kiss him while keeping her eyes tightly shut.

The man in the video Josh watched in supreme disgust was Stephen. He began to kiss Liza. They kissed more deeply as Stephen turned her around to face him and laid her back gently on a bed. Then, the cameraman's voice began providing explicit instructions to Stephen, who obediently carried them out as they were given. Even in his crazed mental state, Josh recognized the cameraman's voice as Gil's.

Josh reached the point where he could barely see any of it because the blood vessels in his eyes were so exerted that it compromised his vision. Then, he started noticing his pulse again, and it felt as though his heart was going to explode out of his chest.

Suddenly, something strange happened to Josh. There was no immediate accounting for it, but his pulse began to decelerate, and his heart slowed from a booming thunderclap to a gentle thump. It fluttered a bit, and he realized he probably had an arrhythmia because of all the strain his heart had undergone from a staggering adrenaline rush in such a short time frame. Nevertheless, his heart slowed. It crawled. It felt like it might stop, and Josh wondered whether he might be entering cardiac arrest.

Josh's mouth had grown parched throughout the past few minutes as he sat speechlessly while Liza was wrung out like a dishrag on the iPad screen. But suddenly, saliva began to flow, so much so that a long strand of thick, syrupy spit had stretched from his mouth to his lap. He reflexively slurped it up and immediately locked eyes with Olivia Knight, who sat across from him with a charming smile as if acknowledging Josh's condition. Almost as though she knew exactly how he felt.

"I tell you, Dr. Odom. There are some brilliant people in this world, and then there are some foolish, trusting souls. They are so foolish that they upload things to clouds as though it's some sort of impenetrable fortress manned by corporations standing guard over it. Oh, I suppose that's somewhat true. If it weren't, those same idiots wouldn't say 'yes' when prompted online by Facebook or Instagram or companies like mine, Fief, as they're asked to allow access to all their photographs. All their videos. All their memories. And, sometimes, all their evil, perverse deeds. Want to know who one of Fief's eight million subscribers is, Dr. Odom? Excuse me, *was* Dr. Odom? Was. One of them was the headmaster of a school. But it turns out he was a different kind of headmaster on top of that. They referred to him as a high priest in a private organization he belonged to. I think you know to whom I'm referring, don't you?"

Yes. Josh knew who Knight was talking about. And he knew *what* Knight was talking about. It further made Josh realize that every bit of insecurity, apprehension, and mistrust he'd had in his marriage to Liza was wholly founded. Among the emotions the barrage of imagery and words elicited in Josh was regret. He regretted not trusting his instincts more. And he regretted his previous unwillingness to entertain his concerns about Liza. Strangely, he also concluded that Liza had very likely screwed Brad Lawrence in college after all.

Knight interrupted Josh again. Only this time, having pulverized Josh's self-esteem and rendered the sanctity of his marriage absurd, Knight intended to address her beef with Josh.

"So, Dr. Odom. Tell me some more things about Lacy. I'd love to hear them. I'd like you to know I've resigned myself to hearing those things before moving forward. I won't rest until I've heard those things, and you, sir, are the only one who can tell them to me. But first, I'd like to ask you a few questions. Yes, let's get back to our Q and A. I'll ask you a few questions, and you'll answer me—that is, while you're still able to answer them."

Josh was horrified as he looked into the eyes of a woman who was more like him than he'd estimated. They could've been twins because they were so similar.

"Let's start by talking about medication. Shall we? You know all about medications, don't you, Dr. Odom? You probably know more than anyone in Shelby County about certain medications because that's just the kind of guy you are. Am I right?"

Still terrified, Josh managed to answer Knight, albeit his speech was labored and slurred, "Yyyesss. I knoow a great deal about ssseveral mezcashunz."

"Tell me, then, Dr. Odom. What is clozapine? What is that drug, and what does it do? And the reason I'm asking you is that the toxicology report for my Lacy girl showed that there was enough of it in her system to drop a Goddamned rhinoceros!" Olivia Knight roared so loudly that Josh tried futilely to cover his ears.

The second transition had happened so fast that it startled Josh, even in his compromised state. And a part of Josh Odom thought it was beautiful to bear witness to. It was the metamorphosis he'd personally undergone only a few times during his life. But it was also one he'd kept in check for several years using the pharmaceutical Knight had just mentioned.

"It…it…it…itsss an antipssssychotic, Mzz Knight. Itzz antishycoticsss..anti-sy-sycotic," Josh slurred.

"Ohhhh. An antipsychotic? Uh-huh, uh-huh, okay. Well, let me ask you this, then. Is that something someone might buy off the street, Dr. Odom? Is there any reason for someone like Lacy to have wanted to take clozapine? Does it offer any sort of a rush or a high or anything like that?"

"Nnnn-nooooo," Josh said as he began to cry.

"No. No, it doesn't, does it, Dr. Odom? You see, I know because I have a friend who told me that, Dr. Odom. He's a really nice man. A nice Christian man who shared aaall kinds of information about drugs with me. In fact, we went down the whole list of drugs that Lacy had been arrested for in the past. But you know what?

Damndest thing. There wasn't a one of those drugs in my Lacy girl's system. Isn't that something, Dr. Odom? Isn't that remarkable? But there was a fuck ton of clozapine, Dr. Odom. And a fuck ton of another drug called a benzodiazepine. Yep, there was a truckload of both of those."

Josh was on the verge of seizing. But that's the moment it occurred to him. Knight had never swallowed her scotch—even after toasting him. Josh had noticed, then immediately dismissed, that Knight stopped short of her mouth and smiled at him. Josh thought that she'd just been waiting for him to pay a compliment to the vintage.

Knight wasn't done with Josh by a long shot, though.

"Something else my Christian friend shared with me, Dr. Odom, were the medications taken by everyone that constituted the pool of sludge my Lacy drowned in. I have to say that I was impressed with everything the government can find out about someone if they want to. If they need to. Ha! If they decide to."

Knight began disclosing information that Josh had thought no one would ever unearth.

"Tell me about Winifred Petro, Dr. Odom. You remember her, don't you? Oh, who am I kidding? You can't tell me a Goddamned thing about her because you can no longer talk, can you, Josh? And it's getting hard to move, isn't it? So difficult. You look like your head is drooping, too, Josh-Kosh-B'gosh. Maybe you'd like a bedtime story. How about that? How about I tell you a nighty-night story?"

Knight was full-on crazy now. She was uncloaked in much of the ways Josh had revealed himself to Winifred Petro, the lonely homeless woman who'd approached him and his father at a gas station for alms when he was a teenager. His father shooed her away, but all Josh had been able to do was view her as an opportunity. He was so aroused by that opportunity that he had to go into the men's room to release the sexual frustration he felt. But it would recharge when he returned to his parent's cabin in Millington. And he'd ride his bicycle back to the gas station with instructions for Winifred to meet him somewhere close by that evening, where he said he'd give her a lot of money if she'd let him do things to her.

Later in life, Josh would satisfy his urges using Blanche Howard. She'd been a librarian in Jackson, where he attended Baker. He'd share what would become Blanche's last cup of coffee with her at Tommy Ray's diner. Then he'd go home with Blanche. Then, he'd have sex with Blanche several times throughout the afternoon. Finally, he would strangle Blanche to death in the bathtub, using her pantyhose.

By the time Lakeshia Miller came along, Josh was a practicing physician with access to prescription meds. He offered some of those medications in exchange for Lakeshia performing sexual acts in the back of his E-320 on a country road. He became a regular of Lakeshia's, building her trust and enriching her addictions, which made it that much easier to slice her throat and haul her carcass into the wilderness at four o'clock in the morning.

And, finally, there was Lacy Knight. It may have been her beauty that initially attracted Josh to her. But that was just a reflexive, sophomoric, and ephemeral response. The more he learned about her, the more his irrepressible urges overtook the passive, docile clinician he'd become by gaining control over those urges with medication. But as her mother was about to relate to him, he'd picked the wrong little girl with whom to act upon those urges.

Knight commenced her fairy tale.

"Once upon a time, there was this arrogant cocksucker named Joshua Odom. And Joshua was so arrogant that he was able to fool everyone—including his broken-down hillbilly parents about whom he was. About what he was."

Josh realized Knight knew everything. She knew it all. But he also knew he could not offer an explanation or anything else by way of discussion because he'd soon go under. And whatever would happen to him after that was at the discretion of the psychotic, heartbroken billionairess that now toyed with him.

Josh had to confess to himself that it was impressive. Not only had Knight taken his heart out and shown it to him, but she'd stomped on it with her revelations about Liza. This woman was as cold and as calculating as Josh was.

Josh no longer concerned himself with what would happen to him because he knew what that was. He just hoped it would be humane. That Knight would go gently and that she'd already assigned his penance via whatever coursed through his circulation.

"Back to the topic of trusting, arrogant simpletons, Dr. Odom. Do you know that company you have cloud storage with? Hacker Bytes? Well, guess what? And I didn't even know this one until recently—but I own it! I own Hacker Bytes and its parent company, DataMark Solutions! Isn't that something?" Knight said, cackling.

"So not only do I have access to the putrid goings on of deviant sex societies, I get to see what's wrong with all of your patients, too! Ain't that a kick in the head, Dr. Odom? Ain't that a hole in the boat, as the old song goes?"

Josh wanted things to be over. He could no longer face the reality of how evil and indulgent a man he'd been. He was the very type of person he disparaged so greatly during his sessions. He wasn't the Messiah of troubled souls. He was their anti-Christ. He embodied all that was wrong with society, and not only had he failed to combat it through his profession, but he had also facilitated depravity through his actions and inaction. He wondered how many people he'd harmed when he'd told himself the whole time that he was helping them. He'd probably created dozens of men just like he was.

But it seemed clear that Knight wasn't concerned with Josh's inward reflection. She wasn't trying to make Josh apologize for anything. But she did want the facts. She'd demonstrated that by going to such lengths to track down the person who'd killed Lacy. And that person was Josh.

"Did she deserve it, Doctor Odom? Don't all whores deserve it in your estimation of things? I know they do because you said that in your notes about Lacy. You said she was a whore and a narcissist and that she could never get better, didn't you? That she'd be better off dead. Isn't that what you said? And then you went and made that a self-fulfilling prophecy, didn't you, Dr. Odom? But even that wasn't good enough for you, was it? You didn't just kill Lacy. You made her suffer, didn't you? You put your fucking medicine in my baby's frozen yogurt sundae from Gracie Bleu, and then you took her somewhere and forced yourself on her, didn't you?"

Knight calmed herself a moment before proceeding.

"You see, I know you did that because they found your despicable seed inside my baby, swirled in with the frozen yogurt. How do I know that one? Well, Josh, that brings us back to poor old Winnie Petro. You remember her, now? She's the one you beat to death when you were only sixteen years old. Wow! That's something else, Dr. Odom! You showed promise early on, didn't you?"

Knight resumed being the crazed, vindictive psychopath whose potential next moves troubled Josh to imagine.

"You took poor old Winnie to the creek near your parent's cabin, didn't you, Josh? The one where you used to fish and hunt with that miserable old drunk that your father was. Gosh! I sure wish he was still around to see this. I wish he could see what I'm going to do to you. Then again, maybe that's a good thing, Josh. Maybe I'd do the same thing to him if he were around, but I'd make you watch me do it first. That's right. I'd make you watch me take his life, just like you took Winnie's, and God only knows who else's life before you took my baby girl's life."

Josh sobbed. He cried and cried—even though he knew it wouldn't do any good.

"It ended up that you weren't as smart as you thought, though, didn't it? No, not nearly as smart. The technology was young, just as you were. But it still existed. And the Shelby County Sherriff's Office believed that one day it might be possible to link the DNA they took from Winnie and match it to whoever had raped and killed her. And they were right! But I bet they'd never have guessed it was little Josh Odom, the Fellowship of Christian athlete and valedictorian of his class. Bet they thought it'd be some drifter or a pervert that would wind up in custody for doing something else. No way would they have predicted this one, Dr. Odom."

Knight squatted to ensure Josh could get a good look at her as she spoke.

"You want to know who *was* smart, though, Josh? Smart like me? Every bit as smart as I am, but maybe even more so? Lacy was smart. She was smarter than anybody thought, least of those being you, wasn't she?"

And then something occurred to Josh. It came crashing into him like a meteorite. And though it was difficult, he managed the ability to speak.

"Oh, mmy-gahhhd…the ppphhone…the phhone. The ph-ph-ph-ph-phone!!" Josh moaned through a lathery, trembling mouth and sobs.

Just like Knight's people had, Josh had found that damned phone after he had difficulty forcing Lacy's eyes to stay open with the duct tape he'd practiced using on himself a dozen times. It rested at the bottom of the Christmas Tree bag next to the crazy glue he'd thrown in for insurance, which hadn't worked either. That was after Josh had beaten Lacy to death with a golf club and after he'd surgically removed her filthy, lying tongue. But it was before he'd noticed the tackle box in the brush a few feet away from where he labored with Lacy's corpse. And it was before he threw stitches in her eyes to keep them open and secure her head in an upright position using fishing line and Big Cat Circle Hooks affixed to the sling chair that he knew he'd find when he arrived. Though he panicked throughout that eleventh-hour catastrophe, things eventually worked out, and he got several exposures of Lacy to use in the next phase of his carefully and wickedly crafted plan.

But, yeah, Josh had found his phone, too. He immediately went to the call log to ensure no numbers had been dialed, which they had not. He was relieved to discover that. But to be safe, he'd stop a mile away and hurled the phone as far into a bog as possible. And that was just how close Clemmie had come to finding Lacy instead of Ardella and Jerome finding her.

Knight started laughing. It wasn't fake or condescending this time, though. It was genuine because she was enjoying herself.

"Yes! The phone! He got it right, folks! Let's all give Dr. Odom a round of applause!" Knight said as she rose and clapped.

Josh's head collapsed onto his chest, but he wasn't unconscious. He wasn't able to hold it up anymore from exhaustion. He struggled with why for a moment, but then he imagined that it wasn't only his meds that Knight had poisoned him with. But it was likely several other things.

"Just sit there and relax, Dr. Odom, while I tell you another story. One whose ending you're going to help me with."

Knight paced back and forth, not looking at Josh as she spoke.

"I bet you thought the phone Lacy found was useless, didn't you, Dr. Odom? And I guess maybe, in a lot of ways, it was useless. At least it was useless to you, wasn't it? No, you didn't need that phone anymore. But somehow, Lacy got ahold of that phone. I just can't figure out how that happened, though. So, I want you to answer that for me, just like I told you before. I'm dying to hear the answer to that. And technically, you're dying to tell me that, too."

Knight lowered her pitch and spoke through gritted teeth.

"Did she get the phone from your house, Dr. Odom? Did you take my baby to your house?"

"Y-y-y-yessss!" Josh wept.

"Oooooh, you did? Well, that was downright brave, Dr. Odom. Brave, brave, brave, brave, brave. And did little Miss Liza know you brought her to your house, Dr. Odom?"

"Nnnoooo."

"Now, Joshua. You might as well tell me the truth. Because I'm gonna find out. You haven't known me long but know me well enough to realize that. Tell you what. Why don't you call her? How about that?"

It hardly mattered, but the woman's voice Olivia's team heard turned out to be that of Daphne Moon, the robust Mancunian physical therapist from *Frasier*. More specifically, they deciphered that it was from Season 6, Episode 20, "Dr. Nora," which was playing in the background as Lacy was murdered. Olivia wanted clarification, but it didn't matter by then. And it wouldn't have mattered even if Knight had determined Liza wasn't involved anyway.

Knight pulled out Josh's ancient Nokia N73 phone, which was fully operational and instead looked brand new. She held it up and pressed the speaker button. Then she dialed what appeared to have been Liza's cell phone because it rang only once before Josh heard her voice.

It was Liza's number. Except it wasn't really Liza who answered. It wasn't she, and Josh could tell that because of the nuanced differences between someone's real voice and their voice as interpreted by Artificial Intelligence. But also because of the things that A.I. Liza offered brightly and cheerfully in her voicemail greeting.

"Hi there! You've reached Liza Odom's iPhone. I can't take your call right now because I'm burning in the depths of hell. But leave your number, and I'll try to call you back. Either that or I'll see you when you get here, Joshua!"

There was a break in the message before the music began playing along with a drum track, and the imaginary Liza started rapping, *"Uhn. So hawny. Uhnn. So hawny. Uhnn. So hawny"*

This continued for another chorus before A.I. Liza repeated sunnily over the background music, "I'll see you when you get here," twice more before its voice changed into Olivia Knight's voice, which affirmed, "I'll see you when you get here," before climaxing in a deep, dark, horrible voice that sounded as though it were indeed resonating from hell.

"I'LL SEE YOU WHEN YOU GET HERE."

With the one eye Josh could keep open, he looked at Knight as she lowered the phone and smiled at him. He could tell her transformation was complete.

"How?" Knight said, smiling, "How did I determine all these awful things you've done? You must be asking yourself that question. Well, I probably oughtn't tell you, Dr. O. Because you don't deserve to hear it. But in this instance, the information is something I can't wait for you to start mulling because you will consider it for eternity."

After a pregnant pause as Knight scowled at Josh, she explained things.

"I got an email from my son, Dr. Odom. This must've been between the time you kidnapped Lacy and the time you killed her,"

Knight was no longer antagonizing. She related things carefully while maintaining a stoic glance that felt like it would burn through Josh.

"It was from an AOL account he used, but even that didn't set off any alarms. Want to know what that address was? It was 'ilove3.1415926@aol.com.' Being the educated man you are, I'm sure you know that email address translates into 'I love pie.' AOL was Tristan's first email account. He came up with that handle or screenname—or whatever the idiots called it—himself at four years old. But he never used it again after they rejected my offer. Ha. A forty-three-billion-dollar write-down, they're bleeding subscribers like water, and seven billion wasn't enough to motivate them. Yeah, they were pretty arrogant too, Dr. O. But you see what arrogance leads to?"

Knight cleared her throat again, preparing to stave off the emotions she was about to feel as she spoke.

"I didn't open that email until after I received the photograph you sent me of Lacy staring at the camera. Turns out you'd already killed her, though, hadn't you? Oh, don't try to speak, Joshua. I know you did because the FBI figured that out for me. "

Knight looked away as though recalling the moments she started to describe.

"When I opened the email, it didn't make much sense. It was just a bunch of garbled text. But once my people pieced things together, we realized it said, 'Mommie help someone got me going to kill me.'

Knight paused for another moment of reflection as tears welled in her eyes.

"That's when we realized the email wasn't from Tristan. It was from Lacy."

Knight refocused on Josh, but it was through the somber, tear-laden eyes of a lunatic.

"She didn't mention any names, though. Because of all the spelling errors, it seems now that she'd typed the email using only her thumbs without being able to look at the screen very well. It's also safe to assume she was terrified."

Knight paused, then reopened with a question.

"Did you take her to your office, too, Josh? Did you bring her here?" Knight asked.

Knight no longer appeared insane, though. She toggled back to sounding like just what she was: a heartbroken mother who had lost her daughter in the worst possible way. She was plaintive but direct and oh-so calm.

"Yyyesss. I diiid," Josh eked out.

At that moment, Knight decided to get the final piece of information she needed from Josh. It was as though she were forcing herself to relive the final moments of Lacy's life as punishment for her not being involved in anything that led up to them.

"Is this where you killed her, Dr. Odom? Is this the place where Lacy died?"

Josh collapsed from his chair onto the floor a few inches from Olivia Knight's Herme's Paris Loafers. He was too far gone to give

Knight the answer. Josh thought that would serve as his last victory in life, no matter how meager or pathetic it was.

Knight's shoes left Josh's sight momentarily, and he heard her rummaging through plastic across the room. A moment later, she positioned herself behind Josh. Josh couldn't see her, but she held a MacGregor five iron. It was Josh's Macgregor five iron.

The golf club had come into Knight's possession earlier that day after members of the Knight regime ransacked Josh's home while he sat alone in Cracker Barrell, enjoying one last Sunrise Sampler. At the same time, another posse was en route to a remote cabin on Dantzler Road, where Stephen and Liza met every Friday. Shortly after arriving, they killed Stephen violently with knives as Liza watched from the brush where she'd run to and hidden after they kicked the door open. But they eventually found Liza. They killed her, too, but they took a little more time than was probably necessary.

Just before that, she'd called Josh and left him a frantic voicemail he would never receive because it would be erased. Liza hadn't even known who it was trying to kill her and Stephen. Nor did she know about those members of Qadeshians whose lives had already been unceremoniously snuffed out.

But even amid her hysteria, Liza contemplated that whoever wanted her dead was probably whoever had Gill killed in prison. Liza was smart like that. But she couldn't leave a voicemail for Josh to that effect. She knew what it would've done to him. So, instead, she bargained on the voicemail for him to call the police so that someone could at least try to stop what she feared was inevitable.

Knight looked down at Josh and posed her final question of the session, for which she'd leave three crisp one-hundred-dollar bills on Josh's back when she left.

Then, the OAK cleared her throat and said,

"Are you frightened? Are you afraid, Joshua?

THE END

ABOUT THE AUTHOR

Charles is a terminally distracted daydreamer who likes to create worlds where someone can escape to occupy a different vantage and encounter people and places a great distance from their routine. His objective is for the reader to feel a complete range of emotions so they're entertained while contemplating how they would have reacted under similar circumstances, which is the essence of escapism.

Charles is a native Mississippian who lives in coastal Alabama with his wife and their two Shih Tzus, Pete and Steve. He loves to cook and is one of those annoying people who takes pictures of the ham sandwich he just made and DMs it to everyone he knows. Please feel welcome to visit his website (Charlessavary.com) and join his subscriber list.

Made in the USA
Monee, IL
27 May 2025

18254603R00218